COBBLE HILL

Center Point
Large Print

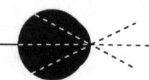

**This Large Print Book carries the
Seal of Approval of N.A.V.H.**

COBBLE
HILL

• *a novel* •

CECILY von ZIEGESAR

CENTER POINT LARGE PRINT
THORNDIKE, MAINE

This Center Point Large Print edition
is published in the year 2021 by arrangement with
Atria Books, a division of Simon & Schuster, Inc.

The text of this Large Print edition is unabridged.
In other aspects, this book may vary
from the original edition.
Printed in the United States of America
on permanent paper.
Set in 16-point Times New Roman type.

ISBN: 978-1-64358-791-2

The Library of Congress has cataloged this record
under Library of Congress Control Number: 2020948177

For Richard and Oscar and Agnes

I am a man who, sauntering along
without fully stopping,
Turns a casual look upon you
and then averts his face,
Leaving it to you to prove and define it,
Expecting the main things from you.

—WALT WHITMAN, *LEAVES OF GRASS*

ONE YEAR AGO

Did you see? People all down the block, waiting for the doors to open. There won't be enough chairs!"

Roy Clarke squirmed uncomfortably. He wanted to stand, but the bookstore owner had supplied a high stool. "I'd better not keep them here for too long then. Just a quick reading, sign a few books, and home."

"They're here for *you*." Wendy Clarke, his wife, had already helped herself to the free prosecco. "Don't be in such a rush. They're our new neighbors. We're all going to be great friends."

Roy unbuttoned his cuffs, rolled up his sleeves, then rolled them down again. While he appreciated Wendy's cheerful optimism, he wondered why he'd ever agreed to this.

On their first stroll to familiarize themselves with their new neighborhood, Wendy had noticed a sign on a scaffolded Smith Street storefront that read SMITH CORNER BOOKS: 2 WEEKS 'TIL OPENING DAY! Without hesitation, she'd stepped around the construction debris and gone inside to introduce herself. Roy lingered outside, pretending to be a smoker, even though he was not. The next day, Wendy forwarded him an email from Jefferson, the bookstore's owner, with the subject *Roy Clarke reading*

11

confirmed for opening day!! The body of the email was all lavish praise and buttering up. Never in Jefferson's wildest imaginings could he ever have hoped for "*the* Roy Clarke" to open his store. Roy didn't mean to be an ass. It was just that he'd wanted to slip into Brooklyn and discover it quietly, be discovered by it quietly. Not bang in—*pow!*—let's welcome the big famous author who, sorry to disappoint, hardly thought of himself as an author anymore because he spent more time making tea and toast than he did writing pages.

Shy Clarke, Roy and Wendy's youngest daughter, age fifteen, contemplated pretending she'd just gotten her period. Shy was nervous about starting at her new American school later that week. She also felt uncomfortable for her father, who she knew was in agony. Shy's older sisters had come up with her unusual name right after she was born because she'd seemed to duck and look away whenever they cooed over her. Right now, Shy sat very still in the front row, her pale bare knees pressed tightly together. She wasn't sure she could endure her father's misery for much longer.

"Unlocking the doors now," Jefferson announced. He wore a heavy black-and-green plaid wool shirt, despite the fact that it was the first week in September and seventy-five degrees outside. His long, bushy brown beard looked like it would make a nice home for a family of squirrels.

An excited murmuring throng waited outside on the sidewalk. Jefferson unlocked the glass door and held it open to let them in.

Roy and Wendy had moved to Cobble Hill, the charming brownstone Brooklyn neighborhood just south of Brooklyn Heights, from London almost three weeks ago. People from the neighborhood had actually stood around with their children and dogs and watched the movers moving in their furniture and boxes of possessions with great interest. Wendy wasn't bothered. She was too busy unpacking boxes and giving orders. Roy watched the neighbors watching them. It was his first inkling that they hadn't moved to the big city at all, but to a very small village where nothing went unnoticed.

Jefferson's neat rows of folding chairs filled up fast. There was a lot of hugging. Everyone in the audience seemed to know one another. Roy didn't know anyone. His agent and editor were both based in London. He hadn't even told them about the event. Wendy was his agent for this one, bless her.

Roy sat stiffly on his stool in a state of faux alertness. Voices faded in and out. Someone touched his elbow. A copy of *Orange*, his most popular novel—the novel that had been adapted into an acclaimed HBO series starring Frances

McDormand, Drew Barrymore, Kristen Stewart, Kevin Dillon, Jonathan Rhys Meyers, and Hugh Grant and had aired for four seasons—was placed across his stool-braced knees. He blinked and clasped the book between his hands. He would read the part about the firemen. It was recognizable from the TV show, a bit racy, and always made him laugh. His agent, a bright twenty-eight-year-old who had inherited the post when Roy's longtime agent died, said it was "endearing" that his own writing still made him laugh. He thought it best to endear himself to his new neighborhood if he could.

A shadow passed in front of him.

"Thank you, friends and neighbors. Welcome to your new bookstore, Smith Corner Books. It's been a lifelong dream of mine to open a bookstore and I'm thrilled so many of you are here this evening," Jefferson began.

Roy shifted on his stool. It was almost time.

"Without further ado, I'm delighted to introduce one of my all-time favorite authors—I'm still pinching myself that he's here in my little store. You know him from *Blue*, *Yellow*, *Green*, *Purple*, and the smash hit *Orange*, which *The New Yorker* described as *Bridget Jones* meets *Waiting for Godot*. *The Guardian* has said of him, 'If Jane Austen froze her eggs and one of them was impregnated by both Albert Camus and Tim Robbins, this author would be the brainchild.'

The *New York Times* calls him 'Kafka for millennials and way, way funnier.' An absurdist and a realist, a master of the microscope. No one understands the tragedy, the humor, and the romance in the everyday better than this guy. If you've read or seen the part in *Orange* when Mark stops up the toilet with marmalade, you know what I'm talking about. Boxed sets of the Roy Clarke Rainbow and individual titles are all available here tonight. Please welcome Roy Clarke."

Roy looked up. Jefferson applauded with the crowd and backed into his seat. His introduction had been rather too swift, Roy thought. He sat up straighter, crossed and uncrossed, then recrossed his legs. Bloody uncomfortable stool. He cleared his throat and looked out at the audience.

At one end of the first row, next to her mother, sat his daughter Shy, her knees squeezed together, eyes on the wooden floorboards, vibrating up and down like she needed the toilet. Next to Shy, Jefferson beamed up at Roy through his beard. Wendy beamed up at Roy from beneath her blond fringe with a sort of pert but docile admiration he didn't recognize. Roy opened his copy of *Orange* and thumbed through it in search of the firemen scene. He didn't know the exact page number, but at some point he'd written a stream of foul words. That was what he looked for.

The firemen were chopping through a burning

building with axes. Smoking embers stung their eyes. They could barely breathe. Like drunken fraternity brothers, they shouted out and explained the dirtiest, most disgusting sexual acts they'd ever heard of with cheerful camaraderie. Later on in the scene they did a full analysis of Julia Roberts's entire acting career, starting with *Mystic Pizza*, which was their favorite. It was this scene that had won Roy's writing critical accolades such as, "witty, sexy fun," and "a man's book you can take home to Mother."

"I think I'll read straight off and get to know you later," Roy said without looking up. Titters of laughter. A few whoops. A whistle. He'd been told that he always came off sounding "very cool" at his readings, which was odd, because speaking in front of large groups of people made him sweat so much he was required to wear black or navy blue so no one would see.

Rusty Trombone. Mississippi Hot Pocket. Dirty Sanchez. Glory Hole. Julia Roberts. Mystic Pizza. Pretty Woman. Notting Hill.

There it was, the Dirty Words Firemen Scene. For a fleeting second Roy worried that Shy was about to be mortified. But she was fifteen. She'd watched the marmalade toilet scene from *Orange*. Nothing could possibly surprise her now. He cracked the spine and began to read.

PART I

SEPTEMBER

Chapter 1

A MESSAGE FROM NURSE PEACHES

Welcome back, PS 919 peeps!

Thanks for returning your pediatric examination forms. If your child has specific medical requirements, please give me a holler.

Moving on to nastier things: EIGHT students have been sent down to me with lice. These are cases that began over the summer and are still lingering. Don't let them linger on your child's head. Now's the time to comb through your child's hair with thick white conditioner such as Pantene. If lice are present, they will be visible in the white stuff. A cursory visual inspection of dry hair is not effective, and those lice treatment kits from the drugstore are full of poison and do not work! Instructions on how to perform a proper comb-through are all over YouTube. Come by my office for a good-quality $10 lice comb. Proceeds go to our PTA. There are also professional "lice ladies" who can remove the bugs and nits from your child's hair for a fee. I have a list of names and numbers. Feel free to call or email me, or stop by my office with any questions or concerns. My main advice: check those heads.

Here's to a totally un-lousy school year!

My very best,
Peaches Park, school nurse
nursepeaches@ps919brooklyn.edu

The warning letter from the new school nurse had come home in Ted's backpack. Stuart felt like the letter was speaking directly to him. And of course now he had lice. They were everywhere—on car seats, in his fellow riders' hair on the crowded F train coming home from work last night, in Ted's hair, on Ted's pillow, in Ted's towel, on the hood of Ted's hoodie, on the leaves that drifted crisply down from the dried-out, summer-weary trees.

Stuart loved Nurse Peaches' tone. Last week, on only the third day of school, she'd left a message on his cell: "You don't know me, but I have your son. He seems fine now, but he puked his guts up after lunch. Better take him home before he pukes on my floor."

When he went to pick up Ted from her office

and first laid eyes on her, he could not stop smiling. Curvy, strawberry blond, merry but cool. Peaches. She was busy with a crying girl who'd scraped her knees pretty badly in the schoolyard, so she'd only glanced up and pointed to the sign-out sheet. Stuart hardly heard a word Ted said as he signed Ted out and led him home. Peaches—it was practically an invitation. Her black T-shirt with the sleeves cut off was an invitation too, or at least a suggestion: there was more to Peaches than met the eye.

"I can't believe you still do that," Mandy, his wife, commented now as he stood in front of the full-length mirror in their bedroom. She was sitting up in bed, wearing the same old mustard-yellow Blind Mice T-shirt she'd been wearing for two weeks. It was his, a collector's item, and he wanted it back.

"Still do what?" Stuart stopped scratching his head and put his hands in his back pockets. His black Levi's were looser than ever, as if they belonged to someone else even though he'd been wearing them since his early twenties. Was he losing muscle now that he was approaching forty? He didn't really exercise, just walked a lot. The jeans were still in pretty good shape too, no holes, zipper still functioning. When did you know you needed new jeans?

Mandy folded her arms over her boobs, which were still massive—even bigger than they'd been

21

in high school—and smiled her foxy, pearly-toothed smile. She used teeth-whitening strips religiously, and they worked. But there was something embarrassing about her boobs and her smile, like they were saying something about him. His songs might be deep, but he himself was shallow, or he had been when he met and married Mandy. Who was even named Mandy anymore anyway?

"Aren't you too old to be like, checking yourself out?"

Stuart looked at himself in the mirror again and then at her mocking reflection. She was the one in bed. Her incredibly shiny, silky black hair—she also gave herself a VO5 hot oil treatment every Friday—was matted flat in the back from lying down all the time. At least Stuart was up and dressed. Ted was up and dressed too, eating Cheerios and watching Cartoon Network. Mandy was just lying there.

"I'm thirty-six. So what? I can't look at myself?"

"Just saying," Mandy said.

She said a lot of things, from bed.

"I think you're even cuter than when you were in the band," she added, a little unconvincingly, Stuart thought.

Stuart's band, the Blind Mice, had been in the top twenty on the *Billboard* Hot 100 list for three years running before they'd broken up ten years ago. Ever since, Stuart had been virtually silent, working quietly for a company that provided music and sound editing for advertisements.

Lately, entertaining Ted had somehow brought out the urge to make noise again. Stuart had even thought of trying to get the band back together to make a kids' album, but becoming *that* dad, *that* guy, *that* band, singing about bubble baths, marshmallows, cement trucks, and poop was not something he was ready for, and he was pretty damned sure the other two Mice weren't ready for it either. Robbie, the charming, handsome guitarist, spent half his time on far-flung beaches in Australia and the other half in Nicaragua, surfing and growing pot. JoJo, the aloof beats genius and techno wizard, produced music in LA and lived in a hotel. Neither of them were married, and they certainly didn't have any kids, or if they did, they didn't know about them. Stuart Little, affable front man of the organization, chief lyricist and rhyme-smith, and not so little anymore, had been the only one to settle down.

"Any plans today?" Stuart asked, the same way he'd been asking for weeks.

"My plan is to do this," Mandy said from bed. It was the same answer she always gave.

"Will you please call Dr. Goldberg?"

For over a month Mandy had been promising to go back to the doctor and get a referral for a specialist. Both times she'd "made an appointment" she'd come back smelling like toasted everything bagels and told Stuart the traffic was so bad she'd missed her appointment, but it didn't matter because she was doing everything the doctor had told her to do back in July, and everything was fine. But she was not fine. She'd gotten much, much worse.

"Today?" he prompted.

"Okay," Mandy yawned.

Stuart glanced at the time on the cable box beneath the large flat-screen TV he'd installed over the summer. "Ted's going to be late again. I gotta go."

Mandy slid back down under the covers. "I love you," she called. "You're totally hot."

Ted was in fourth grade at the small public elementary school on Henry Street that was available only to families who lived within the designated district of Cobble Hill. Ted had turned nine in August and could definitely walk there on his own, but Stuart still took him to school every morning on his way to work, half out of habit and half because he enjoyed it. Three times a week Ted stayed at school for the after-school program, Hobby Horse, an extra two and a half hours of games in the schoolyard or gym, depending on the weather, before Stuart picked him up. Twice a week he went with a group of boys to the Brooklyn Strategizer, where they played complicated board games, like Settlers of Catan, until Stuart picked him up. Every day Stuart would text to see if Mandy was up and wanted to go get Ted herself, but Mandy was never up.

Stuart and Ted rolled their skateboards down Cheever Place and turned onto Kane Street. As usual, Roy Clarke, the famous author, was pacing slowly up the street ahead of them. Later on, he'd sit at the bar inside the Horn and Duck, the overpriced brasserie on the corner of Kane and Court Streets. Stuart had never spoken to the man, but he'd decided that Roy Clarke paced because, according to Google, he hadn't published a book in six years. Stuart also knew that one of Roy Clarke's books had been made into a TV show. Mandy had watched a few episodes and said it was "annoying." Stuart hadn't read the books or seen the show, but he'd always been aware that "the Roy Clarke Rainbow" existed. He knew the books were supposed to be good and that they were named after colors—*Blue, Yellow, Green, Purple,* and *Orange.* At some point he'd attempt to read one and see for himself.

Roy Clarke's gray head bobbed as he paced slowly and deliberately away from Stuart and Ted, hands clasped behind his back, eyes on the sidewalk. Maybe he wasn't thinking about his writing or anything at all. Maybe he was just counting his steps. It seemed like a lot of people in Cobble Hill were very busy doing not a lot.

"Morning," Mr. Swiss Family Robinson greeted Stuart from his doorway. Mr. Swiss Family Robinson was Stuart's nickname for the tall, thin, auburn-haired gentleman who every morning stood at the door of the beautiful brick house on Kane Street, directly across from the schoolyard, wearing a crisply ironed shirt and looking nervous, as if he didn't quite trust the school to take care of his children. Stuart couldn't even remember where the name Swiss Family Robinson came from, but it seemed to fit. The house had a bright blue door with a brass door knocker, matching blue shutters, and immaculately curated seasonal flower boxes in every window. Even the sidewalk was cleaner in front of the Swiss Family Robinson house. It was possible that Ted had gone to preschool at Little Mushrooms in the basement of the local church with one of the Swiss Family Robinson children, but Stuart had never encountered any children or even a wife on these morning walks to school, and he had absolutely no idea what Mr. Swiss Family Robinson's real name was.

Still, every morning, Stuart always said, "Hey."

"Who's that?" Ted asked, right on cue. He asked the same question every day.

"I don't know," Stuart said, as usual. Then he

added, "But we see him every day, so it's polite to say hey."

Ted giggled at the rhyme, and Stuart felt his dour mood lighten. Ted was a quiet boy who hadn't made any close friends yet, but he was a good kid, a *really* good kid.

Stuart picked up Ted's skateboard and followed him inside the school entrance. The skinny, dark-haired boy headed up the school stairs to his classroom on the fourth floor, his army-green Herschel backpack banging against his butt.

"See you later, skater. After a while, chile. Be real cool, fool. Eat your food, dude," Stuart called after him.

He tucked both of their skateboards under his arm and turned away from the stairs toward the dimly lit cafeteria. The school had been built in the 1950s, a mixture of old-fashioned flourishes and uninspired practicality. A sweeping marble staircase greeted visitors just inside the entrance, but the rest of the schoolrooms were prisonlike and drab, with dingy gray linoleum floors, low ceilings, barred windows, and terrible fluorescent lighting. Mothers and fathers in a variety of costumes—business, exercise, Birkenstocks and pajama bottoms, breast milk– or beer-stained T-shirts—straggled by and out the main door. Inside the cafeteria, a mom was crying into a Styrofoam cup of coffee while Miss Patty, the school's sinewy, sleep-deprived, overly made-up assistant principal who commuted there from Staten Island, tried to comfort her.

On the far wall of the cafeteria was a closed door marked with a yellow sign that read NURSE. Stuart knocked twice, turned the knob, and opened the door.

Peaches stiffened at the sound of someone knocking and opening her office door. She'd been totally engrossed with *The Brookliner*'s morning news. A headless female torso had been found in the water behind Ikea, in Red Hook. The torso had a tattoo of a rose on her upper arm.

"How can I help?" Peaches asked without turning around. Her early-morning visitors were most often pukers, kids whose parents had fed them multivitamins, orange juice, and eggs for breakfast.

"Hey," a husky male voice greeted her. "Sorry to bother you. I was thinking of buying a lice comb? It's for my son. Ted Little? He's in fourth grade. In Mrs. Watson's class?"

Stuart thought he detected a crimson flush around Nurse Peaches' ears and jawline when he mentioned his last name, but her blue eyes remained glued to her computer screen. Without even a glance in his direction, she reached down and pulled open the bottom drawer of a filing cabinet.

"That's ten dollars. I can't give you change, so

28

if you don't have exact change now, just send the money in an envelope with your child and his teacher will get it to me."

Her voice sounded stale, canned. Stuart was disappointed. "Sure. Okay." He ran his hands through his wavy brown hair and then realized that she might think that was pretty gross of him, to go around rubbing his hands all over his lice. He stuffed his hands into his pockets.

Unable to resist any longer, Peaches released the scroll button on the computer mouse and swiveled her chair around. It was really him: Stuart Little, from the Blind Mice.

"Wow. Sorry. That was a bit brusque," she gushed, her entire person transformed by shining, flirty exuberance. *You're a married woman,* she warned herself, *and a mother. Plus, you're pushing forty.* "I try to maintain a professional veneer around parents, but I'm really just a former English major, college dropout mom. I have no idea how I became a school nurse."

And now Stuart Little thinks you're insane and *stupid.*

"Hey," Stuart replied, hands still stuffed into his pockets. Whenever he was there, in Ted's school, he felt like a thirteen-year-old kid again—awkward, confused, self-conscious, worried about his armpits smelling, stray boogers on his face, leaving his fly unzipped. He'd never been too awkward, but he'd never really outgrown what little middle school awkwardness he'd had.

"Sorry. That was way too much information," Peaches said, trying to recover gracefully from her outburst. She tucked a few stray strands of strawberry blond hair behind her ears, wishing she'd come up with something sexier that morning than a ponytail. "Just the one lice comb then?"

Before he could answer, she stole a glance at Stuart's left hand, tucked halfway into his pocket. The knuckles on that hand were tattooed with realistically detailed, tiny mouse heads. Oh, the fantasies she'd had in college about Stuart Little's tattooed hand, caressing her all over. Stuart Little. She used to devour everything she could find online about him and study it like it was homework. She was a couple of years older than he was, but so what? She'd taken Intro to Latin in college because of his song "Omnia Vincit!" She'd stopped wearing makeup because of his song "My Girlfriend Wakes Up Pretty." She'd decided it'd be okay to drop out of college because of his song "Fuck College." They'd both had their kids before they'd gotten married. Who'd have thought he'd send his kid to the very Brooklyn public school where she now worked as a nurse? Thank goodness her husband and parents had encouraged/forced her to stop pretending to write a short-story collection or play, take the required courses at Adelphi University, get her nursing degree, and seek out this fulfilling, practical job.

Nurse Peaches was wearing one of those old-fashioned long underwear tops—light blue, with big white snowflakes printed on it. It was tight, pulled over the softness of her upper arms and stomach. The open circle of her belly button was heartbreakingly visible beneath the shirt. She didn't seem to mind. Stuart definitely didn't mind.

He released his tattooed hand from his pocket and ran it through his hair again. "I don't know how to handle the whole lice thing," he began. "My son brought home your letter and I checked him. But I just can't get it out of my head, so to speak. I feel like they're all over me."

"Would you like me to check you?" Peaches offered in the same indifferent, professional tone she'd used before.

"Could you?" Stuart asked, resisting the urge to hug her. "That would be great."

Peaches pulled a LiceMeister comb out of her drawer and stood up. She pointed at her chair. "Have a seat."

Stuart unzipped his gray hoodie, bundling it into his lap as he sat down. "I took a shower last night. Not that it makes any difference."

"It's easier with conditioner," Peaches explained, placing a tentative hand on top of his head.

His hair was soft. Strands of silvery gray were interspersed with the reds and browns. *Thank you Mom and Dad, my dear husband Greg, and my son Liam,* she thought as she combed, admiring the sinewy ridges of Stuart's shoulders beneath his worn black T-shirt. *Thank you for cheering me on through those impossibly humbling hours of nursing school.*

Stuart reached behind him and lifted up the shaggy hair on the back of his neck. "Under here's where it itches most," he explained. "I can't sleep. I can't sit still. I just keep scratching. And the more I scratch, the more it itches."

Rhymes with bitches, he thought to himself. *Sandwiches.*

Back in the day, the Blind Mice used to get in trouble all the time for using the word *bitches* in their lyrics. They heard the scoldings of their critics and agreed that perhaps *bitches* was insulting and degrading to women, but they kept on using it anyway because there really was no better word, except for *chicks,* which rhymed with *dicks,* which opened up doors way worse.

Peaches inhaled indulgently and dug in with the lice comb. His hair was so fine and wavy it was hard to part. He smelled vaguely of smoked meat. Of course he did. He and his kid's mom— whose name was Mandy, Peaches remembered, and who'd once been a teen model—probably went out to those hip new barbecue bars every night and had a rockin' roll of a time, doing shots and snorting lines in their leather jackets and perfectly worn jeans, while she and Greg and Liam stayed home and ate penne with jarred red sauce for the ten thousandth time and binge-watched whole seasons of long-forgotten TV shows like *Fawlty Towers* and *Mork & Mindy*.

"See anything?" Stuart asked with his eyes closed. Even when he'd been kind of a celebrity he hadn't done any pampering, like getting a massage or a cuticle treatment or having the pores on his nose expunged. He took a hot shower once a day and went to the barber for a haircut a couple of times a year. Peaches' comb-through felt awesome.

"So far so good," Peaches said vaguely. "You have so much hair though. This could take hours."

Stuart kept his eyes shut. "I tried to do the conditioner thing on myself, but I couldn't really see what I was doing."

Peaches pulled the top of his right ear out of the way so she could check behind it. There were half-closed holes all the way up his earlobes. She remembered the studs that used to fill them. They looked like screws.

"So, if you didn't always want to be a school nurse, what did you want to be?" Stuart asked.

Your girlfriend.

"Oh, I don't know. A singer or a writer or a musician. Something totally useless."

Idiot. She yanked hard on a hank of his hair to distract him from the fact that she'd just insulted him, but it was too late.

He chuckled. "Maybe I should become a nurse." *Nurse, purse. Rhymes with* verse.

Hot school nurse opens up her purse,
Gives me a Slim Jim for my sick verse!

The Blind Mice were known for their flippant virtuosity and total lack of reverence for one particular genre. Their songs were a tongue-in-cheek mixture of ska, punk rock, pop, and hip-hop, with a lot of New York City private schoolboy thrown in. All three Blind Mice had gone to Bay Ridge Country Day School, the only school in New York City with its own duck pond. The Mice's songs ranged from the angry "I Hate My Art Teacher" and "Driver's Ed," to the sweetly romantic "My Girlfriend Wakes Up Pretty," to the wildly danceable "Omnia Vincit!" in which the Mice shouted rhymes in grammatically correct Latin. The band used to get fan mail from Latin teachers and was featured in *Romulus*, a magazine devoted to ancient Rome. The cover was shot at the Coliseum. For the video, the Mice staged an entire concert with an audience of thousands all dressed in togas.

"What about your wife?" Peaches asked nosily. "She could comb through your hair."

Stuart opened his eyes and then closed them again. "Mandy would help," he said, "but she's having a hard time right now."

"Oh, I'm so sorry." Peaches bit her lip, her curiosity blossoming. Had Mandy gotten hugely fat after the birth of their child? Was she depressed about how fat she'd gotten? Was she too heavily medicated to leave the house? Did they have to raise the ceilings and open up walls to accommodate her?

Stop it, Peaches scolded herself.

"She just got diagnosed with MS," Stuart said. "A couple months ago. It's already worse though."

"Jeez. That stinks," Peaches said. So Mandy was a brave martyr, boldly facing a debilitating disease. And she, Peaches Park, was an asshole.

Peaches drew the comb sideways from Stuart's right temple to the crown of his head. A minuscule brown spec tottered out of the follicles in the parting and skittered off toward the nape of his neck. "Oh!" she cried. "I think I saw one!"

Stuart swiveled around in the chair, yanking his hair out of her hands. "Are you sure?" He shuddered involuntarily, horrified that there were actual bugs in his hair and embarrassed that she'd been the one to find them. "Oh God. What do I do? Should I call a lice lady?"

Peaches wrinkled her nose. "Nah. They all live in like, Brighton Beach, and you have to go to them. Plus, they're expensive and mean."

She smiled her beneficent nurse's smile, the smile she'd practiced in the mirror until Liam gave it his "not too creepy" blessing. "Don't worry, that's what I'm here for. I'll take care of them." She picked up her purse and her denim jacket. "I just have to run to Key Food for conditioner. And I'll need to call your son down. And maybe even your wife."

Stuart checked the time on his phone, unnecessarily. Mandy would be right where he left her—in bed, either sleeping or watching TV.

"Mandy's pretty busy today. Doctors' appointments and stuff." He removed his battered canvas wallet from his back pocket. "But yes, let's do it. Conditioner, check Ted, whatever it takes. I just want to get rid of them." He pulled out two twenties and handed them to her. "Here. Thank you. Buy a whole bunch."

"You don't have to—" Peaches began, but took the money anyway. That was the first rule of working at a public school in a neighborhood like Cobble Hill: always take the money. The parents had plenty because they were educating their kids for free.

"Wait here," she told Stuart. "I'll be right back."

• • •

This was how it started:

One weekday back in early July, after Stuart and Teddy had left for Little Mushrooms summer day camp, Mandy flipped aimlessly through the TV channels, just like she always did. She watched the end of a show in Spanish about some jungle in Colombia where the snakes were so slithery and disgusting, she couldn't look away. Then she watched a show about strange addictions, featuring an elderly woman who was addicted to watching cheesy, sad movies about anorexics—*Kate's Secret, The Best Little Girl in the World, My Skinny Sister*—which Mandy was pretty sure was going to get *her* addicted to anorexia movies. Then she watched *Worst Cooks in America, Celebrity Edition*, a show she always wished someone would nominate her for. When the show ended, she clicked off the TV and floundered around on the perpetually unmade bed, unsure of what to do with herself.

She hadn't always been this way. The obvious turning point had been when she'd gotten pregnant and had Teddy. She'd let herself go, which was such a cliché. In Cobble Hill, though, she was the anomaly, not the norm. Most of the moms in the neighborhood were super fit and looked good in skinny jeans even though they were fifty years old. It just made her hate them, which she knew was uncool. Still, she hated them.

That day in July, as she lay on her back in Stuart's old yellow Blind Mice T-shirt and the same pair of black underwear she'd been wearing for two days straight, she tried to think of something good. Häagen-Dazs coffee ice cream was good. Entenmann's pecan ring was good. Something good about herself though. She turned over onto her stomach, her large chest flattening and oozing into her armpits and against her clavicle. There, that was something good about her. She had great tits. White teeth. Shiny hair. And she was only thirty-five. But somehow that didn't make her feel any better.

The staying-in-bed thing had started the first warm day in May, when she'd put on a pair of old cutoffs and discovered that she couldn't zip them. First, she'd complained of an upset stomach, then headaches, then just plain tiredness. She'd stayed tired into June and then taken to her bed permanently, like a woman in an old-fashioned novel. And whatever it was seemed to be getting worse. She was still tired in July, even more tired than she'd been in June.

Deep down, Mandy knew there was really nothing wrong. It was a fake sickness, all in her head. Nevertheless, that pivotal July day she flipped over onto her back and made the fake sickness real.

Her iPad lay on the bedside table for easy access to takeout menus and movies and TV. She slid it onto her chest and googled *Always so tired, what's wrong with me?!?*

Thirty-seven pages of links came up. The first few were full of mundane tips about diet and exercise and anemia. Further down she found one that interested her: *Signs You Have MS.*

She clicked on it.

> Multiple sclerosis is a neurological disorder that presents itself in a multitude of symptoms. It is more common in females age 20–50 and in temperate climates, such as the United States, Australia, Scandinavia, and Northern Europe. The most common symptoms are fatigue, double vision, a heaviness or tingling sensation in the legs, clumsiness or difficulty walking, slurred speech.

Goose bumps appeared on Mandy's arms. She often felt a tingling sensation in her legs, especially when she got up to pee. Sometimes when she ordered food from Seamless it was hard for her to get to the door in time to buzz in the delivery guy because her legs and feet felt like they were *disintegrating,* like a sandcastle in the rain. She kept reading, feeling the exact same way she'd felt when she'd first heard Stuart and the Blind Mice play "My Girlfriend Wakes

Up Pretty." Like the words had been written expressly for her, because, of course, they had.

Around noon that day her phone buzzed and a text appeared alongside a cute picture of her and Stuart at an outdoor show eleven years ago, when the band was still in semi-existence. Mandy and Stuart weren't even married then. They hadn't gotten married until after Teddy—he sat in the sand while they said their vows. Mandy had never even thought about kids or marriage. They'd never even discussed it. But then her IUD had fallen out while they were surfing—or attempting to surf—in Montauk. She hadn't even noticed until more than two months later when she suddenly craved strawberry shortcake ice cream bars and couldn't stay awake any later than nine. Stuart had been very sweet about marrying her and embracing the whole daddy thing, which should have made it a lot easier, but nothing about their lives was the same or any kind of easy again.

That July day, still in bed, Mandy read Stuart's text.

did you call dr. goldberg?

She found the doctor's number in the list of contacts on her phone, stared at it for a moment, and then went back to Stuart's text and typed a reply.

yup, news is not good

!!! calling u now!

A few seconds later her phone rang and the same picture of her and Stuart, looking tan and young and thin and happy, lit up the screen. She watched it ring and go to voice mail. A few seconds later it rang again.

can't talk waiting for tests

She tossed the phone aside and slipped down under the covers, pulling them up to her eyes. It didn't even feel that weird to lie. It didn't even feel like a lie. She probably did have MS. All the symptoms matched up. She didn't even need to go to the doctor.

She sat up, reached for the iPad again, and googled "treatment for MS." There was a lot of information, stuff about vitamins and injections of hamster placentas and changes in diet. She clicked on a few links and ordered some massive jars of vitamins and green juice powder from Amazon, paying the extra $6.99 so it would arrive the next day.

That was just the beginning. Now it was September and faking it had become almost second nature. The fridge was stocked with green juices, Stuart had changed all the lightbulbs to ones that mimicked rays of real sunlight, and the bedside table was laden with self-help books about coping and parenting with MS. They'd replaced the couch in the open-plan kitchen-living room with a queen-size bed where Mandy spent all her time. Teddy had started playing and reading to himself on the bed so he could be near her. Stuart bought fancy organic frozen meals at Whole Foods or Trader Joe's. The three of them ate dinner and watched movies in the bed. It was nice. But Stuart thought she was deteriorating. He was alarmed. He kept reminding her to call the doctor to set up "another round of tests," maybe get a second opinion. Pretty soon Mandy was going to have to decide whether to continue faking it, or pretend to try some new vitamins or experimental drug and make a miraculous recovery.

The thing was, she'd already gotten so used to pretending, it had become real. The idea of attempting to do anything—walk to the corner deli for toilet paper, open the mail, pay the bills, attend to the Blind Mice fan page, shop online for new clothes for Teddy—just seemed exhausting. She had always been the "responsible adult" in their marriage, the one who made sure the bills and taxes were paid and filed, Teddy's shots up-to-date, Stu's fan mail in order. Now she used Post-its for toilet paper until Stu brought home more. The bills stacked up under the bed, unopened, and the late fees accumulated. The fans continued to post adoring stupid shit whether anyone responded or not. And when Stu took Ted for his checkup, even Dr. Goldberg said Ted's short pants looked fine with long socks.

Besides, she liked it. She liked pretending to

have MS and staying in bed. It didn't feel like she was doing nothing. It felt like she was doing something earned and deserved. She was *resting*.

Breathless, Peaches returned from Key Food. "They didn't have Pantene, but Suave is just as good." She set down a plastic shopping bag containing three bottles of conditioner, a family-size box of Cheez-Its, and two cans of Dr Pepper. "I'm afraid you're going to smell like coconuts for a while. Sorry, it was the only white conditioner they had." She cracked open one of the cans and offered it to him. "I got us a snack too. I couldn't resist."

Stuart put the soda can down on top of her desk. He hadn't moved from her swivel chair since she'd left. Knowing he was infested with lice had immobilized him. He watched her tear open the box of Cheez-Its.

"Love these things." She stuffed a handful into her mouth and offered the box to him. "Please, take them away from me."

"Sorry." Stuart held up his hand. "Not to sound like a total asshole, but I'm trying to only eat greens and drink fruit juices today. Mandy and I are trying to eat healthier." The greens and fruit juice cleanse had been his idea, after reading some WebMD article about how the body absorbs vitamins better after a detox. He wasn't sure he could make it all day, and he was pretty sure

Mandy would cheat, but right now he was kind of digging the hollow feeling in his gut.

> *Starve myself with fruits and veggies,*
> *Pants hang large, don't give me wedgies!*

"Yours is a worthier soul than mine." Peaches threw back another handful of Cheez-Its and tossed the box aside. "Okay." She pushed her hair behind her ears, hoping the electric-orange Cheez-It residue stuck to her teeth wasn't too unattractive. "This is going to be sort of messy." She opened the door to the office closet. Mop. Bucket. Disposable thermometers. Tongue depressors. Ice packs. Paper towels. "I just wish I had some real towels."

Stuart looked down at his T-shirt. He didn't mind getting conditioner on it, but it might put the nurse at ease if he wasn't wearing it. He pulled the shirt off over his head. "Does this help?"

Oh yes. Peaches tried not to stare, but it was useless. For someone with such a boyish face and skinny arms, Stuart Little had a very manly chest, with less hair on it than she would've thought, and no middle-aged paunch at all. His belly was concave.

"Good idea. So helpful. Thank you. That's great. Let's get started."

Stuart swiveled around in the chair. Peaches retrieved a bottle of Suave Tropical Coconut conditioner and a stack of white paper towels. She tossed the paper towels on her desk and stood over him, holding the bottle of conditioner aloft.

"I'm going to squirt a whole bunch of this stuff onto your head and comb through it. I'll wipe the excess off on a paper towel. Hopefully we'll be able to see what we're getting. And hopefully we'll get them all."

Stuart took a deep, shuddering breath. "Go for it."

Peaches popped open the cap, turned the conditioner upside down, and squeezed, ignoring the embarrassing farting and sucking sounds the bottle made as the thick white stuff oozed all over Stuart Little's head. She put the bottle down and began to rub the conditioner into his scalp with her fingertips.

"Run away, little fuckers," she said as she picked up the lice comb. "Prepare to die."

Stuart closed his eyes once more and shivered. "I just want them off me."

Peaches dragged the comb through a section of hair. Conditioner piled up and oozed off the comb, dropping onto his shoulders in clumps, like wet snow. She swiped at them with a paper towel. "Sorry. Told you it was messy."

"Probably should've gone with a professional lice lady," Stuart joked.

Peaches snorted. Emboldened, she drew the comb through another section of hair, letting the excess conditioner ooze down the back of

Stuart's neck, over the slope of his bare shoulder blades, and onto the floor.

She frowned as she combed through another section. "I'm not finding anything. Maybe they're all hiding in one spot, or maybe you only had the one. Or maybe I was just seeing things before and you never had any at all."

"Keep going," Stuart murmured. "It actually feels good."

Peaches smiled and shook her head. Why had she not thought to prop her iPhone in the corner and video this? Not that she wanted to post it on social media or anything, but for her own personal use.

"You know what's going to happen, don't you?" she said. "Some kid is going to come down here with a fever, wanting to go home, and I'm going to be up to my elbows in conditioner." *And you with your shirt off,* she almost added, but didn't, because it had just occurred to her that maybe what they were doing was against school policy. It was very possible that she was breaking some code of staff conduct listed in a booklet she'd been given on her first day of work but had never read.

"It smells great." Stuart rocked the swivel chair gently from side to side. He felt like he was on vacation.

The first sign of Mandy's condition was back in late June. They were watching *Saturday Night Live* and she said, "My legs have felt weird all day, like my feet aren't connected right. They keep falling asleep." Stuart forgot all about it until the next weekend, when he'd planned to bike around Governors Island with Teddy on his new BMX bike. Mandy said she couldn't because she was tired. Then on Monday she said she couldn't walk Teddy to his first day at Little Mushrooms day camp. She went back to bed and stayed there. A week later she went to the doctor, and after that it was like she had a new job, but her job was taking vitamins and sleeping. Even when she was awake, she rarely got out of bed.

Realistically, though, it wasn't that much of a change. Mandy had always been beautiful, but lazy. She had always preferred watching television in sweatpants to getting dressed and going out. Now she had the perfect excuse not to go anywhere or do anything. She was sick.

Back when they were in middle school, Mandy Marzulli had been the first one to develop. In tenth grade, her braces came off and she started modeling. At sixteen she made the cover of the "School's Out" issue of *Seventeen* magazine, wearing a white bikini on a beach in Montauk. Mandy was a junior and Stuart was a senior. Getting together had seemed sort of obvious. Mandy just hung around after one of his concerts and handed him a beer. Stuart took the beer and kissed her, and from then on, they were a couple. They walked out of school every day holding

47

hands. Mandy didn't even finish high school. She went on the road with the Blind Mice, traveling everywhere, drinking a lot and not getting much sleep, taking exotic vacations. It was a whirlwind. Then, at twenty-five she got pregnant. A year after Teddy was born they got married and the band broke up. They were both Brooklyn-born, he from Windsor Terrace and she from Bay Ridge, but they'd bought a place in Cobble Hill because the elementary school was supposed to be good and it looked like a nice place to grow up. Stuart started the same job he had now, and Mandy hung out with Teddy and watched TV.

A photograph was taped messily to the wall behind Nurse Peaches' desk. It was a picture of her playing the drums, her reddish-blond hair pulled up in a 1960s beehive hairdo, a giant grin on her red-lipsticked lips. She looked awesome.

"You play the drums?" Stuart demanded.

"Do I play the drums," Peaches repeated. She dragged the comb through his hair with rapid, jerky strokes. "I do sometimes, yes. At this crazy bar no one ever goes into. I put on music and play along on the drums. It's pretty lame, but also sort of fun."

"I need to check it out."

"No, you don't." Peaches hadn't yet owned up to the fact that she knew who he was. Now was her chance. "You're famous. And I'm really not that good."

Chapter 2

L atin was Shy Clarke's new favorite subject. She'd only started last year, and she'd hated it, but lately she couldn't wait for Latin class.

"Latin is a dead language," her mother, Wendy, insisted. "You should be taking Mandarin. It's the language of the future, whether we like it or not. That's why all the private schools are offering it."

But her father had lobbied for Latin. Shy muddled through the first year, feeling a little insane for trying to learn a language no one spoke. She'd thought about switching to Mandarin. Now she was so glad she hadn't. Second-year Latin at Phinney Collegiate was taught by Mr. Streko. And okay, yes, he had a mustache, which sometimes had bits of dried cappuccino foam in it, and he wore the same light gray V-neck sweater, which also sometimes had bits of food and cat hair on it, almost every day. He had tattoos on his forearms that she couldn't quite make out because his hair was so thick and dark. But he was passionate about Latin—the other students rolled their eyes at him—so passionate, Shy had begun to feel passionate about it too.

She'd hated her new school from the moment she started there last year. The kids rolled their eyes at her, too. They rolled their eyes at her

Gucci sneakers, a spare pair her mother had brought home for her from the fashion closet at work. They rolled their eyes when she didn't understand the people who worked at Just Salad when she attempted to eat out for lunch—what in bloody hell was Buffalo chicken? They rolled their eyes when she didn't know how to play basketball or volleyball. They rolled their eyes when she asked where she could get a cup of tea. Now, a year later, Mr. Streko had changed all that. She felt like a rare butterfly, shedding her cocoon in his classroom.

Today, Latin was just before lunch. They were attempting to translate Ovid's *Amores*—poems about love.

"*Sin, sin, sin*—who has it?" Mr. Streko demanded, his brown eyes flecked with bright orange light, his fuzzy black mustache doing that sad and sexy thing where it went down over the corners of his mouth. Shy wondered if he maintained his mustache on his own or if he had weekly appointments at the barber. "This is a good one," he prompted. "Remember this one on Valentine's Day."

" 'I can't live either without you or with you,' " Shy translated, her long, frail body trembling with the effort it took to keep her voice normal and her eyes disinterested.

"Yes!" Mr. Streko beamed at her with his straight, pearlescent teeth and perfectly curled black eyelashes, shooting out arrows of love that bullseyed her heart, almost knocking her out of her chair.

"For tomorrow, translate the next four lines. Try to use your hearts and minds rather than your dictionaries. Remember, it's poetry, so it has an emotional logic rather than a literal logic."

No other teacher said things like that. No one did. She could have listened to him for hours. But class was over. The other students were already packing up. Shy put her books into her backpack slowly. She planned to follow Mr. Streko and see what he did at lunchtime, if she could find a way to do it inconspicuously. She also wanted to get the hell out of the building while her mom was there.

The meeting with the principal and Shy's teachers wasn't for another fifteen minutes, but Shy could already hear her mother's voice echoing down the hallway, repeating the same diatribe she'd overheard last night while she was brushing her teeth.

"What do you think she does all afternoon? Other girls play on teams or go to dance classes. She isn't interested in anything. And she doesn't 'hang out' with anyone. I'm not sure what that means, but isn't this the age when you're supposed to want to 'hang out'? She only eats bread and Coke. I tried to eat like her for a day and I had to lie down. She's so thin. I just wish she had interests."

Shy didn't hate her mother exactly. She hated this side of her—the meddling, judging, overinvested, insecure side that thought her daughter's grades, looks, behavior, and number of friends somehow reflected her capability as a mother. Why did she care so much? It was impossibly irritating.

Mr. Streko strode down the hall and disappeared into the Latin office. Shy was about to rethink her plan when he emerged again, wearing a green down vest and round, mirrored sunglasses. He was going out.

Walking down Court Street, it was easy to pretend she wasn't following him. He paused outside of Starbucks, but there was a line, so he moved on. He seemed to consider going into the pizzeria, where there was also a line, then looked at his watch and carried on. He walked all the way to Atlantic Avenue and waited to cross at the light. Juniors and seniors were allowed out at lunchtime, but Shy never went this far, preferring to nurse a Coke alone on a random stoop. He was walking in the direction of Cobble Hill and home.

Just past the Trader Joe's, he turned in and pulled open a door. It was Chipotle, the Mexican fast-food place. Shy had never been inside. Should she go in and risk a face-to-face exchange? Would he address her in Latin, the way he sometimes did in class? *"Salve, Shy Clarke."*

And what would they talk about? Poetry? Emotional logic?

She couldn't do it. Instead, she darted into Trader Joe's to buy a demi baguette and whatever the Trader Joe's version of Coke was. The huge store was busy and crowded, the line even longer than at Starbucks. She pulled out her phone to check the time. Her mother's meeting was just getting started. After lunch she had American history, Algebra II, and physics—all of her very worst subjects, taught by teachers who would most certainly not leave her to space out at the back of the classroom now that her mother had told them how clever she was and how she was wasting her potential. School's *over,* she decided. She was almost home anyway. She put back the baguette and ducked outside again.

"*Salve,* Shy Clarke," Mr. Streko greeted her, his Chipotle bag clutched in his fist. "Grabbing lunch?"

"I—I. Um," Shy stammered. She raised her hand in greeting. "*Salve,* Mr. Streko." *Show me your tattoos. Take me away from here. I can't live either with you or without you.*

He grinned in reply, suddenly seeming very young and hip outside the confines of the classroom. He probably played guitar and surfed and ate in those outdoor pop-up barbecue restaurants near the Gowanus Canal with dumb names like Pig Party and Cow Town. He probably

53

had a beautiful twenty-three-year-old girlfriend with a perfect body and amazing hair, piercings in all the right places, and even more tattoos.

"Wanna walk back to school with me?" he offered.

Shy shook her head. "I'm actually going home. I'm . . . um . . . not feeling that well."

The corners of Mr. Streko's expressive mouth turned down in sympathy, his black mustache glinting sexily in the bright sun. He patted her on the shoulder and Shy flinched. He'd never touched her before. Was her face red? Could he tell how nervous and pathetic she was?

"Bummer. Well, get some rest and feel better quick, okay?" He raised the brown paper Chipotle bag in his hand. "Think it's rude to eat a burrito in a meeting?"

Shy shrugged her shoulders and smiled, embarrassed that he'd asked for her opinion on an issue of such grown-up, professional importance and embarrassed that he was most likely meeting her mother.

"*Ita est vita*," Mr. Streko said, which was the Latin equivalent of *c'est la vie*. He said it all the time in class when the students moaned about an upcoming quiz or too much homework. "I get weird when I'm hungry." He chuckled and Shy half smiled back. "Sometimes when I get weird I post dorky Latin quotes on Twitter."

Shy stared at him stoically. She wasn't on

Twitter, but in about thirty seconds she would be, just as soon as they parted ways.

"See ya," Mr. Streko called, striding away to make the light.

His Twitter feed was long and adorable, filled with Latin quotes and links to pictures of his enormously fat black cat in comical situations. In one of the pictures the cat was asleep on its back on Mr. Streko's chest—his *bare,* muscly, elaborately tattooed, very hairy chest! It was enough to send Shy crashing into a lamppost.

"Sorry," she apologized to the inanimate object and kept walking. Still staring at her phone, she continued down Court Street to Kane, then onto Strong Place and home.

As soon as Wendy and Shy left that morning, Roy Clarke had gone out for his morning walk. The sun was bright and the air was crisp and full of promise. Autumn was coming. He loved autumn in America. It was so *American.* Apple pie. Burning wood. Pumpkins. Mulled cider. Tartan shirts and down gilets. *Ambition.* It wasn't the same in England. In England autumn didn't feel like anything, with the exception of Bonfire Night, when there were bonfires and fireworks and everyone got very drunk and stood outside. Roy and Wendy had decided to get married at the bonfire on Primrose Hill. "Let's get married then," he'd said, and she said, "All right," and then the fireworks began and they held hands with their faces turned up to the night sky, murmuring, "Ooh," as each one went off. Pure magic.

This particular autumn day felt so promising that he dashed back inside to retrieve his laptop and set out once more with the idea that he'd go and work on his new novel somewhere in the neighborhood. All the autumn energy might somehow permeate his skull, resulting, hopefully, in words on the screen.

"You can't force these things," he always told Wendy when he tried to explain why he hadn't written a new book in six years. She would nod resignedly as he went on, "It's like a snowstorm, dusting and dusting, building and building, so slowly and quietly, until you look out the window in the morning and find it piled up on the cars and stoops, glistening in the sun, finished and perfect."

The building-and-building part was the challenge. He'd thought starting with a title would somehow inspire him, so he'd come up with *Black and White*—two noncolors, unlike the splashy titles of his previous books. But he'd begun to think the new title felt ostentatious and overly ambitious. He would feel obligated to explore race relations and the history of the newspaper trade. He hated even the idea of research, let alone the actual practice of finding information, taking notes, and getting it into his story properly and accurately. All of his other novels had been chatty and witty and not about anything, really, just people from deranged families, talking. Or deranged people starting families accidentally. He preferred to simply make things up. *Black and White* seemed to build up some kind of expectation that he couldn't possibly fulfill.

Roy walked down Kane Street to the bicycle path that ran along Columbia Street toward Red Hook in one direction and Brooklyn Heights in the other. Deciding which direction to go seemed like a life choice, very Robert Frost, arbitrary yet not. It might mean everything. Red Hook had a reputation for being cool, full of young men with beards making furniture out of salvaged barns and deer antlers, distilling their own barrels of rye, tending beehives on their roofs, or painstakingly smoking cuts of meat from locally sourced livestock. Roy turned right, toward Brooklyn Heights, a staid and pretty residential neighborhood. The sun warmed the path in that direction, beckoning him. *Black and White. Black and White.* The title did nothing but make him feel anxious. *Gold* would be better. *Gold*, like the sun. *Gold* was glamorous and provocative and wide open to interpretation. *Gold.* Yes, he could change it. There was time. He didn't even have a contract for this book, because he hadn't written anything. There was always plenty of time. The problem was putting pen to paper, or fingers to keyboard, and writing something.

Joggers whooshed by him, music blaring from the white pods in their ears, their rhythmic footfalls marching out a mixed tune of Zen and impatience. Roy never felt the least bit guilty amidst the exercising throng. He was trim, in a middle-aged, fleshy sort of way. His clothes from his thirties, when he used to cycle around London all the time, still fit. He was proud of that.

He continued down the bicycle path toward the piers that had been transformed into a sprawling, modern waterside park. There were creatively designed play areas for children—rocky water parks, dangerous-looking rope swings, towering slides, a gigantic soccer pitch, basketball courts, a roller-skating rink, barbecue areas, grassy knolls and beaches, docks for sailboats and kayaks, dog runs, a bridge made of rope and wood, and benches facing New York Harbor and the endlessly entertaining view of the Brooklyn Bridge and Lower Manhattan off to the right, Governors Island and the Statue of Liberty off to the left. Roy had taken numerous photos of the sunset from there when they'd first moved, and sent them to his young agent in London. She'd assumed he'd used an effect of some kind on his camera. It was that breathtaking.

Lower Manhattan was all tall, sleek steel

and glass. Wendy's office was in one of those buildings. The Brooklyn Bridge hung majestically over the sun-dappled water, as if suspended invisibly from a more old-fashioned place, where everything existed in tones of sepia and brown. He'd read the bridge's story, how people had died building it, how the men had wanted to give up and the women had shown their mettle. It was the type of story a more ambitious writer might incorporate into a sweeping mega-saga.

Whether they knew the bridge's story or not, a never-ending queue of tourists tramped across it from Manhattan with no objective except maybe to eat a good slice of Brooklyn pizza. It always alarmed him how many of them there were. Roy turned away from the bridge and circled back toward Cobble Hill. The skyline lowered and his confidence returned. He walked up Congress Street, across Hicks Street and then Henry Street, and into Cobble Hill Park.

It was a tiny, pretty, stop-and-rest sort of park, with carefully tended flowers and protective old trees. A generous number of wooden benches beckoned to him: *"Write here!"* But writing on a laptop out of doors never worked. The sun glared from the screen and made his eyes tear. He was always too hot or too cold. The benches were hard. There were mosquitoes, barking dogs, screaming toddlers.

He kept walking. A couple of blocks down

Henry was a bar he'd passed many times and never gone into. The Horn and Duck was closer to home, but the food was too pretentious—they made their own ketchup; Heinz was better—and the staff were too chatty. He never got anything done there. This bar looked quiet.

Monte—that was the name of the bar. Not Monte's, just Monte, with a Budweiser light glowing tiredly in the window. It was barely noon, but the bar was open. Roy pushed open the smudged glass door and went inside.

"Morning," a cheerful woman with dimples in her cheeks greeted him from behind a set of drums at the back. "Don't mind me." She wasn't drumming; she was looking at her phone.

"Not at all." Roy chose a green vinyl–cushioned stool at the bar and placed his laptop on the shiny wooden bar top. The stool was comfortable, its back just low enough to offer lumbar support, with a perfectly positioned slat across the legs to rest his feet on. He opened his laptop and powered it on. He might just be able to work here.

Gold, he thought, opening a new Word document. *Boris Bowne Books is thrilled to announce* Gold, *the long-awaited new novel by Roy Clarke.* Or perhaps *Golden* was better. No, too 007. His readers would think he'd taken to writing spy novels. Race relations and secret agents—not subjects he could tackle without doing extensive research. Best to stick to what he did best—the quiet humor of two grown children traveling with their incontinent father, a drunk boy driving to pick up the girl he likes, a tedious dinner with an incompetent waiter, a hilariously muddy outdoor wedding.

Gold. Not exactly a title for a family novel. Unless . . . Roy's daughter Shy had a rich Russian-American classmate whose grandmother gave her a solid gold Krugerrand every Christmas, one for every year she'd been alive. Last spring the family had relocated very abruptly to the Bahamas.

Roy appeared to be staring hard at the blank screen, but really there was a scene playing out in his head in which a teenage girl was burying a pile of gold beneath a palm tree.

"There's no bartender," the woman called from the back of the bar, distracting the partially awakened lumbering beast that was his brain. "But I can probably grab whatever you need."

Roy swiveled around. "Tea?" he said distractedly, forgetting he was in a bar and that Americans didn't drink tea constantly, as if it were some sort of vital fuel that one's body couldn't function without, the way most of the English did.

She slid off her drum stool and ducked behind the bar. "Sure, just a sec. There's an electric kettle, I think." She looked up and smiled. "I'm Peaches. I work at the school, as a nurse. You're

Roy Clarke. I read in the real estate section last year that you moved to Strong Place. And my husband went to your book thing at the new bookstore on Smith. How do you like it here?"

Roy hated being recognized. Blustering internally, he hit return twice to demonstrate that he was writing, even though his screen was still blank.

"That was a dumb question, never mind." Peaches pushed a nondescript white mug across the bar. A Lipton tea bag dangled in the steaming water. "We only have that really coarse sugar they use in cocktails, and nondairy creamer." She set the containers on the bar. "I can't find a spoon, but there are cocktail straws there. Help yourself."

She walked out from behind the bar and retrieved her denim jacket from the drum stool.

"I have to get back to work. I was an English major, but now I'm an elementary school nurse. Don't ask." She shrugged on the jacket and buttoned it up. "I have to admit, I own all your books. My husband gave me the box set for my birthday a few years ago. We both genuinely intended to read them, but we never did. Sorry."

Roy nodded. "It's a thing, I understand. My daughter explained it to me. Everyone has my books displayed prominently on their bookshelves, but literally no one has read them. It's all right. The covers are nice to look at. I'm flattered all the same."

The dimples resurfaced on the drumming

nurse's cheeks. "You're a nice man, but don't be too generous with us. One day I'm going to read them all, I promise. I was an English major, I really was. I used to love reading books!"

Something buzzed. She pulled her phone out of her back pocket and glanced at it.

"Fuck. I have to run."

Roy picked up the mug. "Thanks for the tea."

He watched her through the smudgy storefront window as she hurried down Henry Street, sorry to see her go. He was alone in the bar now. Presumably the proprietor was in the back someplace, rotating beer kegs or sorting the whiskeys. Roy didn't mind. He removed the tea bag from the mug, drizzled in some creamer, turned back to his computer, and began to type.

Liam lay on his back in the school hallway, too exhausted to go out to lunch. Besides, he didn't have any money. He never had any money; his parents wanted him to get the free school lunch.

Sometimes the insanity got to him. It got to all of them. He could feel the pressure in the classroom rising, the barometer that was his brain constricting so that his thoughts were not really thoughts anymore but feelings of discomfort: hunger, numb feet, suppressed farts, cranial itching, sweat, shaking hands, exhaustion. Back in middle school they'd all carried spinning devices—fidget spinners—meant to alleviate the stress, but they'd grown out of them. Now the focus was on sex, and, to a lesser extent, college.

Liam's father, Greg Park, had "peaked in college." Liam didn't really get what that meant. It was something his mom always said when Liam's skin or hair or outfit looked particularly bad.

"At least you won't peak in high school, or even in college like your dad. You'll peak later, when it matters."

Somehow in Liam's mind, "peaking" was intrinsically linked to virility, which was how much sex you were having, and he definitely wasn't waiting until after college to have sex.

Some of his classmates had had it, or claimed to, the ones who'd ventured to parties hosted by kids whose parents were never home. "It wasn't that long ago we were the ones at those parties," his parents would say, trying to make him feel better about his stay-at-home lameness. "We know what happens. *You* happened." Most of the time Liam just hung out with them. They watched the same TV shows he wanted to watch anyway. And they let him eat most of the pizza.

There was a girl he liked. She was new last year, from England, with a famous dad. Liam hadn't told his parents about her. He knew they knew about her dad. They were always spotting him, talking about him, acting like they knew stuff about him, when all they really knew was what they'd garnered from the *New York Times*,

Wikipedia, Google, and his book jackets. He was older and English. The mom was American, with some fancy magazine job.

The girl's name was Shy. She was extremely tall and thin and clumsy-looking, like she woke up in the morning much taller than she'd been the night before and had no idea where her arms and legs began and ended. She didn't seem that shy either. They only had one class together, Latin II, and she was always raising her hand, bulldozing her way through readings and translations in her English accent. Their Latin teacher, Mr. Streko, had a thing for her, Liam could tell. It bordered on inappropriate.

"Shy is my best student," Liam could hear Mr. Streko's voice now, resonating down the hall. "I'm surprised to hear she's struggling so much in her other subjects. She's never late, she's always prepared, her grasp of Latin is profound."

Liam sat up and crept closer to the classroom door on his hands and knees. It was a meeting of some sort, about Shy.

"Yes, well, her father is a writer. He must have passed on some of his gift for language." This must be Shy's mother. "But she's not just struggling in her other subjects. She's almost failing."

"And obviously she has the aptitude, given how she's excelling in the one subject." This was Miss Melanie, the principal, friend to all but otherwise pretty useless. The parents loved her until high school, when they realized her passive good nature was not going to help their kid get into college.

"Of course she has the aptitude. She is my daughter; I know what she's capable of. The question is, why is she making an effort in only one subject and slacking off in all the others? Perhaps we should make her drop Latin so she has time for math."

"Uh, I wouldn't recommend that," Mr. Streko said.

There was an awkward pause. Liam sat on the floor outside the classroom and pretended to look for something deep in his backpack. He wasn't even supposed to be upstairs right now, unless he was studying in the library, or in the darkroom, working on his "generic definition" project for photography.

"Most likely she never encountered American history before now," Miss Melanie went on kindly. "And perhaps she could use some extra help in algebra and physics."

"Is it possible she's cheating and you haven't noticed? In Latin, I mean."

Whoa. What mom accused her own daughter of cheating?

"I'm sure it's nothing like that." Miss Melanie rushed to Shy's defense. "You'd have noticed. Right, Sammy?"

Liam almost snorted out loud. Sammy Streko? What the fuck kind of a name was that?

66

"Not at all," Mr. Streko agreed. "I'm a pretty tough teacher, actually. I conduct most of the class in Latin and the kids look at me like I'm a lunatic. Except Shy. She's got a good ear. It's like she can hear the roots, you know?"

Total silence. Poor Sammy.

"Unless she's cheating," Shy's mom insisted. It was almost like she wanted Shy to be more devious than she actually was.

"It's pretty hard to cheat in Latin. The vocab has to be memorized. I ask a lot of open-ended questions. There's no right answer. You just have to be engaged."

"I'll speak to Shy about a peer tutor in algebra and maybe physics," Miss Melanie suggested gently. "That often helps."

"Mmm." Shy's mother didn't sound convinced. "I have to get back to work." There was a rustling as she tied on her trench coat, or whatever rustling item of clothing she was wearing, and swept out of the classroom.

"Honestly," she muttered, nearly tripping over Liam.

Liam leapt to his feet, his last calculus test in his hand. He'd gotten an A minus.

He waited for Shy's unnecessarily frantic mom to rustle away and some of the teachers to wander back to their offices. Then he lunged awkwardly into the classroom.

"Hello, Liam." Miss Melanie offered him her

useless, sunshiny smile. "We were just finishing up a conference. Do you need this room?"

Mr. Streko was typing on his phone. A half-eaten Chipotle burrito rested in his lap. He looked wiped, like Shy's mom had grabbed his mangy beard and dragged him around behind her Mercedes.

Liam took a deep breath. He'd never done anything this bold before. "Sorry, I was totally eavesdropping. I can tutor whoever it is. I do pretty well." He held up his test. "I could use some extracurriculars and stuff. You know, for college?"

"The student in question is female," Miss Melanie said.

Liam shrugged his shoulders as if to indicate that tutoring some dumb girl would be kind of annoying, but he could handle it. "That's okay."

"You know Shy Clarke?"

He shrugged his shoulders again. "Kind of?"

• • •

Torso of Woman Found Behind Ikea Red Hook

A man (who wishes to remain unnamed) was walking his dog along the pier behind Ikea Red Hook early Monday when he spotted what looked like a mannequin in the water. Upon closer inspection, it appeared to be a headless human torso, severed just below the chin and at the waist, with the arms intact. The man called 911.

Torso of Woman Identified by Sister

The dismembered torso of a Staten Island woman was identified by the woman's sister late Tuesday evening. Police had released photographs of a tattoo of a red rose with green leaves on the upper arm of the torso in hopes that it would help to identify the body. A woman has since confirmed that her youngest sister had been missing since late Friday night after leaving the Staten Island restaurant where she worked part-time as a hostess. The woman's house, where she lives with her parents and younger brother, is now a crime scene. The entire family has been brought in for questioning.

Foot in Hudson River Linked to Staten Island Woman. Blood Found in Ex-Boyfriend's Home

Yesterday a foot was found by a kayaker in the Hudson River near Battery Park City. Police have matched the foot to the dismembered torso of the murdered Staten

Island woman found by a Brooklyn man early Monday while out walking his dog. The torso has since been identified by a family member who recognized the rose tattoo on the torso's upper arm. Police have been investigating the woman's family and close friends. The women's ex-boyfriend is now in custody after police discovered traces of blood on the cement floor of his garage. The woman's head and other remaining body parts have not yet been found.

Wendy Clarke rocked back and forth in her expensive, ergonomically correct, springy, gold metal and white leather swivel chair and tapped her manicured nails against the white Italian marble desktop. She clicked her way chronologically through *The Brookliner* links, grimacing as the gruesome story unfolded. She read *The Brookliner* religiously, hoping it would make her feel more Brooklyn-y. Nothing this morbid ever happened in England. England was full of thieves, not murderers. They cleared out your house while you were eating dinner in a restaurant. Wendy's closed office door rattled and she reduced the page, returning to the article she was supposed to write about the history of the French perfume industry. Tanners in Grasse. Catherine de' Medici. Dior. Chanel. The May rose. It was an amalgamation of pieces she'd written before. She reached across her keyboard and squirted two pumps of $130 La Mer hand serum into her palms, as if that would help.

Wendy occupied the coveted southwest-facing office on the thirty-first floor of a five-year-old office tower near the World Trade Center, home to *Fleurt*, one of the few fashion magazines still in print. It had been her idea to move to New York, and she'd courted this job for eight months until she got it, sending witty, erudite emails to Lucy Fleur, its glamorously absent founder—who wore only pale yellow and seemed to exist exclusively at fashion shows—and completely abusing the privilege of being married to a well-known author. Roy had no idea, but he'd basically gotten Wendy the job. Finally, Lucy Fleur had caved, just as Wendy hoped she would. Lucy Fleur just had to have the features editor with the famous author husband, the editor who had once compiled the now infamous *Brexit Suppers*, a series of snarky, irreverent vignettes and alcohol-heavy recipes using only British ingredients, like "Gin and Ewe" and "English Sherry with One French Strawberry Found on the Floor of the Ferry." Never mind that Wendy had always been freelance, with no office at all. Now she was a senior editor.

An excruciatingly uninspired senior editor.

A whole year had gone by. Wendy hid in her

office, reading *The Brookliner* and shopping online, pretending to be extremely busy and acting overly curt and officious toward the assistants. Lucy Fleur hadn't introduced herself to Wendy even once. Their communications had been reduced to Lucy Fleur's cryptic, condescending emails: *Cutoffs, cutouts, cowgirls. Take me to Texas.* Or, *Perfume. Grasse. Chanel. Roses. You know the drill. Make me smell it.*

What kind of person sawed up another person? Was the woman dead when he started, or did he just knock her unconscious and turn on the chain saw? Did she wake up when he was sawing at her waist? Did she look down and see her bottom half fall away? Wendy exhaled noisily, well aware that there was no one to hear her. She didn't know why she was so fascinated, but she felt connected to the drifting dead woman somehow.

Perfume. Grasse. Chanel.

Wendy pumped more hand serum into her palms and rubbed the excess on her neck, which could use all the help it could get. Why couldn't she concentrate? Why had she been so fixated on getting this job and moving to New York when it was clear to her now that it was not what she wanted at all?

It made sense at the time. Roy was floundering. He hadn't published a book in years. The older girls were almost finished at Oxford and Shy was only one year into high school. Wendy had been hosting the same dinner parties and game nights for the parents from her girls' schools, cooking the same meals, complaining about the English winters, writing the same tiredly trendy copy for the same tiredly trendy magazine supplements for newspapers that no one cared about anymore. Roy's longtime agent had died. Two of the couples they were friendliest with had moved away from their London suburb to South Africa and Australia. They needed a fresh start, she'd decided, in New York, where she'd grown up. And once she'd decided, she became fixated, spending all her time searching online for real estate, magazine jobs, and schools. She was going home, where she belonged. Where no one said "prawns and avos" when they meant shrimp and avocados, where virtually no one drank instant coffee, and where she wouldn't have to take a bus to get a fresh bagel. The move had taken up all her time and planning and organizational skills. The new house had five bathrooms! But now that they'd actually moved and had lived in the city for a whole year, Wendy felt more restless and exasperated than ever. Roy still hadn't written anything. Shy was struggling at school and hadn't made any friends. There were no dinner parties or game nights to plan and host. And Wendy's job, despite its title and salary and shiny trimmings, was painfully dull. Over the course of a year, all three of them seemed to have retreated into their discomfort and were more lonely and isolated than they had ever been before. Wendy had always maintained a certain bravado. She was Wendy Clarke. Editor of her Upper East Side girls' school newspaper and NYU's *Washington Square News*. Editor of *Brexit Suppers*. Mrs. Roy Clarke. Her bravado was what had gotten them here. But now that she was here, she didn't know who she was anymore.

There was a light knock and Manfred poked their head into Wendy's office.

"How's it going?"

Manfred was new, one of several gender-fluid editorial assistants at the magazine, but by far the most gorgeous. Incredible legs, perfectly shaped shaved head, beige skin, and wonderful greenish-gold eyes. They were also extremely efficient. The perfume story was due today.

"I'm all right, thank you."

"I'm getting coffee. You know you want some," Manfred offered. "Lucy's not back from Italy until tomorrow."

Not that anyone ever actually saw Lucy when Lucy was "in," but the office got very quiet. The rest of the time, when the assistants ran the place, it smelled like pad thai and squealing was rampant.

"Sure," Wendy agreed. "Coffee would be nice, thank you."

"Milky and sweet, just the way you like it."

Manfred glanced at Wendy's gigantic computer screen, which was split between the dead-woman story on *The Brookliner*, complete with photos, and her perfume story, which was one long, boring paragraph. "Oh my God, have you been reading about the torso?"

Wendy nodded, embarrassed to be caught not working.

"It's so sick."

"There were a lot of pieces," Wendy agreed and then frowned, remembering that she was supposed to be Manfred's superior.

"Creepy boyfriend. He probably thought he was being all sneaky and careful. The dum-dum."

Wendy was still not used to working in an office. There seemed to be a strange combination of the familiar and the formal. Was she supposed to delegate to Manfred or invite them to lunch? She turned back to her computer screen, reached for her mouse, and closed *The Brookliner* window. Sensing that Manfred was about to leave, she whipped around again.

"It's a good story. I still want to know if they find the head."

Manfred's glossy black eyebrows shot up.

"We live quite close to where they found it," Wendy continued. "How could she be living with that man for so many years and not know what he was capable of?"

"You don't seem like the Red Hook type,"

Manfred observed. "Not that I'd know. I go to work and then I go back to Williamsburg. I love Williamsburg."

All of the assistants lived in Williamsburg. They were always meeting up for tacos and tequila or going to spinning classes or buying aromatherapy diffusers for their desks at the Williamsburg outpost of Muji.

"I live in Cobble Hill," Wendy clarified. "It's very safe."

"I hope so." Manfred bit their top lip. "Everyone said you were scary. You're not scary."

They looked at each other in silence for a moment.

"Sometimes I give people the wrong impression," Wendy admitted. When anxious she resorted to snobbery, just like at Shy's school. But she couldn't possibly be snobbish to Manfred. Manfred was perfection.

"There's a rumor that you took a pair of size eight Gucci sneakers from the fashion closet," Manfred went on teasingly. "Only the assistants get to do that, and only if it's not an in-demand size, like a five or an eleven."

Wendy was horrified. The sneakers had been there for almost a month, collecting dust, before she rescued them and gave them to Shy.

"I didn't know."

Manfred laughed. "You're supposed to be able to buy them on your salary, but don't worry about it."

Wendy had the feeling Manfred wanted to say something nice about her outfit now, and was struggling. When she'd started at *Fleurt* she'd decided on a chic and easy uniform—black trousers and a black top. Today's ensemble was particularly unremarkable.

"You have the most beautiful hands," Manfred said finally.

Wendy looked down at her hands. They were her thinnest feature. "Thank you." She looked up. "I like your earrings." Manfred wore tiny, classic pearl studs.

"Back in a few with coffee," Manfred promised.

Wendy watched the door close and reached for her phone. At her most lonely and vulnerable moments she texted Roy or Shy, presumably to help organize them in some way, but really just to garner a response. Should she confront Shy about the meeting she'd had with her teachers? She'd come off a bit more demanding and terse and scary than she'd meant to. But what about that smug, unclean, burrito-eating, overly tattooed Latin teacher? All she wanted was for Shy to succeed. Not as a student per se, but as a person. She began a long, urgent, motherly text.

I know you hate it when I meddle, and I know you like Latin, but you're simply not putting the time into your other classes. The headmistress said something about peer tutors, which I think sounds like a cop-out. We can find you

77

a proper tutor. It's ok to ask for help when you need it.

She read over the text and then deleted it. Shy did hate it when she meddled. Her most meddlesome had been her excitement about the move itself, which Shy had found simply annoying. "What color do you want your new room to be?" Wendy would ask. "I honestly don't care, Mum," Shy would answer. "Should we give away all our old clothes and just get new ones when we get there?" Wendy would ask gleefully. "Why would we do that?" Shy said. "Should we put in one of those taps by the stove in our new kitchen so we can fill up pots for pasta?" Shy didn't even bother responding to that. Should she text Roy? Maybe Shy was in the wrong school. But Roy might be writing. Wendy didn't want to disturb him.

She turned back to her computer and dragged the cursor away from the perfume article and into the search engine. Maybe if she found them a country house they could spend time together as a family on weekends, go apple picking or antiquing. Roy could write in a restored barn overlooking a babbling brook. Shy could have a horse. She clicked on a map of the Hudson Valley. Millbrook, Rhinebeck, Milan, Hudson. There were real estate offices in every town, with websites. Oh, here was a pretty house, in someplace called Ancram—with a pool!

• • •

"Hello? Dad?" Shy called as she closed and locked the front door to their four-story brownstone. The parlor floor consisted of a giant great room with French doors that led to a terrace overlooking the garden. The house had been built in the early nineteen hundreds and had been modernized and remodeled many times, but it maintained its old New York charm. Upstairs were four enormous bedrooms. Downstairs was an entire apartment.

"We could do Airbnb," Shy's father had suggested once. "Let out a room or two to travelers."

"And have a bunch of strangers tromping around, stealing things and stopping up the toilets? I don't think so," Wendy said, ending the conversation.

"I'm home," Shy called again. "Are you here?"

"Here," Roy Clarke called from the library, which was really just the far right-hand portion of the gigantic open-plan living room. Somehow Wendy had convinced them to call it the library because it was where most of the bookshelves were. "All writers have libraries," she declared, and thus it was so.

Roy Clarke was sprawled in his favorite armchair, his bathrobe tied over his clothes, a book in his lap. The TV was on but muted, a cooking show.

"I showered and got dressed and went out this morning. I brought my computer and everything," he announced as Shy came into the room. "I even wrote a few words over a nice cup of tea at the most perfect old bar. I'm so glad I discovered it. I wrote the beginning of a chapter, or the beginning of something anyway. Then I got pretty famished from all the writing, so I went to the supermarket. And then I came home."

"I'm not Mum," Shy said. "I don't care." She sniffed the air. It smelled like cinnamon. "Did you bake something? It smells amazing."

Her father's gray-whiskered face turned pink. "You know those cinnamon buns that come in the tins that you pop open and bake and then squirt that pasty sugary stuff on?"

She nodded.

"I'd never had them before," her father went on. "I went to Key Food for bread and cheese and came out with those. I baked them, and then I ate them all. Marvelous."

"What about that guy's cat, the invisible one?"

"Fed it already."

Shy unzipped her hoodie and kicked off her sneakers. "I'm starving." It was cold in the house. She flopped down on the sofa and pulled the cashmere throw over her legs and feet. By assuming the pose of a sick girl, she now felt a true chill coming on. "Will you make me a cheese toastie?" It was what her father called a grilled cheese and what she craved whenever she had a cold or cramps.

"Are you poorly, my sweet?" her father asked, exaggerating his accent.

Shy missed England. It was so much less stressful. People sat in their sitting rooms watching telly and eating toast soldiers and drinking sweet, milky tea. There was so much less walking. But her mother was from Manhattan and felt very strongly that New York City was the only real city in the world and that they needed to move there. It was her father who'd insisted on Brooklyn because it felt more authentic. Manhattan was just a giant tourist attraction. Her mother resisted at first. "Brooklyn isn't really New York," she'd said. When it turned out living in Brooklyn was so much more fashionable than living in Manhattan, and that they could buy a whole house with a garden instead of living in an apartment, Wendy gave in. As long as Shy attended private school.

Roy Clarke went into the large, open kitchen area, located the electric sandwich press, and set it atop the butcher-block island in the center of the kitchen.

"I'll make you a cheese toastie if you tell me what you're doing home so early."

Shy had hoped her father wouldn't notice. "I don't know," she told him honestly. "Mum was at school, talking to my teachers. I went out for lunch and kept walking. I just wanted to be home. I had Latin this morning."

Roy knew it was wrong, but he liked that his daughter enjoyed his company and was willing to eat in front of him but not her mother. He made two sandwiches. They ate them directly off the kitchen counter, gobbling them up so quickly they didn't have time to talk. Then he made two more.

Gold. Every time he blinked, there it was in 28-point bold italics, centered in the middle of his mind's eye. That hadn't happened with *Black and White*. It was a good sign. His American fans would love it, if any of them were still alive by the time he finished writing the book. If he were still alive. Or maybe *Black, White & Gold?* No, that sounded like a law firm. He didn't do legal writing either. No courtroom dramas or anything too technical. Too much research. Too much room for error. *Black and Gold and Gold and White. White on White with Black or Gold.* Blimey.

Shy never asked about his writing. Either she wasn't interested or she didn't want to nag.

"Hey Dad, do you want to go see a movie?" she asked him now.

"I thought you were ill." He retrieved the cloth from the sink and wiped the sandwich crumbs from the counter.

"I feel well enough to watch a movie." Shy dug

an unopened can of Coke out of her schoolbag and cracked it open. Wendy refused to keep soda in the house. What did she think Shy subsisted on—air?

"I was going to call and check on your sisters, but I'm sure they'd rather I didn't."

Shy's older sisters—Chloe, twenty-two, and Anna, twenty-one—lived in Oxford, where they'd gone to university, and worked in a lab. They were science nerds and extremely dismissive of their father, mother, and little sister. They especially disapproved of the move to New York.

"I'll watch a film with you if it's at the local cinema and if we can get those tiny chocolate buttons with the white sprinkles on them."

"Hold on." Shy looked up the showtimes on her phone. "There's one at one p.m. that looks good. That was like three minutes ago. Leave the crumbs. Come on, Dad, let's go."

"All of a sudden we're in a huge rush," Roy grumbled, but secretly he was grateful. If Shy left him alone he'd feel compelled to try and write something.

They hurried out to the cinema.

"Don't eat them all before the trailers are over," Shy whispered as Roy removed the cellophane wrapper from his box of sweets.

"Hush." Roy slid down in his seat. "You're supposed to be in school, remember?"

Shy hadn't warned him that this was an R-rated French comedy about two bored teenage boys who snuck onto a cruise ship on a mission to lose their virginities. The trailers were all for foreign R-rated films too, full of sweaty naked people drinking wine and throwing vegetables at each other. Roy hunkered down in his seat, imagining the headline: Pervy Author Kidnaps Daughter from School and Forces Her to Watch Pervy French Film.

Shy nudged him with her elbow. "It's okay, Dad. There's no one else here."

The film opened with a scene in which one of the boys was babysitting his little brother. They were watching a strange old film called *The Red Balloon* on TV. The balloon danced and flew over a sagging residential neighborhood of Paris. Its string became snagged in a tree, the balloon so red against the blue Parisian sky.

Red, Roy thought. Not *Gold* but *Red*.

Chapter 3

Cue music. Cue talking cat. Cue voice for cat. Cat sits in chair and slurps spaghetti from owner's bowl. Sated, cat burps politely into his paw. And cut. There was a fraction of time for an ending, some sort of sound better than the burp. He had to get the audience out of the burp and to another, less-gross place. But where?

Stuart liked his job, and he was good at it. Plus, it paid ridiculously well, considering how easy it was. Touring was way harder, but he missed it. He missed the band.

"Wazzup?" Robbie always answered the phone the same way.

"What time is it in Australia? Sorry if I'm calling at a bad time. I just never know," Stuart apologized. He called Robbie and JoJo all the time, like a lonely ex-girlfriend, checking in. He lived vicariously through their adventures in bachelorhood or felt smug about how comfortable his life was now, depending on what state they were in when he called them.

"Fuck if I know. I'm not in Australia. I'm in fucking Indonesia, man. Some island I can't even fucking pronounce. The surf is outrageous and the food is too. I love it here. I'm like, growing tentacles, the water is so warm. It's like a bath, like surfing in the fucking bath." Robbie had an Australian accent now, which was sort of annoying since he was from Park Slope. Stuart kept waiting for him to break into his normal voice, but it had been years now, and he never did. He'd even cut an EP with a song called "G'day, Kanga" on it, featuring an Aboriginal musician playing the didgeridoo. It never made it to the American charts.

"If this is about us getting back together and playing Coachella, sorry dude, but I've got surfin' to do."

Stuart laughed. "You wish. Nope, just checking in. It's my lunchtime and I'm not hungry, so I called you instead." He twirled his chair around a few times. "Any news besides the waves?"

"Dude, that's the thing. I *am* the wave."

Stuart waited for Robbie to say something normal.

"How's the wife?"

"Mandy is . . . worse, actually." Stuart was never completely sure whether Robbie and JoJo liked Mandy or if they resented her. At some point he'd decided not to care either way. "She's pretty bad."

Dead silence.

"Hello?"

"I'm here, mate, I'm here. Christ," Robbie swore. "I am truly sorry."

"It's all right. I just feel bad for her. And Ted."

This wasn't completely true. He liked being the able parent, the caregiver, going out for ice cream cones together and teaching Ted how to skateboard. Ted seemed to like it too. Mommy time had been reduced to first thing in the morning or at the end of the day, when Ted was only partially awake—the way Mandy was all the time—on the big bed in the kitchen.

"Hey, has she tried medical marijuana? It's supposed to really help. Not that I'd have any idea, having never touched the stuff myself."

Stuart laughed. Robbie was a huge pothead in high school. He'd carried Visine and mint gum at all times and subsisted on Oreos and Doritos.

"She'd have to get a prescription." Stuart did not enjoy Mandy when she was high. Annoying didn't even begin to describe it. She liked to wedge herself into tight spaces where she felt safe and give orders from there: *Are there any lemons? Can someone make me some fresh-squeezed lemonade? In a bowl. Please?* But it was worth a try.

"New York State is impossible for that sort of shit though. Red tape like crazy. People die of cancer and AIDS before they get their prescriptions. I know someone who can fix you up. Doctor to the stars, or so I'm told. Music connection. He makes house calls and everything. Just tell him what you need and he'll hook you up. Dr. Mellow. That's not his name, but it's something like that. And I don't think he's an actual doctor, more like a nurse."

"A nurse? I know a nurse." Stuart's mind so easily diverted to Peaches. Maybe she could actually help. How perfect that he'd just been in to see her about the lice. And he'd told her about Mandy. Going in to ask her about this wouldn't seem too random. He just had to loosen up his balls and do it.

"Gotta pick up the kid. I'll let you know if I need that guy's info," he told Robbie distractedly, already standing up and shoving his MetroCard, wallet, and keys back into his pockets. He could surprise Ted by meeting him in the schoolyard when school let out. Ted could play four square with his classmates while Stuart asked Peaches about pot. He'd much rather buy it from Peaches than from some sketchy fake doctor. Not that she was selling it, but she probably knew where to get it.

Roy's mobile phone bleated as soon as he and Shy got home from the movie and she'd retreated to her room. Shy had put his phone on "goat" for when he received texts. Roy meant to ask her how to personalize the noises for each contact. He wanted the Beatles' "Eleanor Rigby" to play whenever this particular person texted or rang, because of all the lonely people Roy had ever encountered, Tupper Paulsen was the loneliest.

Thanks for feeding the cat. He seems happy.

Well, at least the cat was alive. Roy had only fed it the one time, two days ago. He was supposed to go back again yesterday and today, but he couldn't face it.

Tupper had approached him on the street. He seemed a bit desperate.

"Look, I see you all the time, and I know you must be very busy with your writing, but you work from home, right?" he'd said. "I'm Tupper Paulsen. We're the Paulsens." He'd hesitated, as if waiting for Roy to recognize his name. "Elizabeth and Tupper Paulsen. We're on Kane Street, directly around the corner from you." It was a bit creepy that he knew where Roy lived, but then again, so did everyone.

"So, what I was wondering," Tupper had continued nervously, desperately. "Would you mind feeding our cat this weekend? We're going upstate and our cat sitter isn't returning our calls and it would really be so easy for you since we're just around the corner."

Roy's response had been slow. This Tupper fellow was asking him to feed his cat. Not Shy or Wendy, but him. He didn't even like cats. All the same, he appreciated being asked a normal, neighborly thing instead of being stared at, fawned over, or written about in the newspapers.

"Of course, we'd reciprocate when the time comes," Tupper Paulsen added. "Whatever you need. Elizabeth loves cats."

"Yes, of course," Roy agreed, even though he and Wendy and Shy didn't have a cat, or any pets for that matter. "Happy to help." Why not?

Thus, Tupper had given him a key and a few neatly handwritten instructions, including the cat's name. He seemed to be in a hurry, and within a few minutes he started up the pewter-colored vintage Saab parked in front of his house and drove off.

"Catsy?" Roy called when he'd arrived at the Paulsens' the next morning. Nothing. He went about his business, pouring dry cat food into the bowl and refilling the water dish.

"I have to scoop yer shit," Roy called out again. "Nobody likes to scoop shit, but you're obviously used to living in a nice clean house."

Litter box is upstairs in the bathroom outside the twins' bedroom, the note on the counter told him. He mounted the stairs, noting how little they creaked, the absence of dust. The Paulsens ran a tight ship. He followed the instructions on the note, looking for the bathroom on the left at the end of the hall. It occurred to him as he made his way across the sunlit parquet floor that he had no idea how many children Tupper and Elizabeth Paulsen had spawned. Just the twins? More? He thought he might have seen Tupper with a tall girl with white-blond hair, pushing a pram.

The house was orderly and spare. The door to the all-white bathroom stood open and the pungent odor of freshly dropped cat shit emanated from within. It was so strong it almost made him hungry. Not for cat shit—Roy wasn't insane—but for something rich and chocolaty. When he was done here he might head over to the Chocolate Room and have a slice of cake. *One ought to eat more cake,* he thought, and then giggled to himself because he was pretty sure Winnie the Pooh had said that.

He glanced across the hall into the twins' bedroom, expecting to see two cribs or two tiny little beds and a whole host of cute little things in duplicate. Instead there was just a single white bed pushed up against a pale yellow wall. Above the bed was a picture of two little newborn babies swaddled in hospital blankets, nestled side by side in a white wicker Moses basket.

Roy stared down at the lonely bed with its faded daisy quilt and gray stuffed bear. He examined the photograph of the babies again and then began to cough and cough, as if his esophagus were trying to dispel the shocking sadness of Tupper and Elizabeth Paulsen's tremendous loss. One of the twins had died, but they still called it "the twins' room," which meant the child who was left had to live with the hole in the basket that was her sister's little body for the rest of her life.

"I'm clearing out your box and then it's cheery-bye, m'lad," Roy told the invisible cat. Sad things made him nervous.

By now the litter box was probably overflowing with poo.

Can I buy you a drink to thank you?

Roy stared at the texts. Poor bloke. Maybe he'd only asked Roy to feed his cat because he wanted to be friends. He wasn't fame-stalking him, it didn't seem like. He hadn't even mentioned Roy's books or the TV show. He was just a neighbor, being neighborly.

All the lonely people, where do they all belong?

I'm actually headed out to a bar right now if you'd like to join me. Monte on Henry St.

Tupper didn't text back right away. Roy put his coat back on, grabbed his laptop, and called up to Shy.

"Going out again!"

"Okay!" she shouted back.

His screen lit up as he walked down Henry.

Great! See you in 10.

There was no correlation between Tupper's cheerful texts and his dead-infant haunted house. As he walked, Roy googled him. A bio appeared with his neighbor's picture. Tupper Paulsen was an industrial designer, creator of the Macaw—a decorative hollow bird sculpture that could either neatly store all your wires and cables or secretly stash a spare cell phone for surveillance purposes. The most ingenious thing about the Macaw was that it was white, not red like the actual bird, and blended in with the décor of absolutely any room. Stores couldn't keep them on the shelves. Amazon was always sold out. Tupper Paulsen was a genius inventor and his wife, Elizabeth, was a well-known artist. No wonder they lived in the prettiest carriage house in all of Cobble Hill. They also definitely could have afforded to pay a professional cat sitter.

The bar was unlocked and the lights were on, but there was no one inside. It was just as Roy had left it that morning. He poured himself a Guinness, settled onto a barstool, and opened up his laptop. After all these years, he'd mastered the affect of "writing" to perfection.

The word *Gold* glared menacingly from the screen. He deleted it, typed the word *Red* in its place, and stared at it.

Red was bold. Leaves turned red in autumn. Apples were red. Fast cars were red. Red wine was red. But so was blood. He didn't do horror or murders or gore.

"Hello?"

"Hiya." Roy slammed his laptop shut.

Tupper Paulsen slid onto the barstool next to him and held out his hand. It was cold and thin.

"Trying to write in a bar these days. Never done it before."

Tupper nodded. His white shirt was open at the collar, his sleeves rolled up to the elbows. It was a very relaxed look for him. "Is it working?"

"Nah. I don't know. Too early to tell," Roy admitted.

"Well, at least it's quiet, this bar. You couldn't find a quieter one," Tupper said without looking around. He seemed to know the place.

"Odd spot, but I like it." Roy got up and went around the bar. "Here, I'll pour you a beer. What would you like?"

"Gin please. Nothing in it, just gin. It's down to the right, below the dish—"

"Got it," Roy said. It occurred to him that they were in the same business, creating something where nothing had existed before. And they'd both had some success at it.

"So, the Macaw, that was brilliant. Made anything good since?" he asked boldly.

Tupper shook his head. His wavy auburn hair was cut in a way that accentuated his high cheekbones, steely blue eyes, and red lips. If he had been born a girl, he would have been astonishingly beautiful. On a man it was simply off-putting.

"Nothing? Well, that makes me feel better." Roy rapped his knuckles on the bar. He poured Tupper a tall glass of Tanqueray and pushed it toward him.

Tupper picked up the glass and took a small, neat sip.

Roy winced. Nobody drank straight gin except drunk grannies and the children who finished their drunk grannies' drinks after they fell asleep in front of the six o'clock news. But Tupper Paulsen's little child was dead. He deserved a glass or two of gin.

Roy poked around beneath the bar until he located the small fridge with a tray of ice cubes in the freezer. He popped some out and plopped them into Tupper's glass. It wasn't an actual known fact that Tupper's child was dead; Roy had made it up. But the house felt like a shrine to a life that was no more—the invisible cat, the Moses basket, the prettily decorated twin room. And where was his wife? The living child?

Was there something here he could use for *Gold* or *Red* or whatever this new book would be called? Ideas thrashed around in the muddy waters of his head. The family had lost its riches. The parents were hiding out from the debt collectors on their sailboat in the Bahamas. The girl remained stubbornly ashore, burying the only thing she had left—seventeen gold Krugerrands, gifts from her grandmother. Then maybe there was a hurricane or a tsunami or some other kind of natural disaster. The sailboat would be swept away. After the storm the night sky would be so bright with stars it looked like daylight, and that's when his girl—Isabel, he'd always liked the name Isabel—makes her escape. She takes the gold and . . . Mars was red, the planet Mars. *Red*.

Immediately his mind shifted to space. *Battlestar Galactica* was his favorite TV show as a teenager. He and his best mate, Rupert Warwick, watched it religiously. There was even a Marvel comic book series—based on the show, but much darker and creepier—that they bought every month and read in one sitting. The show was hilarious and strange and exciting and seductive. Each episode began and ended with a godlike voice-over that was part cultish philosophy, part nonsensical gibberish. Captain Apollo and Lieutenants Starbuck and Boomer—three strapping space warriors on the last remaining battleship—one impossibly perfect and good, another reckless and wild, the last loyal and brave. Their home planet, Caprica, had been destroyed by the Cylons and now the battleship led a "ragtag fleet" of survivors, in search of a distant planet inhabited by other humans, a place called Earth. All the men smoked and drank and played cards, and the women were beautiful, especially Jane Seymour as Serina—at least, Roy and Captain Apollo thought so.

"I'm not a very good drinker." Tupper spun the sweating glass of gin round and round on the shiny wooden bar top. "I've always been so thin. I get very drunk. And then I vomit."

Roy jolted out of his reverie. He slid the gin away and grabbed a pint glass. "Why don't you drink Guinness then?" He found the tap and filled the glass. "It's got a lot less alcohol than other beers and it's filling, like eating a slice of cake."

Tupper took a sip from the dark, foamy pint. "Yes," he said thoughtfully. "It's possible this won't make me sick."

Roy topped off his own pint. Tupper Paulsen was already beginning to wear on him. He was like an insane person who'd only just been let out. "Working on anything new?"

Tupper got out his phone. Roy sat down on the stool next to him and peered over his shoulder.

"This is the Flounder. It's a very thin mattress that feels very thick. This one's the Artichoke Heart. It's a fancy artichoke-shaped bowl with a tiny heart-shaped bowl inside it. Oh, and here's the Hedgehog. It started out as a vibrating tool to itch your itches and remove dead skin and blackheads, but it's waterproof, so it can also be used in the bath or as a sex toy."

"Naughty," Roy said, shocked.

None of Tupper Paulsen's ideas sounded very good. But then again, neither did a book about a teenage girl in a hurricane in the Bahamas with a backpack full of gold who . . . Could she somehow wind up on Mars? There were meant to be people there eventually. Newscasters were always banging on about it on the BBC. Maybe his book could be set in the future. The first Martian settlement, with volunteers of all ages. People on Earth were watching, feeling hopeful and skeptical. And the absurd thing—the Roy Clarke does *Battlestar Galactica* of it—could be that life on Mars wasn't much different from life on Earth. Basically all anyone ever thought about was food, sex, and going to the toilet.

Roy put down his pint. "Let me ask you this. How far do you take an idea before you decide it's utter shit, or too difficult, or just plain not going to pan out or whatever?"

Tupper took several gulps of Guinness. "I finish everything. You should see my warehouse sometime. I have at least one version of every idea I've ever had."

Roy imagined an airplane hangar full of rubber cows that shot wine out of their udders and battery-operated kittens with massaging paws. "Fantastic. I'd love to have a look."

They sipped their beers.

"Hey, you know, I actually have a camera set up in a Macaw over at my place, like a surveillance thing? It's connected to an app on my phone. I put it in over a year ago when Elizabeth . . . Never mind. Anyway, I know you only fed the cat that one time, because the app shows whenever anyone goes into the kitchen."

Shit. Roy scooted back his barstool. "I'm sorry." He looked down at his feet. "I felt like a burglar in your house. And your cat hates me."

Tupper laughed. "He's a one-person cat. He misses my wife. It's fine. Doesn't matter. I just wanted you to know that I know so you're not carrying it around, you know?"

For all his crisply ironed shirt neatness and insanity, Tupper Paulsen was a pretty nice fellow.

"Where are you from? I mean, originally?" Roy asked. Mars? Uranus? What color was Uranus?

"Maine," Tupper said. "Elizabeth and I, we grew up together in the state of Maine."

Roy pulled his glass toward him. He waited for the story of Tupper's sad wife and single surviving twin, but Tupper just went around the bar and poured himself another pint of Guinness.

"Maybe the Hedgehog should be the Maine Lobster, to make it more personal," Roy mused. He pushed his half-empty glass across the bar for Tupper to refill it. "Or a moose?"

"The Moose. That really sounds like a sex toy."

"Can it make noises? Do moose even make noises?"

"I think they huff and sort of bellow."

"Perfect." Roy laughed.

Tupper came around the bar again and sat down.

"So, it's just you and the cat in the house right now?"

Tupper nodded. "That's sort of the reason I had to rush away. I thought she was close. And that's why I'm using the Macaw. I know it sounds creepy. It's just so I know when she decides to come back."

Roy was confused. "So no one's dead or anything awful?"

Tupper laughed and drank more beer. "No, everyone's fine."

"But your daughters' room. All those sad pictures. The empty bed."

Tupper laughed again. He appeared to be drunk. "That's Elizabeth's work. She's an artist. We don't have any kids."

"I see." A great weight floated off Roy's shoulders, but he was no less confused. "So whose bedroom is it then?"

Tupper huffed, mooselike, into his Guinness. "You really need to come down to the warehouse sometime."

Chapter 4

Ted's face lit up when he spotted Stuart.

"Dad!" He burst out of the huddle of children and ran into Stuart's arms. The other students shuffled over to their minders disinterestedly, or waited for their Hobby Horse teachers to lead them away.

Stuart hugged him. "Thought I'd surprise you. I need to ask someone about something inside the school, and then we can grab a slice of pizza or walk over to Ample Hills for ice cream. Sound good?"

Ted turned his freckled, pen-smudged face up to his father, his green eyes wide. "But Dad. It's Wednesday. I go to the Brooklyn Stragetizer on Wednesdays and Fridays. Remember?"

"Stra*te*gizer," Stuart corrected. "Sorry man, I forgot."

He looked up and saw a pimply teenager wearing a faded *Dark Side of the Moon* T-shirt waving the red-and-black Strategizer flag, the signal that the group would be leaving soon. The boys lined up behind him were pale and scrawny, the kinds of boys who would rather play Dungeons & Dragons than soccer or basketball. Ted was doomed.

"You go have fun. I'll see you after."

• • •

"Hey, sorry to bother you again." Stuart closed the door to the nurse's office and shoved his hands in his pockets. A tall, fat kid lay on the cot with his eyes closed, dried snot around his nostrils, one sneaker off, one sneaker on. There was a hole in the knee of his track pants and the knee was bandaged.

Nurse Peaches swiveled around on her chair. "You find more of the fuckers?" she asked with a dimpled smile. "Sorry, Arnold. Excuse my French."

The fat kid snickered, eyes still closed. They seemed to have an understanding. Still, Stuart couldn't exactly ask her about procuring weed with a kid in the room.

"Uh, maybe." He removed a hand from his pocket and ran it through his hair. "I know I'm being paranoid, but would you mind checking me again?"

Mind? Peaches giggled inwardly. Stuart Little had no concept of the power he had over her. God, he was hot. Hotter than he was Monday. Hotter than he was in his twenties. There was a boyish forlornness to him that she yearned to mother in the most unmotherly way. Because she was a pervert. A pervert with a stockpile of lice combs.

"Sure," she responded, all business. "I'll just check you with the comb." She stood up and patted the back of her desk chair. "We shouldn't need to use conditioner again unless there's been some hatching action."

"God, I hope not." Stuart walked over and sat down. He was trembling for some reason. Goose bumps appeared on his arms. Jesus. This hadn't happened to him since ninth grade, when he'd had a crush on his math teacher. He'd bombed every test just so he could stay after school for extra help and be alone with her. Then one day in May she wore sandals to school and he discovered she had really gross feet. And just like that, he was over her.

Someone was knocking on her office door. Peaches swiveled Stuart around protectively so that his back was to the intruder. "Come in."

"Oh, Arnold." It was Arnold's mom. She was over six feet tall and was wearing a knee brace. She sighed. "Clumsiness runs in the family."

Peaches went over and patted Arnold's shoulder. He was unresponsive. "It's all right. We enjoy hanging out."

Arnold's mom nodded, one skinny eyebrow raised. "Sometimes I think he does it on purpose, just to see you," she said in a loud whisper, shooting a glance at the back of Stuart's head.

Get in line, Arnold, Stuart thought. *She's mine.*

"Well, that would be sweet," Peaches said. "But I think he's just a bruiser. I've seen it before. My son was like that in elementary school. He grew so big so fast he had no idea how hard he'd fall or even where his feet were. I thought he'd wind up playing ice hockey or lacrosse. Instead he's this six-foot, seventeen-year-old math nerd who barely goes outside."

Nurse Peaches has a teenage son? Stuart stared fixedly at the yellow thumbtack holding up her calendar. The month of September featured a depressed-looking bulldog wearing a red tutu.

"I don't know how you can possibly have a son in high school—you're only twenty-five," Arnold's mom said. She didn't seem to care one way or the other though.

"Anyway, I'll let you get back to . . ." She glanced at the back of Stuart's head once more.

"Come on, sweetness."

She frowned at Arnold's still form.

"He doesn't have a concussion again, does he? Liquid diet with a concussion. That's what our doctor recommends. Chewing and crunching stress the brain."

Arnold sat up. "I hurt my hands and knees, not my brain," he protested. "Solid food, please, I'm starving."

Arnold's mom clapped her hands together. "He's alive! Hurry up and get your shoe on. We'll go to the butcher and pick up some steaks on our way home."

As soon as they were gone, Peaches spun Stuart around in his chair. He loved it in

104

her office. He'd gone into a sort of restful meditative state, listening to the distant clanking of the cafeteria staff and the rhythmic footfalls of children on the stairs. He could have stayed there all afternoon.

"I think Arnold's mom is right. They hurt themselves on purpose," he said, staring straight ahead at Peaches' pale clavicle.

It wasn't pale for long. "Ha," she murmured. A hot, red blush crept up her neck to her face. She was going to molest him. It would be all over the news and she would go to jail. "Now, where were we?"

"Lice check," Stuart reminded her.

She reached out and ran her fingers through his wavy dark hair, forgetting herself for a moment. "Lice check," she repeated crazily, and then squatted down to open a filing cabinet and retrieve a comb.

Stuart still couldn't believe she had a big, high school–age son. Somehow it only made her more attractive. They'd both had their children early. She possibly even earlier than he.

"Actually, that's not why I'm here. I was pretending," he admitted. "For Arnold's sake."

Peaches stood up so abruptly her spine cracked. "Oh?"

He'd come to seduce her. It was happening. It was really happening!

Her eyes were so blue and bright, the dimples

in her cheeks so ridiculously cute, Stuart was caught off guard.

Remaining seated, he walked backward with his feet, rolling the swivel chair away from her a foot or two. He was about to bring up Mandy again. He needed some distance so he could think straight.

"It's about my wife," he began. "I was wondering . . ."

Fuck a duck. Peaches attempted to compose herself.

Stuart coughed, jiggled his knee, coughed again. "See, pot, weed, marijuana is supposed to help with MS, right? But she doesn't have a prescription yet, and I think she should try it. I thought maybe since you're a nurse you might have some kind of connection? And like maybe you could hook us up, see if it helps?"

Peaches smiled through her disappointment, distracting him with her dimples.

"Sure," she answered slowly. She had no idea where to get pot, but there was no way she'd ever say no. Maybe Liam could help. He'd told her about the kids who smoked weed through those little vape pen things and pretended it was just herbal apple fumes or whatever. She hadn't smoked pot herself since college. She preferred wine.

"My friend mentioned some 'doctor' who makes house calls. He can bring you whatever you need. I think he called him Dr. Mellow, but that can't be his real name. I haven't looked him up. I thought I'd ask you first."

"Sure, of course." Peaches had no idea who Dr. Mellow was, but he sounded like the type of doctor all those cool arty people in the sixties like Andy Warhol and Edie Sedgwick would call when they'd almost OD'd on amphetamines and hadn't eaten or slept in a year and needed some cocaine and a vitamin B12 shot just to stay alive. "I'll see what I can do."

She closed the gap between them and ran the comb through his hair just because she could, parting it on the side and combing it back behind his ears so that he looked like a little boy on picture day.

"I'll get my people to talk to their people and get back to you," she said vaguely.

Her school phone began to ring. She mussed his hair up with her fingers again and turned to answer it.

"Nurse's office, this is Peaches."

Stuart stood and rolled her chair up behind her so she could sit down.

She sat, tilting her head and flashing her dimples gratefully up at him.

The call was from the mother of another second grader with lice.

"Grab a pen. There are four lice ladies you can contact. None of them do house calls and they're all a hassle to get to, but they'll get rid of them."

"Thank you," Stuart mouthed silently, so as not to interrupt her call.

And without any attempt to curb herself, Peaches winked in reply.

"Pot? Marijuana? Cannabis? Reefer? Herb? Mary Jane?"

Liam blinked up at his mother from the mattress on the floor that served as his bed. He took off his round, wire-rimmed reading glasses, rubbed his eyes, and put them back on again. Had she really just asked him where she could buy weed?

"It's okay. I'm not trying to trick you or get you or your friends in trouble," she said. "It's for a friend. Or actually, a friend's wife. She needs it for pain."

Liam shrugged. He was pretty sure Shy Clarke didn't smoke weed. He couldn't stop thinking about her. He was going to be her tutor. He'd liked her for over a year and now they were actually going to talk to each other. He liked her so much he could barely look at her. He was going to have to get over that.

"Seriously?" his mom demanded, about to go into one of her "I was semi-edgy in high school and you could be too if you just made the effort" gentle tirades. His mom was a good person, but she hated that he wasn't a musician who wore holey black jeans and ripped T-shirts. She hated his neatly trimmed hair and that he kept his pants up with a belt. She hated that he liked salad and was home every night. She hated that when he asked her to test him with flash cards he knew all the answers. She still loved him, he knew that. It was his apparent conformity she hated. "You don't know anyone?"

Liam wasn't about to rat out Bruce, whom he wasn't really friends with anyway. Bruce was high seven days a week, twenty-four hours a day, and he basically supplied the entire high school with weed. He was a brute too. No one messed with Bruce, for fear of pissing him off. He was the El Chapo of their school.

"*Omnia . . . vin-cit*!!" Peaches' husband Greg's boyish yowl resounded from the basement. He was adapting the Blind Mice song for his Phinney Collegiate music class, alternating between the recorder, harmonica, xylophone, and tambourine. They'd both been enormous Blind Mice fans when they met in college. Greg had seen the Mice button on her jacket and hit on her. It was what had brought them together. His basement studio was loaded with Blind Mice memorabilia.

"Maybe Dad knows someone," Liam suggested. "He is a musician."

"Maybe." Peaches hadn't even told Greg that Stuart Little was a parent at her school, worried that he would somehow ruin it. It was her own little nugget of fun, at least for now. "I gotta take the dog out."

While she was out, she wrapped the leash around one hand, took out her phone, and furiously googled "celebrity doctor, house calls, Dr. Feelgood, NYC" with the other. A lot of links came up. Most of it was porn. She remembered Stuart had said his name might be Dr. Mellow, but when she tried that, a series of links to masseuses and hypnotists came up. She scrolled through them. At the very bottom of the list was a website called Cobble Hill General with five-star reviews. "Wonderful," the first review said. "Makes house calls." "Brings you whatever you need," said another. "Discreet." No names were supplied, just a phone number.

Peaches pressed call and leaned against an anemic, tilting tree on Union Street, allowing the dog to sniff the dusty mulch around her sneakers. The phone rang and rang until finally a recorded message picked up.

"I'm out on call," a cordial, deeply resonant male voice answered. "Please leave a brief message and I'll get back to you as soon as I can. Promise."

A tone sounded. Peaches hesitated. "Um, hello. My name is, um. I'll just leave my number for now, I guess. I can explain more when you call. Thanks. Bye."

The dog was pooping anyway. She shoved her phone in her back pocket and looked away, down Union, toward the Gowanus Canal, to give the dog some privacy. When he was finished and had energetically kicked dirt over the poop, she pulled a bag out of her pocket and picked it up. Her phone vibrated and sang. It was the same number. It was the doctor.

"Hi there." His voice was warm and muscular. "Someone called from this number. How can I help?"

What if he was a male prostitute? Peaches wondered, panicking. What if "bring you anything you need" was a euphemism for orgasms?

"Hi," she responded, trying to collect her thoughts. "I was calling . . . It isn't for me, actually. It's for a friend. His wife has MS and he wants to try giving her some . . . pot. But he doesn't know how to get the right kind for her, and since I'm a nurse I thought . . . He just wants her to try it."

"No problem. Is there a time and a place that's convenient for you to meet?"

The drop-off: Peaches hadn't thought about this. She hadn't thought about anything, really. And what about paying the guy? It would probably cost a fortune.

"Now?" Peaches blurted out. The dog didn't care. But she didn't want to meet him on some street corner in case he was a serial killer. She could wind up in pieces in the Gowanus. "There's a bar on Sackett and Bond called Bikini Bottom."

"Love that place."

Peaches tried to keep the tremor out of her voice. "I can meet you there in five minutes. I have my wallet, but I don't have a lot of cash."

"Give me ten minutes. I have a swiper thing. You can pay by credit card. I'll send you a text receipt you can forward to your friend so he can reimburse you."

His instructions were so practical, capable, and normal. Peaches decided to trust him.

She tied the dog to a bike rack outside the bar and told him to lie down. The bar was crowded and full of drunk people playing shuffleboard. Peaches sat down and ordered a beer. She wished she'd gotten Stuart Little's number so she could tell at least one person in the world where she was and what she was doing and make sure he'd pay her back. The school had some sort of complicated online parent directory on its website. She scrolled around on her phone. Maybe it wasn't that complicated. Grade IV. Mrs. Watson's class. Ted Little. Mom: Mandy Marzulli. Dad: Stuart Little. Bingo.

Hey. I'm in a bar, waiting for the Dr. Feelgood guy to deliver some stuff. I'm putting it on my credit card. Just wanted to let you know in case they find my body parts drifting in the Gowanus or something.

Stuart texted right back.

Yikes! Text 911 if u need rescuing!! Thank u, ur amazing. I'll pay u back ASAP.

It was tempting to continue the flirtstream with Stuart Little because Dr. Feelgood was late. Poor dog. Peaches was about to give up halfway through her pint when a silver-haired gentleman wearing a sky-blue linen shirt slid onto the barstool next to hers.

"I have a large dog," she growled at him.

The man laughed. His face was tanned and healthy-looking. "Yes, I saw him tied up outside. How old is he? Fifteen? Twenty?"

"Eighteen," Peaches admitted. "On a good day."

"Dr. Conway." He held out a nicely kempt hand. "At your service."

"Oh." Peaches shook his hand. "I thought it would be a delivery guy, not the doctor himself."

He smiled. His teeth were beautiful. "I do everything myself. Otherwise things get . . . murky."

Peaches nodded. There was nothing murky about Dr. Conway. He was a perfect specimen.

"MS is very difficult to live with," he continued. "But it's not you who has it, is it? It's a friend?" His shirt was very blue and his neat jeans were very white. His silvery gray hair looked like it had just been cut. Dr. Conway was a silver fox.

"Yes, a friend," Peaches responded nervously. She reached into her windbreaker pocket for her wallet. "Thanks for coming so fast. I've never done this before."

"Is she degenerating? I just want to be sure I'm giving you the best fit."

Peaches sipped her beer. Stuart had said Mandy was getting worse. "Yes. Yes, I think so."

He nodded and pointed beneath the bar. A small, benign brown paper bag hung from one of the hooks meant for stashing your purse. "I think that will provide the necessary lift. And if your friend prefers not to smoke it, there's also a method of making butter with it, to put on toast or bake brownies or cookies with or what have you, that works extremely well. There's a lotion too I can provide if needed. It's from Greece."

"Okay, great." Peaches retrieved her credit card and slid it across the bar. He produced his phone, swiped the card through the credit card attachment, and handed it to her to sign with her finger.

A text message appeared on her phone. Cobble Hill General. For services rendered. $350.

And that was that, transaction complete.

"I better go rescue my dog. Thanks so much." She retrieved the bag and stood up. "This was so much more civilized than I expected it to be."

Dr. Conway smiled, his teeth gleaming and white. "I aim to please. Please be in touch whenever the need arises."

Peaches giggled. She had a drug dealer now! "Oh, believe me, I will."

Chapter 5

Hey, so I have this idea." Stuart placed a small brown shopping bag on the kitchen table. He'd picked it up from Peaches' office that afternoon. "I think you should try smoking some weed."

"Stu. You know how I get." Mandy crossed her arms over her chest. "You think I'm a nightmare *now*."

"You're not a nightmare. Besides, this is medical marijuana." Stuart removed the quaint glass jam jar from inside the bag. The jar was stuffed with dull green marijuana buds. He unscrewed the metal lid and took a whiff. "Wow."

"Stu, please."

Pot had always caused Mandy to act severely stupid and overly paranoid, the kind of high everyone hated. Once, in high school, after she and a bunch of other girls had shared a joint in a PE storage closet, she'd burst into the middle of a dress rehearsal for the musical *Cats* wielding a hockey stick and hissing at all the theater kids in their furry cat suits. She also always craved Fritos when she was high—bags and bags of Fritos—and she was already so fat. Medical weed was probably different though. You could tailor the high to your medical needs. But she didn't have any medical needs, because she didn't actually have MS.

Maybe there was some kind of skinny weed, weed that would give her energy instead of Frito cravings, weed that would get her out of bed. Stu would love that. Teddy would love that.

Stuart brought the jar over to the bed and sad down beside her. He held it out for her to sniff.

"Whoa. It's so strong."

"The nurse said you can make butter with it if you don't want to smoke it."

"What nurse?"

It might be wise not to reveal that Ted's school nurse had been the one to procure the pot. "Oh, just someone Robbie hooked me up with. You know Robbie." Stuart sniffed the jar again. "I'll smoke it with you," he offered. "After Ted goes to bed."

The idea of getting stoned together like teenagers was pretty cute. They could sit on the stoop—if she could make it to the stoop—and have their own little private party. Let the neighbors gossip. Worst thing that could happen: she'd get super paranoid and admit her lie. Which would actually be a huge relief.

"Sure. Okay. I'll try it," she said bravely.

Late afternoon light filtered prettily through the linen library curtains. Roy licked the toast crumbs from his upper lip and stared at his laptop screen, hating himself. What in bloody sweet hell was he going on about? Teenagers living on bloody Mars under surveillance with rationed ice cream. Everything he knew about space came from watching *Battlestar Galactica* back in 1979. His own teen years were a smelly, distant riot of drinking too much lager, smoking too many cigarettes, pissing in the rain, and unrequited crushes on beautiful older girls. But for some reason, ever since he'd begun *Gold* or *Red* or whatever bloody title the damned book was going to have, he kept coming up with teenagers. The girl hiding the family gold in the sand with a shovel, and now this space dust–induced spark between a boy and a girl with annoying names— Ceran and Bettina—and no acne because there was no humidity or bacteria or pollution on Mars, which he absolutely did not know for a fact, he was just guessing. What was he thinking? That as he typed all this gibberish into his laptop something brilliant would begin to blossom, like one of Einstein's theories or da Vinci's drawings? It might *seem* crazy and farfetched now, but once he got to the very end, four hundred or so pages later, it would all be so hilariously clear he'd wonder why he'd ever doubted himself?

Perhaps he was having a midlife crisis. Instead of buying a Porsche or having an affair with his personal trainer he was writing an insane, unreadable novel.

Roy thought he ought to talk to someone about it. This was forever his conundrum. Many writers had reading groups where they discussed their work with other writers and workshopped one another's drafts. Some writers had a dedicated, trusted reader, like Stephen King's wife, Tabitha. Some writers had editors who held their hands along the way. *The Great Gatsby*, for instance, would have been double the size and extremely convoluted and wordy had F. Scott Fitzgerald's editor, Max Perkins, not demanded merciless cuts.

Wendy would be honored if Roy asked her to be his reader. But she was a magazine person, used to fitting columns on a page with eye-catching headlines and sexy photographs. Very quickly she would become impatient with herself for not knowing how to shape his pubescent ditherings into a Roy Clarke novel unlike any that had come before, and would take her impatience with herself out on him.

His brilliant young agent was no use to him either. She had gotten married and had two babies since being assigned to Roy and was clever enough to take on fewer and fewer novels and more and more celebrity cookbooks. Roy had recently received a vivacious company email thrillingly announcing the forthcoming *Dining In with the Duchess of Cambridge*, which would most likely be a gigantic hit.

He stared at his laptop screen, muttering, "A stranger comes to town or a hero goes on a journey," the old adage adapted from something Tolstoy once said. Isabel, the Bahamas girl, was the stranger. She appears on Mars and needs to hide her gold. Perhaps she's the daughter of some Elon Musk–type billionaire genius who funded the Mars colonization program, which is now bankrupt. There's no money to bring anyone back, they're stranded. Somehow, though, Isabel and the two horny space-station dwellers, Ceran and Bettina (whose names are so annoying they were probably kicked off Earth), figure out how to get themselves and the gold back to Earth, while Ceran, ever the romantic, struggles with being in love with both girls at the same time. Eventually all three return to Isabel's family compound in the Bahamas to live forever in sin and bliss.

Roy hit return and stared at his screen some more.

He did like teenagers. Shy was endlessly amusing. And so was space, although he really knew nothing about it. He clicked on his search engine and typed in "Life on Mars."

"I really don't need a tutor," Shy told Liam when they met in the empty art room at the appointed time. "I just need to pay attention in algebra. Mr. Streko posted a Latin quote on his Twitter about

119

absurd things. To me, math is absurd. That's why we have calculators."

Liam had a habit of blurting out the thing he most wanted not to blurt out. " 'I carry your heart with me . . .' " he began, quoting the e. e. cummings poem he'd just read in AP Lit, looking askance at the paintings that had been left to dry on one of the art tables because he still could not look at her. He attempted to translate the next part into Latin. " '*Ego autem in corde meo portare*?' "

Shy stared at him and then giggled. It was the best response he could have hoped for.

"Sorry. I think I might have Asperger's," he mumbled at the art table. "Well, not officially, but after reading all her nursing textbooks, my mom and I decided I'm probably on the low end of the spectrum. I'm weirdly good at school and weirdly bad at everything else, so."

"Are you saying 'ass burgers'?" Shy asked, and Liam was grateful. Maybe it was only in the United States that Asperger's was a household blanket term used for weirdos who did well in school. English people were more forgiving. Probably all the great English talents had Asperger's. Peter Sellers, the whole Monty Python cast, Harry Potter. Shy herself was probably on the spectrum, which was why they were already getting along.

"Are you really going to tutor me, or can we

just pretend to do math and talk about other stuff?"

Liam pointed at her Gucci sneakers, which were white leather with little bees in between the red, green, and black leather stripes. "Those are why no girl here ever talks to you. You know that, right?"

There, he'd done it again. What was wrong with him?

Shy looked down at her shoes. "My mom got them for free. She works for a magazine. Also, it's ironic. I mean, look at the way I dress. These are boys' jeans because my legs look weird in girls' ones and my dad's undershirt that he shrank by accident that I cut so it's cropped."

"Well," Liam said, keeping his eyes on her shoes. "They're still alienating. If you were a guy you'd probably get beaten up."

"But this is a rich-person school, right? I mean, I get that feeling." Shy only said this because her mother seemed to have chosen the snobbiest school in Brooklyn, probably because she thought it was the best.

"I guess. I go here for free because my dad teaches music to the little kids."

Shy nodded. That was sweet but also a bit sad.

"And my mom used to be the nurse. She just changed to a public elementary school because they pay better, ironically. But you're right," Liam said. "For spring break and Christmas and

121

summer and stuff everyone goes to like, Vail or Martinique. My family goes camping in the Berkshires or to Rockaway Beach."

Shy had no clue about those places, but she agreed with him anyway.

"See? I bet they have all kinds of Gucci stuff, they just don't wear it to school. If you like something, why not wear it all the time? If it makes you happy. I used to have this leather jacket from Paris that—" She stopped. She sounded even more spoiled than the Martinique spring break kids.

Liam pulled up a chair and yanked a pad of graph paper and his calculator out of his backpack. "So. Algebra. Can I see your homework?"

Shy flipped open her binder and sighed enormously. "Please be nice to me?"

Liam chuckled into the buttons on his calculator, promising himself he wouldn't do something awful like spell out I LOVE YOU backward in numbers and then flip the calculator so she could read the words on the tiny screen.

He looked up, blushing. Shy was staring right at him. He forced himself not to look away. "I'll be nice."

"How 'bout we smoke some of that weed tonight?" Stuart suggested after they'd eaten tortellini and garlic bread on the big bed and he'd read *Harry Potter* to Ted and piggybacked him to his room. He sat at Mandy's blanketed feet and shook the jam jar.

Mandy pressed pause on her iPad and sat up against the pile of pillows. She'd just started a new anorexia movie on Lifetime. "Now?"

"Let's get wasted," Stuart said, tossing the jar into her lap.

"Shhsh." Mandy giggled.

She held the jar up to the light. It certainly didn't look like the pot she'd smoked in high school, which was brown and clumpy and unappealing. This pot grew in fuzzy, forest-green whorls, pretty enough to decorate a sweater with. There was a little white label on the jar with the words PURPLE HAZE written in purple calligraphy.

"I got this, too." Stuart retrieved the little purple pipe he'd bought at a shop on Atlantic Avenue on his way home. It had a USB port and released vapor, not smoke. The guy at the store had showed him how to use it. Smoking a joint was still probably more fun, but this was how everyone smoked now. He was excited to try it. "Why don't I get it set up and we can go down to the stoop?"

"The stoop?" Mandy hadn't sat on the stoop since June. She hadn't left the house in a week. More than that maybe—she'd lost count.

"Yeah, come on. It'll be fun." Stuart walked around to her side of the bed, took the jar out of her hands, opened it up, and sniffed it. "How can you resist?"

Mandy folded her arms over her chest. "I can't," she said, more worried about getting out of bed with Stuart watching than smoking the pot. Her legs probably had a diamond-shaped pattern on them from the mattress.

"You can. Come on. I'm going to do this over the kitchen counter in case I drop some. Then we can sprinkle it on our toast in the morning."

As soon as his back was turned, Mandy heaved her legs out of bed and pushed herself to a stand.

"You need help?" Stuart called out.

"Nope. I got it." At least her yellow T-shirt was big. And her black cutoff sweats hid most of her legs except her calves and ankles, which were huge. "I better put on a bra, in case the neighbors see us," she added and thudded as gracefully as she could into their bedroom. Her bras had been put away neatly, untouched for months. She chose a black lacy one because this felt like a date, like in the old days, before she supposedly came down with MS.

"All set?" Stuart leaned in the bedroom doorway, the purple pipe dangling from his lips. "Let's go."

It was a straight shot through the living room and out the front door. Mandy hovered on the top step of the stoop and clutched the railing. "Whoa."

Stuart took her hand and helped her down the four steps to the middle of the stoop.

"This is good, right?" Mandy stopped and clutched his hand as she lowered her bottom down, already slightly out of breath. "What's wrong with me?"

"You have MS," Stuart answered gently.

Mandy took a deep breath and patted the step beside her. "Come. Sit."

Stuart sat and handed her the pipe. "Take a hit."

Mandy glanced around. The street was quiet. A taxi rumbled by. The air was dull and still. It would probably rain. "Shouldn't we be worried about people seeing us and smelling it?"

Stuart scooted close and put his arm around her. "No one cares what we do anymore."

That was sad, but probably true.

"So I just suck on it?"

"Yup."

She held the pipe to her lips and took a hit. It tasted sweet and warm and almost grapey. She held the hit in her lungs for as long as she could before blowing out the vapor in a thin stream. "This thing is great," she said, examining the pipe. No leaves in your mouth, no burning paper, no matches. "I love it."

"Uh-oh."

She laughed and held it out for Stuart to try.

He took an enormous hit and blew a few perfect smoke rings, showing off. His Adam's apple bobbed up and down.

"More?"

"Yes, please."

They passed the pipe back and forth, settling into the pleasantness. The clouds cleared. Stars were beginning to come out. Smoke curled from a lone chimney across the street. A woman in a black hoodie and sunglasses hurried by with her tiny white dog.

"Do you feel it?" Mandy asked.

"Oh yeah."

Their perch on the steps felt a little precarious. She braced herself against Stuart's strong, skinny arm. "I hope we don't fall."

He wrapped his arm around her and pulled her close. "We won't fall."

Big Boy looked forward to his nightly walk with the family. The enormous mutt was old, a year older than Liam, and these days he walked extremely slowly. They went at night, after dinner, because it was cooler then. It was nice, walking the dog together as a family. Sometimes Peaches walked between Greg and Liam, holding both their hands, feeling truly content.

Tonight the moon was full, the air crisp with the onset of fall and sweetened by the smoke from lit fireplaces. Peaches tried to take Liam's hand but he was looking at his feet, his hands jammed into the pockets of his hoodie.

"Greg, has Liam told you about the girl he's tutoring? She's Roy Clarke's daughter."

"Her name is Shy," Liam said. "Shy Clarke."

"She sounds like a comic book character," Greg observed.

Peaches laughed. "Totally."

Liam glared at them. "Maybe she's faking being bad at math because she's really an evil nuclear weapons specialist about to take over the planet."

"It's possible." Greg chuckled, and for the thousandth time Peaches marveled at the fact that she'd married someone even less mature than she was. Greg was happiest when watching old Bill Murray comedies like *Groundhog Day* or *Caddyshack*, winning at Connect Four, or figuring out how to teach his kindergarten students the words to totally inappropriate songs like "Fight the Power" and "Margaritaville."

Their nighttime walks usually followed the same circuit: over the Gowanus Canal bridge on Union Street, down to Clinton Street and over to Cobble Hill Park, up Henry Street to Kane, past the schoolyard of Peaches' school to Court Street, on to Union Street and then home. Sometimes Big Boy caught a scent and took a detour. Tonight, he decided to veer backward on Kane Street. He stopped at the corner of Kane and Strong Place, peed on the neatly landscaped bushes outside the pretty brick house on the corner, did an about-face, and shuffled on.

"Mom," Liam moaned. "That's the wrong way."

"He knows," Peaches said.

Humoring their beloved old dog, they continued down Kane. At Cheever Place the entire family stopped short.

"Whoa. Someone's having a good night," Liam said.

"How do you know what that smell is?" Peaches demanded playfully. When she'd asked Liam about pot before, he'd acted like he'd never heard of it. She turned to Greg. "Am I wrong to be suspicious? How does he know?"

Greg kissed her forehead. "Everyone knows."

"Kids smoke weed in the bathroom at school all the time," Liam explained. "Not me, per se. Other kids."

"Uh-huh." Peaches inhaled deeply and peeked down the dimly lit street, still feeling playful. "Let's go spy on them."

Mandy's head was heavy on Stuart's shoulder, but it was a pleasant heaviness. He couldn't remember if he'd ever been this high. He felt almost ecstatic.

"We don't even have to move. We can stay here 'til the sun comes up."

"Mmmm," Mandy responded.

A family was walking their huge dog down the street. The woman's hair was a pretty strawberry blond that glowed gold beneath the street lamps. Their dog's fur was the same color. Stuart watched them get bigger and bigger. It was *her*—Nurse Peaches, with a couple of guys and a gigantic hairy animal.

"Hey," Stuart called out a little too loudly. He wanted to say something more formal and stand up and shake everyone's hand and give the dog a biscuit and be charming, but Mandy's head was so heavy and he was pretty sure it was safer to stay put. His mouth and face were not functioning very well.

Nurse from school comes by my crib
Tongue don't work, I can't ad lib!

"Nice night," Nurse Peaches called back brightly. "Guys, this is Stuart Little, and um—"

"Mandy, the mother of our child," Stuart said biblically.

Mandy didn't stir. She was either asleep or completely comatose.

"Their son goes to my school. We've been de-liceifying. Good times!"

Peaches was overcompensating. How had she missed Stuart's address when she'd searched for his number? If she'd known he lived on Cheever, she would never have allowed Big Boy to drag her there.

Stuart wavered on the step. Should he invite them in?

"I'm Greg." The dude who must have been Peaches' husband raised his hand. He was wearing dark denim overalls, a brown bucket hat, and Doc Martens. He was either very punk rock or very weird. "You're *that* Stuart Little?"

Stuart nodded slowly. He closed his eyes and then opened them again. "I guess I am."

"He is," Peaches verified. "Liam," she added, addressing the tall, blond teenager hiding deep inside his hoodie, "Stuart is a famous musician."

"Nice to meet you," Liam's mouth said.

The dog pleaded with his sad eyes. He wanted to go smell things. He wanted to go poo and pee.

"We'd better keep moving," Peaches said. "Big Boy makes some pretty huge poops. I don't want him to mess up your sidewalk."

"Thanks," Stuart said weakly, grateful that they were leaving. "Good night."

Mandy chose that moment to wake up. She lifted her head. "Hey guys. What's going on?"

No one quite knew what to say. The dog sat down again and began to pant.

Peaches wondered if it would be okay to ask about the quality of the pot, since she was the one who had purchased it for them. Liam and Greg might both be sort of impressed. She could even ask to try some. Liam could try it too. Greg used to take off his pants whenever he smoked pot. He probably shouldn't have any.

A face appeared behind the glass pane to the right of Stuart Little's front door. A small hand slapped the glass.

"Ted?" Mandy's green eyes widened. She tried to stand up, reaching for the railing and missing it completely.

"Holy shit." Stuart grabbed her and steadied her before she toppled down the steps. "Just a sec, Teddy!"

"You guys okay?" Greg called up to them.

"We're okay!" Stuart shouted back way too loudly.

"Mom, Dad," Liam whined. "Maybe we should just leave them alone?"

"Come on, guys." Peaches steered Big Boy back the way they'd come.

"That was fucking Stuart Little from the Blind Mice." Greg was clearly miffed. "You know him?"

Peaches bristled. "Yeah, their kid goes to my school." She yanked on the leash, forcing Big Boy to pick up the pace.

"You work at a public school now and the kids get even richer," Greg scoffed.

Anticipating a parental spat, Liam shoved in his AirPods and strode on ahead.

Peaches knew Greg would be weird about it. Weirdly jealous.

Greg had been the big man on campus at Oberlin, at least in the music department. But you don't get rich and famous like Stuart Little majoring in ancient woodwinds and double-minoring in accordion and banjo. You wind up teaching music at a private elementary school to support the younger day student English major from small-town Ohio who liked to play the drums and had to drop out of college altogether because you knocked her up. Greg was so annoying. Hadn't she tortured herself and gotten her nursing degree and the school nurse gig for precisely this reason, to stop him from constantly making comments about money? She was making the big bucks now, picking nits off famous dads and their spawn. Even Liam had two jobs, tutoring that girl and at the Strategizer. Sure, they lived on the wrong side of the Gowanus in a small street-level rental, but they were fine. Getting to know Stuart Little was the highlight of her current existence. Only Greg could turn something fun into a huge bummer.

"I guess they must be rich," she said. "I'm sorry I didn't tell you," she added, even though she wasn't sorry at all.

Chapter 6

It wasn't neat and tidy like his house. In fact, it was kind of a mess, like a storage unit for someone who never threw anything away. That was part of the design process, Roy supposed, creating faulty prototypes and then dissecting them to see what was working and what wasn't. A set of seven white wooden chairs—all in different sizes, their backs adorned with brass plaques bearing the name ELIZABETH—stood in a circle, like something out of "Goldilocks and the Three Bears," only more sinister.

"Those are hers," Tupper explained. "She's interested in Identity."

Roy thought he detected a capital *I*.

"Shifting identities within one person," Tupper went on, as if that clarified it.

"Right," Roy said.

"My workshop is back here." Tupper led the way through the airplane hangar–like space filled with detritus. Roy tripped over a life-size boa constrictor that was wound around a rotten wooden oar. "That was from her Adam and Eve series," Tupper noted as he continued on.

At the back of the enormous studio was a large glass box. Inside the box were two wooden cradles. Nestled in the cradles were two toddler-size papier-mâché dolls with yellow woolen yarn hair, black bird-feather eyelashes, painted red cheeks, and red kissy-face lips. Their lumpy bodies were swaddled in felt and birch-bark patchwork quilts with just the tips of their papier-mâché fingers poking out. The fingers were oddly gray, as if the girls had been playing on the sidewalk before their nap.

Roy stared into the glass box.

"The twins," Tupper explained unnecessarily. "She wheeled them around in a carriage for two years."

Roy followed him through a rusted metal door that led to a bright, spotless workroom with huge windows that looked southwest, toward Sunset Park and Industry City. In front of the windows was a long worktable with a large computer and 3D printer. There were also a potter's wheel, a refrigerator, a kiln, and a wall of shelves filled with white, porcelain figurines. There were elves and unicorns, Arc de Triomphes and Eiffel Towers, parrots and peacocks, cacti and coral, pineapples and watermelons, gorillas and elephants, skunks and squirrels, mice and owls, sea lions and Sasquatches, wolves and polar bears. Lined up against the walls and in the corners were department store mannequins and other humanlike figures, all devoid of faces, clothing, and hair.

"This is where I work," Tupper said.

Roy was entranced. It was a bit like Santa's workshop. A person could really make things here. If only *he* had a workshop. He could go inside and close the door and feel instantly confident that he would achieve things.

Something was nagging at him. He picked up a polar bear and quickly put it down again. "Your . . . this . . . Elizabeth," he said and swallowed. "I hope you don't mind my asking, but where exactly is she?"

Tupper gazed out the window at the gray industrial landscape. It wasn't a nice view, but it was a view.

He sighed deeply. "That's the thing about Elizabeth."

Roy checked the time on his phone, hating to interrupt his lonely neighbor when he might be about to bare his soul. "I'm so sorry, but I have a meeting."

"It's great. I mean, it has the potential to be great. But you've only just begun. You have to keep going, fill it out and finish it." Peaches thrust Roy's flimsy pages across the bar. They were dirtied with what looked like mustard and coffee and tomato soup, and there were scribbles in green crayon, or perhaps eyeliner. "I made notes. Don't feel like you have to listen to any of them."

Roy took back the manuscript. It was even thinner than he remembered. Forty-seven pages was not a book. He sniffed it. Not mustard, curry. He'd given the pages to Peaches yesterday, printing them out and waiting in the bar, pretending to write until she turned up. She'd said she was an English major, and he'd much rather she read it than someone he lived with and had to see at breakfast, like Wendy or Shy. They wouldn't be able to hide their shame and disappointment if it was terrible. Peaches had not been party to his cinnamon bun binges or his ability to look at a blank wall, thinking about Starbuck and Apollo and Cylons and Jane Seymour, for minutes on end. And he never had to speak to Peaches again if he didn't want to. He'd thought about giving it to Tupper, but he didn't want to depress him even more.

Peaches was honored that a renowned author had asked for her opinion. She'd been thinking about Roy's pages all day. They were a welcome distraction from her embarrassment over catching Stuart Little and his wife, high on their stoop, and her annoyance at her husband, Greg, who would not shut up about it.

"The whole boy-girl thing is like *The Blue Lagoon* in space, which I love. I mean, it's genius that they're up there without their families. They are their family now. But at the same time, they have these *urges*. I just think you need to be careful to keep it fresh and not like, too *Blue Lagoon*y. Like, Bettina should not get pregnant and the baby should not eat bad space ice cream and almost die. And maybe neither of them should be white. In the future, no one is white, everyone is beige."

It was too much to take in. Roy shook his head. "I'm sorry, I don't know it. *The Blue Lagoon*, what is that?"

"Oh! Woo!" Nurse Peaches blew her wispy strawberry blond hair out of her face and blushed, presumably because she was making sounds, not words.

She was a very attractive person. Not just because she was dimply and smiley and bosomy and smart, but because she was so awkward and filterless, saying each and every thought, however fragmented, that entered her brain. She made Roy feel almost cool.

"Is it a film?"

"Yeah. It's from the seventies, or maybe early eighties, and kind of so bad it's good. It's about two teenagers who get shipwrecked and have to survive on a deserted island. They're children when it starts, but then they go through puberty. She gets her period and boobs. His voice changes. Eventually they figure out how to have sex. They keep doing it so much she gets pregnant and they have a baby. She breastfeeds it. There's even this weird scene when the baby appears to be swimming in the ocean on its own before it can really walk. I've been pushing for that movie to be shown to the whole fifth grade instead of the dumb sex-ed class they do in like forty-five minutes the second-to-last day of school, but the assistant principal thought it was inappropriate. She's from Staten Island and super Catholic and conservative. I made my son watch it when he was eleven. I think it was sort of liberating for him but also really scary. Your character Ceran totally reminds me of my son—so little confidence and self-awareness he appears almost stupid. But I guess you were a teenage boy once too, not that long ago. You know what you're writing about."

"Not really," Roy disagreed. "Not at all, actually."

Peaches stopped talking. Roy Clarke made her nervous. He was either completely brilliant or just a very lucky clueless person—she couldn't tell. His pages were like a script for a movie that would never get made. But if she tried to write a book, it wouldn't make any sense either. And what was her problem anyway? Did she have to be so critical? Why was she so competitive? Yes, for the five minutes that she'd actually attended college she'd thought she wanted to be a writer, but she was a nurse now. Roy Clarke was a real writer and he'd asked her to read his pages, which was amazing. But it was also confusing. Surely he could have asked someone more qualified.

Roy couldn't believe Nurse Peaches had a son, certainly not a teenager. He'd thought she was about twenty-seven.

"It's on TV sometimes, *The Blue Lagoon*," Peaches rambled on. "Probably no one in England has ever seen it." She crouched down to open the bar fridge, looking for boiled eggs, but the fridge's shelves were bare. She slammed the door closed again and stood up. "It's not, like, good cinema or anything—it's really cheesy. But it is educational."

"I can't believe you have a teenage son," Roy said. "You're what, twenty-five?"

"Thirty-eight," Peaches cut him off.

"And your son? How old is he now?"

"He just turned seventeen. I held him back in kindergarten. He and your daughter are in the same class. He's tutoring her in math. Didn't she tell you?"

"Really? No, I had no idea," Roy said, feeling a bit flummoxed. Shy spoke to him more than she spoke to anyone else, but clearly she didn't tell him everything. This was good news, actually. Great news. Shy would have a friend. A clever boy with a wonderful mother.

"So, is this like a dystopian novel set in the far distant future, or is it set in the near future, based on current space stuff and socioeconomic issues that are happening today?" Peaches went on, still trying to be helpful.

"I don't want to do a lot of research," Roy said stubbornly.

"Okay. But you do need to create verisimilitude," she insisted, making use of her Oberlin creative writing workshop vocabulary. "You still need to draw a vivid picture of the space station or whatever it is they're living in and the kids' schedule of activities in order to make it as believable as possible. I'm imagining it like boarding school in space, except the adults are too busy being astronauts and scientists and doing 'important work' to pay much attention to the kids. So they're raising themselves. They're smart and interesting and horny. It will have all the same everyday tragedies and comedy as your other books, from what I've read about them—part of it just takes place in space."

"Right," Roy agreed despondently. "Or maybe I ought to write about something else."

"No." Peaches pointed at the pages in his hands. "You came up with that for a reason."

She leaned over the bar. Her breath smelled like coffee ice cream.

"Just keep going. The story will become less disjointed. I know it will, because *you* are the connection. I know that sounds so cheesy. But you've done this before. It must feel familiar. It's like, maybe you have to get a certain distance away before you can get into orbit, not to overuse the space metaphor. Then you have to stay up

140

there and complete your mission. And then you have to come back."

She cleared her throat. Just for something to do, she picked up a lemon slice and ate the fruit off it. Then she ate another. They tasted like they'd been sitting out for a long time.

"That makes sense," Roy agreed, feeling slightly resentful because she wasn't the one who had to go into orbit and complete the mission. "I suppose I'd better watch that *Blue Lagoon* film with my daughter."

"Oh God." Peaches snorted. "Forget I even mentioned it. Just promise me no one's going to give birth in space."

Chapter 7

Big Boy had been acting funny all day. He turned his head away when Liam picked up his leash and lay down behind the sofa, panting. Liam's mom thought just breathing some fresh air would do him good. So, after dinner, she and his dad sat on the stoop with the huge old dog and sent Liam out for ice cream.

Ample Hills was only four blocks away from home. Liam wanted a cone, and he'd promised to bring his parents back a pint of Smack Mallow Pop. "It really is smack," his mom said. "I'm going to eat the whole pint."

The weather had been weirdly warm and the place was packed. Bruce Cardozo, Ryan, and Black Ryan from school were in line ahead of him.

"We're going to PS 919 to play basketball," Ryan said.

"You should come," Black Ryan offered.

"Oh, he's coming," Bruce said and punched Liam's skinny shoulder. It was only then that Liam was able to confirm that they were actually talking to him.

They were all big guys, but they'd ordered child-size ice cream cones because they were cheaper.

"We'll wait for you outside," Bruce called, weaving through the crowd with his tiny cone held high.

Liam wasn't sure why they were being so insistent. He liked Black Ryan, but the other two guys—Bruce especially—were total assholes. He didn't know them that well, but they were popular athletes who went to parties. They didn't have to make an effort, so why were they making an effort with *him?* Maybe he was wrong, maybe they weren't total assholes.

He ordered a double kid-size cone but decided against the pint, just in case he really did want to play basketball with Bruce and the two Ryans. His mom would have to suck it up. She was always complaining about the size of her thighs anyway. And it was sort of cool that they'd asked. Plus, it was such a nice night.

Sorry no ice cream for u, he texted his mom. Met up with some guys. Going to play basketball.

Good for u. Good for me. Ice cream is evil, she texted back with a little skull-and-crossbones emoji.

Outside, Liam and the other three boys performed the requisite palm slaps and finger-grab handshakes and then ambled down Union Street, quietly devouring their cones. Black Ryan was the tallest. Everyone called him Black Ryan, even the teachers sometimes. The prevailing opinion was that the moniker wasn't racist; it just made it easier to distinguish between the two Ryans in their grade. There were also three Mayas, but no one called them Freckly Biracial Maya, Asian Maya, and Blonde Maya. Liam wasn't sure why. He also had no idea why they didn't call the other Ryan White Ryan. That would've been funnier.

"I feel like summer never really ended," Ryan said dreamily. He tossed the very end of his cone in the trash can on the corner of Court.

"Right?" Bruce agreed. "It needs to get cold or no one's going to take school seriously. In fact, I'm considering cutting to go to the beach on Friday."

"I love Rockaway Beach," Liam mused. His family used to take the A train out there all the time in the summers. They'd bring a picnic and stay until well after sunset. Sometimes his dad would bring his ukulele and his mom would sing.

"He meant the Hamptons, loser," Ryan said. "He has a house."

The boys walked down Court, four abreast. Passersby averted their eyes and skirted the edge of the sidewalk to avoid them, as if frightened by the pack of teenage brutes. Liam smiled at this. Black Ryan was tall, but his legs were like toothpicks. Bruce was big all over and weird-looking, with bulging blue eyes and straight, dirty blond hair that fell to his shoulders, but he was kind of short. Ryan had the dark shadow of a mustache but a little-boy haircut, and he still wore the dorky yellow polo shirts and khaki pants his mom picked out for him. Liam was Liam Park, medium-tall, skinny, belt-wearing, pimply son of the school nurse and the lower school music teacher. Except for Bruce, the four of them were hardly a threat.

It was dark by the time they reached the schoolyard, but the entire neighborhood of Cobble Hill was safely outfitted with extremely bright white LED streetlamps, so they could see well enough to play. The basketball hoop was on the Kane Street side, right near Strong Place. Dried leaves had begun to collect around the edges of the yard near the tall chain-link fence.

Bruce kicked at the ground with his red Jordans. "Fucking leaves," he growled and dribbled the basketball.

Black Ryan stole it away from him and shot an easy layup. Ryan caught the rebound, faked Bruce out, took a jump shot, and missed. Bruce caught the ball and dribbled it in artful circles. Despite his stocky stature, he was really good at basketball. Liam just stood there with his hands in his pockets, watching.

"You playing?" Bruce called to him as he continued to dribble. Black Ryan ran at Bruce and hurdled over him, laughing, like a hyperactive grasshopper.

"Fuck you, assholes!" Ryan shouted for no apparent reason.

Liam regretted joining them. The ice cream had not agreed with him. "You guys go ahead." He shuffled over to the playground equipment and lay down on his back on the slide. "My stomach feels weird."

"Your face is weird," Ryan joked, but it felt like it wasn't a joke.

"Ha," Liam responded. He closed his eyes and listened to the rhythmic bouncing of the basketball as the boys continued to play. It was nice on the slide. He let his arms flop over the sides, trailing his fingers over the protective rubber mats that lined the playground area. Dried leaves had accumulated beneath the slide. He swished his hands through them, breathing in deeply through his nostrils.

His fingertips met with something hard, a large plastic bottle. He clasped the neck of the bottle and held it up. It was an oversize bottle of vodka, with about four inches of clear liquid left in the bottom.

"Holy shit!" Liam murmured.

Within seconds the other three boys were standing over him.

"We should drink it," Ryan said.

"No way. It might have diseases," Black Ryan said.

Bruce pulled a lighter out of his pocket and

flicked it on. The flame glimmered in the dark and then went out. He flicked it again. "Get up, loser."

Liam sat up and Bruce yanked the vodka bottle out of his hand. He went around to the short metal ladder that led to the top of the slide.

"I've always wanted to do this," Bruce said. "Get your phones ready to video this shit." He climbed to the top of the ladder and shook up the bottle. "This stuff is crap. We're definitely not going to drink it. We're going to set it on fire."

Wendy was working late, so Shy made cheesy pasta and pretended to do her math homework in the kitchen while her dad was in the library, attempting to write.

Roy stared at his laptop. Ceran was messaging his dad about what he would do when he got back to Earth. He wanted to go to the beach and order a pepperoni pizza and play with all the puppies he'd adopted—there were no pets on Mars, only robots, something Roy had stolen directly from *Battlestar Galactica*. Ceran was a bit mushy. If Roy was about to lose his virginity to Bettina, in space, he wouldn't be thinking about puppies.

"Do you want to watch a film with your old dad?" he called out to Shy. "It's a retro teenager film. Someone told me I should take a look at it."

"What's it called?" Shy shouted back.

Roy checked his notes. "*The Blue Lagoon*?"

"Hope it's not about mermaids," Shy responded skeptically. "But I'll try it." Anything to spare her the pain of math. Not that she was doing math. She was checking Mr. Streko's Twitter feed—again. It was addictive. Every Latin quote he posted had so much emotional logic. Mostly, though, she waited for him to post more bare-chested photos of him, his tattoos, and his cat.

Roy turned on the large flat-screen monitor on the far wall of the library and stabbed at the power buttons on the four remote controls that he didn't know how to use.

"Come and help me with the remotes, would you?"

Mandy and Ted had passed out on the bed reading *Harry Potter* while Stuart made his first batch of pot-butter chocolate-chip cookies. The plan was to keep them in the fridge so Mandy could snack on them during the day if her MS was getting bad and she felt weird about smoking on her own. Stuart watched the cookies bake through the oven's murky glass, the glistening dough oozing flat and solidifying in circles on the tray. He scraped the rubber spatula against the sides of the mixing bowl, collecting blobs of cookie dough and licking them off.

The oven beeped. Stuart removed the tray and carefully transferred each cookie to the very professional wooden cooling rack Mandy had bought at Williams Sonoma when Ted was a toddler and she thought she might become the type of mom who baked cookies and cakes every day. The crisp cookies clung to the rack in precise rows. There was one lone extra cookie that wouldn't fit. Stuart tossed it in his mouth and flung the spatula and baking tray into the sink. The roof of his mouth hummed as he chewed. His eye sockets were expanding. So were his ears and his feet. Even his ass cheeks felt weird. Uh-oh. Eating pot butter was way more hardcore than smoking it. All that raw cookie dough and now that whole cookie—he was already super high.

Baked weed cookies for my sweethearty
Ate too many—now it's time to party!

He grabbed his keys and his phone and glanced at Mandy and Ted, asleep on their backs on the queen-size bed. It seemed sort of irresponsible to leave them in such a vulnerable state when he was their protector and provider. But he had to. He had to get outside and walk.

Liam's hands were shaking. He could barely hold his phone in place. His thumb wavered over the record button.

"Guys," he spoke up, his voice breaking annoyingly. "I don't think we should be doing this."

149

They'd already filmed Bruce lighting drops of vodka on fire and practically burning his arm off. Was it really necessary to incorporate the slide?

Bruce screwed the cap back on the vodka, shook the bottle violently, and then unscrewed the cap again. "Speak for yourself. I was fucking born to do this. I just wish I hadn't smoked so much weed earlier. I need to fucking focus."

"What exactly are you doing, anyway?" Black Ryan asked.

Liam glanced at him warily. Black Ryan didn't sound too happy about Bruce's antics either.

"Isn't it obvious, fuckwad?" Bruce demanded.

Ryan chuckled. "You're gonna pour the vodka down the slide, set it on fire, and slide down through the flames."

"Fuck yeah. And you guys are going to film it."

"Holy shit," Black Ryan protested. "What about your balls?"

"My balls will be fine. Jeans aren't that flammable."

"Tell us when," Ryan said eagerly, holding out his phone.

Liam didn't say anything. He wanted to leave, but he also kind of wanted to see what happened.

Bruce squatted down at the top of the slide. He held the bottle in his left hand and cocked it down, ready to pour. His right hand held the lighter. He flicked it with his thumb and a flame sprang up and then died. He flicked it again. And again.

"Fuck, I'm still high," he muttered.

The other three boys stared up at him, mesmerized.

"One, two, three . . . fuck. One, two, three . . . *when!*" Bruce shouted.

Liam hit record. Vodka sluiced down the metal slide. Bruce made contact with the lighter's flame and the whole slide glimmered orangely.

"Here I fucking go!" Bruce yelled and smacked his butt down on the path of fire.

He didn't slide much. He was just sitting there.

"Holy shit, I'm like . . . look at me."

The three other boys couldn't look away.

"Fuck, my shoelaces." Bruce kicked his way down the slide and sat down on the ground. "I think I ruined my pants. And my shoes. That was fun though." The slide wasn't on fire anymore. The other boys stopped recording.

"That was kind of lame," Black Ryan said.

Liam smiled down at his phone screen. It was totally lame.

"I thought it was pretty cool," Ryan said. "We should post it on YouTube or something."

Bruce stood up and smacked at his pant legs. "Yup. These jeans are fucked."

"They smell weird too," Ryan said.

"That's not his jeans." Black Ryan pointed to where smoke was curling up from behind the slide.

Liam squinted in the lamplight. He got down on all fours. The pile of dried leaves beneath the slide had ignited. Something within the pile popped and the flames grew higher. It was quite a fire.

"Oh shit," Liam said.

"No fucking way. This is fucking awesome!" Bruce squealed. "Dudes, come on, we have to split!"

He turned and ran toward the exit. The two Ryans were right behind him.

"Hey!" Liam shouted after them.

Something else popped inside the fire. It sounded like bottles exploding. Sparks rose into the air. The metal slide glimmered hotly.

"Hey, assholes!" Liam shouted, and then wished he hadn't. The boys were long gone. He flipped up his hood and stuffed his hands in his pockets, backing away from the fire, out the schoolyard entrance and onto the sidewalk, his heart pounding.

"Hey, stop!" someone shouted behind him.

Liam stepped into the street and broke into a run.

"Oh. My. God. Pause it, pause it!" Shy grabbed the remote away from Roy and hit pause. She pointed at the screen. "His willy is right there, flapping around in the water. It's—" She giggled merrily. "Sorry, Dad, but this is too funny! It's like the worst movie ever. It's amazing."

"I'm glad you're enjoying yourself." Roy wasn't watching the movie from a critical perspective; he was merely trying to get inspired.

She hit play again and Brooke Shields and the blond boy with the cherubic curls continued to swim naked and spearfish and collect seaweed in tortoise shells on their magical deserted island, pausing only for sex. Once they discovered sex they did it constantly, which was pretty realistic. They were stuck on an island alone; what else were they going to do?

Roy wondered how he was going to accomplish something similar in space. He wanted the book to be entertaining and poignant, not ridiculous or tawdry. Heartbreak and hilarity, those were his specialties. Losing one's virginity without gravity? That would be a challenge.

The kids in *The Blue Lagoon* stumbled upon the remnants of some gruesome native cannibalistic ritual on the "forbidden" side of the island. Maybe Ceran and Bettina could stumble upon some . . . aliens?

Roy rubbed his eyes anxiously as he continued to watch. Brooke Shields was so moody, she was obviously pregnant. Of course the idiot boy just thought she was fat.

"This is like an educational video for what not to do. You're supposed to use protection, be hygienic. They probably have STDs." Shy sniffed the air. "I smell smoke. It's like, not fireplace smoke but it's coming through the fireplace. Do you smell it?"

"Shsh." Roy nodded at the television. "They rarely speak. Let's not miss anything."

The doorbell rang repeatedly. Someone pounded violently on the door.

"Hold on." Shy paused the movie and jumped up to answer it. "If that's Mum, she's either being chased by murderers or she's really drunk."

She peered through the peephole in the door. It was Liam from school. He'd walked her home after tutoring this afternoon, which was nice, even though she did all the talking. Liam was out of breath and crying.

Shy unlatched the door and opened it wide. "Are you all right? Are you hurt?"

"I'm sorry." Liam stumbled inside and stood in the front hall with his hood up, his shoulders shaking. He wiped the snot away from his nose with the back of his hand. "I made a really big mistake."

Roy came up behind them and patted Liam's back. "Shy, why don't you bring your friend into the library so he can sit down."

Shy nodded gratefully at her dad and led Liam to the sofa. The television was paused on an unfortunate image of a mostly naked, fully pregnant Brooke Shields and the totally naked blond guy embracing on a pile of pillows in their palm frond home, but Liam didn't seem to notice.

Shy powered it off. "What happened?" she demanded gently. "What's wrong?"

The flames were beautiful. Stuart wound his fingers through the chain-link fence and watched them dance around the slide and ooze across the playground toward the monkey bars. Tiny tufts of fire floated skyward. They were leaves, Stuart realized, igniting and swirling up with the wind. He thought he'd seen Peaches' son, the boy in the hoodie, run away from the scene, but Stuart was too high to run after him. He was too high even to call 911. This was Ted's school playground. His own son's school was burning. The children wouldn't be able to play there anymore. Nurse Peaches would be pissed. And yet he did nothing. He just watched it burn.

"I told them it was stupid, but they did it anyway," Liam explained.

Shy got up and opened the front door again. She sniffed the air. "That's the smell. I've been smelling it for a while."

"No one's come yet though?" Roy clarified. "Not the fire department or anyone?" He felt he must do something, but he didn't want to get the boy in trouble. "Would you like to call your mum?"

Liam shook his head miserably. "I should have just brought her the ice cream."

Roy stuffed his hands in his pockets and then removed them again. This little episode was so timely and relevant, so Ceran and Bettina. What if there's a fire at their colony on Mars? What if they started it?

"Shall I call 911? Or maybe we should just go over there?"

"No!" Liam said adamantly. He took a great heaving breath to collect himself. "Maybe call and just say that you think you smell something burning and it's coming from the direction of the school?"

The fire trucks were loud. Stuart backed away into the shadows as they came, a whole convoy, their sirens blaring. There must have been eight of them, full of hulking firemen, tapping the hydrants with their hoses and wielding flashlights. Stuart pulled his phone out of his back pocket. He wanted to warn Peaches. He scrolled through his contacts—*N* for *Nurse,* or *P* for *Peaches?*—then put the phone away again. He couldn't find her number. Hoses blasted from all four sides, dousing the flaming slide. Water oozed over the sidewalks and poured in rivers down the street. The schoolyard was totally charred, flooded, and fucked up.

Ate five weed cookies, think I got cursed
Now the school's on fire, don't tell the nurse!

Chapter 8

Mandy woke with a start and threw off the comforter. The microwave clock was visible from the queen-size bed. It was almost noon. She'd slept for more than fourteen hours. Stuart had gone to work. Ted was at school. Sun streamed in through the kitchen windows.

She sat up and swung her feet to the floor. Something was different this morning. She could feel the blood circulating in her veins. She felt . . . *alive.*

Was it the weed? Maybe it was working. Not that she was certifiably ill, but something was different. Maybe it was the sleep. Maybe that's all it ever was. She'd gotten so sleep-deprived when she first had Teddy, she just needed to catch up.

People died from exhaustion. It was a good thing she hadn't died.

She stood up quickly, eager to get on with what would surely be a new kind of day. Whoa, maybe too quickly. Lying in bed watching movies all the time had made her weak. She looked down at her wobbly ankles and doughy knees and looked quickly away. How had she allowed herself to get this fat? Plus, she was starving.

The fridge was full of Stu's gross green juices and Ted's baby carrots. Mandy wanted something substantial, like a roast chicken with mashed potatoes and gravy or shepherd's pie. She didn't know of any place that delivered that sort of food, and she wasn't about to eat at a restaurant all alone. Maybe there was someone she could call, someone with a weird work schedule who might be free. She scrolled through the contacts on her phone. Nothing but doctors she never saw, hair salons she never went to, and a few girls from high school she'd completely lost touch with. Her entire existence had always centered around Stu and his band, and then Stu and Ted. She didn't have any friends. She didn't have much of a life.

Showering was so tedious when she was this hungry, but she made it through by eating half of one of Stu's weed cookies first. By the time she'd dressed, blow-dried her hair, curled her eyelashes, and tied her sneakers, she was buzzing with hungry energy. She took a picture of herself in the mirror and texted it to Stu, showing off how up and at 'em she was today.

Going out, she wrote.

She waited a few minutes but he didn't write back.

There was a luncheonette in Carroll Gardens where all the old neighborhood Italians went. She could get takeout chicken Francese on a bed of linguine with fresh garlic bread, bring it home, and eat it on the sunny stoop.

Her shoes felt tight after weeks of not wearing

shoes, and the brownstone steps were so steep she had to brace herself and take them one at a time, but she made it all the way to the sidewalk. A cute orange truck pulled up in front of the neighbor's house. FULL PLATE, it said on the side of the truck. DELICIOUS DINNERS DROPPED AT YOUR DOORSTEP.

The neighbors were never home. Mandy and Stuart had decided they were Russian spies, trying to blend in. The reason they were never home was because they didn't really live there— it was just a front. Mandy had seen them only a few times, hurrying into a black car with suitcases. They'd probably forgotten they'd even ordered from Full Plate.

The delivery guy placed the box at the top of the neighbor's stoop.

"Have a good one," he said to Mandy as he trotted down the steps to his truck.

The box would probably just sit there for days, unopened, and the luncheonette was on Smith Street, which was pretty fucking far away.

"Excuse me," Mandy called out to the delivery guy. "Um, the couple you just delivered the box to? They're away, and they asked me to take their box. Would it be possible to carry it up to my front door for me?"

"Oh. Oh sure," the delivery guy said with a sympathetic smile. Mandy could tell what he was thinking: there was no fucking way a chubby, out-of-shape lady like her could carry a heavy box like that all the way up to her kitchen. "Just tell me where."

She smiled pleasantly with her hands on her hips and gazed down the street, looking out for watching neighbors and judgers. A police car had pulled over at the corner and a few people were standing around talking to the police. Something must have happened. At least they weren't watching her steal her neighbors' dinner. Man, was she famished. And pretty high from the weed cookie. The Full Plate box was hopefully full of something delicious.

The delivery guy carried the box right to the kitchen. Mandy fished a ten-dollar bill out of her purse and gave it to him. "You're a lifesaver," she said.

She found a pair of scissors and cut through the cute orange-and-white checked packing tape. Inside, the box was fully lined with four frozen gel packs, which must be full of something eco-friendly, otherwise the people at Full Plate were going to hell. There was a neatly wrapped package of frozen, sustainably harvested mahi-mahi chunks from Oregon, a stack of white corn tortillas baked in Queens, half a free-range chicken from the Hudson Valley, diced mango from Puerto Rico, shredded cabbage and arugula grown hydroponically on a rooftop in Brooklyn, some hot sauce, some orzo, a block of Vermont goat-milk feta cheese, and a bunch of beets and chives, both from Long Island. At the very bottom of the box were a ready-made flourless chocolate cake, two bottles of white wine, and two laminated cards with pictures and step-by-step instructions for how to prepare fish tacos with mango salsa and arugula and half a roast chicken with beet, feta cheese, and orzo salad. Score!

Mandy wasn't much of a cook. She could make Bisquick pancakes and grilled cheese sandwiches that sometimes came out burned. She'd certainly never made fish tacos or half a chicken. But the instructions made both dishes look pretty easy, and she had nothing better to do. She'd cook the fish tacos for her lunch and make the chicken for her and the boys for dinner. Ted would go apeshit over the cake. Stu didn't like white wine, so she could have that all for herself.

She expected to feel guilty, stealing other people's food, but she didn't. It wasn't like she was stealing from the hungry.

Stu's face appeared on her phone.

Crazy shit happening over at the school. Did you see?

Mandy's mind drifted to the police car and then back to the mahi-mahi taco instructions.

Don't bother me, I'm cooking.

There was a moment's pause before he replied.

Whoa. Seriously? Can't wait to taste! Sorry, gotta run, client here.

Mandy pulled the freezer packs out of the box.

On each one was a warning label: THESE PACKS ARE FILLED WITH NON-TOXIC POTATO STARCH. PLEASE REUSE OR CUT OPEN CAREFULLY AND DISSOLVE IN SINK. Bingo. Mandy carried them over to the sink to dissolve them. Everything in the box was shrink-wrapped in plastic on a cute blue cardboard plate thing that she was probably supposed to reuse, but she probably wasn't going to. Getting rid of all the packaging was going to be a huge pain in the ass, but she couldn't let Stuart find out she'd stolen the neighbors' food. The taco instructions said preparation time was only fifteen minutes. In fifteen minutes she'd be eating fish tacos for two and fully ready to tackle the pile of plastic wrap and cardboard before moving on to the half chicken. She turned on the TV, just for background noise. The midday local news was in the middle of a report.

"*. . . Police are investigating a schoolyard fire in Brooklyn. An empty liter bottle of vodka and a plastic cigarette lighter have been taken into evidence. Luckily the fire occurred last night after school hours and no children were harmed. A portion of the schoolyard will be closed for repairs.*"

"*We want to know who's behind this.*" Mandy recognized Ted's assistant principal's nasal whine. "*We also want our schoolyard back. This isn't just a playground for our children. It's the hub of the community.*"

Mandy dumped the pre-marinated fish chunks into the pan. They began to sizzle.

PART II

OCTOBER

Chapter 9

Roy unwrapped the second half of a cold onion bagel with cream cheese and bit into it half-heartedly, scrolling up to reread what he'd just written.

Bettina opened the airlock.
"No!"

He snapped his laptop shut and stood up. *Gold?* What a joke. The book was shit.

Wadding up the waxed paper, he threw the rest of the bagel over the railing and watched it drift downriver and then disappear in the dark water. He could never get used to how much dough was stuffed into a bagel. It seemed like such a waste of flour and whatever else was in bagels—cement?

"That's what I love about this river," a woman seated on a bench behind him remarked. "You got worries? You just throw them in that river and they're gone."

Roy smiled grimly at her and continued walking. Oh, he had worries. He'd walked all the way from home, across the Brooklyn Bridge, through South Street Seaport and Battery Park. Now he was at the end of the pier on Christopher Street, in the West Village. His feet ached and he had no reason to walk so far, but walking made him feel like he was writing even when he wasn't.

Why was he killing off Bettina and probably Ceran if they were his main characters? And what about his girl with the gold? He'd barely dealt with her.

Beneath the pier, the Hudson River roiled and churned. The water was so dark here, even on a sunny day. It wasn't green or blue or brown or even black—it was just dark. And deep.

He thought of that poor woman, all in pieces, all over New York. Wendy had read the latest *Brookliner* column aloud to him from her iPad this morning: *"Head Found!"* They'd found it only yesterday, after weeks of searching and waiting. Thankfully there was no picture. Oddly, that annoyed Wendy.

Bettina and Ceran and Isabel were annoyed too. Not just because they were teenagers, but because they were being used. Bettina and Ceran were being used by the scientific establishment as guinea pigs, to see how teenagers develop in space. And Isabel, with her backpack full of gold, felt like life had handed her a backpack full of shit because her parents were cowardly crooks who'd left her on her own.

Roy continued to walk. He did like, or at least appreciate, the dichotomy between the teenagers in space and the one on earth, who were all lucky in their own way—lucky to see and experience

166

what few had seen and experienced, or lucky to have their own island in the Bahamas and a backpack full of gold—but who truly felt that they were unlucky.

Lucky.

Unlucky.

Gold.

Or *Red*.

Every time Roy considered scrapping the whole bloody book, he began to wonder if maybe Peaches was right. If he just plodded on, he'd eventually break through the fog and all would become clear. There was something there—there had to be. Otherwise it was his head they were going to find floating in the river next.

Wendy was strangely excited about the head. Something about this particular murder had captured her imagination.

"Where does one even purchase a chain saw?" she'd asked him. "Do you have to plug it in, or does it run on batteries? Kerosene? Diesel?"

"I haven't a clue," Roy had answered.

"Aha." She laughed. "Covering your tracks."

Roy wasn't sure why this was funny. It seemed unmotherly to be obsessed with the gruesome details of a local murder instead of worrying about the safety of one's own children.

"I bet you can buy one on Amazon," Shy had piped up. And then she and her mother had spent a good hour scrolling through pages and pages of chain saws, selecting the ones that might be best for dismemberment.

"I wish they could put her back together again so she could tell us what happened," Wendy had said wistfully.

Roy had an inkling they were leaving him out on purpose so he could focus on his book, but he still felt a bit ignored.

He continued walking. Whenever anyone on *Battlestar Galactica* visited another planet, they never wore spacesuits or had any trouble breathing. What if Bettina didn't die when she opened the airlock? What if Ceran only thought she was dead and then he kills himself and then Bettina has to kill herself because he's dead and she's lost her will to live, like *Romeo and Juliet* in space—and thus stupidly unoriginal.

What if she tries to die but can't? Because she's no longer human. Neither is Ceran. They've been experimented on for so many years, before and during their time in space, they've evolved into something *else*.

Roy winced. Even within the context of the total shit he'd written thus far this was lunacy. What were they then, mutants? What did that even mean? He supposed since he was the writer he could make it mean whatever he wanted. He was in charge of the situation. He just had to *take* charge.

Roy stopped walking, pressed his palms against

the pier railing, and looked down into the dark water.

Maybe Bettina opens the airlock, expecting to die and possibly kill Ceran, and nothing happens. Nothing. They can both breathe and walk around and do everything as normal. They've been there so long their still-growing bodies have adapted and adjusted. Their keepers on Mars know this, know Ceran and Bettina don't have to stay inside. They've been lying to them, keeping them trapped in the Mars space station to serve a purpose instead of letting them live their lives and roam free. Teenagers hated to be lied to. Roy and Wendy had told Shy they had to move to New York for Wendy's big new job, which wasn't really true. They'd decided to move and *then* she'd found the job. He still felt guilty about it.

Roy backed into a nearby bench, opened his laptop, and began to type.

• • •

Head Found!

The severed head of a murdered Staten Island woman was found amongst discarded soccer balls, bobbing in the water between two Brooklyn Bridge Park piers, less than five nautical miles from where the woman's torso was found weeks ago. The deceased woman has been identified as twenty-eight-year-old Lelani Dimakis of Tompkinsville. Dimakis held a part-time bartending job at Jimmie Steiny's Pub near the Richmond County Courthouse. She lived with her parents and was unmarried. The deceased's ex-boyfriend, Dante Belsito, has been arrested on charges of murder and is being held by Staten Island police without bail. Belsito has a history of substance abuse and was diagnosed with issues involving "anger control" by a middle school psychologist. A 20-inch Craftsman chain saw was found in Belsito's garage. No traces of the victim's DNA were found on the chain saw, although traces of the victim's blood and hair were found in the drain of Belsito's shower. Dimakis and Belsito had been engaged. Their relationship ended more than two years ago when Dimakis began a new relationship with a local attorney and frequent Jimmie Steiny's Pub patron. The victim's family has postponed a funeral until Dimakis's remaining body parts are found. The investigation is ongoing.

The image of a severed head bobbing in the water amongst lost soccer balls was delightfully disgusting. Wendy wished there was a picture.

It was day-old news now, but she could not stop reading about it. Manfred, her former assistant, had a theory that the more mundane your life was, the more you craved the macabre. They were probably right.

Of course, she and Manfred no longer worked together. Wendy had been moved to another magazine.

Yesterday, just two weeks after turning in her excruciatingly dull and mostly plagiarized piece on Grasse and the history of the perfume industry in France, Wendy had received an email from her boss, Lucy Fleur, inviting her to dial into a conference call. Manfred had been on the call.

"A pregnant editor is going on bed rest downstairs and I offered you, Wendy, to replace her," Lucy Fleur announced, forgoing any sort of greeting or small talk. So Lucy Fleur did exist after all. Her accent—from her upbringing in Rome, St. Kitts, and Senegal—was musical, lovely. A voice that launched a thousand ships, or at least one glossy, $23 bimonthly magazine comprised almost entirely of handbag and jewelry ads.

"I see. Thank you," Wendy said, even though this was very definitely a demotion. "Which magazine did you say?"

"*Enjoy!*," said Lucy Fleur musically. "Manfred will show you."

"No problem," Manfred agreed.

"And Manfred, you will take Wendy's place at *Fleurt*."

There was an awkward pause. Wendy wasn't sure whether to laugh or cry. She felt like an enormous failure. What would she tell Roy and Shy? She'd dragged them away from England against their will, only to wind up getting fired? Was it because of the Gucci sneakers? Her boring outfits? Her addiction to reading about the dead woman on *Brookliner*? Wendy glared at the white ceramic bird perched on the top shelf of the glass bookcase opposite her desk. She hadn't put it there. Did Lucy Fleur have a camera hidden inside it? Had she been spying on her?

As soon as Lucy Fleur hung up, Manfred practically kicked her office door down. "You're going to love it at *Enjoy!*," they said. "Gelato on tap. Afternoon yoga. Remember the December chocolate issue last year? I gained ten pounds just reading it."

Wendy did not remember the December chocolate issue. She didn't read the other magazines produced in the building. She imagined *Enjoy!* was one step up from an in-flight magazine.

She clicked back to the Home for the Holidays space she needed to fill in for *Enjoy!*'s upcoming December issue. Examples from previous issues were a feature on homemade throw rugs and one on rearranging your furniture to accommodate extra family members. Wendy thought about the things she and Roy and Shy had brought with them from England. Roy's framed fish portraits, which he'd picked up in a gallery in St. Ives in Cornwall and was completely obsessed with even though he didn't fish for sport and rarely ate fish. His books, which he'd been collecting for forty years and took up most of the moving truck. Shy's pink fuzzy rug, which probably had fleas. Wendy's collection of tacky commemorative royal family mugs. The old chairs. The dining room table with its one tarnished brass leg. Their décor wasn't particularly stylish, but their home looked like a home.

"Shout if you need help." Gabby, with whom Wendy now shared a cramped, windowless office, stood up and did a few squats. Gabby was Wendy's physical opposite, with cascading black curls, huge brown eyes, and an extremely ample midsection. She wore a purple batwing dress. There were pictures of desserts pasted above her desk. *Enjoy!* staff were encouraged to get up from their desks and take a breather whenever they needed to. They were also encouraged to sample recipes in the test kitchen, learn to weave or snowshoe, drink hot chocolate with caramel sauce, and generally *Enjoy!*.

"I love the new chairs, don't you?" Gabby asked.

Wendy rocked back and forth in her padded

white leather desk chair, reminding herself not to sound snobbish. "Much nicer than upstairs," she said, even though they were exactly the same. "The chair in my old office made marks on me bum."

"You're so funny." Gabby laughed and cracked open her second can of Mountain Dew that morning. "Hey, ignore the chopstick piece, okay? One of the assistants did all the shopping and research for it. She can write it and I'll polish it up. Also, even though you're more accomplished and way cuter than I am, I'm technically your boss now. So *you* can write this impossible exposé about some hard-to-get-to tiki restaurant in Tasmania and make it sound all Anglophilic and shit. I tried to call and talk to someone, but he was drunk and unintelligible."

Wendy giggled. Gabby might enjoy dopey photos of cakes and pies, but she was fun to share an office with. "I have friends in Australia. Maybe they can help me."

Gabby pressed a series of buttons on her desk phone, causing it to beep and squawk.

"Hi, Gabby." One of the *Enjoy!* assistants came on the line, on speakerphone.

"Write up the chopstick buyer's guide, please, since you did all the legwork? And also book lunch in an hour for me and Wendy at the yummy Indian place? We're starving." She hung up the phone. "Is that okay?"

"Lunch?" Wendy never ate much lunch. Certainly not Indian food. Lately she'd felt like she was competing with Shy for how little she could eat in a day.

"We eat at this magazine," Gabby said firmly. "Hey, did you see they found the head? There's a picture of it and everything."

Wendy stood up quickly, leaving her chair spinning. The image on Gabby's screen was surreal: gray engorged face, huge blue eyes, tendrils of long brown hair cascading over the seaweed-strewn rocks, pale mouth gaping open, torn neck connected to . . . nothing.

Wendy felt like she was looking in the mirror.

They stared at the picture in silence for a good minute. Then Gabby switched off her monitor.

"Whoops, that was a quick hour. Lunchtime."

Chapter 10

*D*NA test results show the blood and hair found in Belsito's garage match those of the head and torso. Searches for the remaining limbs are ongoing. Belsito has been detained by Staten Island police and will remain in custody. Belsito has a history of prescription medication abuse and was suspended from high school three times before dropping out. He purchased one chain saw at a nearby Lowe's in May, and a second, larger chain saw at Home Depot in August. Strands of Lelani Dimakis's hair were caught in the blades of both saws."

Elizabeth switched off the radio as the hourly stock market report came on. Something about the murder, the body parts, seemed to tug at her, reminding her of Tupper and home. This rarely happened. Of course she thought of him. They had been together—and apart—for a long time. And this tug was not a longing or a yearning; it was more like curiosity. What was Tupper doing? Was he making something new and attractive and lucrative? Was he staying up all night watching television and forgetting to eat? Was their quaint Brooklyn neighborhood sullied by pumpkins and ridiculous Halloween decorations? Elizabeth didn't carry a cell phone, so she had no way of knowing.

She'd have to go back to Brooklyn soon anyway. She needed a bath and a good hot meal and perhaps some human contact. When they were in their twenties, Tupper made her promise to speak to at least two people a day to avoid "getting so sucked into her work that she lost touch with the humans the work was for." Elizabeth hadn't spoken to anyone in almost two months. The cabin she'd rented for this project was unheated and it was getting cold at night. She could go home to Cobble Hill, take a bath, and put on a robe. Tupper would make her a lamb burger with red wine, and he would talk to her. It was so predictable and domestic it was almost unbearable. But she did miss him, or the idea of him.

Besides, she wouldn't stay long. Just until she figured out the next work. This one, this project in the woods, had been good. Each day she'd created a new temporary work made of found objects at the base of a tree and taken a picture with the fancy gold phone she'd been provided with but had never connected to cell service. She'd mail in the phone (she never bothered with uploading or downloading), and the whole series would be projected on a wall at the Apple headquarters in Cupertino, California, and she would be paid handsomely. She'd collaborated with Apple years ago for the launch of another new iPhone. That project was called *Find*

Yourself. Elizabeth built a labyrinth of tunnels that led to end zones where one could collect prizes varying from a wad of chewed gum, to live frogs, to a pair of designer flip-flops, to a hank of horsehair, to the new iPhone itself. It was immensely popular, and Apple was an excellent collaborator, providing expensive prizes and paying her an absurd amount of money.

Elizabeth had always found a way to be paid for her art. She was persuasive in an almost unspoken way—her mere physical presence was convincing enough. Usually she got what she wanted. And she never stopped. Working artists had to work. As soon as she was finished with one project she would move on to the next.

Tupper knew this. He knew her. They'd practically grown up together in Unity, Maine. Starting at age eleven he'd followed her around while she picked up dead bugs and thorny branches. He tried to make a boat out of rocks. They used to see how long they could tolerate walking barefoot in the snow. Her parents were drunk and inattentive Icelandic artists. His parents thought he was gay because he didn't play ice hockey. He'd followed her to every educational institution where she'd sought a degree: a BFA from CalArts, an MFA from the Art Institute of Chicago, an MA from Bard's Center for Curatorial Studies, and a master's and a PhD in the history of consciousness from

UC Santa Cruz, as well as artist residencies at MacDowell, Yaddo, Roswell, and Kala. They were extremely well-educated. Eventually they'd married—a cheesy, quickie wedding in Las Vegas of all places—and Elizabeth changed her name from Elizabeth Fuchsdottir to Elizabeth Paulsen. The very next morning, she'd hitchhiked out of town and didn't see Tupper again until she broke her wrist five months later during her *Rodeo*, when she rode a bucking bull completely naked, covered in live beetles and barbecue sauce.

Elizabeth knew she was eccentric. There were plenty of eccentrics in New York City. The thing about Cobble Hill, the neighborhood of Brooklyn where Tupper had chosen to buy a house with the embarrassing amount of money he'd made and continued to make from his Macaw design, was that everyone knew or thought they knew everyone else's business. The artists all lived in Red Hook, not Cobble Hill. Elizabeth couldn't walk down the street without a staring audience. She was conspicuous, over six feet tall and reed thin—her favorite foods were vodka and vitamins—with a white-blond braid that hung down her back to her waist. She made her own clothes, tearing apart clothing in the sale bin at vintage shops and repurposing it. She liked to wear vinyl because it was durable and warm and waterproof. And she never wore a bra because they were uncomfortable. What bothered her most about their Cobble Hill neighbors—most of them stroller-wielding parents; their children were their works of art—was that they were so *content*.

And then there was Tupper. Beautiful, adoring, nervous, and anything but content. Sure, she and he had attempted contentment for a time. They'd bought their house. They'd prepared for a child, children. When the children didn't come, she refused to succumb to the clichéd and obvious rabbit hole of fertility treatments, or adoption, or depression. She refused to discuss it at all. She simply made them. She made twins. Out of papier-mâché and birch bark and wool and felt. Then she staged their illnesses and untimely deaths—the one project she did not get paid for—and stashed them in a glass box. And then she moved on.

But she did need to go back. Tupper was probably wasting away, fretting over some quirkily adorable contraption like a penguin that dispensed mini marshmallows into your cocoa or a Chihuahua that farted hot sauce. And perhaps she was being too hard on their Cobble Hill neighbors. Perhaps she could *incorporate* them in some way. Perhaps they'd even be useful. More than anything, she needed the landline. Any day now the recipients of the MacArthur Fellowship "genius" grants would be announced. Elizabeth had been making culturally relevant work for over twenty years. She was certain this was her time.

Roy read and reread the last paragraph he'd written, pressing his back against the stiff wooden barstool. Now what was he on about? Well, it was obvious, wasn't it? A storm. Something powerful enough to get Isabel up to Mars. A magical tornado, or a tidal wave, the crest of which would reach the Milky Way.

It would take about a year to get to Mars in a spacecraft—he'd looked it up. But since Isabel was traveling by natural disaster, she could pop up whenever he wanted her to. Because she was special and he was in charge. Now all he needed was for Ceran to get both girls pregnant. And for the bad guy—who was either a Russian stowaway or a mutant scientist—to swoop in and hold them hostage. Maybe the bad guy hides in the food-restocking rocket ship amongst the crates of bananas—no, bananas wouldn't last—grapefruits and oranges and bags of rice and sultanas, and emerges on Mars, pretending to be a new scientist. He assimilates and slowly begins to kill everyone. Then, like a pack of stealthy coyotes, Ceran, Bettina, and Isabel lure him outside into Mars's atmosphere, to which they are immune, and look on triumphantly as his head explodes.

Oh hell.

The bar was dark and empty. Would it not

be wise to put the book down for a bit and go home and make a snack? Perhaps he could plan a magnificent meal for Shy and Wendy, go to the shops, and spend the rest of the afternoon cooking in their wonderfully equipped kitchen. He'd never been much of a cook though. He'd never done much of anything besides write books. He was useless, really. How Wendy and Shy put up with him he'd never know.

The bad guys must have a laser gun. Roy couldn't actually call it a laser gun, though, that was silly. If this were a TV show, the guns would be called something cool and futuristic. Zapper. Taser. Faser?

Roy jumped off his barstool and aimed his index finger at a bottle of gin.

"Watch out! He's got a faser!"

"Where'd you get this anyway?" Shy passed the joint back to Liam. Neither one of them had ever tried weed before. They'd almost bought a little vape pen, but they were so expensive and she'd always wanted to try rolling a joint, so they'd bought rolling papers instead.

Liam inhaled deeply and then coughed out the smoke. "My mom. She has a dealer. Actually, I think she might *be* a dealer."

"Seriously?" Shy was impressed. Her parents were so boring. Well, maybe not boring, but old-fashioned. "How do you know?"

"I found a giant jar full of pot in a paper shopping bag in her closet. I was looking for the dog leash. And now it all makes sense. I mean, she's always been really weird. Now I know why."

Shy nodded. "I already feel weird."

"Me too," Liam said and put his arm around her. They were huddled on a bench in the playground next to the entrance to the BQE. It was sort of a clichéd thing to do, but where else could they go, Starbucks?

Shy put her head on his shoulder and they looked up at the darkening sky. It was a little after five o'clock. Stars appeared one at a time in the expanse of azure, twinkling brightly, like they'd been switched on.

Shy pointed at a freshly glowing pinkish-red dot.

"Mars is the Roman god of war."

She'd garnered this fact from Mr. Streko's Twitter feed, which she'd decided to be more strict with herself about and not look at more than four times a day so as not to become an obsessive teen stalker. Also, she was starting to really like Liam.

"And also a candy bar," she added with a giggle.

Liam snorted and actual snot came out of his nose. He pulled his arm away from her and wiped at the snot with the back of his hand.

"Ugh. I can already tell I'm not going to like my mom's weed."

Shy didn't move. "I like it."

Liam shoved his hands into his jacket pockets and jittered his legs restlessly.

"I know it's been a few weeks, but all I can think about is the schoolyard fire. I can't sleep. Black Ryan wants to confess. *I* want to confess. But then Bruce will kill me. He'll kill both of us."

"But you didn't really do anything, right?"

Liam shook his head. It was exhausting just thinking about it.

Shy sat up and turned to face him. Her blue eyes were enormous. She looked pretty in the twilight, but also a little fucked up. "Then you should be the one to confess first. Just tell someone what happened. Exactly the way it happened. You won't be punished for being honest. Forget about Bruce. He's disgusting."

"Yeah," Liam said. "I guess." And the more stoned he felt, the more he decided what Shy said was right. He hadn't started the fire, he just happened to be in the wrong place at the wrong time with the wrong people. He had to come forward and confess so he could get a decent night's sleep.

"Oh God." He grabbed Shy's hand and squeezed it hard, bouncing his feet up and down, overcome by paranoia and nervous exhaustion.

"How does my mom smoke this stuff? She's a maniac. Seriously. I'm freaking out."

Shy walked Liam home and then went home herself. She was still so high, and trembling with cold, and trembling because she was pretty sure Liam wasn't just her tutor anymore. They might even be in love. In the dimly lit library, her father sat very straight in his chair. He looked like he was concentrating.

"Hi, Daddy." Shy walked up behind him and read the words on his computer screen. "Mars, really? Did you know Mars is the Roman god of war?"

Roy was in deep space with Ceran, Bettina, and Isabel and didn't notice how stoned she was.

"Is it?" He ruminated on this little factoid, wondering how he could work it in. His teenage Martian colonists were at war with everyone on Earth who had stolen their privacy and with the rich Russians who were trying to steal their gold.

"It was on Mr. Streko's Twitter. Oh, and I'm thinking of joining the table tennis team. Mr. Streko is the coach, and Mum said I need extracurricular activities for college."

"That's fine. Sorry, I'm distracted. Did you have a nice afternoon?" Her father looked up with a vague smile. "How's Liam?"

"He's a mess." Shy yawned. "I'm going to go stare at my homework. Wish me luck."

"Good luck."

Shy had homework, that was good. He'd come home from Monte intending to make an elaborate sandwich and read the newspaper, but had wound up eating only a few crisps before going back to his book. Ceran and Bettina were having sex outside the airlock in a sandstorm, while Isabel messaged Earth in fluent Russian. Soon Wendy would be home from running *Fleurt* and they'd heat up the delicious lamb stew she'd made over the weekend, or order Thai curries from Joya and drink white wine.

Roy hit return.

Chapter 11

A MESSAGE FROM NURSE PEACHES

Dear PS 919 parents,

As you know, our beloved schoolyard was vandalized last month. The identity of the perpetrators has since been revealed and a suitable punishment has been assigned—by me. The vandals themselves have agreed to pay for repairs to the schoolyard. They have also agreed to personally apologize to each and every classroom of children in this school for the damage they did that night. And they have agreed to weekly community service within the school from now until winter break.

The apology will take place this Friday, starting at 8:55 a.m. I will need a few parent volunteers to help me walk the vandals from class to class. The whole process should take about three hours.

Repairs, on the other hand, will take longer. A few contractors have made bids. I'll keep you posted.

Thank you for your help and support.
We will have our schoolyard back soon!

My very best,
Peaches Park, school nurse
nursepeaches@ps919brooklyn.edu

Stuart followed Nurse Peaches down the fourth-floor hallway to Ted's classroom. Behind him Peaches' son, Liam, and his teenage vandal cohort shuffled dutifully along.

"Dad!"

Stuart was a parent volunteer. "Hey, bud." He hugged Ted's head to his hip.

"Ticktock," Ted's slightly loony septuagenarian homeroom teacher, Mrs. Watson, called out.

"Applesauce!" Ted and the other nine-year-olds responded dutifully and took their seats at their tables.

Liam, Bruce, Black Ryan, and Ryan stood in front of the sunny windows, staring down the lint balls on the round blue classroom rug with nervous exhaustion. They'd worked their way through the grades, missing a whole morning of classes and lunch at their own school. Ted's was the third to last classroom to hear their guilty plea.

"These big boys have something to say to all of you," Mrs. Watson told the class. "So I need you to be all ears and open hearts."

Stuart wanted to hug her. Something about her

188

heavy Brooklyn accent and smoker's voice using a term like "open hearts" made him feel mushy all over. Maybe it was the massive amounts of THC in his system from the pot he and Mandy had been constantly eating and smoking, or maybe it was the presence of Nurse Peaches in the sunlit classroom, her dimples popping despite her efforts to frown.

"Go ahead, boys," she said. "Liam, why don't you start?"

Liam glanced at his mom and then at Mrs. Watson and then down at the rug again. Ted and his classmates wiggled impatiently in their chairs. Half of them had food on their shirts and untied shoelaces. The room smelled like farts.

"Yeah. So." Liam looked up at the classroom full of boys and girls. He knew three out of every ten boys in every classroom in the school from his after-school job at the Brooklyn Strategizer, which made this even more humiliating. "Um."

It occurred to Stuart that the son had inherited none of his mother's cuteness. He was awkward and gawky like his dad.

"So, me and my friends—" Liam glanced at the other three boys, who looked away. "We were hanging out in the schoolyard. At night, when it was dark outside. And we found a bottle of vodka that someone had left under the slide. And vodka is mostly alcohol, which is flammable, so that gave us an idea."

He hadn't gone into such detail in the other classrooms, but the morning had worn him thin. He hesitated. Was he teaching these kids bad things? Oh God, what an idiot.

"Um, one of you guys want to take it from here?"

Black Ryan cleared his throat. "We weren't doing anything bad at first, just hanging out. But then we decided it'd be cool to make a video of flames pouring down the slide. So we—"

"I did it. It was all my idea." Bruce stepped forward with his hands in his jeans pockets, his weird eyes bulging. It sounded like he was bragging. "I poured the vodka down the slide and lit it on fire."

Ryan kicked at the rug with the toe of his Converse sneaker. "And I took a video. We were going to put it on YouTube. But then the leaves started to burn, and the rubber mats on the ground melted, and the little tree caught fire, and—"

"And we're sorry," Bruce interrupted him impatiently.

"We're so sorry," Black Ryan said.

"Yeah, we are," Ryan said.

"I'm really, really sorry," Liam muttered, glad that it was almost over.

"Thanks, guys," Peaches interrupted them. "It's always hard to admit when you did something wrong." She turned to the class again. "These guys will be helping out in school a few days a week until the holidays, so you'll be seeing them around."

The class applauded for no apparent reason—almost every class had applauded—and then everyone began talking at once. Except for Ted, who raised his hand.

"Ticktock!" Mrs. Watson shouted.

"Applesauce!" the class shouted back and then sat silently in their chairs.

"Ted has a question," the teacher said. "Go ahead, Ted."

Stuart stared at his son. This hadn't happened in any of the other classes.

Liam glanced at his mom for assistance, but she was smiling at the boy who'd raised his hand. The boy's name was Ted. He was a nice little kid. Liam was teaching him to play Settlers of Catan at the Strategizer.

Ted put his hand down. He sat very straight and didn't seem nervous about talking in front of his whole class and a bunch of adults and big boys.

"Did you guys have fun?" he asked.

Liam shook his head. That night had not been fun. It was a total nightmare. But the other boys chuckled.

"Yeah," Black Ryan spoke up with a slow smile. "It was pretty fun." Peaches glared at him and he cleared his throat. "For a few seconds anyway. We didn't mean to ruin the whole playground."

"The fire was awesome," Bruce said. "I can't deny it."

"Yeah," Ryan agreed. "It was pretty cool."

Peaches scowled. This was not how this was supposed to go. There was nothing cool about it.

"Well, thanks to their fun, cool time, you will all have to put up with recess and after-school playtime in a much smaller area until we get the playground fixed up, which could take until spring or even next fall. How cool is that?" she said.

"Not cool at all," Stuart remarked. It was the first thing he'd said.

All eyes shifted to Stuart.

> *Burn our shit and you're in stitches*
> *Your cool trick pissed off my bitches!*

"Fire is bad," he continued recklessly, already disagreeing with himself. There was nothing wrong with fire; fire was fucking awesome. "Fire is bad when you destroy other people's property with it."

"My dad got mad when the landscaper burned leaves in our backyard," Lily van Dusen spoke up. Her family lived in the corner house on Tompkins and Degraw. It was one of the envies of the neighborhood.

"We have a firepit. For s'mores," another girl said.

"I set my cat's tail on fire by an accident," a boy named Loden said. "With a blowtorch."

Peaches was pretty sure it wasn't an accident. Loden was a psychopath. He had once ground his own forehead into the bricks of the school building because he wanted to look like he was built out of *Minecraft* bricks.

"Anyway, we still have part of the schoolyard," Ted announced, breaking the tension. He hugged Stuart's side. "Bye, Dad. We have to go to art now."

"Later, skater," Stuart said. Ted was such a good kid.

"It is what it is," Mrs. Watson announced sagely to the room. She clapped her hands and shouted, "Onward!" The children hurriedly lined up in ordered pairs in front of the door. "Leaders, lead us to art!" she cried, and the children filed out of the room.

"Amen." Peaches sighed. "Come on, boys. Just the fifth grade and then you're done."

Mandy had just finished roasting the duck from 4 Cheever Place apartment 2A's Farm to Front Door box. It was a little burned on the bottom and the kitchen smelled like sizzling hair because she'd singed her arm hair removing the duck from the oven, but still. Who would have thought she'd ever manage to cook a whole duck?

Now it was time to toss the shaved beets and

Jerusalem artichokes in their sesame oil and ginger vinaigrette dressing and add a sprinkling of chopped peanuts and scallions for garnish. There was a single duck egg in the box that Mandy wasn't sure what to do with. The little illustrated instruction card for the egg seemed to have slipped out the seam of the box and gotten lost.

Her cell phone rang on the kitchen counter. It was a Brooklyn number, possibly Ted's school. Mandy took the call.

"Mrs. Little? This is Billy from the Brooklyn Strategizer."

"Oh, hi." Mandy broke off another morsel of pot cookie and tucked it into her cheek so she could chew while he was talking. Usually she hated it when people called her "Mrs. Little." That was Stu's mom's name, and Stu's mom was a total c-u-n-t. Mandy's name was Mandy Marzulli. But she didn't say anything.

"Yeah, we've been having some issues with Ted today. Uh, sometimes we burn scented candles in the bathroom, like for when someone makes a huge stinky doogie?"

Mandy giggled. The guys at the Brooklyn Strategizer were all man-children. They wore sticky-looking T-shirts and never tied their shoelaces and stayed in the store playing Dungeons & Dragons and Settlers of Catan until two in the morning, drinking homemade root beer and eating caramel popcorn. She and Stu had seen them through the Strategizer window walking home from restaurants in her better days.

"Anyway, today Ted took the burning candle out of the bathroom and brought it to a table in back without anyone seeing. He had one of our Jenga sets, which are made of wood, and he was like, torching the pieces, one by one."

"Seriously?"

"Yup."

"All by himself? Or was it, like, a group of boys?"

"No, just him."

"I'm so sorry."

"That's okay, we caught him before he burned the building down or injured himself. But I'd like for someone to pick him up now. And I told him he can't come back."

"What? Like, ever?" Mandy spat the last bit of cookie into the sink, preparing for a fight.

"Mrs. Little, we have strict rules to avoid chaos. Your son was inciting chaos. This is our protocol." He sounded like he was quoting a video game.

"I'm sorry," Mandy snapped, annoyed. "Let me call his dad."

"Jesus Christ," Stuart said when she told him the news. "I know what this is about. He was so into the whole playground fire apology story this morning. Fucking pyromaniac assholes."

195

"Stu, you're talking about our kid."

"No, the boys who burned the schoolyard down. They came to talk to the classrooms this morning. To apologize. And Ted thought what they did sounded *fun*."

"Oh."

"Yeah. Fucking monsters. All right. I'll go get him. It'll only be an hour earlier than normal by the time I get there."

Mandy pulled a piece of crispy duck fat off the sizzling duck body and stuck it in her mouth. It was salty and delicious.

"It's actually good you guys are coming home, because I made a duck."

"Whoa. A duck? You're amazing."

"Thanks," Mandy said. "I don't know why, but I'm really into cooking now. Except there's this funky little duck egg in the box, but I think the directions for it slipped out, because there's no mention of it in the instructions."

"The duck came in a box with instructions?"

Mandy clapped her hand over her mouth. Fucking weed. "You know, the recipe." Time to change the subject. "Anyway, go get Teddy. The sooner you go, the sooner we can eat!"

"You want to keep your development options open, right?" Liam asked Ted.

"Yes," Ted answered, hovering over the board with earnest concentration.

Liam felt bad that Ted was getting kicked out. He was a good kid, and of particular interest to Liam now that he knew Ted's father was that semi-famous weed-smoking dude from the stoop the other night. So what if Ted had set something on fire? Stop putting candles and matches in a bathroom where there are little kids if you don't want them to set stuff on fire. Stop smoking weed on your stoop in front of your kid.

Because his dad taught music to the younger grades, Liam got to attend private school for free. But his mom said if he wanted "a private school wardrobe and fancy private school tossed salads and wraps for lunch," Liam had to get an after-school job. He'd been working at the Brooklyn Strategizer twice a week for the past year, picking up kids from the PS 919 schoolyard, walking them the five blocks to the store, and teaching them role-play and board games. He made them homemade sodas and popcorn and swept up and Lysoled the bathroom before the adult evening sessions. At first the place made him feel uncomfortable and unclean. The tables and chairs and floor and doorknobs were sticky, and the other guys who worked there were much older than he was and pretty weird. Danner wore black leather chaps with metal skulls dangling off them and had a tattoo of a frog on his nose. Billy identified as "a wizard" and had stringy purple-and-green hair that hung down to his kneecaps.

But they were really nice. Liam made sixteen dollars an hour. It was a good job.

He leaned over the game. "Then don't start so close to the corners. Start toward the middle. Okay, I'm going to trade you my bricks for your three sheep."

"No way."

Settlers of Catan was Liam's favorite game. You got to build settlements and trade resources, and it was a sort of race to see who could take up the most geographic space on the board. He liked how simple the game was; it was easy to teach. Ted was pretty dumb at Catan though. He became too attached to the materials.

"I like my farm how it is," he insisted. "I'm keeping my sheep."

"That's not how the game works. You have to build and expand. It's progress, dude."

Ted sat back, suddenly losing interest. "You know when you started the fire in the schoolyard? Were you guys smoking weed?"

Liam felt his face turn bright red. This kid, holy shit. Still, he didn't want to lie.

"Actually yeah, some of the other guys were before we got there. I wasn't though. I'm not really into that." *Unlike my mom and both of your parents,* he added silently. Except for that one time with Shy.

"Have you ever smoked weed?" Ted persisted.

Stuart pushed open the glass door. The

Brooklyn Strategizer was so nerdy it almost gave him hives, but he knew he would have dug it as a kid. "Let's go, buddy. I heard you did something bad."

Ted looked down at the floor and shrugged his shoulders.

Liam stood up while Ted collected the game pieces and put them in the box with the game board. Strategizer protocol dictated that each player had to clean up and put away his game neatly. "Yeah, Billy had to take off, but he said he called you. Ted can't come back. At least, not this year."

Stuart glared at him. "Pretty harsh, but I get it."

"It's stupid," Liam said. His lower lip trembled, and for a moment he thought he might cry. Ted's dad so obviously hated him. And Liam hated that he was now part of the asshole group who'd set fire to the little kids' schoolyard.

Stuart continued to glare at him while Ted found his backpack and coat.

Liam held out his fist for Ted to bump.

Stuart felt like a dick. Peaches' kid seemed pretty decent.

"Your mom is cool," he said before they left, because he wanted to be nice.

Chapter 12

"What would happen if I drank all the vanilla extract?"

"You'd feel ill. And probably a little drunk," her mother said. "Remember when you used to call it vanilla 'abstract'?"

Shy was making Toll House cookies. Wendy had taught her and her sisters when they were little. No one in England knew what a Toll House cookie was. They had to go to Tesco in Kensington to get the right chips.

Shy stuck her tongue into the hole at the top of the tiny bottle and puckered her lips. "Wine is better."

Wendy took it away from her. "This restaurant is getting an F rating." She poured a bunch of vanilla into the bowl of butter and brown sugar without measuring it.

"Dad, do you want me to put nuts in some of them? I think we have pecans," Shy called out.

There was no answer from the library.

"Don't bother him. I think he's writing—like, actually writing. It's been a while since he's been this productive."

Wendy had just returned from her own chair in the library where, instead of getting up the courage to tell Roy she'd been fired from *Fleurt* and was now filling in for someone on maternity leave at *Enjoy!*, a lifestyle magazine full of beautiful bathtubs and decadent desserts, she'd attempted to paraphrase a Malcolm Gladwell piece from *The New Yorker* that questioned the whole movement to legalize marijuana. Wendy hated pot—the odor, how slow everyone got when they smoked it, the need to eat afterward.

"Finally, someone with some sense," she'd said to Roy's profile as he stared fixedly at the blank screen of his laptop. "Not nearly enough research has been done. There haven't been enough studies. It's simply a disaster waiting to happen. How will planes and trains run on time? How will UPS deliver anything to the right location if everyone is high? It causes impotence, too."

Roy did not respond.

A disaster waiting to happen, he repeated silently, still staring at his screen. *Impotence.* He hit return.

Wendy left him alone.

Shy stuck both hands into the bowl and squeezed the raw egg yolks until they popped and oozed between her fingers. She preferred not to use an electric mixer or utensils of any kind.

"Mr. Streko got a new tattoo," she told her mother as she churned and kneaded the bowl of sweet goo. "On his neck."

He already had so many tattoos, half of which she hadn't seen. There were some on his back—

he'd told the class—and some on his legs. Monday he'd come to school with a bandage on his neck and a few days later had revealed an orange-and-blue baseball with legs and a toothy face. He said he'd made a bet with a friend at a baseball game in college. "If the Mets don't win the World Series in the next ten years, I'll get an ugly tattoo that everyone can see." It was pretty crazy of him. Shy hated it, but she also sort of loved it. Mr. Streko's skin was very tan and his body was so covered in black hair that his tattoos were like faint background patterns that you didn't notice until you stared really hard at them.

"I remember he had a lot of tattoos." Another thing Wendy hated. Why would one want to deface one's body? She wondered if she should tell Shy about her new job before she told Roy. "It's completely inappropriate for a teacher," she added, chickening out.

"I don't mind." Shy was used to her mother's declarations about what was appropriate or inappropriate. She ripped open the package of Nestlé chocolate chips and poured them over the batter. They resounded against the metal bowl like beach pebbles.

Wendy grabbed a chip and popped it into her mouth. "But how can you pay attention when your teacher's body is scrawled all over with ink?"

Shy refused to take her mother's bait and begin

an argument. "Oh, did Daddy tell you? I joined the table tennis team. Mr. Streko is the coach. Practice is every afternoon starting Monday, and we have our first match next Thursday. You told me I needed extracurriculars for college."

Wendy opened the fridge and poured herself a glass of white wine. She didn't like how obsessed Shy was with her teacher.

"What about that nice boy? How will you have time for a boyfriend if you're playing table tennis all the time?" She put her glass down and lined up the baking trays next to the mixing bowl.

"Liam?" Shy scraped her hands against the rim of the bowl to remove the excess dough. Her mother had no idea that Liam had been involved with the schoolyard fire, she realized. That he stole pot from his mom. He was not a "nice boy." She was pretty sure her mother wouldn't think so, anyway. "He's not my boyfriend."

"He's not her boyfriend," Roy repeated from the doorway, holding his laptop against his chest. He'd gotten in the habit of carrying it around with him from room to room. They made them so small and light these days it was no trouble. "I made the same mistake. Apparently if he hasn't officially asked her to be his girlfriend, it's not official. Therefore they're 'just talking,' which means they actually talk and probably kiss, but he's still not her boyfriend."

"You've kissed him?" Wendy demanded. Of

course she was the last to know. When it came to Shy, she was always the last to know.

"Dad," Shy protested.

"I'm just guessing from the look on your face," Roy said. "I'm not a writer for nothing. I notice things."

"That's great, Dad," Shy complained. "Thanks." She wasn't about to give them any information.

"It's not my problem you're 'just talking' to one of the known perpetrators of the playground fire. He's an arsonist, which you probably think is sexy, in your twisted way. For all I know, you're carrying his little arsonist child. I don't mind, really. Girls far younger than you are getting married and raising children in some countries."

"Ha!" Shy shouted.

"Settle down you two," Wendy said jealously. Roy and Shy could have these little I'm-only-pretending-to-hate-you-spats because they were so close. She and Shy never had spats. Shy's older sisters had always been jealous of it too. "What do you mean he's an arsonist?" She was having trouble processing all this information at once. Her brain was still hung up on the Latin teacher and his tattoos.

"Never mind," Shy grumbled, glaring at her father as she began shaping the cookie dough into balls and placing them in neat rows on the trays. It was always easier to keep her mother a little bit in the dark. Now her dad had spoiled it.

"Did any of your teachers have tattoos?" Wendy asked Roy, and Shy was relieved.

He laughed. "None."

Wendy was so good at compartmentalizing. She couldn't be bothered about Shy's possible boyfriend because she was focused on Shy's crush on her Latin teacher, which was alarming, but perfectly harmless. Wendy was so capable, too. In a moment she'd be minding the clock, making sure the cookies weren't burned. She never got so preoccupied with the unnecessary that she couldn't function. Unlike himself. He hadn't even gotten dressed yet and it was what, six o'clock? Meanwhile Wendy was running *Fleurt*. Before they were married, Wendy wrote a feature a day, supporting him through the writing of *Yellow*. She didn't even insist on a big fuss of a wedding. They were both too busy. They did it at the Kensington and Chelsea registry office. It took fifteen minutes.

"Maybe you should take a pottery class instead," Wendy told Shy.

"Instead of what?" Shy pointed at the oven and Wendy slid the trays in and set the timer on the microwave for eleven minutes.

"Table tennis."

Shy clattered the mixing bowl into the sink and whirled around. "I've already signed up for it, Mum. I'm trying to get involved in things like you said. For college."

"Did you know," Roy interrupted, trying to

dilute the tension, "that one of the best subjects to study at college as far as jobs and salary is pharmacology? The worst are education and social work, that sort of thing. There are too many of them and the pay is shit."

He stopped talking. His wife and daughter were staring at him.

"I've become somewhat addicted to Google," he admitted. "You can find everything on it. You just type in a question and loads of answers pop up."

"Welcome to Earth." Shy rolled her eyes and sucked the cookie dough off her fingers.

Roy rolled his eyes in response, a poor imitation. "I would never want to be your boyfriend."

"Thanks a lot."

Wendy watched the cookies spread and glisten in the heat, feeling left out in her own kitchen. Roy was completely absorbed with his new book. Shy was becoming a typical American teenager. They were both thoroughly stuck in.

"Pharmacology," she repeated, and sipped her wine.

"Hey! Excuse me? That's mine!"

Mandy froze. She knew if she put down the Farm to Front Door box it would be an admission of guilt. Instead, she clutched it to her chest and turned around to face her accuser, an auburn-haired man wearing a neatly ironed white shirt and navy-blue suit pants. Aside from the permanently wounded look in his sad eyes, he appeared to be the type of Cobble Hill resident who could afford to donate a few boxes of food to her cause.

"Um, I order from here all the time." Mandy jutted out her chin in defiance. "I have a subscription. How else could I shop and make dinner for my family? I have MS."

The man frowned as he approached her. He was tall but also sort of small. He peered at the box. "Yes, but I'm pretty sure the label says T. Paulsen. That's me."

Mandy squinted at the label, shifting into clueless mode. "Oh yeah." She put down the box. "Sorry. Wow, what a screwup."

T. Paulsen made no move to pick up the box. He shoved his hands into his suit pants pockets and looked over Mandy's head, scanning the street with his wounded blue eyes. "Did my wife put you up to this? Elizabeth?"

Mandy was ready to go back inside. Scrutiny was not her thing. Neither was chatting on the street. Neither was feeling unkempt and dumpy next to a tall, skinny, well-dressed guy.

"Who?"

"Elizabeth Paulsen. The artist. She's my wife."

"Sorry. Don't know her."

"She's close, I can feel it."

As if things needed to get any weirder. Mandy did not enjoy conversing intimately with strangers.

"I was just picking up my dinner. Which turns

out not to be my dinner. I better go call"—she glanced down at the box—"Farm to Front Door. Let them know they fucked up my order."

T. Paulsen squinted at her. He flexed his fingers. "So this is not one of Elizabeth's pranks?"

Go home, Crazypants. "Nope. I just got the wrong box. Sorry for the mixup."

Mandy headed back down Kane Street. Never again would she round the corner for food boxes. She was only trying not to milk her direct neighbors dry. But they were never home and were quite possibly Russian spies. She could keep on milking indefinitely, helping out her country by starving the enemy.

"If you see her, tell her I'm cooking!" T. Paulsen shouted after her.

Mandy turned the corner, her sights already on the orange Full Plate truck with the nice driver, just pulling up in front of the house next door. Mandy had been enjoying Full Plate so much she'd even logged onto their site to write a five-star review: *"I used to be scared to use the stove,"* she wrote. *"Your recipes are so easy and so, so good. The meal choices for next week look amazing too. Yum. Can't wait to cook!"* —Jodi, West Virginia

"They're in the Bahamas!" she called to the driver. "I don't know why they don't just cancel."

"Want it upstairs again?" he asked, like they were an old team and he knew the drill.

"Yes, please," Mandy said. "You're the best."

Chapter 13

This sucks," Black Ryan complained. He leaned back against the bathroom door and gazed forlornly at the wet-toilet-paper-strewn floor. "It smells so bad."

Liam had been hanging out with Black Ryan a lot recently. Both boys had pretty much the same take on what had happened in the schoolyard that night: Bruce was an asshole, and all of this was his fault. Bruce was the only one who really owed all those kids an apology, and he alone should be doing community service at the school to make up for it. But Bruce's and Ryan's parents had chipped in five thousand dollars apiece for repairs to the schoolyard so their sons wouldn't have to clean toilets and could "choose their own" fake community service. Liam's and Black Ryan's parents weren't about to cough up five thousand dollars. They wanted them to be punished. So here they were, cleaning the kindergarten boys' bathroom.

"It smells like ass," Liam said.

Black Ryan shook his head. "Not my ass."

Liam turned off the hot-water tap and heaved the bucket of sudsy gray water out of the sink and onto the floor. He plunged the mop into the water and then thwacked it down on the tiles.

"Hey, you're not going to mop without picking up all that paper, are you? That's disgusting, man."

Liam was sort of hoping that the toilet paper would just disintegrate into the water and disappear, but Black Ryan was already dutifully putting on a pair of blue rubber gloves. Liam dropped the mop and put on a pair too.

They began to scoop up the damp, dirty toilet paper and chuck it into the garbage.

"Oh, that's nasty. That had streaks on it. Actual shit streaks," Black Ryan moaned.

"Pigs," Liam said. "Hey, I've been meaning to ask, do you mind when people call you Black Ryan? I mean, does it offend you?"

He'd been wondering this forever. Ever since he'd met Black Ryan in ninth grade homeroom and heard everyone, including Mr. Vonn, their homeroom teacher, call him Black Ryan.

"They call me that?"

Liam glanced at him in shock. He had to know. He had to have heard it.

Black Ryan smirked. "I'm joking, you idiot. They call me that to my face. I'm pretty sure *you've* called me that to my face."

Liam picked up a particularly nasty wad of brown paper towels, gum, and hair. "But does it bother you?"

Black Ryan shook his head. "I don't know. It's confusing. Why not call the other Ryan White

210

Ryan, right? And me just Ryan? Is Ryan a white name that I appropriated, so just to clarify things let's call me Black Ryan?"

Okay, so it did bother him. And he'd thought about it a lot.

"Yeah, I don't know. It's stupid." Liam pushed the full bucket out of the way with the toe of his sneaker. "From now on I'm just calling you Ryan."

"Whatever," Ryan said. "Hey, after this do you want to get pizza? I can't really think about food right now, but I know I'm hungry."

Liam was supposed to report to his mom after he finished in the bathrooms.

"Yeah, sure. I have to meet my mom first though. She's the nurse here, remember?"

Ryan grinned. "Oh, I remember. Your mom is cool, but she hates us. She wants us to lick this bathroom clean."

Liam laughed. "She does. She totally does."

When he'd shown his mom the crappy dark video of Bruce attempting to slide down the schoolyard slide through a puddle of flaming vodka, all she'd said was, "Idiots."

"My mom is always talking about how nothing bad has ever happened to me. Like, we didn't have to relocate to a refugee camp where I had to walk ten miles barefoot through the snow to learn math. She's hoping this is the thing that will make me not take my 'privilege' for granted."

Ryan chucked a tiny stray SpongeBob sock into the trash. "Your mom and my mom sound like they're both smoking the same hookah. Actually, she calls me Black Ryan sometimes too, kind of making fun of our school and all the assholes who go there. She'll be like, 'Time to set the table, Black Ryan,' when I'm on PlayStation too long, or, 'Black Ryan, did you read your Dickens?' My dad would not think it's funny at all, but he doesn't get to have an opinion because he doesn't even live here."

Liam knew Ryan's parents were divorced. His dad lived in Florida.

"I told my mom it's not funny, it's offensive. Like, maybe if I came up with the name myself it'd be funny and empowering, but I didn't."

"Yeah." Liam was sorry the whole Black Ryan thing was even a thing.

"Okay, I'm going to start mopping now, so we can get out of here." Ryan retrieved the soaking-wet mop from the bucket of gray sudsy water and slapped it down on the grimy tiles. "There's a Sublime drop tonight. Like a Silenciaga collaboration?"

Liam had heard other kids at school talk about these drops, but he'd never been.

"Yeah, I was hoping to get there and spend some of my Strategizer money," he said. His mom was always insinuating that he looked like a math nerd, and now that he was hanging out with Shy he wanted to dress better. After all, she wore Gucci.

Ryan whistled. "How much money have you made? That shit costs like nine hundred dollars for one hoodie, you know that, right? When I buy stuff I have to put it on my housekeeper's credit card and beg my mom to pay her back. She gets so mad. It's fine though. It's worth it."

Liam blinked at the floor for a moment. *My housekeeper's credit card?* It seemed like everyone at his school was rich except for him. Ryan did have some really cool clothes though. "Maybe I'll just get a belt or a beanie or something."

Ryan grabbed the jumbo aerosol can of Lysol. "I'm gonna spray the shit out of the toilets and flush and pray they don't overflow. At least it'll smell better in here."

Liam shook his head as he swirled soapy gray water over the brown linoleum floor. "Can't believe we have to do this 'til December."

Ryan flushed all three toilets and wheeled the cleaning cart out of the bathroom. Liam backed out after him, mopping as he went. The bathroom was practically gleaming. As much as he complained about it, he actually enjoyed seeing how much better they'd made it.

"Boys?" His mom's voice echoed down the school hallway.

Liam swung around, mop in hand.

She shot him her favorite new look of withering disdain. "You done already?"

Liam shrugged his shoulders. "I think we're done."

"We're definitely done," Ryan said.

"Well, do you have plans tonight?"

"Maybe." Liam didn't really want to explain the whole drop thing because she clearly didn't think he deserved to do anything fun or interesting ever again.

"Whatever," his mom responded.

It had been almost a month, but she was still so angry with him and his "entitled asshole friends" that she still wasn't really speaking to him. Not like before.

"I offered for you to babysit Ted Little tonight, but his dad turned me down. Obviously he doesn't think it's a good idea for his son, who might be a tiny pyro, to hang out with a big pyro like you. He told me he already had a sitter, but I could tell he didn't. Anyway, you can get your own dinner. I'm going out. Your dad has his music group tonight. I expect you to be in bed when I get home."

"Okay," Liam said, refusing to engage. It wasn't like he didn't feel bad. He'd confessed. He'd *told* her he felt bad. But she thought he needed to feel worse. "See you later, Mom."

"Nice meeting you," Ryan mumbled as they shuffled past her to put away the cleaning cart.

• • •

Peaches noticed the handwritten sign in the window of Monte that morning when she stopped by on her way to work: KARAOKE TONIGHT. 8 P.M.–.

Elizabeth was back.

She'd left a typically cryptic note for Peaches on the bar: *Please invite friends and open up by 8. I'll do the rest.*

Dutifully, Peaches took a picture of the sign and sent it in separate texts to Stuart Little, Roy Clarke, and Dr. Conway.

Dr. Conway was the first to respond.

Fun! Let me know if you want me to bring anything ;)

Roy replied with a series of dollar signs, ampersands, and hashtags. Peaches wasn't sure if he was trying to indicate expletives, as in, "Holy fucking shit!" or if he just didn't know how to use his phone.

When his phone bleeped on the subway, Stuart took a screenshot of Peaches' sign and texted it to Mandy. Mandy loved karaoke—not the singing so much, but watching other people make asses out of themselves. If Stuart got drunk enough, he would sing and make an ass out of himself too, which she especially enjoyed.

Mandy texted back a thumbs-up emoji and the words, if you can get Ted a sitter!

Stuart was just happy she was up for it. Mandy had crazy amounts of energy lately.

Almost immediately Peaches texted him with, Liam is available to babysit if you need him.

Stuart knew she meant well, but he couldn't accept. Liam was a bad influence on Ted. Thanks, he texted back. Sitter situation already taken care of.

And for the rest of the day, he couldn't concentrate on the cat food commercial he was composing for. He really wanted to go out tonight, and there were so many teenagers in the neighborhood. Surely one of them could hang out in the house while Ted—who was no trouble—ate chicken nuggets, played a game on the iPad, and went to bed.

He left work early to pick up Ted from the after-school program in the school gym. On their way home, he saw her.

Stuart had seen her in the neighborhood many times, walking to school or grocery shopping with her father, the author Roy Clarke. She looked about sixteen or seventeen. A teenager who helped out her parents and was never late to school. She seemed pretty responsible. It didn't seem that weird to follow her on their skateboards to the corner of Kane and Strong, grab his and Ted's boards, and call out to her.

"Hi. Excuse me. You live around here, right? You're Roy Clarke's daughter?"

"Dad, why are you yelling at her?" Ted whined.

He was always whiny after Hobby Horse at school. He missed the Strategizer.

"Shhh," Stuart said and squeezed his shoulder.

The girl stopped and turned around. She had long legs like a baby giraffe, and she seemed to have trouble keeping her head up, making eye contact difficult. She was clearly not fully formed. But then again, neither was he, and he was thirty-six.

"I'm Stuart Little. This is Ted. He goes to PS 919, right here. Anyway, our sitter for tonight kind of didn't work out, so I was wondering if maybe you would hang with Ted while we're out? We won't be far away and we won't be out very late. Say, eight to eleven. Twenty dollars an hour?" Even though she was only a teenager, he thought he ought to offer something above minimum wage. He smiled a goofy, friendly, harmless dad smile. "I'm sorry, I don't even know your name."

She smiled then, not at him but at the neighborhood in general. "It's Shy. Shy Clarke." Her voice was low and her accent was very English. He hadn't expected her to sound so English. "I can babysit for you. I just have to do my homework and check in with my parents." She held out her long arm and impossibly long fingers. "Give me your phone. I'll put in my number and you can text me the address."

Obediently Stuart handed over his phone. She

was weirdly direct. There wasn't anything fake or pretentious about her. He liked that.

Shy wasn't sure why she'd said yes. She'd never done any babysitting. Twenty dollars an hour seemed like a lot though, and she'd been in a weird mood ever since she and Liam had smoked his mother's weed in the park. She felt restless, like she needed to be out of the house, away from her dad and his cheese toasties and cinnamon rolls and tea.

"I'm a big admirer of your dad's," Stuart said.

She grunted, typing rapidly with her thumbs. Something about this dad and his mini-me son with their faded black skinny jeans, high-top sneakers, and matching skateboards made her feel a bit obnoxious.

"It's okay. You don't have to pretend you've read his books. No one has." She thought of mentioning the fact that she had no babysitting experience whatsoever, but then decided it would be unprofessional. "I'm in there now." She handed back his phone. "Under *C* for *Clarke* in your contacts."

"So you'll do it?" Stuart asked. "It's kind of important. My wife has been sick and she doesn't get out much, but she's been feeling better so . . ."

"Sure." She glanced down at the boy and tried to smile at him without being too creepy, but he was staring intently at a crack in the sidewalk and didn't seem to be paying any attention at all.

"Great. Thanks so much. I'll text you," Stuart said and hauled Ted hurriedly away.

Roy was staring at his computer screen again. He hated when he did that. Sometimes he even nodded off. It was embarrassing. He felt so old and stupid.

"A Russian assassin on Mars," he said aloud so that the pain of his humiliation would be even more acute. If only he could put on a hair suit and flog himself.

"Dad, I'm babysitting tonight!" Shy shouted when she came home from school. "They're paying me loads of money!" She charged upstairs and slammed the door to the bathroom.

Roy continued to stare at his screen. Peaches would be at the karaoke thing. Peaches could help him. He hoped Wendy wouldn't be too busy at work to come. She loved parties and going out and they never went anywhere anymore—which was entirely his fault. He reached for his phone.

There's a fun-sounding gathering at a bar in the neighborhood tonight. Meet me there?

Chapter 14

The bar was unlocked. A karaoke machine with two microphones, a large screen for reading the lyrics, and two huge speakers stood beside the drum set. The wooden bar top gleamed and the whole place smelled of Murphy Oil Soap and something else Peaches couldn't quite nail down. She checked the bathroom. The white porcelain toilet and sink were bleached clean. Ten individually wrapped rolls of fresh toilet paper were stacked on a shelf. The paper towel dispenser had been filled and the wastebasket emptied. Elizabeth had been busy.

Peaches' relationship with Elizabeth and Monte began in August, when she was required to show up at the nurse's office every day, even though the students would not be in attendance for almost a month. Once she'd ordered supplies and arranged her office, she had nothing to do except attend staff meetings and make copies of emergency contact forms. She took long lunch breaks and went for walks. One day, she walked past Monte and spied the drum set through the window, just sitting there collecting dust. The bar was open— at least, the door was unlocked—so she went inside. There was no one around. The bass drum had been set up wrong and the cymbals were missing a screw. Peaches wiped the drums down with a Kleenex from her bag and fixed the bass drum. Then she sat down and played a Pretenders song with two ballpoint pens, really whacking the drums hard with them because it was only Wednesday and her work week had been so long, hot, and boring. When she looked up, Elizabeth was standing behind the bar, pouring herself a shot of vodka, wearing nothing but a black bikini top and black vinyl shorts, splattered head to toe with metallic silver paint, looking ten feet tall and scary as hell. But she was civil to Peaches.

"I'm Elizabeth," she said. "You can come in and play whenever you like. I'm here very infrequently."

"Sorry about the pens, I didn't see any sticks. I'm Peaches," Peaches said. "I'm supposed to be the school nurse, but it was not necessarily the correct career path for me."

And so it began.

The bar was a welcome escape from Peaches' smelly office. Elizabeth would leave notes with instructions on the drums. *Would you mind meeting the beer guy? He comes from 3 to 5.* Or, *Toilet paper, paper towel, and napkin truck dropping off boxes today 4 to 6.* She'd disappear and then reappear again. They rarely spoke and then only cursorily. Elizabeth spent most of her time in the basement. The week before school started, she'd disappeared altogether—until now.

Formaldehyde, that was what she smelled. A heavy thud resounded beneath Peaches' feet, followed by a muffled, exasperated growl. Peaches had been instructed to never enter the basement. Elizabeth would be up when she was ready.

She ordered pad thai from the Seamless app on her phone and sat down behind the drum set. She'd been playing drums since her boring but weirdly intuitive parents put her in a Girls Rock summer day camp at the age of nine. The crazy thing about it was, despite being married to a musician, she didn't know how to read music. She didn't even know the official terms for anything she did. Her music teacher at the camp had been all about "feeling it," so she'd always just listened for the rhythm in a song and felt her way, trying out different things until she got it. For the last month she'd been working on the Talking Heads song "Burning Down the House." She played the song quietly on her phone, on repeat, and played along, getting louder as she gained confidence. She could keep up the pace now that she'd been practicing. It was faster than she'd first thought.

A guy on a bike arrived with her pad thai. She sat at the empty bar and ate it as the big, round, rose-gold sun dipped behind the old hospital buildings across the street, falling into New York Harbor only to be run over by the determinedly orange Staten Island ferry. That was the best thing about Cobble Hill. With its proximity to the water, its low buildings, and gradual, gently rising streets, the sunset was clearly visible and always startlingly beautiful.

The high, whiny vibration of an electric tool resounded from below. Elizabeth was either cutting tile or mixing cake batter.

A shadow darkened the window. Then it brightened again. A woman wearing gigantic sunglasses, her body and head shrouded in an enormous black rain poncho with the hood pulled up, darted behind a nearby tree and then slunk away again. Probably an actress, Peaches thought, paranoid about the paparazzi. There were quite a few of them in the neighborhood, but none so famous that they needed to hide behind trees. The bar door swung open and the rain poncho woman stepped inside. Her black hood fell away, revealing white-blond hair pulled back in a severe braid, a severe jawline, and a severely downturned mouth. It was Elizabeth.

"I need your help in the basement," she announced. "We'll enter from the street. The stairs in here need to stay clean."

The Sublime drop began at eight. Liam and Ryan arrived at six thirty. They'd gone out for pizza after cleaning the toilets and felt sort of gross, but they knew they'd feel less gross outside than they did inside, so they decided to go into Manhattan and stand on the sidewalk outside the store with all the other losers and wait.

The popularity of Sublime amongst boys between the ages of eleven and seventeen was not something any of the boys could explain. It was all about the logo, which was big and basic and just plain cool—the word SUBLIME in Futura Bold Oblique font, white text on a purple background. The clothes and accessories were hideously ugly, or weirdly complicated, or so simple they were simply not at all special, but that was part of their appeal. A black T-shirt with a bloody squirrel printed on it. A hat with tusks. A brown hoodie with eight rows of felt shark teeth around the hood. A red leather wallet with eleven zippers. Gold velvet boxer jock underwear. A plain white T-shirt. A plain gray T-shirt. White tube socks. An itchy black wool ski hat. Joggers with purple camouflage print on one leg and red and white stripes on the other leg. A black sleeveless T-shirt. A light pink skateboard.

Liam examined the shop's website infrequently but somewhat eagerly, not because he wanted or needed anything that could be found there, but because all the other boys at school were always wearing Sublime or talking about what they were going to get at Sublime. He thought he should be able talk about it too, and maybe even wear something he'd bought there, if it wasn't too expensive or ugly. Some of the kids at school had bots that bought the stuff for them and when they got it they sold it through their social media for way more than it was worth. That was too time-consuming and involved for Liam. And thus the rich got richer and the poor got poorer.

From what Liam had garnered from the talk in school, attending the drop was more about standing in line and being seen in the line than about actually buying anything. This particular drop was a collaboration with Silenciaga, with prices starting at ninety-five dollars for an iron-on patch. A T-shirt cost three hundred dollars and a hoodie cost seven hundred dollars. There was no way anyone could be buying much, except maybe Bruce, who had a black AmEx card. Another reason to hate him.

Liam and Ryan got off the F train at Broadway-Lafayette and wandered east on Houston, looking for the line of bored-looking guys staring at their phones. They didn't have to look far. It was getting dark. Illuminated by the Bowery streetlights stood a hushed and orderly throng that spanned the four blocks to the store. They walked alongside the line of boys, compelled to check out the store itself before heading back to wait.

"Hey, assholes."

It was Bruce, a third of the way down the line. He'd left school early, claiming he felt sick. Now they knew why.

"Hey," Liam said sourly. It was a little difficult to stomach the notion that he and Ryan had been scraping poo and bubble gum off a bathroom floor while Bruce posed on a street corner, playing *Fortnite* on his phone.

"Thought you were sick," Ryan grumbled.

"Black Ryan, my man." Bruce held up his hand to high-five Ryan.

Ryan did not hold up his hand in return. "Come on," he told Liam. "Let's go see if we can cut this line."

"Good luck with that!" Bruce shouted after them.

The line was so long. Liam wondered if they shouldn't just turn around and go home. "Why are we here again?" he asked.

"Because your parents have plans tonight and you've always wanted to witness a drop," Ryan said. "Plus, your 'not my girlfriend' will be impressed if you actually managed to score anything. We ate like a whole pizza before we came here. We can stand up for a couple of hours."

Roy Clarke was the first to turn up at the bar. "So what's with the invisible barkeep then?" he asked. "Is he, like, disfigured or something? Does he wear a mask?"

Peaches poured him a pint of Brooklyn Lager. "He's not a he."

"She then. Is she you?"

"No. I just work here. For free. I keep it clean and meet the deliveries and play the drums and offer people drinks if they're brave enough to come inside. Usually they just open the door and look around and then walk out again. You were the exception. It's not really a full-fledged bar. More of a 'space.' She put up the sign for karaoke tonight though, not me. She's an artist and she travels a lot. I'm sure you'll meet her later."

"I see." Roy took a sip of his drink. "What's her name?"

"Elizabeth Paulsen."

"Aha," Roy replied. It figured. How could someone so mysterious be so ubiquitous? "Does it smell like formaldehyde in here to you?" he asked, sniffing the bar top.

Peaches pressed her lips together and nodded. Elizabeth had amassed a fuckload of weird shit in the basement. It was all part of her *Birth*.

"Maybe," she replied coyly. "I didn't smell it 'til you said it."

Liam flipped up his hood. It was colder than he thought it would be. Ryan was still marching toward the store, ignoring the annoyed glares of the lined-up, waiting boys.

"If we're waiting on line, don't we have to go to the end?" Liam asked when he caught up.

"I hope not. I have an idea," Ryan said determinedly. "I did it once before, at the North Face store when they released a new line of limited-edition parkas."

Liam glanced at his friend. "Did what?"

"Well, it might be different this time. My mom knows the CEO of North Face. Anyway, we're going to pretend to be models."

"Models?" Liam stopped walking. He was tall and skinny and had pimples and a sort of perpetual half-asleep expression. His childhood barber still cut his hair, so he looked kind of like a Roman emperor. "Yeah, right."

Ryan kept walking and Liam hurried to keep up with him.

"They like real-looking models. We just go up to the door and say, 'Hey, we're the models.' Just let me do the talking, okay?"

"Okay." Liam was pretty sure this wasn't going to work, but the worst thing that could happen was they'd get sent to the back of the line, which was where they'd wind up anyway.

The Sublime storefront was totally nondescript aside from the distinct purple logo in the window. The windows themselves were papered over to keep bystanders from peeking inside and taking pictures of the drop. Two enormous bouncer guys in navy-blue bomber jackets stood at the door.

Ryan went right up to them. "We're the models," he said.

Liam couldn't believe it. His face felt hot. Good thing it was dark.

"What models?" one of the bouncers asked. His thick mustache turned up at the corners. He looked like an inflated bullfighter.

"We're modeling the drop," Ryan explained patiently, like the bouncer was stupid for asking.

"Oh," the bouncer with the mustache said.

"Let them in, Jimmy," the other bouncer said impatiently. He was young and had a very thick neck. "They're late."

Two pints later, dark had set in. Peaches and Roy were still the only ones in the bar. Then Stuart pushed open the door and held it open for his wife.

Peaches had never officially met Mandy, except for that one time when Mandy was passed out on Stuart's shoulder on their stoop. She'd expected her to look sick. She'd expected a wheelchair or a walker or a cane. She certainly hadn't expected Mandy to be flawless and rosy-cheeked with a curvy ass and incredible boobs. She hadn't expected Mandy to be beautiful, with gleaming black hair, milky pale skin, luminous green eyes, a red bow of a mouth, and super-white straight teeth. She looked like Snow White on steroids.

"Hey," Stuart greeted Peaches a little nervously. He was worried she'd act overly familiar with him. What if she mentioned all the times she'd checked his hair for lice? Or selling him pot? What if she hugged him? He realized a split second too late that it was he who was being overly familiar. What made things even more confusing and awkward was that Peaches was sitting and talking and drinking with Roy Clarke, whose daughter happened to be babysitting Teddy that night, yet he and Mr. Clarke had never actually met.

"Stuart Little." Stuart held out his hand.

"Roy. Roy Clarke," the man said with a charming sort of sputtering English embarrassment.

Stuart glanced at Peaches and touched Mandy's elbow. "And this is Mandy, my wife."

Peaches hopped off her barstool and kissed Mandy once on each cheek. She couldn't help herself. She just had to feel the powdery white softness of Mandy's cheeks. She had to know firsthand what Mandy smelled like.

"It's so great that you're here."

She smelled like a forest. Not floral, more musky. Like the woody, barky smell of mulch in people's gardens at night after a summer rain. Or maybe she just smelled like pot.

Mandy kept smiling brightly even though she had no idea who this cute, dimply, friendly, cool-as-fuck woman with the drumsticks in the back pocket of her ripped jeans was. She turned to Stuart for help.

"Peaches Park, the school nurse. You met before on the stoop," Stuart explained. "Ted's school nurse."

"And bartender. And drummer. And DJ or master of ceremonies, or whatever you call the person who womans the karaoke machine," Peaches elaborated. Whenever anyone introduced her as the school nurse, she felt like she had to elaborate. "Sorry about the smell. Some new cleaning product."

She was stalling. Elizabeth had told her not to get things started until the bar was full of people.

Roy wished Wendy would arrive. She was so much better at meeting and greeting. He held onto his beer and shook the man's hand and nodded at his attractive, curvy wife, who looked like she still thought she was seventeen and had never done much besides drink lager and put on mascara, although apparently she had a child. He recognized Stuart Little not by name but by sight. He saw him every morning with his small son. And he was vaguely aware that it was Stuart and Mandy's small son Shy was babysitting for tonight. Cobble Hill certainly was an odd and tiny place.

"You're the author," Mandy said, because she knew. Everybody knew.

"Yes."

The door swung open and Roy was heartened to see Tupper, wearing his signature navy-blue suit and tie, his auburn hair freshly combed, his femininely handsome face freshly shaved.

Mandy recognized the well-dressed man whose dinner she'd almost stolen the other day.

"Is she here?" Tupper asked Roy anxiously, ignoring the others.

"Not that we've been able to detect," Roy responded honestly. It was possible that Elizabeth was hiding in a closet or under the floorboards, although from what he'd garnered from Google images, Elizabeth was an extremely tall woman. She'd be easy to spot.

"Actually," Peaches interrupted. Tupper had been by the bar a few times in the last month or so, asking after his wife. He never hung around long, insisting that they "respected each other's work." "Elizabeth was here . . . recently. Hasn't she been home?"

Tupper's home Macaw footage had revealed a meowing display of feline excitement—Catsy adored Elizabeth. His work Macaw footage had shown Elizabeth raiding his studio. At home, he'd found a "body" in the bath, which was full of red paint. Elizabeth had staged her own death, her jokey way of announcing that she'd finally come home.

He went around the bar and poured a pint of Guinness. "Only on camera, through the Macaw. She's teasing me," he added miserably. "She hates surveillance."

"Sorry, mate," Roy said. It must be difficult to be married to an artist.

"Shy, the girl babysitting Ted right now. She's his daughter," Stuart whispered in Mandy's ear. "The English writer dude, not the freaky one in the suit."

"Yeah, I got it," Mandy whispered back. She felt a little left out. Stuart knew all these people, and she knew no one. But that's what you got for pretending to have MS and hiding in your house with boxes of other people's food and a whole lot of weed.

Stuart put his arm around her. "You look so beautiful tonight. No one would know you were sick."

I'm not, fuckwad, Mandy thought, feeling suddenly defiant. Maybe this was part of the problem. She was tired of being Stu's useless, wifey ornament. She was like one of those decorative hedges outside the mansions in the Hamptons. All she ever needed was pruning and watering and she made the mansion look awesome. Except now she had a disease. "I feel totally normal," she said. As if that were a normal thing to say.

"Really?" Stu pulled away and eyed her up and down. "That's great. Maybe something's working. Maybe it's going into remission. Maybe we should get you some more tests."

"Yeah," Mandy said. "I think for now I'm just going to drink some wine."

233

• • •

"You're both a size extra small," Trey, the manager of Sublime, chucked a black $850 zip-up hoodie at Liam and a $1,200 baby-blue down parka at Ryan. He was huge, with bleached, gelled hair and a black goatee. "We like them tight, so they don't puff out when they're unzipped. Take everything off on top and put those on." He pointed at Liam. "We're getting you some other pants and some decent shoes." He sneered at Liam's stained gray Urban Outfitters jeans and the too-small, navy-blue Converse sneakers he'd been wearing since the beginning of tenth grade. "Those are fine." He nodded appreciatively at Ryan's skinny black Champion sweatpants and red Adidas EQTs.

"You want me to wear a parka with nothing on underneath?" Ryan asked.

"You're getting paid, aren't you?"

Trey's assistant appeared from downstairs with a folded-up pair of orange camouflage pants and a hideous pair of size eleven Nike AF1s in purple and silver patent leather. "Try these," he said breathlessly, and handed them to Liam.

"Sweet." Ryan grinned merrily. "You are going to be one hype beast."

Trey pointed at a red-curtained dressing room in the corner. "But hurry. We need to do your tattoos and get you out there."

"Wait," Liam demanded. "Out where?"

"Didn't the agency tell you? In this age of protest, we can't just sell clothes. Your generation likes to speak out. That's why there's a broken gun and the words 'Fuck Guns' on your sweatshirt. That's why your jacket says 'Still Alive' on the back. Every day is a protest. Your job is to look good while doing it. To be fashionable activists."

Liam was probably the least politically active kid at school. He didn't even recycle for fear he'd do it wrong.

Ryan was undeterred. "Fuck guns. Yeah, that's cool."

"Gotta go change my pants." Liam's voice wavered as he headed into the dressing room.

"So, your husband told me what's going on. MS sucks. I'm sorry. You look amazing though. Like, better than amazing," Peaches gushed.

Mandy had already decided that Peaches was annoying. She clearly had a crush on Stu and possibly the writer dude and probably flirted with all the dads at Ted's school. It was gross.

"Can I get a glass of red wine?" she said in response. She'd done her research. Wine was full of antioxidants. If she was going to drink alcohol in public while allegedly sick with MS, wine was the correct choice.

"Totally," Peaches said, feeling like she was sixteen and trying to make friends with the coolest girl in high school. "I'll open you up your own private bottle."

The agar-agar and formaldehyde would not coalesce. Luckily Elizabeth had stored an entire case of Saran Wrap in the basement. She'd have to make a good seam, one she could tear apart with her fingernails—quickly, at just the right moment—if she ever made it upstairs.

Other people from the neighborhood were trickling into the bar. Peaches thought she recognized a few parent faces, but out of the context of the school she couldn't be sure. Roy Clarke had taken up the position of bartender, which suited him. She joined him behind the bar, ducking down to look for a bottle of red wine.

"This would be the perfect thing to do when you're not writing," she said. "You can observe people, listen in on their conversations. Watch them misbehave."

Roy stood to the side so as not to tread on her. "Tending bar, you mean?" He had never considered this. "I'm hiding, don't you see? Mingling has never been my thing."

Peaches located a dusty case of Malbec and pulled one of the bottles from the box. Now she had to open it—with what, her teeth? She was tempted to tell Roy about Elizabeth's *Birth*, but decided he couldn't be trusted not to spill the beans.

"What're we supposed to do about money? People have been handing me twenties at random intervals. I put them in this." Roy flapped a plastic bag in front of her. "I didn't give them any change."

"Seems reasonable." Peaches hadn't discussed such particulars with Elizabeth. The basement was Elizabeth's priority. The bar itself was a vanity project or an experiment of some sort. It reminded Peaches of the coffeehouse at Oberlin. People wandered in to bake cookies and vegan muffins and make flavored coffee or herbal tea and would wind up doing improv or playing the guitar. Money was not the point. The point was to bring people together and see what happened.

The bar was getting crowded now. Peaches followed Elizabeth's instructions and put on music—the Rolling Stones, Duran Duran, Prince, Wham, Beyoncé, and the Go-Go's—to jumpstart the karaoke mood.

Neither she nor Roy could locate a corkscrew. There was a drawer full of pink plastic flamingos and a drawer full of tea candles. There was a box full of what looked like brown M&Ms and a box full of mousetraps. And there was a wooden container that had once held a wheel of French Brie but now was full of extra buttons.

"Tupper?" Roy called to Elizabeth's useless husband, drinking pint number four of Guinness at the end of the bar.

Elizabeth had warned Peaches that Tupper was a lightweight and would soon be very drunk. He would drink out of frustration, Elizabeth said. Peaches felt sorry for him. If she were married to Elizabeth she'd drink too much too.

"Come back here and help us, would you?"

Tupper stood up and came around the bar. "I installed a Macaw." He pointed at the large white ceramic bird perched between two bottles of Cîroc vodka. "She's around here somewhere," he told them grimly. "She's just being coy."

Roy smiled a sort of fatherly, patronizing smile, as if he didn't believe what Tupper said was true but didn't want to discourage him.

"What exactly does the Macaw do?" Peaches asked.

"His masterpiece." Roy patted Tupper's shoulder. "It hides surveillances devices and wires. He puts a camera in it connected to an app on his phone so he can spy on his wife's comings and goings. Except she never comes."

Tupper sighed. "She mostly goes."

Peaches admired his navy-blue silk tie. He clearly didn't want to be underdressed when Elizabeth finally decided to return. It was sweet.

"She's definitely around," she assured him. "She set all this up. She even cleaned the bathroom." She wasn't giving any of Elizabeth's secrets away. She was just trying to be nice.

Tupper checked his phone, then tucked it into his back pocket. "No one's allowed downstairs," he said firmly.

Peaches could tell he was very tempted to go down there and kick in the door.

Roy gave up trying to find a corkscrew. He pointed at the bottle of wine. "Here you go, Mr. Macaw. You're the inventor. Invent something to open this."

Tupper reached into his pocket and pulled out a red Swiss Army knife. He opened the corkscrew attachment, twisted it in, and expertly pulled out the cork. "There." He unwound the cork and put the knife back in his pocket.

Tupper was far more capable than he let on, but then again, he was from Maine. Watching him got Roy thinking about the gadgets they'd have up on Mars. Perhaps his urine-sanitizing water fountains wouldn't serve fresh drinking water exclusively. They could serve all sorts of other beverages as well. Wine would survive just fine on the long journey from Earth to Mars. Grapes might like to grow there. Potatoes meant vodka. If the urine sanitizers malfunctioned, alcohol might be the only safe thing to drink. The scientists would all become mad raving drunks. Chaos would ensue. And then the restocking capsule would arrive with the baddie inside. Roy picked up his glass and finished off his pint. He hadn't brought his laptop with him.

Peaches reached for the wine and poured Mandy Marzulli an enormous glass.

"My husband used to carry a Swiss Army knife in his pocket in college. I think he thought it would attract girls." She searched the crowd for Mandy and found her, hugged tight to Stuart's side, talking to a petite, well-groomed blond woman in her fifties wearing an expensive-looking trench coat and carrying a huge Macy's shopping bag.

Roy followed her gaze. "That's my wife, Wendy," he said. "She came straight from work."

Behind them, Peaches spotted Dr. Conway, dressed immaculately in a crisp white shirt and dark denim jeans, doing tequila shots in the back of the bar with a group of young moms she sort of recognized from the school.

"Whoa," Peaches breathed. "This is weird. It's like all the pieces in the jigsaw puzzle of my life are showing up tonight. Roy, come introduce me to Wendy. Tupper, you're in charge here."

"Marvelous," Tupper moaned, his face sagging.

Down in the basement, Elizabeth oozed and jiggled. Her scummy, Saran Wrapped surface sweated out a fishy gray mucous that caught the light with a waxy sheen. The consistency was perfect.

Chapter 15

Wendy had brought an entire double batch of homemade pumpkin apple cider mini donuts made by the *Enjoy!* magazine staff in the *Enjoy!* test kitchen. The donuts were caked in powdered sugar and individually wrapped in clear cellophane bags with football helmets printed on them. There were fifty bags. Well, forty-seven now. She and Gabby and Manfred had each eaten one on the taxi ride to Brooklyn. She'd also brought twenty "game-night mini dinners" from Full Plate. They'd been sent to the *Enjoy!* office to be reviewed. She thought it might be amusing to leave them out on the bar tables and eavesdrop as people ate and discussed them.

"Shy was so excited to babysit your son," Wendy told Stuart after she'd introduced herself. She never would have recognized him herself, but Shy had texted her that she was babysitting for Stuart Little from the Blind Mice, with a link to his picture and bio.

"Shy wears Gucci sneakers," Mandy said. It was the first thing she'd noticed when Shy came to babysit.

"I stole them from work," Wendy whispered mischievously. "They're not too pretentious, I hope."

"I didn't even notice them," Stuart said honestly.

"Is that food?" Mandy pointed at the Macy's bag.

Wendy pulled one of the Full Plate boxes out of the bag. "We should try these right now. They're 'game-night mini-dinners,' whatever that means."

"Oh! I saw them on the website. They're not supposed to be available 'til Super Bowl weekend. I can't believe you got them." Mandy clapped her hands together. "I love Full Plate."

Stuart spotted Nurse Peaches and the author, Roy Clarke, winding their way through the crowd. They seemed very comfortable together, which bothered Stuart for no good reason. What did Nurse Peaches have to do with Roy Clarke?

Roy was so glad Wendy had come. The move and her big job at *Fleurt* had nearly swallowed her up.

"I didn't bring any forks," Wendy was saying to the pretty, plump wife of the famous musician fellow. "But 'game night' implies finger food, doesn't it?"

"Darling, this is Peaches Park, the elementary school nurse and reader extraordinaire I was telling you about . . . or perhaps meant to tell you about at some point and then forgot?" Roy realized as he was speaking that he had never so much as mentioned his interactions with Peaches to Wendy or anyone else. He blushed and then covered it up by handing Wendy an overly full glass of wine.

Wendy was a little surprised by and a little jealous of how many people Roy already seemed to know. "What an unusual name." She shook Peaches' hand. "I like your dimples. Have you met the gorgeous Mandy Marzulli?"

Mandy giggled despite herself. Wendy Clarke was funny. Or maybe she was still a little high.

"Yes, we met earlier. Your wine, madame," Peaches offered Mandy the full glass with a dramatic flourish.

"Brilliant," Roy gushed, because Wendy's adroit party charm was infectious. He was a bit worried she'd be standoffish. She did that when she was nervous. But she seemed to be in her element.

"Cheers." Wendy clinked glasses with Mandy.

"Mazel tov." Peaches raised her bottle of Brooklyn Lager and took a sip. Any moment now Elizabeth would burst out of the basement and things would get weird.

Peaches was very mellow for someone hosting an entire community gathering. Stuart wondered if she'd been sampling Dr. Conway's merchandise. Stuart certainly had. He'd been eating pot cookies nonstop. And he was still jealously curious about the connection between Peaches and Roy Clarke. Then again, Mandy was probably wondering how he'd become so friendly with Peaches himself. She was a very friendly person.

"I should text Greg," Peaches muttered to herself and pulled out her phone. He never went out and this was so low-key. Although he hated crowded rooms full of noisy, talking people. It aggravated his tinnitus.

Stop by Monte after your music group if you can. Fun times.

"How'd you two meet?" Stuart asked, slouching casually in her direction.

Peaches pressed her beer bottle against her flushed cheek. "Who, me and Greg?" she asked. "He's not here. He's not into crowds."

"No, you and Roy Clarke," Stuart clarified. Only when he said it did he realize it was a weird question. How did anyone meet anyone, and what business was it of his? Roy Clarke was helping his wife and Mandy pass out containers of food. He was a congenial man, he was famous, and he was around, it seemed like, all the time. Why wouldn't Peaches have met him?

Eat pot cookies now my brain's all sweaty
Staring at the nurse like she's Apple Brown
Betty!

Was Stuart Little jealous of Roy Clarke? Peaches wondered in amazement. Oh yes, he was. Even in the throes of Elizabeth's crazy artist weirdery, Peaches found she could still flirt with him.

She cocked an eyebrow. "It's a pretty small neighborhood."

"Um, what exactly are we protesting again?"

Liam lay on his back, shirtless, while a woman named The Professor painted a giant "tattoo" on his bare torso.

"Is the tattoo words or pictures?" he asked, as if it made any difference.

"Both." The Professor tucked one paintbrush into her purple-and-gray dreadlock bun and extracted another. "You don't work out or wax. I worship that. In a model, I mean. Model boys all look the same, all muscular and hairless."

"Thanks." Tears streamed from the corners of Liam's eyes. She was hurting him, but he didn't think he could say anything. He turned his head to glance at Ryan, stretched out on his back beside him. The Professor had already painted a tattoo of a bleeding tiger cub all over his entire torso and the words ENDANGERED SPECIES across his chest. He was waiting for the ink to set, his shoes off, eyes closed. He seemed to be in his element.

"Hey," Liam whispered at him.

Ryan opened his eyes. "Hey," he said back. "You're cool," he added, as if sensing that Liam was uncomfortable. "Remember, we could be doing something really boring right now like playing *Fortnite*."

If only, Liam thought. He lifted his head. His chest was painted with a neon-red target. The word BULLSEYE was written in black glitter paint above it.

When the ink had set and The Professor had gelled their hair and applied lip gloss, concealer, face powder, eyeliner, and mascara, and they had donned their sneakers and shrugged on their new Sublime apparel over their bare, tattooed chests, the boys were released outdoors. There was a flash of cameras.

"Models, hello?" Trey clapped his long, thin hands together, as if to signal that he meant business, they were working. Liam elbowed Ryan hard in the upper arm, but Ryan refused to look at him. Ryan looked like a total freaking pro in his baby-blue parka, unzipped to reveal the bleeding, flaming orange-and-black tiger cub on his chest, his cheeks glittering with gold makeup. Liam was pretty sure he didn't look quite as good.

"The boys lined up out here think they're waiting for a drop. Really, they're props. We're staging a protest to advertise the merchandise and feed the frenzy on social media, etcetera. You two are the leaders. You rile them up. The photographers take pictures. You look perfect." He nodded at Liam. "Love the pimples. Now go. *Go.*"

Ryan dashed fearlessly into the crowd. Liam had no choice but to follow him.

"What are we doing?" he shouted.

Ryan stopped halfway down the block next to the long line of boys waiting to get into the store. He planted his feet and fanned out his baby-blue Sublime parka behind him like a peacock's tail, flexing his chest muscles.

"Fucking A!" one of the boys in line cheered loudly. "No more fucking guns!"

"Bullseye!" another boy yelled and pointed at Liam. "Bullshit!"

Liam wasn't sure if this was good or bad.

"No more bullshit. No more bullshit!" the photographers chorused as they snapped pictures.

Ryan just stood there looking sad and glamorous, modeling. Liam tried to imitate him but he felt like a freak. His pants were falling down, his shoes were ugly, and the body paint was itchy.

"One Mississippi, two Mississippi," he counted silently in his head, the way his mom used to count and pat his bottom soothingly at bedtime when he was little. He wished he was home, not playing *Fortnite* necessarily, but maybe talking to Shy on FaceTime and eating Ben & Jerry's.

"More, Pimples! More!" Trey barked from behind him.

Liam raised his arms overhead like he was under arrest and faced the crowd. "Don't shoot. Don't shoot."

The result was stupendous.

"Yes. Shoot video *now!*" Trey hissed at the photographers.

Not to be outdone, Ryan mimed taking a bullet and fell down on the sidewalk. The boys in line hit the lighter apps on their phones and drew around him in a circle, holding a vigil over his prone form.

"*Bullshit!*" the boys chanted, their voices loud and furious. "*Bullshit, bullshit, bullshit, bullshit . . . !*"

"*Bullshit!*" Ryan shouted from the sidewalk, eyes closed, the veins at his temples bulging sweatily. The word echoed down the Bowery, ricocheting against the buildings and resounding in the cold night air. It felt like all of Lower Manhattan was filled with chanting boys. It was thrilling, powerful.

A siren wailed and a police car pulled up, lights flashing.

"*Bullshit! Bullshit! Bullshit!*" every boy on the sidewalk except Liam shouted. He zipped up his hoodie and flipped on the hood. He did not sign up to get arrested. He had school tomorrow. Homework to do. He wanted to speak to Shy, kiss Shy, maybe even eventually lose his virginity with Shy. He couldn't do that in prison.

"Everybody up!" Trey shouted. "Models inside. It's not real, folks. Sorry, just a promotional thing. Go home. Drop starts online tonight at midnight. Your bots will sell out everything in thirty seconds as usual. Go home. Get out of here. I'll deal with the police. And don't forget to hashtag Sublime in your posts!"

Roy felt a little drunk. He'd had those two pints with Peaches before anyone arrived, and was now on his fourth. Something about Wendy and Peaches introducing themselves to each other had made him feel even drunker.

Worlds collide.

"Roy? I'm having trouble with the name of the bar in London we used to go to before the girls were born, where they had karaoke. Soho Sugar something, wasn't it? Roy?"

"I actually met Roy for the first time in here," Peaches explained. "He was looking for a place to write out of the house. I made him sugary tea."

Roy was vaguely aware that they were talking about him.

Worlds collide.

That was the problem with his book. He needed the worlds to *collide*. Right now they were just sort of lying limply in close proximity to each other, like discarded tissues. On *Battlestar Galactica* planets were always colliding and blowing up. He needed to blow something up.

"I think I am having an epiphany," he said. "I've had several since I got here." He'd begun to sweat. He needed his laptop.

"That's fantastic." Peaches patted his arm. "But could you stay, at least for a little bit? I have to get the karaoke started, and Tupper needs your help at the bar." Elizabeth would be horrified if their most distinguished guest left early.

"He doesn't need me. Look, he's got help."

A cheerful group of bearded, plaid flannel shirt–wearing men were behind the bar now. They looked like hockey players, grinning and bumping up against each other. They'd probably drink the place dry, but Peaches could restock. Or was it Elizabeth who did the restocking?

Restock.

"Roy, do you want to go home to your computer?" Wendy asked gently. She'd seen this faraway look plenty of times before. He was writing.

"It's fine for now. I'll just take notes on a cocktail napkin or something."

Peaches wasn't listening to them anymore. She'd noticed a change in the music. It was still the Go-Go's, but there was a trancelike overlay that she hadn't heard before, a rhythmic throb that made her teeth vibrate.

It was Philip Glass, she realized, her absolute least favorite composer of all time. Greg loved him. He took showers and did sit-ups and sun salutations to him. But to Peaches, listening to Philip Glass was like being anesthetized and endlessly prodded in the back by oboes and clarinets.

The sound system was near the basement stairs. Peaches could just make out the toes of a battered pair of silver Converse high-tops and a long platinum braid poking out of a gray heap of primordial ooze. A beached walrus. A newborn humpback whale.

Elizabeth had made it upstairs.

Peaches approached the karaoke machine and ducked behind a speaker to address the ooze. "I hope this is okay," she said loudly, because Elizabeth's ears were encased in Saran Wrap and gunk. "Not sure how big you wanted to go, but the room is pretty full." She shuddered involuntarily. "My husband worships Philip Glass."

The "head" of the ooze turned slowly and stared up at Peaches with cool gray eyes. Elizabeth's gross costume or artwork or whatever the fuck she wanted to call it looked like a massive dinosaur placenta. Peaches had asked her about the stench of formaldehyde. Apparently, the giant goo blob she'd encased herself in was partly made from fat cells of reptiles pickled in formaldehyde that she'd ordered in cans from a website for biology teachers. The other part was agar-agar, a jellylike sea substance from the health food store. The two did not mix well, and now that she was upstairs, the stench was almost unbearable.

It seemed like a lot of trouble to go through for a somewhat questionable result.

"Your husband is pretty worked up," Peaches warned her. "I think he might be drunk, like you said."

Elizabeth had forgotten to make a mouth hole. She couldn't speak.

"Nnnngh," she replied.

"Okay if I make some kind of announcement to get things rolling?" Peaches asked.

"Nnnngh."

Peaches took a seat behind the drums. She wasn't exactly sure when Elizabeth was planning to burst out of her nasty sac, but she didn't want to be standing over her when it happened. She leaned into the microphone.

"Looks like we're ready to get started with the karaoke portion of our evening. Just write your song selections with your first name on the pieces of paper stacked on the bar and on the tables by the window and drop them in the fishbowl over here, next to the karaoke machine. If anyone feels inclined to play the drums while someone sings, they're here. We also have a tambourine. First I'll get the ball rolling with a little drumroll."

As instructed, she tapped out a military-style drumroll that segued into the beat of "Here Comes the Bride."

Elizabeth rolled and oozed forth, exuding a gag-inducing odor. Members of the crowd began to notice her and took a startled step back, clutching their noses.

"Nnnngh," Elizabeth moaned from inside her casing. "Nnnngh!"

The crowd took another murmuring step back. Peaches continued to thwack out the beat of "Here Comes the Bride." Behind the bar, Tupper Paulsen looked very fragile and very pale.

"Nnnnghaaaa!!" Elizabeth burst out of the revolting gray heap of slime and rose to her full height, wearing only a black bikini. The bones of her hips and shoulders protruded from her torso like dorsal fins. Her ribs and vertebrae were easily counted beneath her glistening white skin.

As instructed, Peaches dropped into a mellower roll.

Remnants of gray ooze speckled Elizabeth's thick black eyebrows and clung to her platinum-blond hair. Her face was not beautiful, but stately and ageless, with deep frown wrinkles and a thin mouth so downturned it almost looked like it had been put on wrong. Everything about Elizabeth seemed to defy possibility. She was like Stonehenge in human form.

Tupper made his way out from behind the bar and walked unsteadily through the staring crowd.

Peaches stopped drumming. "Introducing your host, the artist Elizabeth Paulsen," she said into the mic.

Elizabeth bowed formally. Her social skills

had suffered while she was away but her hauteur had not. "Sorry about the mess," she apologized huskily to the rapt room. "My husband and I will clean it up while you sing."

Tupper held out his hand and she stepped forth out of the goo, a messy Venus entering an awestruck, unprepared world. The merry, drinking crowd applauded and snapped pictures on their phones, thrilled to have been a part of one of Elizabeth Paulsen's infamous works of art. They would embrace her now. If that's what she'd been going for, she'd achieved it.

Chapter 16

Roy shifted his feet in the tight space and scribbled more notes. Wendy had found him a little closet and a legal pad and pen. On the other side of the door a bass drum pounded, cymbals clashed, and a woman growled, *"Why can't I get just one kiss?"*

A literary critic from *The New Yorker* had written once that "the everlasting appeal of a Roy Clarke novel, however limited in scope, is his awareness that we are all in this together." The critic had gone on to say that even though Roy's books "all take place in a bubble," Roy had an "uncanny ear for irony and the absurdity of life," and that was what made reading his novels "feel like stroking an affectionate cat."

He needed to blow things up and stroke the cat.

Roy's pocket jolted violently. He retrieved his phone and read the text message from Tupper.

Where are you? You're missing everything. She's HERE!

Someone knocked on the closet door and Roy opened it, eager to escape his scary book and even scarier thoughts.

"We're singing soon," Peaches announced. "I put our names down."

Roy enjoyed singing, but only in his head. "Must I? I'm not sure that I can."

Peaches ripped the notes he'd written out of the legal pad and tucked them into his jacket pocket. "Think of it as research. And anyway, you have to meet Elizabeth. She came out."

Elizabeth's birthing of herself had stolen the show, but only briefly. Stuart was watching Mandy now. Something about her was different. Was it really just the pot? Or maybe it was he who was different. Mandy sat at a small table to the left of the door, looking beautiful and confident, talking to their neighbors, snacking on fancy snacks, sipping wine. Her black hair was shiny, her skin flawless, her smile bright. She was still chubby, but in a hot way. She wasn't yawning or complaining, she was laughing. Stuart was intrigued. Maybe it was because he was high and drunk and had just sung "Purple Rain" with a bunch of strangers, but the Mandy over there in the chair was not the same tired and sullen Mandy stuck in bed for the last few months. She was someone completely shiny, sexy, and new. She was gorgeous.

Ted had eaten fourteen tater tots. Two more meant sixteen, which was how many he'd asked Shy to cook for him, but they were so salty and greasy, and he was so thirsty and full. Lately his parents had either been eating weirdly fancy gourmet food, or snacks like tater tots and Oreos. They used to order in a lot. Now they never ordered in, not even pizza. His mom was always cooking. They even made their own personal pizzas, with prosciutto and arugula on them. They were supposed to have capers on them too, but Ted picked them off. Two hours after bedtime he woke up to pee and found them sharing his box of Cocoa Puffs, shoveling them into their mouths with their hands like they were starving. Ted found this new behavior worrisome; he was thinking of asking the school nurse about it.

"You want the rest?" he offered his babysitter. She'd said her name was Shy, but that wasn't a real name.

Shy grabbed the tater tots from off his plate and tucked one in each cheek. "I'm saving them for later." She stood up from the kitchen table and gestured for him to follow her. Ted was a lot like her when she was younger. He thought he didn't need anyone and was happy to just read and play games on his own. Really though, he was lonely. Together, they explored the two-story town house, looking for the next activity.

"Is there a game you want to play?"

"No," Ted said. The only games he ever played at home were on his iPad. He wished he had Settlers of Catan, like at the Strategizer, but it was so complicated, he wouldn't have been able to explain how to play anyway.

"Really? I love games. I like making up games. Like, I used to walk around our house in England counting all the green things. And then I would do it again and count all the blue things. Maybe there's something wrong with me."

"I used to line up my mom's nail polish bottles and count them. She has forty-three. Two are clear and the rest are colors."

"So you don't have any games in your room or anything?" Shy asked. Their house was small compared to her spacious brownstone. Ted's room was messy, with just a single unmade bed and a round green table with two low blue stools. It wasn't messy cozy, either—it was just messy. In one corner stood a laundry basket full of unfolded clothes. Shy knew she was spoiled. Nena came to clean and do their laundry every Monday. But was it really such a big deal to wash and fold Ted's little skater-boy T-shirts?

Ted kicked the legs of one of the stools and it fell over. "I mean, we could *make* a game."

"Okay."

Ted grabbed a coffee can off his bookshelf and emptied its contents onto the table. There were some mini pencils, some tiny, grotty neon-green Post-its, loads of broken crayons, and about ten dollars in pennies, nickels, and dimes.

"Draw a lot of roads with trees and an ocean

and fields on this piece of paper," he ordered, pushing a piece of wide-ruled loose-leaf in front of Shy. "The whole point of Catan is that you're trying to expand your settlement and use all your resources and keep your enemies out."

Shy did her best. She was not a skilled artist, and she hated crayons. They smelled like throw-up. She drew connecting pathways and lumpy bushes and puddles, sort of modeling it after Chutes and Ladders.

"We need sheep," Ted said, drawing on a Post-it. "And wood and wheat. I'll draw those."

"Okay."

"Draw huts that look like they're made of straw," he told her. "Not too close together."

Shy bit her lip and drew four droopy square houses with triangular roofs and round windows. They looked very postapocalyptic.

"Does our game take place in the future, or is it, like, old-fashioned times?"

Ted didn't seem to hear. He drew pointed ears on his brown sheep. "What kind of tails do sheep have?"

There were sheep all over England. Shy used to see them from the car window when they drove to the seashore or to the home where her grandma sat staring at the television, drinking gin and eating chocolates until she died.

"Little dinky tails, like the very end of a dog's tail." Shy had sort of hoped that Ted would want to go to sleep soon. "Do you want to watch a movie while we're drawing?"

He shook his head adamantly. "No, we're going to play our game. Ours is actually better because we customized it."

"I'm just going to get a glass of milk," Shy said, because she knew milk sometimes made her sleepy. "Do you want some?"

"Okay," Ted said. "But don't touch the cookies in the jar in the refrigerator. They're for grown-ups only."

Shy found a carton of organic milk, filled up two glasses halfway, and returned the carton to the fridge. At the back of the top shelf was a large metal jar with a screw-on lid. She retrieved it and screwed off the lid. The jar was full of lumpy, homemade-looking chocolate-chip cookies. She held the open jar to her nose and took a whiff. The skunky, man-sweat odor was unmistakable. The cookies were laced with weed.

Shy located the kitchen drawer containing useful items like Saran Wrap and tinfoil, and procured a Ziploc sandwich bag. No one would notice if she took two cookies. She stuffed the bag with the cookies into the pocket of her hoodie and returned the jar to the fridge.

"I'm all done with the sheep!" Ted yelled from his bedroom.

Shy returned to the bedroom and handed him a glass of milk. "Drink it all up so you don't spill on our cool game." She sat down with her milk and examined the insane drawings and various crayon-scribbled Post-its all over the round table. "So how do we play? Do we need dice or something?"

Ted chugged his milk and set the glass down on the floor. "You're a better babysitter than my parents," he said, and burped loudly.

Shy picked up a sheep Post-it and stuck it to a window on one of the houses she'd drawn, just for fun. "Yeah, well, they are paying me. No one pays them."

Ted seemed to consider this as he arranged his Post-its. He removed Shy's sheep Post-it from the house window and handed it to her. "Okay. Let's play."

Roy knew the minute he laid eyes on Elizabeth—a towering blonde wearing paint-spattered white painter's overalls over a black bikini and silver high-top sneakers—that he would never be able to sing in front of her. He was afraid to even introduce himself.

"Love shack, baby," Peaches purred hyperactively in his ear as she dragged him toward the microphone stand set up in front of the drums. She seemed to have lost her sense of decorum.

Elizabeth glanced in Roy's direction as she fiddled with the dials on the karaoke machine and smiled. Her teeth were yellow and her mouth was downturned, like a tortoise's.

She rose to her full, monumental height and addressed him. "You're Roy Clarke."

"Hello." Roy nodded at her because she hadn't offered him her hand. "Thank you for having us. It's quite grand of you. Oh, and Tupper and I are old chums. He showed me round his studio." When Roy was nervous, he became more British.

"Bully for you," Elizabeth replied.

"Smashing," Roy said.

"Love shack, love shack, love shack!" Peaches squealed.

Roy stood on tiptoe to search for Wendy. She was nibbling on something, offering plates of food around. Roy waved at her over the sea of drinking heads. He waved again, with both arms.

She held up what looked like a mini hot dog. *"Hungry?"* she mouthed.

He nodded vigorously, counting on the fact that she would march straight over with a plate of food.

"Any chance I could pick the song?" he asked Peaches and Elizabeth together, because it was now unclear which of them was in charge.

"Not feeling the shack?" Peaches asked. She was beginning to get on his nerves. "Come on—"

"Course you can," Elizabeth interrupted her. "Isn't that the point? Or don't sing at all."

"Do you sing?" Roy asked curiously. She didn't look like she sang.

"Darling. I brought you some snacks. Are we singing?" Wendy pushed a plate filled with disgusting-looking mini meats and corn chips beneath Roy's nose, knowing full well he wouldn't want them. She was a bit peeved with Roy. He'd made all these friends and seemed to enjoy flirting with the school nurse. Meanwhile, she'd been working at *Fleurt* all year—or at least pretending to—in a boring office all by herself. *Enjoy!* was better. She was actually starting to enjoy it. But she still hadn't told Roy. It just seemed so demeaning. Was she really that much of a snob?

"We could do our song," Roy said.

Roy and Wendy's song was "Candle in the Wind" by Elton John. They were both completely tone-deaf. Shy shouted at them whenever they tried to sing.

Roy glanced at Peaches. "Do you mind?"

Peaches shrugged her shoulders. She did seem a little disappointed.

"Aren't you going to introduce us?" A tall, androgynous person with glowing tan skin, a shaved head, and the most perfectly symmetrical eyebrows Roy had ever seen was hovering near Wendy, holding a glass of clear stuff. "I've been wanting to meet your husband since the day I picked up *Purple* in the bookstore a million years ago."

"It's all right if you didn't finish it." Roy held out his hand. Male or female? Not that it mattered. He was a modern person. "It's my longest book. No one ever finishes."

"Sorry, sorry," Wendy cut in. "This is Manfred."

Roy shook Manfred's hand. Masculine or feminine didn't matter. Manfred was Manfred. "You're from the magazine?" he guessed.

"*Fleurt*," Manfred said. "We *were* comrades in armed, ergonomic swivel chairs."

"Manfred keeps me on deadline," Wendy said breezily, shooting Manfred a look.

Manfred blew her a kiss, as if to say, "It's not my business what you choose to tell or not tell your husband, I love you anyway," and Wendy blew them a grateful kiss back.

Roy smiled grimly at the disgusting plate of greasy game-night snacks. All he really wanted was to go home to his laptop. "You wouldn't happen to know the words to 'Love Shack,' would you?"

But a new song had already begun, and it was Elizabeth who took the mic. It wasn't "Love Shack," either. She was moaning, and the music was slow.

"Oooooh," Elizabeth crooned. *"Love to love you, baby."* She licked her downturned lips and waggled her eyebrows suggestively across the room at Tupper, who had tucked himself back in behind the bar.

Tupper's face turned pink and then gray.

"Oh!" Elizabeth shrieked.

Tupper ducked down, pretending to search for something beneath the bar.

Elizabeth continued to growl and moan. She put the microphone between her teeth, got down on her hands and knees, and crawled across the floor. The crowd parted ways to make room for her. There was a lot of cheering and whooping. Tupper reappeared with a full pint of Guinness in his hand.

"Oooh," Elizabeth cooed on all fours. She seemed to enjoy the spotlight.

Tupper chugged his Guinness.

Elizabeth was aware of the fact that she was dominating the room. She reminded herself that tonight was not meant to be exclusively about her; it was meant to be about the neighborhood. She pointed at Peaches, signaling her to change the music.

"Say what?" Peaches screeched into the extra microphone.

Roy was relieved to hear "Love Shack" begin without him.

Manfred danced around Peaches with a tambourine while Peaches banged on the bongos and sang.

"Funky little shack!"

Then Stuart Little joined in. He rolled up his T-shirt sleeves and grabbed a mic, his mouse tattoos in full force.

"Glitter on the mattress," he sang, waggling his shoulders a little too enthusiastically at the school nurse.

An extremely handsome silver-haired gentleman wearing a crisp white shirt, dark denim jeans, and expensive-looking brown suede loafers danced groovily nearby, flashing his Rolex watch.

Roy glanced at Stuart's wife. She sat alone in a chair, eating a plate of Wendy's snacks and staring at her phone.

"Gabby, my other friend from work, is here somewhere," Wendy shouted at Roy through the din. She felt ridiculous for not telling him about *Enjoy!*. "There've been some staff changes recently," she began, but she could tell he couldn't hear her.

Roy didn't know why Wendy was even attempting to hold a normal conversation. The bar was far too noisy. Besides, he'd drunk too much lager.

"Would you excuse me for a minute?" he said, and slipped away.

Greg pulled off his headphones and observed silently from the door as Peaches sang and banged on the bongos, her voice slightly out of tune, her drumming slightly behind the beat. His sensitive ears rang with the feedback from the speakers. "Love Shack" was Peaches' favorite song. Hearing her sing it, karaoke style, with Stuart Little from the Blind Mice, in a bar full of strangers was perplexing though. It felt like a display of dissatisfaction, restlessness, and ennui. She was showing off, flirting outrageously, overcompensating for being nervous, getting louder by the minute.

Greg thought things were better now that she'd chosen a career and was out of the house, away from her notebooks full of unfinished short stories, broken drumsticks, and partial to-do lists. He thought she was past this—whatever this was.

"Bang bang, on the door baby!" Peaches and Stuart Little shouted gleefully into the same mic. When had she gotten so chummy with Stuart Little?

A silver-haired dude in dark denim shimmied over and bumped his butt against Peaches' hip. Peaches bumped him back, grinning as she continued to sing. Stuart Little wrapped his arm around her shoulders and bumped his bony ass against her other hip.

"Bang bang!" Peaches sang ecstatically.

She wasn't acting out or making a point, Greg realized. She was having the time of her life— without him. Greg was shy around new people, sensitive to loud sounds, and generally awkward. It seemed to get worse with age. He would never be as successful or rich as Stuart Little. He would never have the groovy savoir faire of the handsome silver-haired dude with the Rolex. Instead of joining in, he backed out the door and into the night.

Mandy was not sad. She was surreptitiously videoing Stuart for his fan site, which she was supposed to be in charge of and hadn't even checked since last spring. Stuart was singing and that was a good thing. He needed to sing. She, on the other hand, was trying to keep a low profile. How many boxes of these people's food had she stolen? The guy who'd literally taken his box out of her hands out on the sidewalk was right there behind the bar. She felt both mortified and smug. No one suspected the lumpy lady in the chair.

But the people here were nice—in a weird, unexpected way. She felt bad about stealing from them. The older English writer was on his way over to her now, bearing yet another plate of snack food.

"Quite a party this is turning out to be," he observed, offering her the plate.

"Yup." Mandy slid her phone beneath the plastic plate and nudged a piece of turkey pepperoni away from a smoked mozzarella stick. The game-night snacks from Full Plate were a more gourmet version of the food she used to eat when the Blind Mice were on tour. "It's great."

"I don't enjoy singing," Roy said.

Mandy gazed up at him, wondering if he was

only paying attention to her because he'd heard she had MS. "Me neither," she agreed.

"But maybe we could pretend to dance?" Roy held out his hand.

Mandy giggled and tossed the plate onto the table beside her. She took his hand and stood up.

"We don't have to do any twirls or lifts," he joked. "I'm heavier than I look."

"I'm supposed to be sick anyway," Mandy said, because she was pretty sure Roy Clarke didn't care either way. "So I probably shouldn't overdo it."

"Love shack, baby, love shack!" Stuart chorused as he watched Mandy sway from side to side with Roy Clarke, throwing her head back and arching her pale, supple neck. She looked healthier and sexier than she ever had in her life, healthier and sexier even than during her modeling days in high school. The pot, the good food they'd been eating, the vitamins she was taking, the sleep she was getting—it was working.

"Damn. Our school MetroCards are no good after eight p.m."

The walk back to the subway was kind of a comedown. Sublime had let Liam and Ryan keep the clothing, but they didn't want to draw attention to themselves by actually wearing it. Instead, they turned the hoodie and parka inside out and tied them around their waists.

269

"I have a twenty," Liam offered.

"You should be rich now," Ryan said. "You're a famous model."

But since they weren't real models, they would never be paid.

"At least we could maybe put it on our college applications," Ryan said. "I saved a picture of my tattoo on my phone. So if there's a college question like 'What did you do for whatever cause?' I can show the picture and say I was, like, an activist."

Liam hadn't thought about this. "That's pretty genius."

"Maybe we'll be in the news," Ryan added. "Which would be somewhat cool, but also sort of embarrassing. I'm sure my mom will have something rude to say about it."

"Mine too." Liam wondered if his mom would be impressed or angry. Either way, she would definitely have something to say.

"What a fucking waste," a boy their age complained as he pushed his way past them.

The sidewalks of Houston Street were teeming with boys. The drop had never happened. It was like the anti-drop.

"I don't even want this anymore," Ryan said, tugging on the sleeves of the expensive parka at they walked. "I think I'm over Sublime. It's too commercial."

"Yeah," Liam said, disappointed. He'd finally

scored a Sublime hoodie only to find out that it was too commercial?

"Whatever. I can probably sell it for twice what they're asking," Ryan said.

Someone grabbed Liam by the shoulders and shook him hard. It was Bruce. He tugged on the hoodie tied around Liam's waist. "Hey, did you losers actually get stuff? That's totally unfair."

"Hey." Liam pulled the hoodie out of Bruce's hands.

Ryan tightened the knot on the baby-blue Sublime parka. "That was lame," he said. Liam knew he'd said it just so Bruce would stop bothering them. "We came all this way for nothing."

"But I saw you guys go in," Bruce said. "I was standing there for like five hours, and you guys just walked right in."

"No," Ryan said. He glanced at Liam.

"We tried. They knew we were full of shit," Liam said vaguely.

"Yeah," Ryan agreed.

Bruce yanked Liam's hoodie from around his waist and reversed it. "What the fuck is this, then? I fucking saw you guys. I don't know how you did it, but this thing is worth like seven hundred bucks or more and I don't even know how much that jacket costs—probably as much as a car. I waited five fucking hours and I'm fucking keeping this fucking hoodie."

Liam could feel his face getting red. Before the schoolyard fire he'd felt sort of ambivalent toward Bruce, but he hated him now, especially after having to wipe five-year-old-boy pee off the seats of the bathroom at the elementary school.

The thing was, he really didn't want the hoodie anymore.

"Eight hundred bucks," Ryan said flatly, as if reading Liam's mind. "For sixteen hundred we'll let you have both."

Bruce glared at Ryan, probably thinking something racist, because he was the worst kind of asshole. "Look at Black Ryan, acting like he's in charge."

Ryan straightened up to his full, significantly taller-than-Bruce stature. "You saw us, we were in the store, and these parkas are selling for over a thousand dollars each. We're giving you a deal. You want this shit or not?"

"Let me see it?" Bruce asked, and Liam could tell he was caving.

Ryan untied the parka and dangled it in front of Bruce. "Limited edition. Already sold out in preorders online. It's a collector's item." He glanced at Liam. "Or we could just hold on to them and sell them in a year for double what we're offering you."

Bruce took hold of Ryan's parka, licking his lips greedily as he turned it inside out and examined the washing instructions for authenticity. Typos meant it was a fake. He was all theirs now.

"I take Venmo," Ryan said. "You can transfer directly into my bank account."

"Huh?"

"Give me your phone and your credit card," Ryan said impatiently.

It was all Liam could do to keep from snickering. Ryan was treating Bruce like a child. It was classic.

When he was done with the transaction, Ryan handed over Bruce's phone and credit card along with the hoodie and parka. "There. You just paid me." He nodded at Liam. "I owe you half. I know you don't have a credit card. Don't worry, I'm good for it."

Liam nodded coolly. "Thanks man."

"Yeah, thanks." Bruce hugged the clothing that probably wouldn't even fit over his ugly, stocky body, like an obnoxious asshole version of Linus from *Peanuts* with his blanket.

Finally, Ryan smiled. So did Liam. They couldn't help it. They'd just copped a shit-ton of money from Bruce. "No problem," they said in unison, knowing they were going to be laughing about this for the rest of their lives.

Chapter 17

Shut your mouth," Elizabeth crooned into the microphone, impersonating David Bowie at his most removed and sultry. She'd drawn lightning bolts on her cheeks and forehead with the type of blue pen surgeons use to mark up a body.

A drunk guy with a beard and an ugly orange neck tattoo danced lazily in front of her. There was black cat hair all over his gray sweater.

Wendy and Roy stood side by side, holding their drinks, watching and not talking.

"That's Shy's Latin teacher," Wendy observed finally. "The one she has a crush on. I ought to go have a word, tell him not to encourage her. She never had the slightest interest in table tennis before now."

"I think I'm off," Roy said. "Best get home to my laptop. I've made all sorts of notes tonight."

Wendy didn't seem to have heard him. "The tattoos. The beard. The cat hair. He's so unclean. I'm going to say something."

Roy grasped her elbow. "Better not. Have fun with your new friends. Shy is babysitting. She's fine."

They continued to watch Elizabeth, and the crowd watching Elizabeth. It was impossible to look away, but nothing about her invited you in. As far as Roy could tell, Elizabeth had been too busy performing to properly greet her husband. What an odd marriage. But of course, all marriages were odd. Even he and Wendy were a bit off lately.

"Anyway, Shy has a crush on the nurse's boy," he reminded her. "Remember?"

"That's not a crush," Wendy corrected him. "If the person reciprocates, it's not a crush. That boy is so awkward, he needs Shy just to cross the street."

Roy didn't respond. Wendy was being cruel. It was the wine. After a few glasses, the hospitable hostess always turned on her guests.

"You have a crush on the nurse," she added. "It seems all the men do."

Peaches did seem to be enjoying the company of the famous singer who'd been in a band once. They were both wearing black jeans. She kept smiling, showing off her dimples, and he kept grinning back at her and tousling his hair with those ridiculous tattooed hands, the twit.

"Yes," Roy agreed, because what Wendy said was true.

She looked up at him searchingly and then looked away.

"I'll give you eyes of blue . . ." Elizabeth crooned deeply into the microphone.

Roy peered over the crowd, looking for Tupper. He was still behind the bar, leaning on his elbows and nursing another Guinness. He looked like he might be coming down with flu.

"And then there's the fat wife of the musician," Wendy went on mercilessly, still voicing her tipsily cruel thoughts. "She's so beautiful. If she didn't have MS I'd send her to an agency for plus-size modeling. Even with the MS. She's probably always played second fiddle to his music career, and then she got fat having a child, and then she fell ill," she mused. "I'm going to help her."

Roy wasn't sure Mandy required any help, but Wendy had always needed to feel needed. At least she wasn't focused on the Latin teacher anymore. Tupper was more worrisome. His eyes were slits. His face glistened with a grayish-green sheen.

"And I'm going to help *him*," Roy said, starting toward the bar.

Monte was crowded now and stuffy. The sound system twanged with feedback. Someone put on the song "She's Not There" by the Zombies.

"Well no one told me about her. . . ."

Roy bumped shoulders with Stuart Little.

"Hey man," Stuart said. "I just texted your daughter to see how it's going with Ted. She texted back a thumbs-up, so I guess it's all good."

"Mmm," Roy said, still edging toward the bar. "Would you ex—"

"I'm actually just coming over to check on our bartender," Stuart continued. He jutted his chin at Tupper. "He doesn't look so good."

Roy had Stuart marked as a self-absorbed nob,

but now he was changing his mind. Besides, rescuing Tupper might be a two-person job. "Too right." He slipped nervously into over-Britishness again. "I was just having a wee bit of a surreptitious peek at him meself."

They reached the bar just as Tupper squeezed his eyes shut, bent over double, and threw up on his shoes.

"Easy there, tiger." Stuart dashed around the bar and grabbed Tupper by the elbow, catching him before he fell. "Don't worry about it. I have a kid. Stuff like this doesn't bother me."

"We'll get you home," Roy soothed from behind them. He took off his jacket, thinking he might throw it over the vomit. It was his Burberry one. Wendy would kill him. He put it back on again. "Is there a back door, do you think?"

"I'm not sure. I'll ask." Stuart texted Peaches while Tupper swayed and wavered in his puddle of puke. He wasn't even lucid. He'd passed out standing up.

Roy tried not to be jealous that Stuart had Peaches' number plugged into his phone. He held it up so Roy could read Peaches' reply.

School nurse on her way!

"Should we notify his wife?" Roy asked.

The two men shared a bewildered glance.

Tupper's head fell onto Stuart's shoulder. They were both standing in puke.

"I'm all right," Tupper murmured drunkenly.

"No, you're not," Stuart assured him. "But it's cool."

He texted Peaches again.

Hurry up.

Shy's drunk, hairy Latin teacher shimmied up to the bar, his horrible neck tattoo glistening sweatily. "I love your work," he slurred at Roy. "And your daughter's da' bomb," he added creepily.

Roy winced and squared his shoulders. "She's your student, and I'm her father," he said haughtily.

The Latin teacher laughed, taking Roy's bluster for a joke. The smiling orange-and-blue baseball on his neck bobbed up and down. Black chest hairs squiggled out of his V-neck. Wendy was right. He was a pervy git who needed taking down.

Roy lunged over the bar and growled into the teacher's face. "You keep your smarmy tattooed mitts away from my daughter."

"Hey, sorry man." The Latin teacher held up his hands and backed up a step. He swallowed nervously.

"Roy?" Peaches scolded from behind them. "No fighting in the schoolyard, please."

Roy whirled around. His face was hot and his armpits were damp. "Right. Sorry," he mumbled, although he wasn't sorry at all. He felt quite good actually. He might even have punched the guy. The Latin teacher had retreated. Problem solved.

"Please don't bother trying to find her. . . ." The Zombies song was just wrapping up.

"Oh wow, my favorite." Peaches grimaced when she noticed the puke. She held her nose, grabbed a roll of paper towels, and began ripping them off the roll and tossing them at Stuart and Tupper's feet. "What did he eat for lunch?"

"Tuna fish," Tupper slurred, drooling on Stuart's shoulder.

Wendy, Mandy, and Manfred began to sing that sad, sultry song "Lovefool" by the Cardigans. Stuart recognized Mandy's honey-sweet voice right away. He admired her over the sea of heads as they helped Tupper out of the bar. Glittering green eyes, sleek black hair, milky white skin, sexy red mouth. If he wasn't already married to her he would have hit on her.

"I better tell Elizabeth." Peaches threw down more paper towels and searched the crowd for the monolithic blonde. But Elizabeth had disappeared.

"I'm okay," Tupper said, his knees sagging.

Roy and Stuart grasped his elbows. Peaches led the way to the back door, and the three staggering men followed.

The doorway to the Paulsens' neat brick carriage house was old-fashioned and narrow. Roy had a key. Leaving Peaches and Stuart out on the stoop, he unlocked the door and led Tupper inside. They staggered through the dimly lit living room to the gray linen sofa, where he released his hold on Tupper and watched the man recede into the soft cushions, hands between his knees, head bowed.

Across the room, Elizabeth was sprawled in an armchair, asleep. The red paint on her overalls looked like blood. The cat was curled tight against her thigh, yellow eyes in slits, obviously ecstatic that she'd come home. A huge jug of maple syrup stood at her feet.

Tupper's ginger hair was matted and his neat white shirt had come untucked. Roy wondered if he should remove Tupper's shoes. He felt nervous leaving him there with Elizabeth. She was almost scarier asleep than awake. And what were they going to do with all that syrup?

Peaches and Stuart perched on the stoop to wait. It was a cool night. Peaches had left her jacket at the bar. She huddled against Stuart, not even thinking about whether or not it was okay.

"I love how everyone just came out and did their thing tonight." She looked up at the stars and the sliver of moon and shivered. "Fuck, I'm cold."

"We can go back," Stuart said. He wanted to listen to Mandy sing. And then he wanted to walk her home and pay Shy Clarke for babysitting and get into the queen-size bed in the kitchen with Mandy and kiss her and tell her how good she looked and how glad he was that they were still together after all these years. He started to stand up.

"Wait." Peaches tugged on the back of his T-shirt.

He sat back down.

"I'm embarrassed." She rested her head on his shoulder. "But I've been wanting to do this forever, so I'm just going to do it." She turned her head and kissed him.

Yo, it's bad, don't kiss your teachers!
Lips so sweet they taste like peachers!

Stuart was surprised and also extremely confused. A moment ago he'd wanted to kiss Mandy. Mandy was his wife. But he liked Peaches. Peaches was pretty. Peaches was smart and funny. She played the drums. She was a badass nurse. And kissing her was weirdly exciting because she wasn't Mandy. But at the same time, he loved Mandy. Mandy was hot.

He leaned in and kissed Peaches again, just to check.

"Blimey," Roy said, catching them in the act as he came out the front door.

Of course the rock star got to kiss Peaches. Was it just starting now, or had it been going on for ages? Wasn't it strange how you could live in such close proximity to people, speak to them every day, and still not know them at all?

"Ahem." Roy pretended to cough and pulled up his socks.

Peaches and Stuart broke apart and looked away into the dark. Then Peaches reached out and squeezed Stuart's knee. They might never kiss again. She hoped they would. But if they didn't, it had been a great kiss, maybe the best kiss of her life.

"Time to collect our trouble and strife and climb the apples and pears, I should think," Roy announced, so nervous he'd resorted to Cockney rhyming slang. "I need my bed."

Peaches' hand slid off Stuart's knee as he stood up and descended the steps to the sidewalk.

"I think I left my skateboard . . ." he began.

He'd abandoned Mandy at the bar. That was pretty uncool of him. Plus, Roy's daughter was at his house, waiting for him to come home and pay her for watching Ted. This night was so confusing.

"I'm not sure what I'm doing," Peaches said aloud. She'd meant to think it, not say it.

A man wearing noise-canceling headphones over a khaki-colored fishing hat wandered across Henry Street at the far corner and turned up Kane Street, hands tucked into the pockets of his beige fleece vest.

"That was my husband," she observed. "Do you think he saw us?"

PART III

ONE WEEK LATER

Chapter 18

Mandy was exhausted. She'd been exhausted for an entire week, ever since the karaoke shindig at the bar. It felt odd that the day after that big, busy night was a regular, normal weekday, just as it always was. Ted went to school and Stuart went to work. Then it was the weekend and they did their normal weekend things—cooking, eating, and watching TV. Then it was Monday, Tuesday, Wednesday. She googled things about living with MS, watched more anorexia movies, stole her Russian spy neighbors' food, cooked it, drank their wine, and ate pot cookies. Karaoke night seemed significant enough to have changed everything, but everything was exactly the same.

It was Thursday now. A whole week had passed. After the boys left, Mandy lay on her back on the bed in the kitchen and considered what to do next. She could tackle the stack of bills under the bed. She could deal with Stu's fan site. She could find another movie to watch, or try to go back to sleep. Each day she'd been living with the preposterous lie that she had multiple sclerosis, she wondered what to do next. She'd come up with the disease in the first place in order to not feel guilty about staying in bed. Now she felt not guilt but exasperation. She was not a stupid person, but she had done a stupid thing.

For Mandy, the most significant takeaway from karaoke night was how often people told her how beautiful she was. Even people who didn't know that she was "sick." And Stuart seemed more attracted to her now. He could not stop touching her last night. He'd been sending her random flirty texts. Work is boring, i miss ur boobs, or, u r my dream girl, or, u really do wake up pretty, or just, hello beautiful.

Was she? Was she beautiful?

She was shallow, clearly. Why did it matter so much to her?

Wendy Clarke had given her the name and number of some model agent person.

"My friend Manfred thinks he'd go crazy over you," Wendy promised. "They said he's always looking for new faces."

"But I'm old and fat and—"

Manfred—of the perfect eyebrows and incredible legs—stepped in at this point.

"Stop it. You're what? Thirty-one? That skin! That hair! There aren't enough working plus-size models. He is going to die."

There was no harm in calling. The worst thing that could happen was he'd say no thank you, and she'd feel embarrassed for five seconds, and then immensely relieved, and then forget it altogether. She reached for her phone and scrolled through the contacts, looking for the agent's name. Kramer Lamb. What kind of name was that? *Todd and Mary Lamb welcome their new baby, Kramer.*

Plus-size model. Plus-size model. Plus-size model. It just sounded so *fat*. But also maybe kind of cool? Maybe. It wasn't every day that she met a woman—especially in this not-exactly-edgy Brooklyn neighborhood—who was a plus-size model, or any other kind of model. She wasn't sure how the other women in the neighborhood occupied themselves, but whatever they did seemed to involve reusable grocery bags, nine-hundred-dollar Canada Goose parkas with real coyote-fur hoods, yoga mats, group walks, skinny jeans and clogs, and fancy Swedish bicycles with enough seating for six children.

If only she could call someone to discuss the pros and cons of contacting the modeling agency. But the only person she ever conferred with was Stu, and Stu would make fun of her. Or maybe he wouldn't. It was just so embarrassing.

Plus-size model. Plus-size model.

Was she really that fat?

She could call her mom, but she would definitely be mean about it. Her mom was never kind. Nancy Marzulli weighed ninety pounds, smoked a pack of Salems every day, and ate fruit cocktail straight from the can. At night she drank vodka and Crystal Light lemonade and ate sardines straight from the can. She was a single mom, but she had never taken much interest in Mandy, and Mandy had never taken much interest in her. Maybe one day soon her mom would be at the supermarket buying more fruit cocktail and Crystal Light and she'd see Mandy modeling a bathing suit on the cover of *Vogue*. Then she'd call—to tell Mandy how fat she was.

Stu might actually be impressed. To start a new career with MS was pretty brave. She clicked on Kramer Lamb's name again, and pressed call.

"Thank you, Madame Jesus," he said after she'd introduced herself. "Wendy Clarke already sent me a sneaky pic of you in some dark bar. When can you come in? I'll send a car."

Mandy still felt sort of hungover from last week. She'd drunk a lot of wine and eaten a lot of Wendy's game-night snacks and talked to so many people on top of eating pot cookies every single day before and after. She felt like she was still recovering. But what else did she have to do?

"I need to take a shower," she told him.

"I don't want you to feel rushed. I don't want to inconvenience you at all. Why don't you text me the address and I'll come to you, take a few nice shots? Don't blow-dry or put on any makeup or fancy clothes. We need the real deal. How 'bout tomorrow, five o'clock?"

That would give her time to tell Stu, and time to cancel if she changed her mind.

"I can do tomorrow."

"I thought they wanted a view," Elizabeth commented.

"I love this view!" the dopey orange-skinned woman crowed. Her hair had been styled for the show so that she looked like a bridesmaid.

"That is not a view," Tupper scoffed. "That's a parking lot, you idiot."

"Great double vanity in the master bath," the woman's simple-faced husband remarked.

"Why don't we have a double vanity?" Elizabeth pretended to complain.

"Because you hardly ever brush your teeth," Tupper remarked, which was true.

Watching HGTV house-hunting shows together had always been one of their favorite rituals. It had been a very long time, and so they'd done it every morning that week. Once again, Tupper made blueberry pancakes, smothered in maple syrup from the two-gallon jug Elizabeth had brought home with her.

"So, the new project," Tupper continued the conversation they'd begun during the last commercial. The Macaw—at his studio and at Monte—had caught Elizabeth with full black trash bags. "You ransacked my mannequins."

Elizabeth smiled her rare, Elizabethan smile.

He knew she disliked discussing the work. And the truth was, she didn't have a solid plan for a new project yet. She was home to check in on Tupper and receive the MacArthur.

"You're not going to explain it to me, are you?"

Tupper knew her well enough not to push for an answer. The couple on HGTV was looking at the second option now, a square brick box of a house on stilts, built on a hill overlooking a swampy bay.

"This view is to die for," the husband said, blinking his dull eyes in the sunshine.

"Absolutely," his wife agreed. "Look at that water."

"It looks like a place where you'd go to die," Elizabeth said. "It looks like a place where your wife poisons you and dumps you in the weeds."

"That's what you'd do," Tupper said.

"That's what I'd do," Elizabeth agreed. "I'd do it in pieces. Like that Staten Island girl they found floating in the harbor."

"You always do enjoy a treasure hunt," Tupper said.

Elizabeth had not stopped thinking about the torso of that murdered girl and her still-missing parts. Staging her own murder in their bathtub had been an elaboration of sorts, but that was private, for Tupper's eyes only. She could do better, *more*.

A sort of excitement radiated from her. Tupper picked up on it immediately.

"You could do that. A treasure hunt of manne-quins."

"To make what point?" Elizabeth snapped, annoyed at his intrusion. His role as a mate was not to suggest, not even to encourage, but to stand well out of the way while she took her work from idea stage to final execution. Surely she never made suggestions for any of his creations, which were all unfathomably crafty and commercial, but seemed to satisfy his impulse to make things. When he created his skunk salt and pepper shakers, she never said, "Why not badgers instead?"

The phone rang and she jumped up to get it. At last, the MacArthur Fellowship was calling to offer her its "genius" grant.

It was the New York City Ballet, offering a discount on tickets for their winter season. Elizabeth hung up the phone in disgust.

The HGTV couple had decided against the last option, a pink stucco bungalow with a questionable thatched roof. They decided against the brick house on stilts, too, and went for the safe, tired apartment with the "amazing" parking-lot view.

Elizabeth dunked her thumb in maple syrup and licked it. "I'm not sure how long I'm staying."

Tupper felt more nauseous now than he had the morning after karaoke night. Elizabeth's presence had always done weird things to him, but he'd allowed himself to forget how it felt. He didn't want her to leave. He wanted her to take off her clothes and get in the bathtub so he could look at her long bones and bring her things. But then there was the constant feeling of impending doom. She was here now, but would eventually leave.

Of course, this was the game they'd always played. Elizabeth liked the tension, the thrill of things being not quite right. It was the disquiet that excited her. She used the French word for it: *frisson*.

"Did you hear about the accident? This morning, before dawn?" Tupper asked because he knew if he didn't contribute to the *frisson*, she would leave immediately.

"What accident?"

"A guy in his flashy convertible. He overshot the turn off the BQE onto Columbia Street. Half flipped the car. His exposed head hit the guardrail with such an impact it was knocked right off, severed completely."

"Oooh." Elizabeth's enormous gray eyes widened in delight. She grabbed a pen off the side table and a junk envelope from the huge stack of her unopened mail. "Let's draw it."

She sketched a car with the top down and a driver wearing Ray-Bans, motoring happily down the highway. Then she drew a bunch of arrows and a sharp exit turn with guardrails on both sides. Next, she sketched the bottom of the car, upturned against the left guardrail so the driver was obscured. In the sky she drew a soaring head wearing Ray-Bans with a seagull flapping by.

She was so brilliant. If Tupper tried to sell the sketch on eBay, it would probably fetch a fortune.

"Have they located the head?"

"I believe they have," Tupper said, loving how much she enjoyed the story.

She put down her pen. "Maybe we should collaborate."

Tupper shot a nervous glance at the television. Man and wife were hugging and grinning happily on their new terrace, gazing out over the parking lot with its cracked blacktop and lone palm tree. Elizabeth had never involved him in her work. He put his sticky plate down on the coffee table and wiped his mouth with a blue-and-white checked napkin.

"But you never collaborate." He stopped himself, careful not to dictate or predict too much.

Elizabeth picked a blueberry out from between her front teeth. "Why not?" she said. "Let's try it."

"I'm flattered."

"Yes. Well." Elizabeth had never been able to exchange compliments or pleasantries. Had she suggested they collaborate out of some nauseating marital urge to make her partner feel included? She certainly hoped not.

"Thank you," Tupper said. "I think."

Elizabeth laughed. "Come here."

He got up and sat beside her on the narrow love seat. She took his wrists in her hands and squeezed them. She'd always liked his wrists. They were bony and long, almost canine. He reached up and smoothed down one of her thick, dark eyebrows. She closed her eyes and rested her forehead against his. When they were kids, learning to drive in Maine, he used to chase down rabbits just to please her, but he never ran over them.

"Your breath smells sweet," she said.

He kissed her downturned lips and smoothed her other eyebrow. Why was he so anxious? Being together didn't have to be difficult. The couple on TV wept happy tears and embraced. Maybe the miserable view from that ugly apartment was their *frisson*, their severed head. The phone rang again and Elizabeth jumped up to get it.

A set of second-grade twin girls with blotchy red rashes on their faces waited blearily on the bed in her office. Peaches paid no attention to them.

What had she done?

All week long she rehashed it. She'd kissed Stuart Little of the Blind Mice, something she'd wanted to do since she was nineteen years old. It was a great kiss, too, but now it was over. Now she could go back to being nurse, mom, wife.

But what if she was in love with him? What if he was in love with her? Maybe this wasn't just a little crush. Maybe they were meant to be. Of course, she hadn't seen or heard from him all week, so it was really fucking difficult to know.

"I have to pee," one of the twins whined.

"Mommy will be here soon," the other twin said.

The mother arrived, all in a fluster because she thought she'd have a twin-free day. "I hope it's not contagious."

"It's very contagious," Peaches assured her, and ushered them away.

Her phone vibrated as a text arrived. Finally, the text she'd been waiting for. She resisted the urge to read it in its entirety until she was up and out of her swivel chair, out of her office, down the passageway outside the cafeteria, and out the back door that led to the schoolyard.

The sun was bright and a crisp fall breeze blew. The melted and burned playground equipment was cordoned off with yellow police tape. She hugged her sweater coat around her and read Stuart Little's text.

I don't want things to be weird. Want to have dinner?

Anyone not crazy in Peaches' situation would have responded with something like, *Probably not a good idea. Don't text me anymore.* Peaches texted back right away.

Sure

Stuart Little replied immediately.

Good. I know it's late notice but does tonight work? 6:30? 10 Cheever Place, #2.

Peaches' heart slowed.

Oh fuck. He meant come over to his house for dinner. He meant hang with him and his wife and kid. Unless he meant fuck in his bed while his wife and kid were out? Her heart sped up again.

Ok.

Liam sat up in bed and pulled back the window blind. He watched his dad head out to teach, sheet music flapping out of his black canvas CBGB tote bag. His mom would have already left. It was Thursday. Liam had double free first two periods and then lunch, which meant he didn't have to be at school until 11:43. He didn't know how he'd scored this scheduling gold mine. It was awesome, and usually he slept straight through until eleven, but not today.

Last Thursday night, his dad had been waiting on their stoop when he finally got home from grabbing tacos with Ryan on Smith Street after the Sublime drop/photo shoot/fake-protest craziness. Their big old dog lay on the sidewalk, panting.

"Hey, Dad," Liam had said. He was tired. He wanted to take a shower and wash the bullseye off his chest and see if Shy was done babysitting so he could tell her what happened.

"Your mother is still out," his dad had said, removing his headphones. He looked pretty worn out too, like he'd been walking for miles in his Birkenstocks.

"Where is she again?" Liam's mom never did much of anything besides put Band-Aids on little kids and walk their old dog and go grocery shopping and make dinner and drink wine and ask him how school was and get mad at him about burning the schoolyard or leaving his shoes directly in the way of the front door or not hearing what she said because he had earbuds in or getting water all over the bathroom floor when he took a shower. Oh, and hoard jam jars full of weed.

"I'm not sure. There was a party at a bar. She seemed to know everyone there. I went in and then I left because there was karaoke."

"Seriously? That's so lame."

"Seriously. It was like a karaoke nightmare, and with my tinnitus, I had to escape."

Greg had developed tinnitus playing the piccolo in his New Jersey high school marching band. It worsened at Oberlin, where he'd fronted two experimental rock bands, a Dixieland jazz ensemble, and a Philip Glass synth symphony. Ever since, he'd had to wear noise-canceling headphones when out and about. Teaching music to small children who sang in breathy voices and barely made a sound when they blew into their recorders didn't bother it much, but he couldn't go to a live concert or anyplace where the music was loud without tremendous suffering.

"Your mom was singing and dancing and having a wonderful time. She didn't even notice me. I left without speaking to her, but then I went back because I was hoping to talk to Stuart Little from the Blind Mice. He wasn't there. Neither was she. They . . . they'd already left."

There was a sadness in his voice that Liam hadn't heard before. His parents were nerdy and annoying, but they were usually nice to each other. They held hands at the movies and got each other weird gifts at thrift stores.

"Were you wearing that?" Liam gestured at his dad's rolled-up Dickies overalls, black Doc Martens, and khaki fishing hat. His dad had explained to him that his style of dress was a tribute to some early-eighties band called Dexys Midnight Runners, but it didn't really work for him. "No wonder she didn't want to talk to you." He was trying to lighten the mood. His dad didn't respond.

"Want me to call her?" Liam offered. He pulled out his phone. The battery was almost dead. "Let me go inside and plug it in."

"No, don't," his dad said.

"You sure?"

His dad nodded, staring dejectedly at the dog. He looked up at Liam again. "Would you be at all interested in transferring to a public school?"

Liam frowned. It wasn't like his parents had to

pay any tuition. "Not really. I mean, I'm a junior. It's probably not easy to change schools this far into high school. Why?"

His dad shook his head. "No real reason. I was just thinking that maybe if I got a better-paying job your mom wouldn't have to work so much and we could do more things together as a family. But if I change jobs you can't go to private school anymore. Which could be a good thing. It might be good for you to go to a school with more economic diversity."

"Yeah." Liam shrugged his shoulders. "I mean, I like my school. And it's a pretty good deal we have. Plus, I'll be leaving for college after next year."

His dad nodded. He looked like he was going to cry. "Wow. That's soon."

"Uh-huh," Liam said.

His dad leaned down to scratch the dog between the shoulder blades. "Never mind. It's not important." The dog didn't move.

Liam went inside to take a shower. His dad stayed outside. After his shower he'd texted Shy, but she couldn't talk because she could hear the parents of the kid she was babysitting coming home. Liam passed out pretty soon after that.

Now his parents were avoiding each other without admitting they were avoiding each other. It was like sharing an apartment with roommates who never spoke.

His dad was a morning person. He usually woke up first and put on music and fixed breakfast and danced around nerdily while Liam's mom stared at him and drank her coffee before stumbling off to work. This morning and every other morning that week, his dad left late, after his mom, without making breakfast or any noise at all except the front door slamming behind him.

Liam stared at the sunspots on the wall and enjoyed the silence. Then he picked up his phone and texted Shy.

Hi.

She texted back right away.

wtf mr streko hates me now—went to his office to get chocolate b4 2nd period like always and he said I'm not a vending machine and shut the door in my face. wat a cunt.

We don't use that word here, like ever

not sure i even want to be on his cunty table tennis team

Hey are you free later or are you babysitting again?

those people are weird. i got a surprise for us—meet me after school?

They walked from school to the playground on Congress Street. Shy sat on a bench and pulled off her gray fleece jacket. She wore a black jumpsuit with the name MARK sewn in green script on the chest pocket. Her long, thin legs looked less gawky beneath the loose, thick material.

"Nice to meet you, Mark." Liam held out his hand.

Shy gave him the finger. "Hey, look at the sun."

The days were getting shorter. Already the sun was sinking and the sky had begun to pinken.

"Pretty," Liam said.

Shy handed him a chocolate-chip cookie. "Eat that. I'm already almost finished with mine."

Liam shoved the whole thing in his mouth. "Did you make them?" he asked as he chewed.

Shy laughed. Her blond hair was pinkening too. "No, I took them out of the fridge at the people's house where I babysat. The kid told me not to touch them. I've been hiding them in our freezer ever since. They're pot cookies. Smell."

She held out the last bite of hers and Liam took a whiff. The cookie smelled like chocolate with an underlayer of skunk.

"What's it going to do to us?" That time they'd tried his mom's pot, Liam could barely walk.

"I don't know. Eating it is probably different from smoking it, and this is different pot. Come on." Shy jumped to her feet, popped the rest of the cookie into her mouth, and led him over to the swings.

"I have a calculus test tomorrow," Liam complained.

"I'll help you study," she joked. Shy was so behind in math she'd probably never take calculus. She pumped her legs and swung back and forth, looking cute and spidery in her black jumpsuit and Gucci sneakers.

Liam tried to relax. Why was he thinking about calculus?

He sat down on the swing next to hers and kicked it back and forth. "Fifteen minutes and then I better head home to study."

Shy twirled her swing around and around so the two chains it hung from twisted. Then she let it unwind, spinning fast and violently, her pinkish-blond hair flying out around her head. "In fifteen minutes you won't want to go anywhere."

Liam kicked at the ground some more. "Have you done this before?"

"No," she said simply. "But the dad is famous. I don't think his stuff is weak."

Peaches had gone home to shower and change the minute school got out. She'd emailed Greg and Liam to tell them she wouldn't be home for dinner. Texting was too immediate. Whenever she didn't want her family members to hear about something right away but wanted them to know she'd made the effort to keep them informed, she sent an email. Greg wouldn't be

302

home until seven. By then she'd be naked in bed with Stuart Little or eating canapés with Mandy and Stuart and Ted. What did one wear to sleep with a man she'd just kissed, or alternatively, eat dinner with his wife and child? Were her V-neck maroon sweater dress and knee-high boots too un-nurse-like? Fuck it. She left the house again before she could change her mind. What should she bring? Flowers? No, flowers were in poor taste if Mandy was sick and wasn't ever getting better. Wine seemed like a worse idea. Peaches kissed people who were not her husband when she drank alcohol. She'd bring dessert, a key lime pie.

Never before had she felt this nervous. Her hands shook as she passed a twenty to the checkout guy at Union Market.

"Do you need a bag, ma'am?"

"Mmm?" Her mind kept wandering. What was the purpose of this dinner exactly? To normalize their relationship, she assured herself. Whatever that meant. Should she have gotten a healthier dessert? Clementines? Raspberry sorbet? Did Mandy know? She hadn't exactly been friendly at the karaoke party. Her beautiful smile was reserved for the select few: Stuart; Roy Clarke; Roy Clarke's wife, Wendy—she seemed to like her a lot. Peaches had gotten the brush-off—the vague smile, the cursory nod. Well, she was only the school nurse, after all.

"Will you be needing a bag today?"

"No, no bag," Peaches said, and carried the pie out of the store. A green taxi raced up Court Street. She could have sworn she saw Liam's friend Ryan with a tiger painted on his bare chest in a poster in the advertising box atop the taxi's roof. The word SUBLIME was stamped in purple above his head.

She was half an hour early. Stuart Little's place was only three blocks away. If she wandered the streets nearby, she'd risk bumping into him. She decided to walk down to Congress, over toward the water, and then circle back up Kane.

The sun was low and the sky was streaked with violets and pinks. Peaches carried her pie down the hill and across Hicks Street. Van Voorhees Park was just ahead, more a large playground with slides, monkey bars, and swings than an actual park. The younger grades at Liam's school had their end-of-the-year picnic here because there were sprinklers and enough benches for the parents and teachers to sit down. Last year, Peaches had had an awkward conversation with the mother of a third grader. She wanted advice on how to make her daughter "cool." She worried her kid would suffer in middle school because she liked hats and refused to wear denim.

"My husband likes hats," Peaches told her. "And he doesn't own a single pair of jeans."

There were two teenagers on the big-kid

swings, a boy and a girl, kissing. Peaches looked away and then looked back again. She'd washed those gray pants over the weekend, that blue NASA T-shirt. It was Liam with Roy Clarke's daughter, Shy. They weren't kissing normally, either. They were really going at it and sort of licking each other. Peaches ducked behind a tree. The pie trembled in her hands. She didn't like to spy, but she'd never seen Liam with a girl before.

"Grrr," she heard Liam growl. Then he licked the girl's neck.

"You are so high!" the girl squealed. She was wearing the type of jumpsuit gas station attendants wear. It was pretty cool.

"Grrrr," Liam growled again. The girl pushed him away and he fell on the ground.

"Holy shit!" he exclaimed. "Get down here and look up at the sky!"

Peaches watched them for a moment, lying on their backs, side by side. She didn't want to interrupt. They were teenagers, having fun. And Liam seemed cooler to her now. He was high and with a girl and not worrying about preparing for his AP Calculus test or picking his pimples. Was she a bad mother for feeling this way? At least he wasn't home, wondering where his mother was, resenting her for not being there to fix him dinner. She slipped away and back up the hill, unnoticed.

Stuart had only just convinced Ted to take an early bath and put on his red plaid pajamas when the doorbell rang. Mandy was on the bed, painting her nails. A ham and mushroom quiche was in the oven. She'd already made garlic bread and kale Caesar salad. Tonight's box was from Grandma's House—stolen from the power-walking, knit-their-own-sweaters, two-woman couple across the street—and she was pretty sure it was going to be her favorite so far.

"Who's that?" Mandy asked without looking up from her nails.

"I'll go down and check," Stuart said, and dashed out into the hallway.

Bitches got me jumpin', I'm in distress
Balls are shrinking, got to clean up this
*   mess!*

The lyrics shouted themselves in Stuart's head as he opened the wood-framed glass doors at the top of the stoop. A Blind Mice pin featuring a picture of Stuart's mouse-tattooed fist was stuck to the collar of Peaches' leather jacket and she was holding a pie.

She handed him the pie and pointed to the pin. "The mystery is gone. I decided to completely geek out on you. I've had this pin since sophomore year in college."

Stuart knew he was supposed to feel flattered. Instead, he was simply bummed out. Why had she chosen to reveal her great, longtime fandom at this particular moment in time? To render herself harmless? To show him that she'd always loved him? To somehow align herself with him and Mandy? Her intentions weren't clear. But then again, neither were his.

"You're probably wondering why I asked you over here." He hadn't moved from the doorway. He hadn't told Mandy that Peaches was coming. He hadn't told Ted. It occurred to him that he didn't even have to invite her in.

"Kinda," Peaches admitted. "I'm pretty sure it's not to announce to your wife that you're leaving her."

Stuart stared at her. She was blushing and there was a sort of terror in her eyes. He had all the power in this situation and he didn't want it.

"No," he said.

"You just wanted to hang out?"

He shrugged his shoulders. "I was just hoping to not ruin a perfectly good friendship. I thought maybe if we all hung out and you were just, you know, Nurse Peaches from school, we wouldn't like, feel what happened was a threat. Like the kiss could just be a kiss on a stoop on a confusing night and we could leave it at that."

"Oh." Peaches' face fell. She made as if to take the pie away from him and then put her hands in the pockets of her leather jacket instead. She took a deep, shuddering breath and shook her head. Her blue eyes were glassy and faraway-looking. "I think this was a bad idea," she said in a flat voice. "I'm gonna go."

"Who was it?" Mandy asked when Stuart came back upstairs.

Mandy was on the floor doing crunches, her wet-nailed fingers fanned out behind her head.

"Just the neighbors. Their Full Plate box gave them an extra pie."

"Twenty soldier jumps," the voice on her ab workout app instructed.

Stuart put the pie down and watched her. He'd never seen Mandy exercise in his life, and now she was doing military-style core curls with jumps he wasn't even sure he could attempt without spraining something.

"Whew. That felt good." She took a sip of whatever green juice she was drinking and smiled coyly. "I have a surprise for you."

"What is it?" Stuart asked.

Mandy jogged in place and took another sip of juice. "I'm thinking about modeling again."

Stuart removed the quiche from the oven and cut it in sixths. Mandy had been cooking the most awesome food lately. "Seriously? Shouldn't you check with Dr. Goldberg first?"

Chapter 19

W e want it to look realistic," Elizabeth had instructed. "Don't just scatter the body parts clean. We need dirt and leaves on them. Blood. It needs to look authentic. You're not used to this sort of risk, but authenticity requires risk. Just don't get arrested."

What sort of "authenticity" were they going for? Tupper wanted to ask, but didn't. She might question his ability to collaborate.

Elizabeth was reluctant to leave the house in case the MacArthur people called again. She was certain she'd already missed several of their calls while they were at Tupper's warehouse in Red Hook, collecting more limbs. Over the years he'd amassed a huge selection of human forms. They were all experimental, all failed designs, but they were perfect for their collaboration, which Elizabeth had decided to call *The Hunt*.

There were people in the park—a couple of teenagers horsing around on the swings, a man with a toddler on the baby slide, two guys shooting baskets—but Tupper paid no attention to them. Whistling, he rolled a pale white calf with foot attached in the mulchy dirt beneath a hedgerow and left the foot displayed, as if the rest of the body might be hidden somewhere beneath the branches. Next, he knelt down in a pile of dried leaves adjacent to the tennis court and removed the canvas pack from his back. Inside was the torso from one of his oldest fabrications: "Friend." It was supposed to sit in your house and keep you company in an unthreatening, undemanding way. It wasn't supposed to be cute like a stuffed animal, or needy like a live pet; it was supposed to be human-*ish*. The skin was a sort of brownish gray, like the color of a mouse, and had dimpled with age. With its featureless, hairless head and rigid limbs hacked off, Friend looked like a target for shooting practice.

Tupper stood it up in the leaves, and then knocked it down again. He dragged it around and kicked soil and leaves and sticks over it. The torso was almost completely camouflaged, but perhaps that was best. Ironically, Friend was the most artificial-looking body part in his collection.

Was there a connection between Elizabeth's staging of her death and rebirth and this trail of body parts? Tupper wondered. What was her intention? Maybe that was part of the process—part of the hunt—to wonder, to feel confused.

The man was strapping the toddler into its stroller now. They were leaving, which was good, because Tupper wanted to dangle a leg from the top of the big winding slide, let go, and see where it landed. The monkey bars would be perfect for an arm.

"Don't go overboard," Elizabeth had warned. "Just a light touch. This isn't a carnival show. Be provocative, not obvious. Best-case scenario, no one even notices them for days and it rains and green stuff starts to grow on them. The more integrated into the environment the better."

Weedy vines grew up the fence behind the big-kid swings. If only the teenagers would leave. The sun had set. Soon it would be very dark. If he creeped them out enough, they might take off.

He dragged the trash bag full of limbs across the rubber mats of the playground. The teenagers, a boy and a girl, both long-limbed and skinny, were lying beneath the swings, batting at each other like kittens and laughing their heads off.

Tupper sat down on a bench and tried to look threatening. The teenagers took no notice of him. He cleared the mucous from his throat and spat into the dead leaves. Nothing. He reached down, pulled a foot from the bag, and cradled it in his lap.

"We have to wait 'til dark," he told the foot in a loud, creepy voice. There was ketchup in his bag, for blood. He took it out and squirted some on the foot.

"Hey, see that guy?"

"The one talking to his food?" Liam pushed himself up on his elbows and peered through the dusk. "He's not homeless. His clothes are too nice."

"I know. He's still weird though. What's he eating anyway? It looks like a foot."

"Should we go?"

"Are you okay to go?" Shy asked. Liam's eyes were slits and he could barely talk.

"I don't want to go home. Can we go to your house?"

"Yes. My dad might be home though." Her dad was always home.

"Can we have sex?"

"Maybe."

"Seriously? Okay, let's go."

Tupper's scary-man act had worked. The two teenagers got to their feet very suddenly and ran out of the park, holding hands and shrieking. They'd left their schoolbags beneath the swings. All the better. It was a nice effect, the abandoned schoolbags, the scattered limbs, the darkening sky. Just for fun he'd leave a head.

Roy slammed his laptop closed and sank back in his armchair. The notion that he could pull off a Russian assassin in space detained by oversexed—possibly pregnant—teenagers with a backpack full of gold and urinals that made Evian water out of piss was completely ludicrous. He was once a beloved, prolific author, but the current mess on his laptop was a not very subtle sign: his authoring days were over. Time to get a proper job like Wendy and end the misery.

Roy had always admired Wendy's attitude toward work. You got it done and then had a glass of wine. Roy could never quite leave a book alone. Once it was in his head, it stayed there like an infection or a tick, niggling at him, filling him with guilt and dread, or inspiration and elation. Writing novels was like walking endlessly up a hill made of shit, stopping to eat the shit along the way and deceiving oneself into thinking it was cake. Each night when Wendy came home from work, poured herself a glass of wine, and switched on the news, Roy would follow her into the kitchen and pour himself a glass of wine too. But no sooner had he finished the glass than he was filled with self-loathing. At most, he'd written yet another stream of shit that day, even runnier and smellier than the last. What on earth did he have to celebrate?

"Oh, this part always makes me cry," he heard Wendy say in the kitchen.

Wendy was preparing dinner and watching her new favorite TV show on her computer, *A Royal Week*. If she missed anything about living in England it was the royal family. She knew it was dopey of her, but she just ate it up, every last fascinator and footman. Right now, they were doing a recap of Prince Harry and Meghan Markle's wedding at Windsor Castle. The show was focused on the changes to the family as a whole since then, including the couple's escape to America, and the fortitude of the Queen's husband, HRH Prince Philip, Duke of Edinburgh. Meghan herself appeared in a brief interview in what looked like the doorway of a school. Was she or wasn't she pregnant again? Her red coat was too billowy to see.

"During our last conversation, my grandfather-in-law, Prince Philip, and I talked about how much we love Bonfire Night. The bonfires, the fireworks, the good cheer. Guy Fawkes was trying to blow up Parliament, but he did not succeed. What's been made of that event, Guy Fawkes Day or Bonfire Night, is always so thrilling, with everyone outside celebrating around massive bonfires. This fall, in honor of Prince Philip, Harry and I will be hosting our first Bonfire Night party in our new home. It's going to be magical. I'm inviting all my American friends and Harry's inviting his Royal Air Force buddies. We're going to party all night." She smiled her perfect smile. "And there will definitely be fireworks."

Wendy didn't think Meghan sounded like a pregnant person. She wasn't staying in and nesting; she was planning to stay up all night partying.

"Roy!" Wendy called. "Roy!"

Roy had just decided to jump ahead in time and

make both girls pregnant. Meanwhile, the people on Earth were watching their every move, like they were the stars of a reality show. Like Tupper with his Macaw.

"Roy?" Wendy bustled into the library. "I'm sorry to interrupt your train of thought, but I've just had the most wonderful idea."

"So have I," Roy said. "Your program inspired me. I don't know if I've mentioned that much of my new book takes place on Mars. And what could be more delightful to those of us plebs on Earth than a wedding on Mars? It would be televised, so we could watch it. I'm not sure of the science of it, the time delay and all that. I don't think it would quite be in real time. Still, can you imagine the excitement here on Earth? The first Mars wedding! And I was thinking it could be a double wedding—well, two wives anyway—because the rules are different on Mars. Up there everyone's sort of tribal. I haven't thought it through." He clutched his head in sudden agony and pounded his fist on the arm of his chair. "Oh, this is madness."

Wendy wasn't really listening. Roy always babbled nonsensically when he was writing. The fact that he was writing was what mattered. She should have fessed up about her demotion to *Enjoy!* by now, but she didn't want to distract him when he was finally writing again. "Can I tell you my idea?"

"Sorry." He closed his laptop and looked up at her. "Yes, what is it?"

"Bonfire Night. Guy Fawkes. We're going to have a Bonfire Night party here in our backyard. We can invite all our new Brooklyn friends. We can even drive to Delaware or somewhere and get fireworks—I think they're illegal in New York State."

"Illegal is good," Roy said. "The police will be thrilled. And what will we burn? There aren't many trees to cut down in our garden. Shall we pull all the doors off their hinges and burn them?"

"I'll get the burning things," Wendy said, annoyed at his mocking tone. "The bonfire has to be massive, as big as we dare. Maybe we can ask your artist friends to make us a Guy. Harry and Meghan are doing one in LA this year, their first one ever. That's what inspired me."

"Naturally we must keep up with the Windsors."

"Ours will be even better," Wendy said haughtily. "Manfred and Gabby and I will plan the whole thing. Maybe I can somehow spin it into a story for the magazine so they can pay for it," she added without mentioning exactly which magazine. "All you have to do is invite the locals."

There was a loud thump upstairs and a distinctly male exclamation of surprise or pain or jubilation.

Wendy froze and stared up at the ceiling.

"Do you think they're having sex?" she whispered.

"Sounds like they might be trying on a little Posh and Becks," Roy responded uncomfortably. He liked Liam, but Shy was his daughter. She was meant to eat cheese toasties and go to movies with him for the rest of her life.

"I think it's good," Wendy said uncertainly. "I mean, he could be scary and there could be massive clouds of drug smoke coming out of her room and loud music. He could be from some other neighborhood we don't know. He's a nice boy from school who's good at math and wears clean clothes."

Roy was trying very hard to unwatch *The Blue Lagoon*. Why on earth was Wendy choosing not to be uptight about this when she was uptight about almost everything else?

"Hope they're being careful," he grumbled.

Wendy snorted. "His mum is a school nurse. She probably started giving him responsible-sex talks in kindergarten."

Sensing a brainstorm, Roy turned back to his computer. A nurse like Peaches was exactly what he needed. Not human, though, an android nurse. She would be Ceran, Bettina, and Isabel's confidante and his literary device. Through her, the reader would come to know what was really going on on Mars—how the scientists on Earth were manipulating the teenagers. Maybe the nurse could give Ceran a little sex *lesson?* The fact that she was not actually human would give Roy more leeway with her. Yes, it might read as android porn, but what teenage boy wouldn't want sex lessons from an android nurse? It ought to be required.

He reopened his laptop and hit return several times. He'd have to go back to the beginning, or at least to an earlier section, and revise. Was Shy really having sex? Should he go up there and bang on the door? Best not. Best focus on the things he could control and not the things he couldn't.

"I'll leave you to it," Wendy said.

"Mmm," Roy replied distractedly.

Elizabeth sent Tupper out to scatter various body parts in the local park knowing she'd already washed her hands of the project and was ready to move on. Allowing Tupper to get involved felt like a door closing rather than a door opening. The *frisson* was gone. Perhaps it was the lack of funding. She was no idiot. She preferred to get paid for her work. She had no real intention for the project anyway. She just wanted Tupper to feel useful. She had cooked an easy one-pot meal, now he could do the dishes.

It was possible she was going through some sort of midlife creative crisis. But those never lasted long. To distract herself, she spent the afternoon opening her mail. One inquiry piqued her interest, a formal letter from a wealthy art collector in Iceland. She wanted Elizabeth to come and be a part of her world-renowned "living gallery." Elizabeth had never been to Iceland. It seemed as good a choice as any.

She began to pack, mentally composing a note to Tupper. Changing her mind, she decided not to pack anything all. Instead, she pulled a Post-it from the stack and stuck it to the kitchen counter. With a pencil she wrote, *Keep chasing rabbits, my love,* and tucked the note into her poncho pocket.

As soon as the moment presented itself, she would leave. She glared at the phone, daring it to ring.

Upstairs in Shy's bedroom, Shy and Liam were not as naked as her parents suspected. He had taken off his shirt, because they'd run home and he was sweaty. And she'd unzipped her jumpsuit, because it gave her a wedgie when it was fully zipped and she was lying down.

"My chest is so lopsided," Shy said, frowning down at herself. "One is round. The other is pointy."

Liam turned his head and examined her chest in what he hoped was a casual way. "It's nice."

"Thanks." She looked up at him and giggled. "I can still see a faint outline of a target."

Liam crossed his hands over his underdeveloped pecs. There were weird white bumps on his upper arms that he'd been meaning to ask his mom about. Hopefully Shy wouldn't notice.

"That whole thing was such a waste. I wonder what happened when the real models showed up."

Shy stared at his mole-speckled neck and dug her toes into the comforter. "I still feel a bit strange."

Liam shivered. He was cold now but still sweaty. "Um, I have supplies in my backpack."

"What do you mean, supplies?" He must know she wasn't serious about having sex. She pulled the comforter up to her chin. She was freezing and starving. She needed her dad to make her a cheese toastie.

"The day I turned sixteen my mom went to Costco and bought a huge box of condoms. I put some in my backpack, just in case."

Liam looked askance at her bedroom floor and then at the door.

"Shit. Where is my backpack?"

Chapter 20

Look away. And now back at me. Good. Look away again and now back. Left foot forward a bit. Cock your left hip. Not too much, just a hair. Good. Now look straight at me and pout your lips. Uh-oh. Wow. Okay, now smile like you just won a million-dollar contract with L'Oréal. Because you're worth it, baby."

Mandy had expected Kramer Lamb to be slick and fashiony and intimidating, dressed head to toe in black couture. Instead, he was a super-friendly dork wearing a turquoise mohair bow tie, pleated khaki pants, and pink Adidas pool slides with gray rag wool socks. And he obviously loved his job. She would have to send Wendy Clarke flowers or steal her a pie for recommending him.

Mandy straddled a kitchen chair the wrong way around and leaned her chin on the back of the chair. She pushed her bottom lip forward in a pout. Poses seemed to come naturally to her, and she didn't feel self-conscious at all in her own home.

"Stop it!" Kramer Lamb yelled, snapping pictures. "Stop it, stop it, stop it!"

Mandy giggled. "You know, I don't even like clothes very much. I just wear my husband's old T-shirts." She was wearing one right now, the plain black V-neck one that Stu always said looked sexy on her.

"Modeling isn't about clothes. Or makeup. Or hair. It's about the *je ne sais quoi*, and you have it." Kramer Lamb pulled the camera away from his face and squinted at it. "You're a goddess with a heart-shaped mouth *and* a heart-shaped face. Even your nose is sort of heart-shaped. So is your butt. And your cleavage. You're insane!"

Who knew flattery could be so exhausting? Mandy flopped down on the bed. The streetlights came on outside, streaming white light through the kitchen windows. She hoped he wouldn't notice the enormous stack of unopened bills beneath the bed.

"Oh my God," Kramer Lamb exclaimed, snapping away. "Kim Kardashian is so going to want to use you for her new lingerie line. Stop it. Stop it, stop it, stop it." He took a few steps back and looked around. "I love that you have a bed right here."

"She has MS."

Stuart stood in the kitchen doorway with Ted, watching them. He'd been trying to keep Ted entertained in his room, but Ted was hungry.

"We're almost done here." Kramer Lamb didn't appear to have heard what Stuart said, or if he had, he didn't care.

"So, what happens next?" Stuart demanded.

Kramer Lamb blew Mandy a kiss as if to say, "Your husband might be famous, but he's a pushy dick."

"Next, you let me do my job and send these pictures out and I call you with seventeen trillion offers and you buy yourselves a country house with a swimming pool!"

"And a dog," Ted said.

"Okay." Mandy wasn't sure. "Can I see if I like it first? I mean, if someone wants me, then I'll try it, and if I hate it, can I just stop?"

"Or if her MS gets worse," Stuart said. He really was being sort of a dick. "Maybe we should check with her doctor first."

"I already did," Mandy lied. "He says it's fine."

Kramer Lamb held out his fist. Mandy made a fist and bumped it against his.

"No worries. Worry makes wrinkles," he said. "From now on, I worry for you. Yes, my beautiful one?"

Mandy giggled and hugged her pudgy knees on the bed. "Don't I need to go on a diet? Or like, do something different to my hair?"

"No! Please. Whatever you're doing is working for you. Just keep doing it!"

It was Friday. The women who lived across the street always got meals with salmon and potatoes delivered from Grandma's House on Fridays. Last week it was salmon moussaka—yum.

Mandy just had to get Stuart and Ted out of the house so she could steal it.

"Can you go to the store for me, Stu?" She asked sweetly. "Take Teddy too, so he can pick out his snacks."

Elizabeth's eyes were closed. "Why are there so many English people in Brooklyn? I hear their voices everywhere. There was a whole pride of them in the liquor store."

She lay full length on the couch, her bare size-twelve feet draped over the arm, Catsy curled comfortably between her protruding pelvic bones. Tupper was on the floor trying to straighten out his back. They'd been awake the entire night before, gathering more limbs from his warehouse in Red Hook. When Tupper had returned from scattering them in Cobble Hill Park, they'd made love and ordered sushi and shared a bottle of wine. Now they were both more relaxed than they'd been in years. Elizabeth never mentioned Iceland.

Tupper's eyes were closed too. "Maybe they feel at home here," he replied. "It's not so different from London."

"That English friend of yours, Roy Clarke," Elizabeth went on. "His books are not as *'important'* as everyone thinks. If a woman wrote them, they'd be considered chick lit, not absurdist masterpieces or astute social satire."

"I keep meaning to read them," Tupper

said. "Well, it's nice to hear they're not full of testosterone and bullfights. Maybe it's a good thing."

"No, it's not."

"You've read them?"

"Yes, every color of his Rainbow. You know I read everything. What will be the title of the new one?"

"*Gold*," Tupper said. "Or *Red*. He hasn't decided. He seems very excited—"

Someone knocked loudly on the door. Elizabeth jumped to her feet. It was the MacArthur people, come to deliver the news in person.

"Who is it?" Tupper called out gaily, his eyes still closed. He imagined it was Roy, wanting to meet up for a quick drink. They could sit outside on the stoop. Elizabeth could nap.

"Police," said the voice on the other side of the door.

It was Monday. Stuart was at work, but he wasn't paying attention to anything he was supposed to be doing. He was supposed to be composing music for a "healthy" macaroni and cheese commercial featuring animated dinosaurs. Instead, he was obsessing over Mandy. Her recent energy and behavior were just so inconsistent.

Girl's so hot her limbs are fired
My lazy lady used to be so tired

He decided to call Dr. Goldberg.

"Hi, it's Stuart Little, Mandy Marzulli's husband?"

"Mmm," Dr. Goldberg said. "The man with the mouse tattoos. How can I help?"

Stuart immediately felt guilty for not going in for a checkup in at least three years. He probably had something dire like skin cancer or fatally high cholesterol.

"Yeah, well, I was just wondering if all the activity she's been doing lately is okay. I know you have her on some kind of new medication and she's like, so much better. Plus, and I don't even know if I should say this, but I got her pot and she's using it. We both are. Anyway, it's like—and I don't even know if this is possible— she's cured. Maybe you want to do some more tests?"

"Tests for what exactly?"

"Like, to see if she still has MS. I mean, like a month ago she couldn't get out of bed, and now she's bouncing around and modeling again and cooking and carrying heavy boxes."

Friday night, after Mandy had sent Stuart and Ted away to shop for food, they'd come home to find her hauling a huge, heavy box up the stairs.

"I totally forgot," Mandy had said, "I signed us up for Grandma's House!" And then she'd cooked them an incredible meal of salmon shepherd's pie.

"I mean, I just don't know if the modeling thing is such a great idea," Stuart went on. "She'll be traveling, not eating right, standing up all the time and putting her body in weird positions. I guess what I'm concerned about is, with her condition, and with her already being so exhausted—well, she was exhausted *recently*—shouldn't she be resting more? Can you tell me what you recommend?"

He heard the sound of papers rustling and the beep and click and whir of a computer. The doctor cleared his throat.

"I have no record here of Mandy having any existing condition, certainly not MS. She had a sinus infection a year and a half ago. That was the last time I saw her and the last medication I prescribed."

Ted's parents had forgotten that the Brooklyn Strategizer had kicked him out. Used to be, Danner from the Strategizer picked him up in the schoolyard with the other boys who went there after school. Now no one picked him up. Now, two afternoons a week, after the nannies and mothers and fathers and grandparents had picked up his schoolmates, Ted messed around in the corners until the air got cold and smelled of fireplaces and the sky turned royal blue. Then he walked home by himself.

Except for today. Today, as he was kicking

around in the corners of the schoolyard, foraging in the dried leaves and garbage, he found, amongst other things, a lighter. The lighter was small and green. When he flicked it, a tall flame, taller than he'd expected, rose up and wavered, hot and glorious. The other things he found were a half-full bag of Lay's potato chips, an unopened pack of watermelon gum, an almost-full water bottle, a pink-and-white polka-dotted lunch bag monogrammed with the name DAKOTA in lime green, and a paper subway map.

Ted sat down cross-legged on the ground, the weight of his full backpack pulling him down. He glanced over his shoulder to see if anyone was looking. One of the moms had brought her Great Dane puppy into the schoolyard, on the far side by the basketball hoops. Dogs were not allowed, but the three or four kids and one nanny who remained didn't seem to mind. They pet the dog and talked to its owner. No one noticed Ted.

He flicked the lighter, causing it to spark but not light, and put it in the pocket of his Adidas track pants. Then he pulled it out and flicked it again, harder. The flame rose and swayed in the purpling light. When it died, he flicked it again. It was addictive.

His parents had matches lying around their house. His dad brought them home when he picked up takeout from restaurants and used them occasionally to light candles. A lighter was better. You could stare at the flame and it didn't burn your fingers. When it went out, you could just light it again.

He wanted to hold the lighter to the corner of the subway map and watch it burn. He could put the fire out with the bottle of water. He wanted it so badly, his mouth hung open and he drooled a little. But the people admiring the huge puppy were still there, across the schoolyard, and the lame principal and strict lunch ladies and even stricter librarian were still inside, preparing for tomorrow. He pushed the lighter back into his pocket, its heat against the top of his thigh, and opened the subway map. Here was Brooklyn, there was Queens, there Manhattan, the Bronx. You couldn't take the subway to Staten Island but it was on the map because it had its own subway that wasn't connected to anything. He pretended to study it, waiting.

• • •

Halloween Hijinks

Call them pranksters, call them artists, call them Halloween devotees to a crazed degree. Someone went overboard this year. In the lead-up to Brooklyn's favorite holiday, someone scattered the limbs of dolls, mannequins, stuffed animals, and porcelain figurines in parks and gardens around Cobble Hill, giving members of the community quite a fright.

"The ankles looked just like my husband's," said Plum Brenner of Amity Street. "He's been dead for seven years."

The fun of it is, no one knows who's behind it. But we prefer it this way. Maybe it'll become a yearly thing, like the spiders crawling up the houses on Verandah Place, the piano that plays itself on Clinton Street, or the tiny pumpkins stuck all around the prongs of the wrought-iron fence on Kane.

(Cue evil laugh).

Happy Halloween!

PART IV

NOVEMBER 3

Chapter 21

Wendy said she would buy the firewood herself.

It was Friday. The party was Sunday night, which meant she had all weekend to prepare, but she'd taken the day off work to get a head start. She'd found the name of a woodcutter in Staten Island. Finding him would be an adventure. Wendy was excited. Parties were her specialty, and this was their first in Brooklyn. Roy couldn't be bothered; he was too busy with his book.

She'd rented a U-Haul van to pick it up. A cord of wood, just over the Verrazano, which was the impressive-looking bridge over the whitecapped bay that you could see off the Belt Parkway on the way home from JFK. That was about all she knew. Wendy wasn't big on driving. She'd quit altogether in England because they drove on the wrong side of the road and the roads were narrow and fast. The only time she'd tried, she'd sideswiped an entire hedge and made permanent fingernail gouges in the car door trying to find the gearshift.

The U-Haul place was a much longer walk than she'd expected, up Union Street, across the Gowanus Canal, up and up to Fourth Avenue and then over to Fourth Street. She could have taken a car service, but the staff at *Enjoy!* were encouraged to walk.

The U-Haul van was basic and raw and empty in back, modern and full of gizmos in front. A screen barked at her when she backed up, showing her a picture of what was behind her and the dangers therein. The GPS never shut up. The E-ZPass allowed her to zip through tolls. Wendy drove in a dutiful daze, following the GPS instructions.

She'd get the wood and maybe even some fireworks, she thought as she crossed the Verrazano Bridge.

The view was vast, with water everywhere. She rolled down the windows so she could taste the salty air, the blue sky, the brown beaches. Oh, Staten Island, here comes Wendy Clarke of *Enjoy!* magazine. Mrs. Roy Clarke. Mother of Shy, Chloe, and Anna Clarke. Seagulls hovered in the misty air, their beaks open in silent yawp. Below the bridge, the deep water tossed and sucked. Wendy's tongue tingled with the rankness of it. Her nostrils flared.

Yes, fireworks. There had to be someplace that sold them. Staten Island had everything.

Elizabeth had been arrested for serving and selling alcohol without a license, a misdemeanor criminal offense with up to one year of prison time. It hadn't even occurred to her that Monte was a real bar serving liquor to the public and that bars had certain rules. She'd received notices with threats of fines when she'd taken over the site months ago, but she'd thrown the notices away without even opening them. The police had ransacked the bar and confiscated the liquor. The odor of dead fish in the basement and "evidence of foul play" down there made them even more suspicious. They put a dead bolt on Monte's door and sealed it with yellow police tape.

Tupper tried to be helpful.

"It's art," he protested. "She's an artist." He supplied the authorities with video footage from the Macaw—proof that her unusual behavior was all in the name of the work.

Elizabeth was kept in a holding cell on State Street until the police had taken their statements and reviewed the video. In the end, the fact that she was a renowned artist and Tupper a respected industrial designer helped quite a bit. The New York City Police Department wanted to appear open-minded. Elizabeth was sentenced to only five days prison time and fined thirty thousand dollars—more than twice the cost of a New York State liquor license.

Due to overcrowding at the holding prison, Elizabeth was transferred to Rikers Island for the last three days of her detainment. Tupper visited her the first morning, traveling from Cobble Hill to Pier One by Citi Bike, Pier One to Wall Street, and then on to Queens by NYC Ferry, and the rest of the way by kayak. As he paddled across the murky, swiftly moving water, barely escaping death by ferry collision, trash floe, or the charge of a barge, he saw how easily one could deposit a body, or anything else, in the cold New York–area waters. There were so many islands, so many marshes and canals and inlets. Determined to continue his and Elizabeth's work despite this little hiccup, he'd taken a wooden arm with him in the kayak. He released it in a ferry's wake and paddled on.

How wonderful that he knew just where to find her. She was locked in a cell, right where she'd been deposited the night before. He knew it was wrong, but he'd even been a bit coy with the lawyers, not returning their calls right away, giving them only limited information, because he'd really almost rather she stayed in jail than leave him again.

• • •

Bettina had read ~~The Handmaid's Tale~~. She knew about having babies against your will.

"I just got accosted by some kind of weather specialist," Isabel announced. "He asked me all these really bizarre questions like, 'Did I feel any fragmentation?' And then he put his hand on my stomach. Scientists are so creepy."

• • •

Much to Tupper's disappointment, Elizabeth's jail time was cut short. Her concerned patrons, including the CEO of Apple, the Italian politician who'd funded her last show at the Venice Biennale, some rich art collector in Iceland, and Roy Clarke himself, bailed her out early. They also wrote letters, lauding her work and clearing her of all malintent, that were published in the *New York Times*, *Artforum*, the *Wall Street Journal*, and Italian *Vogue*.

Tupper brought her home from Rikers that very day. He cooked a late lunch of fish and noodles and demonstrated his latest prototype.

"It's the Money Pit," he explained. "Sort of a cross between a peach pit and a sea sponge."

Elizabeth stared at it and hugged her bowl. She forked a pile of noodles and fish into her mouth.

The Money Pit was a wallet made from a spongy material that literally absorbed your bills and change into its pores and then flattened in your pocket. It was revolutionary. He'd gotten the idea while trying to conceal a Barbie arm in the bark of a dead, rain-dampened tree.

"Look." Tupper stuffed a few quarters and one-dollar bills into it and then flattened it with his fist. "It'll come in colors like pink or green or red or briefcase brown. I developed the material myself. It's one hundred percent biodegradable and compostable."

Elizabeth grabbed it and tucked it into the front of her orange prison jumpsuit, which she'd asked Tupper to purchase from the jail so she could wear it home.

Tupper laughed. "That won't work. You don't even wear a bra."

Elizabeth let the Money Pit drop into her jumpsuit and continued to eat her noodles. It fell through to the crotch area, where it bulged masculinely. Tupper wondered how long this prison behavior would go on. She'd only been "inside" for three days. Every time Elizabeth went away and came back, he felt like she was experimenting with a new persona—affectionate Elizabeth, distant Elizabeth, hungry Elizabeth, surly prisoner Elizabeth. He had news, but he didn't want to deliver it until she appeared to be paying attention.

"Why don't we go out and celebrate?" he suggested. "It's unusually warm for this time of year. We can go to that upstairs bar outside in the park."

"All right," she agreed. "I just need to wash my feet."

It was Friday afternoon and the bar was packed.

"Get vodka," Elizabeth commanded, choosing a grubby, newly vacated table in the corner. "A whole bottle." She was still wearing her orange prison jumpsuit. People stared. One man gave her a thumbs-up.

Halfway to the bar, Tupper turned around to make sure she was still there. Elizabeth had turned away to take in the view. Ferries crisscrossed the harbor from Manhattan to Brooklyn and Staten Island and beyond, leaving frothy white wakes. In the far distance, the Statue of Liberty towered greenly, symbolically. The sun was low, bathing the silvery buildings and dark water in golden light.

Tupper's nervousness made her restless. The boats made her restless.

It wouldn't be long now.

Tupper brought the vodka back to their table with two shot glasses.

"Icelandic." Elizabeth admired the bottle. "Perfect."

Tupper had noticed the letter from Iceland on top of her stack of mail and the particular interest the rich Icelandic art collector had taken in freeing Elizabeth. He poured them both shots, reminding himself to say what he had to say while his head was still clear and he wasn't about to throw up everywhere.

"I'm guessing that's where you're headed next—Iceland?"

Elizabeth's downturned mouth turned down even further. She tossed back her shot.

Tupper knew he was cornering her, but he was tired of her performative antics and complete self-involvement. She hadn't asked about *The Hunt*. She didn't seem interested in the Money Pit. She didn't care that Monte was closed, even though their neighbors liked it there. She hadn't even noticed that he'd joined Full Plate so that they could dine on delicious meals for two. It was possible to be an artist and a nice person, but Elizabeth didn't even try. If she wanted to go, she could go.

He threw back his shot and poured himself another.

"I was awarded a MacArthur," he said, finally delivering his news. "They called last night."

Elizabeth gray eyes widened. "For *The Hunt*? That was a collaboration."

Tupper grunted. Of course she'd believe the award was somehow meant for her.

"They said it was for my promise as a designer. They can't wait to see what I'll make next."

Elizabeth drank two shots in a row and poured herself another. Out on the harbor the Staten Island ferry blasted its horn. She'd underestimated him. She was always underestimating him.

"I'm not going anywhere," she said, deciding it on the spot.

Tupper pushed his glass away. "But I want you to go. I want to make things, you want to make different things. It's better if you go."

"No." Elizabeth gritted her yellow teeth determinedly and folded her arms across her chest. At last, it was back: the *frisson*. At least for now. "No."

340

• • •

Her mum was probably right. Shy should have dropped the idea of table tennis and signed up for a pottery class instead. Mr. Streko was so different now that the season had started. He took table tennis far too seriously, as if they were training for the Olympics. Practices were every day, and only Mr. Streko and the senior captains were allowed to speak. Table tennis was a game of concentration, like chess, he said. Talking distracted the players. Sometimes Shy would forget and ask him a question or giggle and make a self-deprecating remark about her own clumsiness. Mr. Streko would just shake his head and turn away.

It carried over into Latin class too, as if he was intent on training her in and out of the gym. He never called on her anymore. He never even smiled. Shy was worried about him. He seemed preoccupied. Maybe someone in his family had died. Maybe his cat was sick. But the last thing she wanted was to let him down. So she dug in and practiced hard. She did squats and bench-pressed the weighted bar. She learned to serve backhand and forehand and tried to be quick on her feet. To her surprise, she enjoyed table tennis. She liked the rigor of it, the concentration, and how it was exercise without too much exercise.

Today was their first away match, against the Berkeley Carroll girls' team. Sun Kim, one of the captains, always warmed them up. Sun was tiny and never stopped smiling. She also had the quickest volley on the team. She was an inspiration. Mr. Streko was always saying, "Watch Sun. Watch Sun." Shy kind of hated her.

"Fifty laps, fifty crunches, then fifty jumping jacks!" Sun shouted gleefully, and the team took off, running around the Berkeley Carroll gym in their matching white Under Armour quick-dry polo shirts and black mesh shorts.

Shy trailed behind them. She hated running. Bruises dotted her bony shins. Her skin looked gray. She'd almost invited Liam to the match but then decided to wait until she improved her game. Liam was being weird anyway. He'd gotten a bad grade on that calculus test—which for him meant an 89 instead of a 100—and she felt certain he blamed her.

The girls circled the gym, jogging in a silently determined clump. Mr. Streko and the Berkeley Carroll coach, a wiry woman in a red tracksuit with a smoker's voice and a dyed-red pixie cut, volleyed back and forth at one of the two tables set up in the center of the gym, the *ping* and *pong* of the ball echoing loudly.

"Your point," the woman growled at Mr. Streko in a Russian accent as Shy staggered by.

"*Non vincere omnes*," Mr. Streko called back.

To win is not all. Was he flirting? Shy wondered.

The girls finished their warm-up and collapsed on the bench to sip water from matching water bottles and receive the lineup from the coaches.

"Sun and Suraya, you're first," Mr. Streko called, making notes on his clipboard. "Jill and Danielle go second. Then Amy and Kylie. Then Sun again and Tati. Suraya and Jill are last. Go team!"

He hadn't said Shy's name. And Suraya was a freshman. Why did she get to play twice?

"Mr. Streko?" Shy asked, breaking the code of silence.

He ignored her, already standing at the ready beside the table, clipboard in hand, bushy black eyebrows furrowed deep in concentration.

Beep, beep! The other coach blew her whistle. "First match."

Shy jumped to her feet. "Go Phinney!" she shouted. If she couldn't play, she could at least show some enthusiasm.

Immediately, Mr. Streko pointed at her, shook his head, and then pointed at the bench. She sat down again and kicked off her black team Nikes, which made her hideously pale legs look even paler. No playing, no cheering. This was so much fun.

Ping, pong. Ping, pong. Tic, toc. Tic, toc. Table tennis was the most boring game in the world to watch. More boring than regular tennis, or American football, or golf.

Kylie nudged Shy's arm with her elbow. "Hey, your grandfather is here."

"Hello, darling." Roy sat down next to his daughter, marveling at how a school gymnasium in Brooklyn could smell exactly the same as a school gymnasium in the middle of England. Sweaty socks, sticky floorboards, and exhausted fluorescent lightbulbs.

"We're not allowed to talk, Dad," Shy said through her teeth. "What are you doing here anyway?"

"I was curious." Roy had never mentioned his altercation with Mr. Streko at Monte. "Just offering a bit of moral support."

Beep, beep! Mr. Streko blew his whistle and pointed at them to be quiet.

"They're good, aren't they?" Roy went on, ignoring Mr. Streko completely. "And I like their red tops. It's a good, deep red. I do like a good red," he mused.

"The reds are the other team. Shush, Dad. You're going to get kicked out."

"Go girl!" Berkeley Carroll's coach shouted after a particularly brutal serve. Why was she allowed to yell?

Berkeley Carroll won all four of the first matches. Then the next one was called.

Beep, beep! Mr. Streko blew his whistle. "Sun, you sit out. Shy, you're up," he shouted without even looking at her.

Shy almost peed her pants. She slid her feet into her shoes and hurried to tie them.

"Exciting." Her dad rubbed his hands together the same way he did when he watched Wimbledon or the Tour de France on TV. "Show us how it's done."

"Don't get too excited, Dad." It occurred to Shy that Mr. Streko was only letting her play because her father was there and they were losing the entire match. "I think I kind of suck."

Beep, beep! Mr. Streko pointed at her and then at the table where Tati, a senior from Berkeley Carroll, was holding her red paddle and shifting impatiently from foot to foot, her hair pulled up in a tight ponytail with a matching red scrunchie. She looked scarily competitive and mean.

"Come on, black and white!" her father yelled like an ardent Premier League soccer fan.

Shy approached the table. She picked up the black paddle and the Berkeley Carroll coach rolled her the ball. She took a deep breath and tried to remember everything she'd learned about serving. She was pretty crap at it, but she'd do her best.

Toc! The ball flew sideways, just skimming the net. Tati assumed it was out, but it hit the table in-bounds, and she lunged for it at the last minute. It ricocheted off the edge of her paddle and flew straight into the air. Tati lay across her side of the table, moaning dramatically. Shy had scored the first point.

345

"Get up, girl!" Berkeley Carroll's coach yelled hoarsely. She didn't seem to know any of her team members' names; she just called them all "girl." "Play, play, play!"

Roy had expected Shy to be gangly and clumsy, but she was rather good. Of course the Latin teacher git Streko offered no words of encouragement whatsoever.

Roy had wasted the entire morning searching the bookshelves in the library for a poem he'd read long ago, something about "a new planet." The poem was by Byron, or Keats, or Shelley. He'd texted Peaches, but she'd yelled at him grumpily, via text, that he was the one who'd read English at Oxford. Then she'd found it for him anyway. It took her about ten seconds to google it. The poem was by Keats.

Then felt I like some watcher of the skies
When a new planet swims into his ken

Now that Roy had it, he had no idea what to do with it. He'd written a paragraph comparing Isabel and Bettina to the women in *The Handmaid's Tale*, and then deleted it. He'd read and reread the previous paragraphs he'd written, and then deleted them too. He'd written the bulk of the story—he was in the homestretch. But why this absurd plot and not some other? Why these characters? Why these sentences? Why these words?

Because, he'd told himself. *It's what you do.* If Shy could suffer the indignities of high school and Wendy could take a crowded subway to run a magazine in Manhattan every day, then he could stop asking so many stupid questions and just get on with it. But instead of getting on with it, he'd come to the match.

"Go, girl! Pick up your feet!"

Roy stood up. Shy had scored again with her impossible serve. It looked like she was holding the racket completely wrong and the ball was going to hit the floor, but miraculously it landed on the table, just barely in.

"Come on, black and white!" he yelled again, delighted that he'd made the effort to come and cheer her on. Shy's smarmy Latin teacher refused to even look at him, even though he was the loudest person in the gym.

The girls took a water break. Shy jogged in place as she sipped from a bottle of Poland Spring. She flashed Roy a smile and he winked at her. His other daughters had played field hockey and tennis, but he'd never watched them. Perhaps that's why they hated him.

The girls in his book could be sporty, he thought as he sat down again. And table tennis would work perfectly on Mars, if they could fit the table in a spacecraft. The girls would request one and be super excited when it came. Ceran would be hopeless, but the girls would play constantly. That's how they'd keep fit during their pregnancies.

Beep, beep!

Mr. Streko blew his whistle and pointed at Shy, his orange-and-blue neck tattoo bulging. He carried himself differently at table tennis than he did in Latin, she noticed, more upright and bossy. His black Phinney T-shirt stretched tight across his sturdy, muscular chest. It was kind of hot.

"Eye of the tiger," Roy said, redirecting his daughter's attention.

Shy picked up her paddle and bit the inside of her cheek in concentration.

"Go, girl!"

Chapter 22

W E HAVE RABBIT said the handwritten sign taped to the window. A little bell jingled when Peaches opened the old shop door.

Hasslachers was the oldest butcher in New York State. It was famous for its always-been-here, low-key vibe and its unfussy presentation. The head butcher was the grandson of the original Hasslacher and had trained his young assistants since they were teenagers. The maleness of the place always intimidated Peaches and so did the meats. What was the difference between a sirloin tip and a Newport strip? But it was Friday, the school week was over. She wanted to drink a bottle of wine and cook something delicious for dinner—part of her pact with herself to make the best of what she had, which was a lot.

She squinted at the display case and eavesdropped on the butchers' conversation behind the counter.

"She's a great actress though, Nicole Kidman. You ever see that one where she plays the newscaster with Matt Dillon? She's hilarious. And the one where she plays Virginia Woolf? She wore a prosthetic nose. You forget it's her. She's brilliant."

Peaches was startled. It was not the sort of

conversation she imagined butchers would have. Why was she such a snob? Just because you were a butcher didn't mean you thought about meat all the time.

"Can I help you, miss?" The youngest butcher offered. He wore a mustache and had elaborate arm tattoos.

Peaches shook her head. "Sorry, I'm not ready." She wished they would keep talking. What other movies had they seen? Maybe she should forget about dinner and go to the movies. Liam and Greg could order in.

Today had been a weird day. It was warm, so warm it felt like September, not the first Friday in November. The morning had begun with two kindergarten girls scratching their heads with such frequency during circle time that their teacher sent them down to Peaches' office. Sure enough, the girls were infested with lice. Half the kindergarten was infested with lice, including three of the teachers, plus the art teacher, the gym teacher, and the parent coordinator, who even had nits in his beard. She'd been so busy combing through hair and sending children home she'd only eaten Cheez-Its for lunch and she felt rotten. Several times during the day Roy Clarke had texted questions pertaining to his book. "What's another name for 'anus'?" "Do people get the clap anymore?" And finally, "Do Russian dogs get the rabies vaccine?" Peaches was too busy to respond. At two o'clock Stuart Little's son came in with a rash and threw up on her floor. Mandy came to pick him up.

"I made clams last night," she said by way of explanation. "They were in the box, out on the stoop in the sun. Teddy loved them so much Stu and I barely ate any. Guess they were bad?" She looked different. She'd done something to her eyebrows and trimmed her hair and her outfit looked current. Was she still sick? Was she taking new meds?

"You look amazing," Peaches said jealously while Ted retched on the little cot. "It might be the clams. Or it could be fifth disease. It's a virus with a fever and a rash. But who knows? I was an English major."

The two women stared down at Ted.

"Should I take him to the pediatrician?"

Peaches shrugged her shoulders. "Maybe? Or just wait it out."

Mandy nodded. "It's Friday anyway."

She seemed so relaxed, Peaches was envious. After they'd gone, she tried to clean up her office so she wouldn't come back to a mess of lice combs and vomity paper towels Monday morning. Then Stuart Little himself showed up, skateboard clenched against his side, mouse tattoos stretched tight against his knuckle bones. He looked totally stressed out.

"Ted's home. Your wife came to get him. He

needs rest and rehydration. He'll be fine very soon."

Stuart sat on the cot and ran his hands through his hair. This was not the reaction she'd expected.

He blinked wearily at the dirty linoleum floor. "I got all inspired. I started writing kids' music. Some of it is pretty good, maybe. I started writing a song based on that famous Shel Silverstein poem, 'Sick.' You know, the one where the kid lists all these things wrong with him that are totally preposterous?" He looked up. "I think Mandy's faking. I don't think she has MS."

Peaches spent the next half hour trying to talk him down, or up. He had all these theories, but Peaches found it difficult to care. Somehow it didn't matter to her one way or the other. Everyone had their foibles. What if Mandy had lied? Maybe she needed to lie. At least she was creative. Pretending to have MS was sort of badass when you thought about it.

She could hear the children leaving for the day and then the teachers. She didn't want to talk to Stuart Little about his wife anymore. Clearly they needed boundaries. If he wasn't there to sweep her off her feet and elope with her to Mexico, she wasn't interested.

"I think you need to talk to her," she said finally and stood up. "I'm sorry, but I have to go."

She didn't really have to go anywhere, but she

did need some protein and some wine. As soon as Stuart left, she headed to the butcher.

"She is by far my favorite actress. By far," the older butcher said now as he wrapped up a pile of pork sausages. His horn-rimmed glasses looked expensive. His hair was cut expensively too.

"The Newport steak is great," the younger butcher told her. "How many people you cooking for?"

Peaches looked into the case at the Newport steak. It was thick and lean, except for a strip of fat on one side. Greg hated steak. He wasn't a vegetarian, but he ate like one. Liam was almost a vegetarian out of laziness.

"Do you happen to know what's playing at the movie theater?" she asked the young butcher.

He rolled his eyes. "A bunch of kid stuff. What a waste. Marvel and Disney. They used to show good films there—Tarantino, Woody Allen."

"I don't care what people say about the guy. *Hannah and Her Sisters*, best movie of all time," one of the other butchers said as he wrapped up a pile of tenderized chicken breasts.

"Or today we have premade shish kebabs. Nice lamb meat. Fresh onion, peppers. All you need to do is grill them," the young butcher suggested to Peaches. "Four minutes on each side, so they stay pink."

Peaches didn't have a grill. It was difficult to focus on the meat. The decision seemed enormous, exhausting. She was so hungry, and she really needed wine. And a vacation. Why was everyone always coming to her all the time, demanding things? She couldn't hide in Monte anymore either. It had been impounded.

There had to be one decent movie playing. She could buy a mini wine bottle with a screw top, get a sandwich from Union Market, and take them to the movie theater. Even better, she could text Cobble Hill General and tell Dr. Conway she was stressed out and needed "a prescription."

She studied the glass case, working her phone with her thumbs. "I'll take the rabbit," she said finally.

It came wrapped in brown paper tied with white cotton string. "Don't overcook it," the young butcher instructed. "*Herbes de Provence* and radicchio, or blueberries and coriander give it a nice flavor."

Dr. Conway texted back right away.

I have what you need. Something new, from Corfu!

The firewood man was fantastic. Wendy's U-Haul was now full of nicely split firewood, two old doors, and a dismantled picnic table. She had no idea if it was even legal to burn such large items in one's garden in Brooklyn, but what was the worst thing that could happen? If a neighbor called and complained, Wendy would simply invite them to the party. The more the merrier.

Next on her agenda: fireworks. Much to her frustration, she'd been unable to find any online, even on the "dark web" sites that sold hand grenades and Tasers that Manfred and Gabby had sent her links to. Her name was probably on a watch list now. The FBI, CIA, KGB, and MI5 had probably staked out her office. News of it would trickle back to Lucy Fleur and Wendy would be banned from the building.

Pulled over in the U-Haul in Staten Island, she googled "buy fireworks near my current location." A single address appeared.

She hadn't realized how rural parts of Staten Island were. Growing up on the Upper East Side, she'd snobbishly thought of it as a network of landfills and ugly, close-together houses with vinyl siding, but it wasn't nearly that bad. Winding her way to the fireworks salesperson, she passed pretty brick houses with tree-lined driveways, a horse farm, an apple orchard, and lots of signs to the beach.

The U-Haul bumped down a weedy dirt road.

"Your destination is on your right."

The structure was more of a temporary shelter than a house or storefront. Cinder blocks on the bottom, metal roofing for sides, and clear plastic sheeting for a roof. The word FIREWORKS was painted in red on an old piece of plywood.

Wendy pulled over and stepped down from the van.

"Hello?" she called out. "Hello?"

A person emerged. He was fortyish and unkempt and carried a shotgun. Only then did it occur to her that she should not have come alone. No one knew where she was. Her phone probably didn't even have service.

"Police? Press? FBI?" the man demanded. The words SEE YOU IN HELL . . . were tattooed in neat calligraphy along his collarbone. He wasn't pointing the shotgun at her, but it was in his hand. He held it casually, like a lit cigarette he was tired of smoking. "How'd you find me?"

"Google," Wendy explained. "I'd like to buy your fireworks. Whatever you have, I'm sure they'll be fine."

"I didn't put anything on Google."

He was holding the shotgun more tightly now. His muscular forearms were streaked with dirt. His teeth were straight but discolored. His greasy hair was curly and long. He might have been attractive if he were clean and not so paranoid.

Wendy pointed bravely at the sign. "Aren't you selling fireworks?"

The man seemed to notice the sign for the first time. "Huh. I don't know. Maybe?"

Wendy looked at her watch, even though she'd stopped wearing a watch years ago. "Well, that's disappointing." She sighed, trying to sound like a normal person who wasn't scared to death. "I'll have to call around and see if I can find them somewhere else."

"No." He waved the shotgun around and she almost screamed. "Let's look for them. If we find them, you can have them for free. Finders keepers."

He turned and went into the shelter. Wendy really wanted the fireworks. Against her better judgment, she followed him.

It was a murderer's lair, that much was certain. The actual discarded dirty clothes and shoes—women's shoes—of his victims and more randomly, a collection of hairbrushes, lay on a blue plastic tarp on the ground.

"I'm trying to gather enough stuff to open my own vintage shop." Of course he was lying. That's what all murderers said. "I wanted to collect typewriters, but they're so heavy."

"Mmmm," Wendy said, too frightened to speak actual words.

A tall, lidded garbage can stood in the corner. It was probably full of body parts. The man removed the lid.

"Oh, here you go." He pulled out a long, thin cardboard box printed with red and yellow Chinese characters. "Bingo. It's full of 'em."

How had he not noticed this before?

He picked up the garbage can by the handles and carried it out of his lair. "I can't do anything with these. They're illegal to sell. I don't want to draw attention. You understand."

Wendy followed him to the U-Haul. He was still carrying his gun. If she said one wrong thing, he could change his mind, shoot her in the head, and steal her hairbrush, which was in her purse.

"I'm trying to stay under the radar," he went on.

He heaved the garbage can into the van and propped it against the dismantled picnic table. Wendy did her best to smile.

"Thank you very much. I was never here," she said, and walked in what she hoped seemed like an unhurried, unafraid fashion to the driver's-side door. "Good luck."

He waved his shotgun in the air. "See you in hell!"

"I miss home."

As soon as he'd written the words, Roy sat back in his chair and wondered: Did he miss home? Did he miss England?

England's climate was cool and damp. The rooms were always cold, no matter how well the heating worked. The tap water was not as tasty as Brooklyn tap water. The dryers took forever to dry anything and shrank your socks. There was less pressure to work late and exercise and more of an inclination to meet at the pub for a pint or have a nice cuppa and a biscuit and relax in front of the telly.

Did he miss it? Yes, sometimes. He was fifty-six years old and he did still sometimes miss home. But if they hadn't moved, Shy would never have learned to play table tennis and he never would have thought about Mars or written *Red*. Or *Gold*.

Definitely *Red*.

He'd made great progress in the few short hours since Shy's inspiring table tennis match. Both girls were pregnant and had married Ceran in a tacky, overly publicized Martian wedding with vaguely pagan undertones. They'd stolen a rover and run away and discovered a crater full of frozen water, which they'd melted to survive. And the Russians were coming, a whole rocket-load of them. Not to kill them, but to rescue them. Isabel's rich Russian family were criminals with hearts of gold.

But they missed home. There was only a chapter or two to go. Roy had to get them home.

By the time Liam and Greg came home, Peaches was high as a kite and cooking a rabbit.

"Dinner won't be ready until I don't know, midnight, but it'll be worth it," she told them loudly, brandishing a glass of white wine.

"I smell pot," Liam said.

"Oh, do you now?" Peaches giggled.

"Mom!" he whined. He looked like he'd been crying.

"*Herbes de Provence*, that's what you smell."

"Are you stoned?" Greg asked. He seemed impressed.

"Very," she admitted.

It was hot in their apartment. She'd taken off her sweater and jeans and was cooking in just her T-shirt.

"Mom, please put on some pants," Liam whimpered.

Her phone bleated. Another text from Roy Clarke. Greg stared at the phone where it lay on the counter.

Then the phone rang. It was Stuart Little. It rang and rang. Her ringtone for when he called was set to the opening drum sequence of the Blind Mice song "Omnia Vincit!" It was pretty obnoxious.

Peaches gulped her wine and snorted, horselike. "I'll go find some shorts."

When she came back, Greg and Liam were seated at the kitchen table, waiting for her. This was odd. They never gathered around the kitchen table except to eat.

"We have something to tell you," Greg announced.

Peaches didn't know if she was being paranoid because of the pot, but it sounded like they were trying to freak her out on purpose.

"Guys," she protested, "I already had the worst possible day."

"Well, it's about to get worse," Liam said.

Peaches' lower lip trembled. When had her only child learned to be so mean?

"It's the dog," Liam said. "He's dead."

"We came home around the same time," Greg explained. "He was lying in front of the door. We carried him to the clinic but it was too late. His heart stopped."

Peaches hadn't even noticed that the huge dog was missing. She sat down next to Liam and took his hand. Greg reached for her other hand across the table.

Tears spilled from the corners of her eyes and rolled down her cheeks. "He was a good dog." She hoped she didn't sound stupid and high. "He was my friend."

Letting go of their hands, she tucked her palms beneath her thighs and rocked back and forth in her chair. Her chest shuddered. A stream of snot dripped from her nose.

"We got him when I was pregnant with you." She sobbed in Liam's direction. "He was your brother. When you had to go to the pediatrician, I used to say I was taking you to the vet."

Her sobs were loud and uncontrollable now. News of the dog's death and perhaps smoking a shitload of pot while gulping white wine had uncorked all her bottled-up emotion. How did she get here? She was supposed to be a girl drummer in a cool indie band, dating Stuart Little. Instead she was an overworked school nurse, Liam's mom, Greg's wife, chief cook and bottle-washer of the family, and the owner of an enormous, old, dead dog.

Greg watched her across the table, regretting that they were no longer holding hands. Liam's eyes were screwed miserably shut. He was inconsolable. They both were. Greg stood up.

"Can I help with dinner? Do you need more wine? Liam, can you set the table? Maybe start by getting us all some big glasses of ice water."

Nobody moved.

"I hate this kitchen." Peaches sobbed. "There's no ventilation. Maybe we should move. I want to move."

Liam opened his eyes. "Mom. Stop."

Greg knew Liam had every right to be miserable. Liam was a teenager. But Peaches. He hated to see her so sad. It wasn't just the dog—he was an old, old dog. She was sad before they even got home.

Greg began to clank around the kitchen, putting away clean dishes, opening another bottle of wine, cutting bread, taking out the butter, making a salad. Whenever Peaches was incapacitated, he became hyperefficient. There'd been so many sad, restless, dissatisfied days before she became a nurse. They'd brainstormed possible solutions—move, have another baby, go to cooking school, go to plumbing school, train for a marathon. Peaches had fond memories of her own elementary school nurse. She made the kids toast and gave them Coke for an upset stomach. When Peaches finally decided to go to nursing school, Greg was thrilled. He made lists of the courses and exams she needed to take and the closest universities. He created study schedules for her. He shopped for groceries and cooked all their meals. He quizzed her and bought her a new pillow so she'd be well-rested before her exams.

"He would have liked to try the rabbit," Peaches whimpered softly. She wiped her nose on her sleeve.

Greg lifted the lid and peeked into the pot. He gave it a stir. Legs, thighs, and a little pointed head. "You're cooking a rabbit?"

She nodded and snorted into her arm. Her shoulders shook. Was she laughing or crying?

"I got him at the butcher. Rabbit must be the meat of the week or something. I know you won't eat him. But I'm going to try him. Oh, and we need to watch more Nicole Kidman movies. They're huge fans."

"Who?" Liam wasn't crying anymore.

Peaches wiped her nose on her shirtsleeve again. "The butchers."

Liam stood up and took three glasses out of the cupboard. "Mom, you're high. It's embarrassing. Remember that time you asked me where to get pot? Was it for you?"

"No." She waved her hand at him. "That was for Stuart Little. His wife was sick."

Greg refilled her glass of wine. "I know you have a huge crush on him. I guess I always have too. I've been thinking about him a lot lately."

Don't waste your time, Peaches thought bitterly.

"I was wondering if I could give you some songs to share with him. I think they're pretty good, but I'm not a hip enough musician to make them sound cool. I think he could. They're kids' songs. For a kids' album." He dispensed a cube of ice from the freezer, popped it into his mouth, and sucked on it. "I feel like you owe me this."

Peaches gulped her wine. She decided not to say anything about Stuart trying to turn the Shel Silverstein poem "Sick" into a song. What did Greg mean, she owed him?

Greg dipped his index finger in the rabbit pot and licked it off. "They're sending us the dog's ashes." He smacked his lips together. "Tastes like blueberry jam." He pulled a little notepad and pen out of the back pocket of his khakis and jotted something down. *"Rabbit, grab it. Blueberry jam,"* he sang to himself.

Peaches watched him with stoned dissatisfaction. She pushed her wineglass away. "Stuart told me once he'd never do a kids' album. It's too middle-aged and obvious."

"Oh, he told you that, did he?"

"Yes. He tells me lots of things." Peaches wasn't sure what she was doing. Last time she'd seen Stuart Little, she'd basically told him to go home to his wife.

"Why don't you ask Stuart Little to come over and eat your rabbit with you?"

"Maybe I will," Peaches responded.

"Guys," Liam pleaded. "Stop."

"I saw you kiss him," Greg said.

"Yeah, and I enjoyed it."

"Mom?"

Greg ignored his pleading son. Liam was seventeen, he could handle it. When Peaches was in labor with Liam she'd growled at Greg like a rabid dog and shouted expletives at him. Somehow it helped. If Peaches needed to fight now, he could fight.

"Fuck your flirting. And fuck your rabbit," Greg said ridiculously. He tore off his socks and hurled them across the kitchen, inside out, to rile her up even more.

"Dad!"

"Fuck *you,*" Peaches snapped. "It's your fault the dog died."

"Mom, please."

But they kept on ignoring him, and Liam fled the room.

In his room, Liam fumed. Why was everything so messed up? His dog was dead, his parents

365

hated each other, and he'd totally messed things up with Shy. They were practically about to have sex and then he'd left his backpack in the park and got so worried that someone was going to steal it and his calculus textbook with it that he'd basically abandoned her, half undressed, without any explanation. He'd gotten an 89 on his calc test the next morning, which was totally unacceptable, his lowest grade ever, and he'd been in a foul mood ever since. Not that he blamed Shy.

Fucking Bruce, that's who he blamed. If Bruce hadn't burned down the schoolyard, his mom wouldn't have been mad at him all the time and he wouldn't have developed this complex that he didn't deserve to have things work out, that he deserved things to be fucked up and to not be able to talk to or even text an apology to his girlfriend. Okay, so he hadn't officially asked her to be his girlfriend, but fuck that, she was his girlfriend. If she didn't already know that, she was an idiot. She was too busy being obsessed with their Latin teacher anyway. Fuck him. Fuck her.

Liam's phone vibrated and he pulled it out of his back pocket. It was a selfie from Ryan, who was in London now, being a model. He was at a pub, a full pint glass of beer pressed against his grinning, expensively moisturized cheek.

#nodrinkingage the text read.

Sublime had gotten in huge trouble for their

offensive mock protest and using the anti-gun movement to sell merchandise. They'd had to take down all their posters and every social media post from "the drop." But Ryan had already been scouted and picked up by a modeling agency by then. No sixteen-year-old had worn a dying tiger on his chest so well. He'd put school on hold until the new year and was actually using the name Black Ryan professionally. He kept sending Liam annoying texts with pictures of himself wearing cool clothes, sauntering down some famous London or Paris street: Fish and Chips and Chanel on Carnaby Street! Je t'aime trés bien asshole! He'd already done a photo shoot on a yacht in the Mediterranean for Vilebrequin swim trunks and driven a McLaren in Monte Carlo. Get out here, bruh! he urged. Milan is next! But no one at any modeling agency had invited Liam to London or Paris or Milan.

Liam kicked the legs of his bed and the back of his desk chair. He sat down on his bed and then bounced back up again.

"Fuck," he muttered to himself. "Fuck, fuck, fuck."

His cell phone vibrated again and he leapt at it. It was Shy, finally.

I fucking won a fucking table tennis match you cunt!

She sounded happy. Liam didn't answer. He didn't want to be a buzzkill. Luckily his dad had introduced him to the Smiths, whose music was moody and morose. He stuck in his earbuds and put his phone on Do Not Disturb.

"I almost died today," Wendy announced when she finally returned home to Strong Place with the U-Haul.

Roy was exactly where she'd left him six hours ago—in the library, furiously typing on his laptop.

"I'll need your help, and Shy's too, unloading the U-Haul van. I have to return it by nine p.m." She poured herself a glass of white wine and drank the entire glass standing up. "I'd like to do it soon so I can take a shower."

Roy did not look up. He was completely engrossed in his writing, which was nice to see, but also infuriating. She really had almost died.

"I believe the person who dismembered that woman whose body parts they've been finding in the water is alive and well and living on the far side of Staten Island."

"Almost finished," Roy said without looking up. He'd been typing like a madman ever since the table tennis. He'd come to love Isabel's Russian family so much he'd decided to pare down the assassin nonsense and amp up the amusement of sneaking her family members onto Mars. He'd also thrown in a lot of pregnant table tennis. There were some sad bits too. Now he was working on one of his trademark optimistic endings.

"Where's Shy? Oh, of course, she's at a match," Wendy said, answering her own question. She really did need a bath. The essence of serial killer was all over her. She poured herself a second glass of wine, wishing Roy would get out of his chair and embrace her and make her sit down and put her feet up and tell him all about her near-death experience while he fixed her a Kir Royale and Camembert and crackers.

"Done," Roy announced, triumphantly hitting a final key and closing his laptop. "I might need to tinker with it and add a brilliant last line and pad it out quite a bit, but it's mostly there. I'd like to give it to you to read. See what you think."

"I almost died," Wendy repeated. She tossed aside her phone and gulped her wine. She didn't want to read the rough draft of Roy's new book. In fact, that was the last thing she wanted to do. He always said he threw out about 75 percent of his first drafts because they were completely inane. He could show it to his school nurse friend, his reader, the one all the men in the neighborhood seemed to lust after. Or his skinny, nervous, suit-and-tie-wearing friend who couldn't handle his liquor. Or his friend's crazy artist wife. Or his twenty-eight-year-old agent, for Christ's sake—that was her job.

For the first time Roy noticed that his wife looked particularly harried and even a bit drunk.

"Was the traffic awful? I thought it might be on a Friday. I can unload the U-Haul and return it to the garage if you'd like to have a bath," he said gently.

Wendy stared at him. What was the point?

The front door clicked and Shy flounced into the house. She ran the kitchen tap and drank straight from the stream.

"I won at table tennis." She slurped some more water. "I'm starving. What are we having for dinner?"

"I went to watch for a bit. She's quite good," Roy shouted from the other room.

"Mr. Streko has been a bit of an arse lately, but at least he let me play. I thought maybe his cat was sick, but then he posted a picture of his cat looking totally fine. I asked Dad to leave because we were having a team meeting after," Shy explained breathlessly. "I still can't believe I won. The other girl was pretty crap. But maybe it's my talent. Maybe I'll go to the Olympics."

"The team could do with a proper coach," Roy put in from the library. He didn't like that Streko, not one bit.

"I almost died," Wendy said for the hundredth time.

Shy snatched up her mother's wineglass and

took a sip. "I'm going to take a shower," she announced and dashed upstairs.

"I'll unload the wood," Roy said, and began collecting his keys, jacket, and shoes.

Wendy retrieved the bottle of wine from the fridge and took it upstairs with her. They didn't care whether she worked at *Fleurt* or *Enjoy!* or the *National Enquirer*, or that she'd just survived a terrifying encounter with a serial killer. In fact, the problem with having a family at all was that nobody noticed if you were dead or alive until dinner went unmade and they found your torso floating in the dirty water behind Ikea.

PART V

NOVEMBER 5

Chapter 23

C ome in, come in!"
     Roy Clarke led the group of newly arrived neighbors into the house, through the kitchen, and into the library.

"I should say, 'Come out.' The party is outside in the garden, just through the French doors. It's a bit chilly, but the fire will take care of that. It's going to be enormous."

"Thanks so much for doing this. What a treat." A chubby man wearing thick glasses, a plaid wool shirt, and hiking boots held out his hand for Roy to shake. "Your wife stopped by the store yesterday. She said you've written a draft of a new book. I'm excited."

Roy could not remember ever having met this man.

"Yes, yes. Good to see you. I gave the draft to Wendy to read." Roy shook the man's hand, trying to place him. He seemed like the type to own a store that sold complicated backpacks, freeze-dried camping meals, and mosquito netting.

The man laughed and patted his puffy pink cheeks. "It's Jefferson. From Smith Corner Books? I shaved, I shaved. No beard, no beard!"

Aha. Jefferson, owner of the not-so-new-anymore bookstore where Roy had made his

Brooklyn debut over a year ago. Roy had only been inside the bookshop maybe once or twice since moving in. Wendy went all the time—just to browse, she said, although he suspected she was really making sure they kept the Roy Clarke Rainbow in stock.

"Full disclosure: Wendy forwarded the manuscript to me. I read it yesterday in one sitting. 'Blast Off, Roy Clarke!'—that's the headline of the prepublication review I'm going to submit to *Publishers Weekly*. You really outdid yourself this time."

Roy was horrified. Wendy had sent the bookstore man his possibly terrible new book?

"Shabba Ranks for your help, Claire," he mumbled nervously in Cockney rhyming slang.

But Jefferson had already barged past him and into the library. He threw his arms wide and spun around in a circle. "I'm in the home of one of my favorite living authors!" he shouted exultantly before dancing out the French doors.

Roy hung back as more guests followed Jefferson outside. They knew who Roy was, even if he wasn't quite sure he knew them, but they were either too intimidated or too rude to stop and introduce themselves.

He could not mistake the hairy, tattooed creature skulking past him and making a beeline for the food tables in the garden: Streko. Shy must have invited him. Well, he had nerve.

"Food's over there. Drinks by the fence," Roy shouted aggressively after him. "Take as much as you like, there's plenty!"

The garden was large and had been designed and planted by a botanist from the Brooklyn Botanic Gardens, a former tenant of the previous owners. Two enormous rhododendron bushes, their leaves still green and shiny, divided the brick-walled space into thirds: a slate-paved patio area featuring a massive teak table laden with food; a grassy area where the drinks table was—large enough for groups to mingle, lounge on various weathered wooden benches, or duck behind an evergreen completely out of sight; and a potential vegetable patch, where the bonfire had been erected.

Gabby and Manfred had insisted that Wendy hire a caterer, even though Wendy wanted to order all the food from Full Plate and prepare it herself. "It's not dinner," she insisted. "Just nibbles and wine and beer."

"That's what caterers are for," Gabby had advised.

Gabby and Manfred had been called away to LA by *Enjoy!* and *Fleurt* to cover Meghan Markle and Prince Harry's Bonfire Night party in person. Wendy should have been annoyed that she hadn't been called away to LA too, but in fact it was a relief.

Wendy's nerves were fried. She'd stayed up very

late last night trying and failing to read Roy's book. It was either brilliant or awful, she couldn't tell. Did it have to be set on Mars? Why not in Marfa, Texas? Or Lima, Peru? Was Mars a metaphor for something she didn't understand? Roy had gone to Oxford. She'd only gone to NYU.

Roy kept shooting her anxious, hopeful glances—even in his sleep. She knew he was waiting for a report. But the truth was, just like so many of his so-called fans, Wendy had never been able to get all the way through a Roy Clarke novel, not even *Orange*.

How would she tell him? There were so many things she needed to tell.

She stood by the food, rearranging the cheese knives and gulping champagne. Was it the cheese, or did the garden smell like pot?

Oh, what were they doing? Americans didn't even celebrate Bonfire Night—they didn't even know what it was.

One person was definitely celebrating. Ted Little was having a blast, lighting small objects on fire and tossing them on top of the still unlit pyre. He'd even found an aerosol can of insect repellent and was repeatedly spraying it and lighting the spray with the lighter he'd found in the schoolyard.

Ted couldn't believe no one was yelling.

"That's a cool trick," the school nurse said appreciatively. "I'm glad you're feeling better."

"Do it again," said the nice mom of his babysitter. It was even her house.

"Again!" his mom panted while doing jumping jacks. Lately she was always doing jumping jacks. Or giving herself facials. Or plucking her eyebrows.

Off in the corner, his dad smoked a little purple pipe, his skateboard propped up against the garden wall.

"Dude," a hairy man approached him and reached for his purple pipe. "Your song 'Omnia Vincit!' is what made me want to be a Latin teacher."

Ted lit another shot of insect repellent, then another, and another.

Liam sat cross-legged on the grass, half-hidden by a rhododendron bush. Shy spotted his worn gray pants and old Converse sneakers from her bedroom window and came down to talk to him.

"Mum can't be happy. The whole garden stinks of weed. Why didn't you come up? Why're you being weird?"

"I'm not being weird," Liam grumbled, even though he knew he was.

"You never answered my texts. Are you mad at me?"

"Yes. No. I don't know," he said miserably.

"Hello, Daughter." Shy's father stood over them, wielding a cocktail glass, looking larger and older than usual. A button was missing from his cardigan. "Did you invite that git of a Latin teacher to our party?"

"Dad," Shy complained, "Liam and I are talking. Also, the whole neighborhood is here. It's fine. I can invite who I like."

Liam hadn't noticed Mr. Streko arrive, but he saw him now, stuffing food into his mouth, gross neck tattoo bulging. He wished Shy hadn't invited him either.

"I'm hoping he'll make me captain next year," Shy observed. "I thought I should make an effort."

Mr. Streko glanced over at them, tossed his half-eaten plate of food into the unlit fire, and headed in their direction, already holding a hairy paw out to Roy.

"*Salve*, Mr. Clarke. I just wanted to let you know there's no hard feelings."

Roy's limp grasp grew firmer as he took in the ridiculousness of the man's orange-and-blue tattoo of a smiling baseball.

"You weren't going to let my daughter play that match before I turned up."

"Dad," Shy complained from the grass.

Liam appreciated the fact that Shy's father seemed to hate Mr. Streko as much as he did. Go, Mr. Clarke.

"Yeah, but it turns out she's pretty good. So I'm going to have to let her play." Mr. Streko pulled his hand away from Roy's iron grip and gestured toward the unlit bonfire. *"Ignis aurum probat."*

Shy jumped to her feet. " 'Fire tests gold.' Seneca. It was one of your tweets."

Roy sucked in his stomach and swizzled the weak gin and tonic around in his glass. Mr. Streko was just like the scientists in his book, except smarmier. He was diabolical.

" 'Fire tests gold,' " he repeated. "I like that." The book was only a rough first draft. He could still work it in.

"Dad." Shy imitated her mother's controlled, bordering on controlling tone. "Why don't you go see if Mum needs help."

Roy peered down at Liam. He seemed even more glum than usual. He'd interrupted something, a lovers' quarrel. "I'll leave you to it."

Mr. Streko backed away toward the drinks table. "Great party," he said to no one in particular.

Wendy had just poured herself a second or third or fourth glass of champagne. Five o'clock. The sky was darkening. The garden was nearly full of happily chatting people. The caterers had everything under control. The bonfire was piled high and ready to be lit. There was the neatly stacked firewood, the old door, the broken chairs, the dismantled picnic table, and the "Guy," supplied by Roy's friend Tupper and his extremely odd, extremely tall, artist wife. It was a broad-shouldered, yellow-haired, orange-faced papier-mâché "Guy" wearing a flammable blue tie and a shiny gray flammable double-breasted suit. He looked very much like the recent president, whose name no one spoke out loud. They'd strung him from a rope tied beneath his arms and hung him from the upended leg of the picnic table, where he dangled helplessly, head down, shoulders stooped.

She'd asked Roy to give a brief explanation of the meaning of Bonfire Night before the fire was lit. Roy said it wasn't necessary, but Wendy didn't want the whole neighborhood to think they were psychotic bonfire worshippers. Criminals, actually, considering the fireworks. She was about to go tap him on the shoulder and remind him to say a few words, but Roy was deep in conversation with Tupper and Elizabeth Paulsen, so she stayed away.

Stuart was with Mandy tonight, but not *with* Mandy. Since discovering her fakery, he'd maintained an imaginary distance. He even taunted her a bit, just to test her.

"Which is better, beer or wine, to mix with your meds?" he asked. "I hear unpasteurized cheese is dangerous for MS sufferers."

Mandy was unruffled. She'd been faking so long, she'd become an expert. "Dr. Goldberg says it doesn't matter, as long as I take my vitamins and eat well and get plenty of sleep and sunshine."

She looked beautiful tonight. If Stuart wasn't so angry he'd write a song about her.

> *You lie like a rug, like a kick to my face*
> *But I see you, girl. Fucking pump that bass!*

He'd installed one of Tupper Paulsen's Macaws in the kitchen, to record the extent of her deceit. She had a CrossFit trainer now. They pushed the bed out of the way to get his equipment in. Other than working out, getting the mail and stuffing it under the bed, and cooking elaborate meals from boxed gourmet food delivery services, she still spent most of her time in bed on her iPad. Watching the surveillance footage was actually really boring.

Their son Ted was eating a huge pile of macaroni-and-cheese balls and poking the "Guy" in the foot with his fork. Had they raised Ted wrong? Stuart wondered. Was he fucked up too? It was difficult to know, but Stuart suspected their son was badly behaved. How did you socialize an only child? Going to parties like this was probably a good start, except there were no other young kids, just Roy's daughter and Peaches' son, who were sitting very close to each other on the grass with their limbs intertwined and their heads bowed, talking.

That used to be Stuart and Mandy. They used to be all over each other. And he was still hot for her, or would be if he wasn't so angry. Spending almost all your time in bed for no reason was not cool, not when your husband was working at a job that bored him and your son was getting picked up from school by weirdos who taught him to play Dungeons & Dragons and tempted him with fire. How could she lie to him? In what scenario was lying to your husband/best friend/roommate/only person who really cares about you in the world/father of your kid about having a major debilitating disease a good idea? He had to tell her how pissed off he was. It was just so selfish and lazy and crazy of her. Wasn't it? Wasn't it?

Mandy's black hair was so shiny. Her dark blue denim jacket looked fantastic against her pale skin. Her black eyebrows had a fierce new upward slant. She had it going on tonight.

"What are they waiting for?" Mandy demanded. "It's pretty darn dark already." She leaned into Stuart and took a swig from her beer. "I feel good tonight. I feel like I'm twenty years old."

"Why wouldn't you feel good?" Stuart muttered bitterly.

Mandy took a step back. "What's up? Are you mad at me?"

Stuart didn't know where to begin. He wasn't just mad, he was affronted. He and Mandy and the guys in his band used to pull pranks on their teachers and friends in high school all the time. Mandy was still his best friend. Couldn't he at least have been in on it?

"Remember the first time I got pot for you?" he said, deciding to take it slow. "You hadn't been outside in a while. We went and sat on the stoop. It was a nice night."

Mandy smiled. "It was a really nice night." She looked up at the darkening sky. A star or two twinkled overhead. "Tonight is a nice night."

"Wendy? Should I fetch a torch?" Roy shouted from an open window above their heads. A few people laughed. Roy Clarke was so hilariously English. It was fun to be in his home.

"I'll get it, Daddy," Shy Clarke shouted back.

"It was nicer for me when I didn't know you were faking it," Stuart finally said. Fuck taking it slow. "Your MS. You don't have MS. You never did."

Mandy sucked in her breath. Stuart knew. It sounded like he'd known for a while. She felt so stupid. But did he really have to be such a dick about it? If she'd gone to all the trouble to formulate such an elaborate lie, she must have been in a bad place to begin with. Where was his compassion?

"I don't know, maybe I've watched too many bad movies, but it made sense to me. I wanted to stay in bed, so I gave myself a reason to stay in bed."

"So you fucking lied to me about going to the doctor and all the vitamins you had to take? And what about the prescriptions; you faked those too?"

"Yeah, I just put Midol and vitamin C in old prescription bottles," Mandy admitted. "I did leave the house though. I got better. All those great meals I made?" She left out the part about the stolen food boxes. Maybe stealing was a side effect of lying. Anyway, she'd just paid for her very own Grandma's House subscription. The first box was coming tonight.

"But you lied. To me and Ted. And what about the pot? You kept telling me how much it was helping. Helping with what?" Stuart could hear his voice getting louder and louder but he couldn't stop. A few people moved away from them and closer to the bonfire, which Roy was dousing with lighter fluid.

"The more I think about it, the more I realize I just *needed* to," Mandy said slowly. She and Stu had been together too long for her to get defensive and make up a whole bunch of reasons for pretending to be sick. "I don't really know what else to say. I feel better knowing that you know, if that makes any sense. At first it was sort of fun, sneaking around, but then I just felt crazy."

"It is crazy. It's fucking completely fucking crazy!" Stuart was yelling now.

"Sorry to butt in, but are you guys okay?" Peaches listed over to them with a creepy smile on her face. She looked disheveled and drunk. Every time Stuart thought he was in love with her he realized Mandy was maybe fatter, but much hotter.

Peaches could feel Greg watching them from the terrace. She'd been avoiding him since they arrived. He so desperately wanted her to introduce him to Stuart Little.

"She knows," Stuart growled. "I mean she knows I know."

"Uh-huh," Peaches tossed her beer bottle into the still-unlit bonfire, smashing the glass. "So maybe it's not such a big deal."

Mandy hated the irreverent, flirty, I-don't-have-to-kiss-your-ass-because-I-know-you-have-a-crush-on-me way that Peaches always addressed Stu. It was so inappropriate. She was Ted's school nurse. What was she trying to achieve anyway? It wasn't passive aggressive, it was just aggressive. Peaches was a mind-fucker, but then again, so was she.

"What's not a big deal?" Wendy Clarke trilled, picking up fallen paper napkins and discarded glasses as she moved toward them. She obviously got off on being a hostess. She was in high gear.

"Mandy doesn't have MS," Peaches explained flatly. "Sorry, Mandy, your husband told me a while ago. People come into the nurse's office and they say things. It's weird. It's like I'm Lucy in the *Peanuts* cartoons, in my little shrink's hut, waiting for people to unload their problems." She tugged on the zipper of her leather jacket. "And their lice."

Stuart ran his fingers through his hair. He felt ganged-up on. This was supposed to be a big confrontation with his wife. He wished the other women would just butt out.

"When I was in fifth grade, I told everyone I had a sister who was sick at home, just like in *Little Women*. I kept the lie up all the way through middle school," Wendy said. She'd just remembered this.

"We're lighting it, Wendy. Is that all right?" Roy shouted from the other side of the garden. Tupper held a Zippo lighter beneath Guy's feet.

"I've never read any of my husband's books. Not one. He has no idea," Wendy blurted out. "Also, I got fired from my job and never told him."

Mandy giggled. "Wendy!"

Wendy took Mandy's beer and finished it. "That bonfire is never going to light. We need gasoline or something."

"Vodka," Peaches said, and snorted.

"Ted would love to light it," Mandy said. It was such a relief having Wendy and Peaches there to diffuse the tension. Stuart was too distracted to be angry anymore.

"Where is Ted?" he said.

"You know, my husband, Greg, is dying to meet you," Peaches told him disparagingly. "He's a musician. He wants to make a kids' album with you."

"Oh yeah?" Stuart wasn't sure if he was just pretending to be interested or if he was actually interested. How could he make a kids' album when his mind was so fucking full of fucking pissed-off expletives, bitch?

"Here we go!"

With a fiery whoosh the Guy burst into flames, crackling and burning thrillingly fast. The orange features of his face disappeared first, then his heavy blond wig, his shiny gray suit. Soon he was just blackened twigs hanging from a smoldering rope, and the picnic table, door, and chairs were alight.

"That was some Guy," remarked a hairy man with a hideous orange-and-blue baseball tattoo on his neck. "Did you know that during the Great Fire of Rome, Nero just watched from a hilltop, singing and playing his lyre, like he was thrilled the whole damned shithouse was going up in flames?"

The man was addressing her, Elizabeth realized. She inhaled and then exhaled slowly. She could do this. She could make chitchat with the natives.

He swigged his beer. "I like your outfit."

Elizabeth was wearing her orange prison jumpsuit. "Thank you. I got it at Rikers."

"*Neque fimina amissa pudicitia alia abnuerit.* Tacitus. A woman after losing her virtue will hesitate at nothing."

Was he hitting on her? Elizabeth was at a loss.

Tupper returned from stoking the fire and wound a skinny arm around her waist. "I keep hearing compliments about our Guy."

"You made that? Seriously?" the hairy man marveled. "So cool to be able to make stuff. I'm a Latin guy. I teach Latin."

Elizabeth ignored him. The fire had set her mind ablaze. Why had she never worked with fire? There were dormant volcanoes in Iceland. She could bring fire to them. It would be a huge project. She'd need helicopters. Except she wasn't going to Iceland.

"Remember *Deus ex Machina* at Bard?" Tupper said. "We went to a discount Christmas place and bought out every elf in the shop."

Elizabeth rested her long cheek on his bony shoulder. She didn't have to go to Iceland alone. He could come with her. There was nothing keeping them in Cobble Hill. With his MacArthur money they could go anywhere.

"What are we celebrating again?" Tupper heard someone ask as the fire crackled and roared.

"That time when Big Ben almost got blown up but didn't. It's a big thing in England."

"This is way better than Halloween," someone else said. "Except for that crazy trail of arms and legs someone did this year. That was fucking awesome."

"It's definitely better than waiting on hold for two hours while Full Plate tries to figure out what's been happening to our orders."

"Hey, our orders have been messed up too!"

Above their heads, on the landing outside the kitchen, Roy Clarke banged a fork against a glass.

"I just wanted to thank you for sharing this fun English tradition with us. If you have old shoes, useless children, or too-tight jumpers that need getting rid of, you are more than welcome to throw them into the fire. And please help yourselves to more food and drink. Wendy loathes leftovers. Thanks very much. Enjoy!"

Roy descended the stairs and joined Tupper, Elizabeth, and the abominable Mr. Streko beside the fire. "I see you've met Shy's Latin teacher."

"*Salve*," Mr. Streko said and swigged his empty beer bottle uncomfortably.

Roy had never been much of a bully, but he enjoyed making Mr. Streko nervous. It distracted him from the fact that Wendy was avoiding him. Roy was becoming all the things he hated tonight—a bully, an insecure husband, an overly confident host. Or maybe he'd always been all of those things and he was only just discovering it.

"These two are brilliant artists," he blathered on. "They created the Guy."

"Brilliant," Mr. Streko agreed and shook his empty beer bottle. "Good thing you guys have five bathrooms. Hey, is that your weed I'm smelling?" he asked Elizabeth.

"So, we're still friends, platonically speaking?" Shy didn't mean to be pushy, but something about Liam brought out the pushy in her.

"I guess." Liam ripped up handfuls of grass and tossed them behind him.

"Good." Shy eased her butt off the ground and into his lap. She settled her shoulders against his chest. It wasn't very platonic.

Her Gucci sneakers were muddy and her black jeans were torn and frayed. Liam ran his thumb over her skin through one of the tears. "I'm sorry. I've been in a bad mood all weekend. My dog died. My family sucks. I didn't want to drag you into it. Congratulations on the Ping-Pong tournament or whatever."

"Shhshh."

Liam stopped talking.

"*Volo enim vos eritis mihi in amans?*"

"I have no idea what you just said."

"That's probably because I'm failing Latin now. I asked you to be my boyfriend."

Actually she'd asked him to be her concubine, because there was no word for "boyfriend" in

Latin except *amasiunculus*, which sounded like a disease that made your penis fall off.

Liam shifted his weight. Having Shy in his lap was almost impossible to endure bonerless. "I thought I already was."

"Okay, good."

Shy leaned back against him. Across the grassy area of the garden Mr. Streko was hungrily watching some guy who looked like he'd just stepped off a yacht in the South of France roll him a joint. She wasn't in love with Mr. Streko anymore, she realized. She might still follow him on Twitter, and she might consider taking AP Latin with him next year, but Mum was right—his neck tattoo was gross.

Liam rubbed his chin against her hair. He didn't know why he'd been so bummed out. He was in an absurdly good mood now.

The party was crowded and boring. The big man-doll thing had melted too fast, and now the fire was boring too. Ted shoved an aerosol can of insect repellent into his sweatpants pockets, picked up his father's abandoned skateboard, and walked down the little side alley that led out of the garden and onto the sidewalk.

The streetlights were bright. He rode the skateboard down Strong Place and up Kane Street toward home. He turned on Cheever and tucked the skateboard under his arm. A blue-and-white checkered box from Grandma's House was on his stoop. Cardboard was paper, so it probably burned.

Crouching on the stoop beside the box, he sprayed a corner of it with insect repellent, flicked his lighter, and held it close. The box caught fire. It burned even better than he'd thought it would. The flames weren't small and lame. They were tall and blue.

Now the whole top of the box was on fire. The white label with his mom's name on it turned black, curled off the box, and flew up into the air like a smoking bird.

Something inside the box popped. "Pop, pop, pop!" It sounded like popcorn from the movie theater.

Ted backed down the steps and sat on the bottom one. Was the whole box going to blow?

Instead, the box seemed to implode. Little burning bits trailed up into the night sky, like fireflies. There was a lot of smoke.

"Holy shit."

Bruce Cardozo, master of the epic light-the-slide-on-fire-with-vodka trick, was riding his bike around the neighborhood. Nothing made him feel so free and independent and fully fucking alive as when he was on his bike in the dark, just cruising. Plus, it was nice to get away from his older sisters, who told him he smelled

like dirty underwear and called him "the fat kid."
He stopped when he saw the smoke. The house
was dark, lit up only by the glow of a single
streetlight.

"Hey, little kid. Get away from there. That
house is burning."

"That's my house," the kid said. He pointed
upstairs. "The label went into that window. It was
on fire."

"Are your parents home?"

The kid shook his head. "They're at a party.
There was supposed to be a huge bonfire, but I
thought it was lame."

"Can you show me where they are?"

The little kid shook his head no. Bruce
straddled his bike, wondering what to do. There
were actual flames coming out of the upstairs
window now. The block was eerily quiet. The
houses were all dark. There was no one around.
They were probably all at the party. Bruce turned
back to speak to the kid, but the kid wasn't there.
The front door of the house stood open. The little
fucker had gone inside.

"Ladies."

The scent of warm cashmere permeated the
air. Peaches looked up from where she, Wendy,
and Mandy were huddled around the bonfire,
drinking.

"Dr. Conway!"

The doctor looked even more perfect than usual in the firelight. His silver hair glistened. His teeth and skin were flawless.

"Guys, this is Dr. Conway, aka Dr. Feelgood," Peaches introduced him. "He's the best."

The doctor had wonderfully soft hands. "And what kind of doctor are you exactly?" Wendy asked, already thinking she could do a feature on him for *Enjoy!*.

"Actually, he's more Mandy's doctor than mine," Peaches said. "Mandy's the one with MS," she clarified.

"Except not really." Mandy shook the doctor's hand. He seemed more amused than anything.

"And is there anything I can help you with right now?" he asked, his blue eyes twinkling.

"Oh, you betcha." Peaches backed away into the shadow of a rhododendron bush.

"Anyone else?" the good doctor offered, following her.

"Absofuckinglutely," Mandy said, following right behind them.

"Oh." Wendy understood now that Dr. Conway wasn't a medical doctor. "I probably shouldn't—"

She stole a glance at Roy, chatting with Tupper and Elizabeth on the other side of the bonfire. Someone had put on music—the Eagles. She loved the Eagles.

"Wait for me!" she called, following her new friends.

Chapter 24

Ted?" Stuart padded down the upstairs hall-way. The Clarkes' house was huge. Empty bedroom. Empty bathroom. Linen closet. Another bathroom. He came to a closed door and stopped. "Ted?" he called out again and opened the door.

It was Roy Clarke's daughter's room. She was under the sheet with Peaches' son. Clothes were piled on the floor beside the bed. Her Gucci sneakers had been kicked askance. A purple lava lamp cast a bacchanalian glow.

"Sorry."

Shy giggled beneath the sheet. "Is he gone?"

"Sorry." Stuart backed into the hallway and closed the door.

Peaches' hat-wearing husband was alone in the living room thumbing through a shelf of vinyl records, a pair of noise-canceling headphones slung around his neck.

"Hey, man," Stuart greeted him. "Have you seen my kid?"

"No. No, I haven't." Greg gestured at the record collection. "It's impressive they own vinyl. Their sound system is amazing. But their taste in music is terrible."

Stuart walked over to examine the records. The Eagles. Elton John. Eric Clapton. Cat Stevens.

Harry Chapin. The Beatles. "Eric Clapton's cool." He held out his hand for Greg to shake. "I'm Stuart. We haven't officially met yet. You're Peaches' husband."

Greg nodded, unsure whether to punch the guy or shake his hand.

"Yeah. Greg Park." He shook Stuart's hand. He was not going to pass up this chance. "So hey, I've been sort of aware of your career and like, the fact that we're practically neighbors and I was wondering. I've written a bunch of kids' songs? But I kind of need, like, a collaborator."

Peaches had already warned him, so Stuart was not surprised. "That's cool."

"I want it to be very cool, you know, not boring," Greg went on excitedly. He took off his hat and ran his fingers through his curly, graying hair. "I want to sort of reinvent the kids' album. I want it to sound like, I don't know, Jimi Hendrix and Woody Guthrie meet like, the Clash, meet like, the Blind Mice," he added with a smile.

Stuart sat down on the arm of a sofa. "Wow. Okay. Do you play an instrument?"

Greg grinned giddily. "Sure. I'm a music teacher. I play everything."

"Fire!" Bruce shouted, circling blocks on his bike.

Where the fuck were the parents of that sicko fucking idiot kid?

"Fire!"

• • •

"I'm against it, usually." Wendy took another hit on Mandy's nifty little steam-pipe and blew out a tremendous stream of skunky vapor. "I mean, how will the trains run on time? How will FedEx deliver the next day? How will doctors finish medical school and transplant lungs, if everyone is high?"

She passed the pipe to Peaches, aware of the fact that she was repeating herself but unsure now with whom she'd broached this topic before.

Peaches handed Dr. Conway the pipe. He took a quick hit and handed it back. He seemed like he'd had a lot of practice.

"I haven't smoked this stuff since college," Peaches said, taking another hit. "It's smoother now, seems like."

"I'm glad you like it, it's—" Dr. Conway began.

"I feel weird," Mandy said, cutting him off. She sounded anxious. "This is different from what we got before."

"It is," Dr. Conway said. His voice was velvety and smooth. "It's the party version."

A blond head loomed just beyond their little gathering.

"Elizabeth." Wendy coughed hoarsely. "Come join us!"

Elizabeth had left Tupper and Roy to set up the fireworks. "Hello," she said.

"Hello. Hello," Wendy trilled. "I'm glad you're out of prison."

"Totally." Peaches handed Elizabeth the pipe. "This neighborhood would be so fucking boring without you."

Elizabeth took the pipe and held it between her lips. Wendy Clarke caressed her orange jumpsuited elbow. A carefully dressed man with perfect skin and teeth was watching her closely.

"Careful, it's pretty strong," he warned.

She inhaled deeply, holding her breath as she passed the pipe to Wendy. Wendy took a hit and handed it to Pretty Man. He took a hit and handed it to Snow White in Denim. She waved it away.

"I need to get inside," Mandy said. It was more of a demand than a request. "*Now*, please."

"We can go inside." Wendy released her hold on Elizabeth and linked arms with Mandy. "I think there might still be some leftover lasagna in the kitchen."

"No. Not inside *your* house. Inside *my* house," Mandy insisted.

Roy stabbed the pointed stick-end of one of the larger firecrackers into the grass. "Shine the torch over here a moment, would you?" he told Tupper.

Tupper and Roy were unwrapping the fireworks from their colorful Chinese paper wrappers and setting them up in the dark, grassy area at the foot of the garden near the brick wall. The empty lot behind Roy and Wendy's house belonged to a church and was used for parking. It was almost possible they might get away with their Bonfire Night extravaganza without disturbing the neighborhood at all.

A *torch,* Tupper thought, feeling suddenly inspired. A real torch. He could start with a blowtorch and alter it. Dragons breathed fire, but that was too obvious. It might be more fun if it were something innocuous breathing the fire, like a ladybug or a panda or even a non-animal thing, like a fork or a shoe. A sock? He couldn't wait to get back to his studio to try it out.

"What are we lighting these with?" Elizabeth demanded, crashing out of a rhododendron bush. She wished she had the wooden oar from her *Adam and Eve* series. A burning oar would be perfect.

In her stoned artist's mind she'd already set off a volcanic eruption and interrupted the Icelandic weather patterns. They could track it via satellite. She'd have to get NASA or some government weather command center involved, which would have been easier if she'd been awarded a MacArthur, but that was where Tupper could be of use.

"I'll make something we can work with," Tupper offered. "A real torch." He began to whittle a large stick with his Swiss Army knife and, using his belt and an old nail, fashioned it into a barbecue lighter that would stay permanently lit.

Tupper was so capable, Elizabeth thought. He just needed to stretch himself. Iceland called. It was calling them both.

Roy Clarke caught her eye and handed her an enormous firecracker. "You're the resident criminal," he joked. "If anyone comes to arrest us, we'll just say it was you."

"Don't anyone get too close to the fire, because it's very big and very hot," Roy heard Wendy caution from the other side of the garden. Her voice sounded slow and hoarse, like a record put on at the wrong speed.

Roy ripped open another firework wrapper and stabbed the end into the dirt. She must have thought the new book was terrible. That was why she was avoiding him.

Elizabeth broke his train of thought. "Look." She pointed up at Shy's bedroom window. "Shadow puppets."

Wendy couldn't leave her own party, especially not before the fireworks had even been lit, and Dr. Conway "had business to attend to," so Peaches had offered to walk Mandy home. Wendy took methodical, stoned sips of her white wine and stumbled deliberately around the fire toward Roy. She didn't know if she could talk to him or anyone else right now, but she needed to be near him.

Roy looked so strong and ebullient, stabbing at the ground with fireworks as he chatted with his artist friends. He needed tasks to perform at parties; otherwise, he hid. Roy was a good man, really. He liked clean clothes and was generally neat. He might not appear to notice things, but from reading snippets and reviews of his books, it was quite clear he noticed everything. He could sit on a cold, empty beach and watch the waves. He liked to leave the window open and listen to the rain. He pretended not to mind that their older daughters, Chloe and Anna, didn't seem to like their parents very much and only appeared for Christmas, but there were versions of Chloe and Anna in every book he'd written. He would rather eat at home than in a restaurant. He did not enjoy parties.

Wendy loved parties and crowded places where she could people-watch. Abandoned beaches bored her. Sitting bored her. Reading lengthy novels bored her. She loved to read restaurant reviews and became extremely irritated when Roy wouldn't try them. It occurred to her that perhaps she was the difficult one.

An animal noise in the dark startled her. It was the Latin teacher, Streko, curled up in the farthest, darkest corner of the garden, half obscured by an evergreen bush. Empty beer bottles lolled in the grass near his tattooed form. An overturned plate leaned against his sneakered foot.

"Wendy? Is that you lurking? Are you all right?" Roy called out to her.

Wendy leaned casually against the garden wall. "Just taking a break," she said, like it was a very normal thing to be standing alone in the dark at your own party. She wondered if she should call his attention to the Latin teacher. She didn't mind it really. Maybe he was tired. Teaching teenagers must be exhausting.

"I'm not sure you're going to like this," Roy said. "But I think something's happening upstairs."

Wendy walked unsteadily toward him, her eyes fixed on Shy's third-floor window. The venetian blinds were closed, but the light was on, casting shadows on the blinds. The shadowy hulk of the bed with two bodies on it was fully visible.

"Oh," Wendy gasped. "Oh."

Roy put his arm around her. "Remember how nice you said it was? Right here in our house. Not at some party with a boy she'd never laid eyes on. He's the school nurse's son and therefore probably very clean?"

Wendy shuddered involuntarily and leaned into her husband. "I did say that."

"It's all right, just don't look up." Roy sounded a bit too delighted. Even in her foggy state, Wendy recognized that note in his voice—when something he'd written actually happened in real life.

"At least they're here, safe with us, and not on Mars," Wendy said, playing along.

Roy squeezed her shoulders. "So, what did you think, anyway. About the book?"

Wendy wished she had more wine or more pot to smoke. It was unavoidable now. She'd have to say something.

"I only skimmed it sort of partially. I noticed there were lots of factual things about space. Words I didn't recognize." Was she slurring? "I thought you hated research."

"I do," Roy harrumphed. *She'd only skimmed it?* "But Google makes it so easy. Scientists are quite serious about us colonizing Mars. I didn't want to offend them. Did you know the atmosphere there is full of water? NASA's got this system called MOXIE to extract it and in the process they can produce oxygen for the people to breathe and to oxygenate the rocket fuel. And if we have water and oxygen, we can probably grow things. There'd be no meat, maybe just grasshoppers and root vegetables and that sort of thing."

Wendy felt guilty that she hadn't tried to read the draft more carefully. Roy was so excited.

"I gave it to Jefferson. He thinks it's genius."

"Yes, he's rather Sheffield United. And I'm quite chuffed. But you only skimmed it."

"I like the idea of turning pee into water," Wendy said, her eyelids drooping.

Roy blanched and stepped away from her so that she staggered backward. Was she making fun of him?

"It's rubbish, isn't it? I should toss it and give up. Maybe I can get a job as a barkeep or something."

Wendy pressed her spine against the bricks of the garden wall in an attempt to maintain her dignity. "I don't know, Roy. I've drunk too much wine and I smoked pot out of a pipe and I have to confess I've never fully been able to read any of your books."

Roy stared at her. "Not even *Orange*?"

Wendy's gaze shifted to the upstairs window. There was no movement on the bed now, just a big lump. Then the lump reared up and she averted her eyes.

"Also, I got fired from *Fleurt*. I work for another magazine now. It's called *Enjoy!*. It's a huge demotion and not even permanent. I'm covering for someone on maternity leave. Oh, and the pay is shit. It's a magazine for people who don't mind spending an entire day at Macy's. But I like it."

"Hey, excuse me."

It was Stuart Little, prowling around in the grass near the Latin teacher. "Sorry to interrupt, but have either of you seen a skateboard? I'm pretty sure I left it right here."

"Our place is just down Kane, left on Cheever," Mandy told Peaches.

"I know." Lately Peaches felt like she knew

406

everything. It was not a good way to feel. It irritated her that she had all the answers and everyone else seemed so lost. She was also quite drunk and very high, which skewed things slightly. "I walked my dog by your house that time. Our dog died. He was a hundred years old."

"I need to cross the street," Mandy commanded. "There's a tunnel attached to the slide in the school playground. I'm going to get inside it."

"Seriously?" Peaches said, but Mandy was already crossing the street.

It was dark now. They peered through the schoolyard fence. The red metal tunnel had survived the fire and remained intact. Trees rustled their dry leaves. The clear, cool November air smelled of smoke from the neighborhood fireplaces.

Mandy led them into the schoolyard, ducked under the police tape, and dove headfirst into the tunnel. It was half the length of her body. She lay on her back with her knees sticking out, her feet on the ground, and sighed contentedly. "It's cozy in here."

"I could use some of these," Elizabeth said, holding a blue firework in place while Tupper lit it.

Tupper felt like he was on vacation. He'd spent so much time alone with Elizabeth, it was a relief to be out with her amongst his neighbors and friends. He'd thought she might scare people, especially after birthing herself out of a smelly sac of goo and then going to prison, but Elizabeth was as much a part of Cobble Hill as Roy and Wendy. If anything, the neighborhood was proud to claim her.

They backed away and the firework shot into the air, exploding into a series of smaller Roman candle–like bursts that went off in rapid succession, hung like blue stars in midair, and then swayed slowly earthward.

"We could do a fireworks show together," Tupper suggested excitedly as he lit the next one. "Maybe up at Bard. Over the Hudson. With lemmings."

This is what separates my work from his, Elizabeth thought. *He always reverts to cute rodents or exotic birds.*

"Maybe," she responded with effort.

She'd thought she would stay or take him with her, but she couldn't. He was happy here. This was where he'd done his best work. He'd earned a MacArthur. And her best work was done separately, elsewhere.

"Who wants to light the red one?" Roy called out. He'd lost track of Wendy while he was helping Stuart Little hunt for his skateboard. They weren't done talking. It was all right that she hadn't read his books. Join the club. And it was all right that she'd been fired from her job if she hated it anyway. Tonight was supposed to be romantic. He and Wendy had gotten engaged on Bonfire Night, a million years ago. She should light the red one.

The fire was enormous. The whole garden was alight. There was Streko, the bum, asleep in the grass. And there was Wendy, talking to a dapper silver-haired gentleman in expensive leather shoes. Wendy looked a bit undone, her eyes drooping at half-mast, her hair wild. She'd been partying like a teenager, but she deserved it.

Elizabeth lit the red one. It shot up into the night sky as she strode toward the house.

"Loo's just through the kitchen," Roy called after her. He looked up at the sky as Tupper set off another one. Shy was missing the fireworks. Maybe Isabel, Ceran, and Bettina could see them from Mars. And maybe he'd throw out this draft—or most of it anyway—and start again.

Fireworks exploded in the sky. Mandy slid down the tunnel so that her head stuck out the bottom. There were red ones that burst into spinning red stars, blue ones that made trippy, slow-falling streaks, white ones that rocketed straight up and burst into perfect circles that sparkled slowly down.

"Whoa," she breathed. "Hope Stu got Ted outside to see this."

She'd asked Wendy to tell Stu to bring Ted home when he was ready. She was operating under the assumption that Ted was in a room somewhere, watching TV.

"Fireworks were invented in medieval China," she said. "To scare away the evil spirits." She'd learned that from Ted.

"Where'd they get these anyway?" Peaches marveled. Greg would be covering his ears right about now. He hated fireworks. "They must have cost a fortune. And I thought they were illegal to buy in New York State."

What the fuck was with the fucking fireworks? Bruce wondered as he peddled furiously up Degraw Street. No one was going to hear him now.

"Fire!"

He felt like fucking Paul Revere.

"Fire!"

"Roy," Wendy called out hoarsely. "Come meet Dr. Conway." It was such a relief to have told Roy what an immense disappointment she was. But Roy and Tupper were busy lighting more fireworks. The fireworks Wendy had retrieved from that Staten Island madman were magnificent, surely stolen from some special display for the Olympics or the coronation of a queen. It was all very professional. Manfred and Gabby would have been impressed. The Windsors would be jealous.

"That's our friend Tupper Paulsen," she explained to the doctor. "He and his wife are very creative. He just won a MacArthur. And she went to prison," she added in a whisper.

"Nothing beats fireworks," Dr. Conway observed, gazing up at the sky. His skin was almost opalescent. He reminded Wendy of the flawless male vampires in the movie *Twilight*, which she and Gabby had just watched in their office one recent afternoon, lying on yoga mats while sampling gelato.

"Roy and I got engaged on Bonfire Night," Wendy told him. "On top of Primrose Hill." It seemed like a hundred years ago, or it could have been yesterday. She sighed heavily. "I'm sorry. I've been in quite a state all day."

"Here."

Dr. Conway handed her a gummy lozenge. Wendy put it in her mouth. She'd decided to succumb to everything tonight.

"I just bought a new banjo," Greg said. Damn these fireworks. Was he talking too loudly? Could Stuart Little hear him at all? With his noise-canceling headphones on it was impossible to tell. "There's a store in Nashville I like to order from. They'll let you try any instrument for a week, free."

"Cool."

Greg had invited Stuart to check out the instruments and recording equipment in his Gowanus basement. They walked up Kane Street toward Court, away from the schoolyard, while fireworks continued to burst overhead.

I bet Ted is loving this, Stuart thought. He assumed Mandy had taken Ted home. He'd texted her to let her know what he was doing and wasn't surprised when she didn't text back. They were both still pretty mad at each other.

Greg was walking quickly. The fireworks seemed to cause him pain.

"Wait up," Stuart called. He wished he'd found his skateboard.

Shy and Liam had spent a lot of time beneath her sheet, reading the hilarious step-by-step instructions inside Liam's battered box of Costco condoms without actually using any of them. They still had on their underwear and most of their clothes. Shy was sure that at any minute her parents were going to bang on the door and ask her to do something completely unnecessary like put the kettle on or rake the leaves. The fireworks were over. Laughter and pot smoke wafted up from the garden.

"I'm starving," Liam said from beneath the sheet.

"Me too," Shy agreed.

"Do you think your parents would mind if we ordered pizza?"

Shy threw off the sheet and reached for her phone.

"I smell something," Mandy said when the fireworks had finally ceased.

"I bet you do," Peaches said. "A bunch of stupid private school teenage assholes including my own son burned this place up last month. It still smells like burning rubber."

How much longer would she have to stand here, waiting for Mandy to get out of the tunnel and go home? There were stars now. The air was cold and clear. She sniffed, then sniffed again, her nose raised like a dog catching a scent.

"Actually, I smell meatloaf. And caramel popcorn. And chocolate cake."

"You just described my entire Grandma's House order," Mandy said from inside the tunnel. "Minus the mashed potatoes and spinach salad. Hey, does anyone have any Fritos?"

Wendy lay on her back in the grass. The fireworks were over. Tupper and Roy and Dr. Conway and the other remaining guests conversed in low, soothing voices. The stars glimmered. The air smelled of fireplaces. The bonfire crackled. Wendy made a mental note to ask Roy if it wouldn't be interesting to have the teenagers in

413

his Mars book smoke Mars-grown marijuana. It seemed plausible. And once their inhibitions were loosened they could do something really crazy, like steal a rover or a rocket or whatever they drove up there and discover new, unknown life-forms.

A stocky teenage boy straddling a bicycle rolled into the garden from the alleyway. Roy must have left the gate unlocked. Wendy pushed herself up on her elbows.

"Fire! Fire! Fire!" the boy shouted. He was red in the face and his eyes bulged.

"Shshh." Wendy heard someone say. Or maybe she'd said it.

"Fire!" the boy shouted again. "There's a kid in the house," he sputtered, his face impossibly red. "I think he's trapped in there. His parents are at a party."

"It's Bonfire Night," Wendy told him.

The boy stared at her with wide, bloodshot eyes. A fire truck roared by, its siren wailing.

"Fire!" he shouted again.

Peaches shivered and squinted up at the stars. Mandy was sure taking her sweet time in the tunnel. She could tell Mandy she'd kissed her husband—that would get her out fast.

A gigantic ladder fire truck whooshed down Kane Street, sirens blasting. It ran the light at Clinton and flew over the speed bumps.

"Dudes," Peaches complained, "this is a school zone. They're going to run over someone."

Inside the tunnel, Mandy checked her texts.

I don't have Ted. I thought you had him.

No, I'm outside with Greg. I'm sure he's fine.

Mandy slid out of the tunnel.

He probs went home by himself. I'm in the schoolyard.

Turning around. Meet you in a sec.

"Sorry, I can't hear you," Greg told Stuart, who had suddenly turned around and was half running, half walking back the way they'd come. "I'd take these off, except those fire trucks are really loud."

Tupper went indoors. Elizabeth had not returned. She must have been chatting with someone in the kitchen.

"Elizabeth?" he called into the empty rooms.

Most of the other guests had left when the fireworks stopped. The caterers were scraping leftovers into tidy Tupperware containers for Wendy to take back to the office to nibble on during the week.

"Have you seen Elizabeth?" Tupper asked them.

"Elizabeth? Tall blonde in the orange prison suit?"

Tupper nodded.

"She just left."

Tupper checked the downstairs bathroom and master bathroom just to be sure. He checked the basement and the towel cupboard and the coat closet. But it was just as the caterers had said. Elizabeth was gone.

"Shy?"

It was her father, right outside the door.

"Don't come in!" Shy and Liam shouted together.

Shy envied the marooned couple in *The Blue Lagoon*. They had way more privacy. Not that she and Liam were doing anything. They'd segued from reading condom instructions to ordering pizza to checking out Black Ryan's recent social media posts. He'd snorkeled in the Seychelles wearing a diamond Chanel necklace and held a blue snake in Australia wearing a tiny red Armani Speedo. Now he was in Texas, making a gun-control PSA. Only celebrities made PSAs. Liam's friend Ryan was famous.

"Leave them alone, Roy!" Shy's mum shouted up the stairs.

Wendy had rallied and shifted into high gear again. There were fires to put out and boys to rescue. If Shy got pregnant tonight, they would deal with that disaster tomorrow.

"Dad, please do not open the door."

"It's all right," her mother called. "We're going out for a bit. You just carry on."

"Thank you, Mum," Shy called back.

Roy peeked out the hallway window, which looked onto the garden. The bonfire had already died down considerably. The man from the bookstore and his girlfriend were toasting marshmallows with the Latin teacher, who, miraculously, was still alive.

"There're a few guests outside," he told Shy through the door. "They're in charge of the bonfire. It's dying down, but I don't want to leave it untended."

"That's fine, Dad. We just ordered pizza."

"Thanks, Mr. Clarke." Liam's crackly teenage boy voice followed Roy down the stairs, causing him to wince.

Kane Street was crammed with fire trucks and heavy-coated firemen. A ladder truck had been implemented. Spotlights had been erected. Fire hoses were connected to every available hydrant. There was a lot of smoke. The air smelled like charred wood and wet carpet.

When it became apparent that the fire was

around the corner on Cheever Place, Stuart, Mandy, Peaches, and Greg began to run.

"That's my house," Stuart sputtered breathlessly at a fireman carrying a walkie-talkie. "My son—do you have him?"

"We're on it, sir," the fireman said. "Please stand on the other side of the street so the men can do their jobs."

Stuart and Mandy backed away. Clinging to each other, they watched the spotlit scene in a confused haze. One of the side effects of Dr. Conway's pot was that it was difficult to concentrate on more than one thing at once. They'd been distracted by the party and Ted had gone home and set it on fire? It hardly seemed possible. Ted was at the bonfire with them. He was having a good time. There was also their shared belief that nothing bad could ever happen to Ted.

The others were not so easily deterred.

"I'm a nurse," Peaches offered. "I'm their nurse."

Greg threw down his headphones and hat. He kicked off his Birkenstocks and unbuttoned his shirt. He was going to help save Stuart Little's son. He was going to help save Stuart Little's house.

There was a lot of shouting from the ladder.

Greg rushed past the firemen and into the smoke.

"Greg!" Peaches shouted after him.

"Ted's fine," Mandy said, clinging to Stuart.

"He's fine," Stuart said into her hair.

A walkie-talkie crackled.

"They're coming out!" someone yelled.

The front doors had been propped open. The glass was broken. Greg emerged in his sooty sock feet carrying a small body wrapped in a bright yellow Ikea blanket. A dark head poked out from the blanket. Ted.

Stuart and Mandy sat on the bottom step of their neighbors' house with Ted between them. Greg sat behind them, the yellow blanket covering his shaking knees. His pant legs were caked in ash. Peaches gave him small sips from a bottle of water and listened to his lungs with a stethoscope.

Roy and Wendy Clarke, Tupper Paulsen, and a stocky, red-faced teenager straddling a bicycle stood behind a police barricade across the street.

"Everything all right?" Wendy shouted.

Peaches gave her the thumbs-up.

Stuart remembered the Macaw. He pulled out his phone and played back the footage. A swath of something burning flew into the open kitchen window. The bills beneath the bed caught fire. Ted came upstairs and poked at the fire with various kitchen implements. Ted left the fire. The fire grew. Firemen peered into the windows and began hosing things down. Greg burst in with his shirt off, grabbed a gallon of organic milk and a gallon of extra-pulp orange juice from out of the fridge and poured them all around the bed.

"Jesus Christ," Stuart said.

Then Greg walked through the kitchen, carrying Ted.

It wasn't as bad as it could have been, the firemen said. Structurally everything was sound. There was a lot of water damage. Good thing some of the windows were open and that kid on his bike had dialed 911.

Mandy rubbed the space between Ted's skinny shoulders. Ted was fine. Their house was fucked, but Ted was fine.

"We're lucky," she said.

"Yeah. Thanks, man." Stuart reached behind him and fist-bumped Greg's foot. It looked like they might have to move out for a bit. Not from Cobble Hill though. His son was a pyro and his wife was a beautiful, lazy liar, but this was their home and these were their people.

The ladder was lowered. Firemen continued to tromp in and out of the house with axes and rolled up their spent hoses.

Stuart rubbed his knuckles against Ted's bony knee. "Better get you to the hospital so they can check you out for smoke inhalation and all that cool stuff."

"Do we have to?" Ted whined.

"The fact that he's whining probably means he's fine," Peaches said.

"Just in case, though." Mandy stood up and held her hand out to Ted.

"Better to err on the side of caution," Peaches agreed, and stood up. She bent down and brushed her lips against Greg's ear—the way she used to when they ran into each other in between classes at Oberlin. Then she crossed the street to talk to Bruce.

"You did the right thing," she told him. "For once."

"Does this mean I'm exempt from community service?" Bruce asked. He shook his inhaler and pumped it into his mouth twice. "FYI, that's not why I did it."

"You're exempt," Peaches said. The kid was still sort of an asshole, but so what? Everyone was an asshole some of the time.

It occurred to Tupper that Elizabeth might be at home. She might be taking a bath and packing her things. She might be booking cars or boats or trains—she rarely flew—and talking to sponsors. He wouldn't let her sneak off again. This time he wanted a say.

Go, he'd tell her. *I want you to go.*

He checked his phone's Macaw footage. Nothing. But there was something on the coffee table—a Post-it with a note. He zoomed in. It said something about rabbits.

"I'm just going to check our place," he announced, and hurried down the street.

Wendy was shaking. Roy put his arm around her. Despite the fires and fireworks, the sky over their little patch of Brooklyn was clear enough to see the stars. From out on the harbor the Staten Island ferry sounded its low, mournful horn.

ONE YEAR LATER

B efore we begin," Jefferson began, "I'd like to thank you for coming. I'd also like to invite you to stay after the reading. There will be wine and beer and hard-cider mini donuts—courtesy of *Enjoy!* magazine—plus cheese and crackers and some extremely entertaining live music by Greg Park, Stuart Little, JoJo Biederman, and Robbie Catchpoole of the Blind Mice, whose recent hit collaboration, 'Sick,' needs no introduction—it's on the radio all the time. Congratulations, guys.

"Now, without further ado—Actually, why not? I'm going to make some ado. This guy is a god. I just heard he got a MacArthur 'genius' grant—there are actually two MacArthur recipients in the audience tonight. He didn't keep the money though. He donated it to 718 Reads, an amazing organization that provides individualized reading instruction to low-income Brooklyn kids, so they could set up a new outpost in that impounded bar on Henry Street. We're here to celebrate his new book. Buy it, read it, love it. Buy two! It's truly an honor to welcome Roy Clarke, my favorite author, here to share with us his new masterpiece, *Gold*. He describes it as *The Blue Lagoon* meets *Battlestar Galactica*. Need I say more?"

The audience whooped, whistled, and applauded.

Roy smiled from his high stool. "Thank

you, Jefferson, favorite owner of my favorite bookshop." He was glad he'd gone with the title *Gold*. His agent liked the new title because it stood alone and couldn't be lumped into the Roy Clarke Rainbow. Besides, *Gold* had more gravitas than *Red*. Red was the name of a pony.

He wasn't as nervous as the last time he'd stood before an audience in this shop. He'd found the perfect passages to read. He was going to skip around, really give them a taste of the book so they didn't have to read it at all if it was too much trouble. At least they'd have an entertaining evening.

As with his others, now that the book was finished and in print, he had misgivings. He could have done more. The book could have been longer or shorter, the names less annoying. He could have had a glossary of Martian terms, a Russian dictionary, and an introduction by someone from NASA. He could have written something more sensible and less inane. Best not to think about that now.

"I want to express my sincerest gratitude to you all for coming tonight."

Roy recognized almost every face in the shop, as if all of the guests from Bonfire Night had been squashed into one room, plus a few extras. Nurse Peaches, her musician husband, Greg, and their son, Liam, Shy's boyfriend, with their rescued three-legged greyhound at their feet. Wendy's friends from work, Manfred and Gabby, who'd made the donuts. Stuart Little, his beautiful wife, Mandy, and their pyromaniac son, Ted. Stuart Little's rock star bandmates. Shy's Latin teacher and table tennis coach, who was really rather brave to show his hairy face. The handsome doctor, who'd brought another very handsome man with him. Jefferson, the bookstore owner, and his girlfriend. That big knucklehead who'd started the schoolyard fire and helped rescue the little boy. Tupper, wearing his signature navy-blue suit spattered with plaster because he was working on something new, and beside him an empty chair with a piece of paper on it that read THIS CHAIR LEFT INTENTIONALLY VACANT. Christian, the Scottish student currently renting their newly renovated Airbnb basement flat. Shy and her sisters, Chloe and Anna, whose stroppy glares had not worn off since they'd arrived at JFK. And, of course, Wendy.

"Thank you for being such wonderful neighbors. I'd like to thank my youngest daughter for learning to make those cinnamon buns out of a tube and for eating some of them so I don't eat them all. I'd like to thank my other two daughters for deigning to be here."

"Don't forget Mum," Shy whispered loudly.

"How could I possibly forget?" Roy whispered back even louder, setting off a ripple of laughter.

"The writing of this book and all the others, my

brilliant daughters, my brilliant life here . . . are all thanks to Wendy. Would you mind standing up please, my darling?"

Whistles and applause. Wendy half stood, waved modestly, and sat down again.

He paused. Whenever he tried to explain to anyone why'd he'd written *Gold*, how the idea of teenagers stuck on Mars had come to him, he drew a blank.

"When I lived in England, I wrote about America. When I moved here, rather logically, I found myself writing about Mars."

Encouraging titters of laughter.

"Someone asked me if this was a young-adult book. Someone else asked if it was dystopian. Honestly, I have no idea."

More titters of laughter.

"I'll let you decide."

Roy opened the book. The room fell silent. He began to read.

An extremely tall, thin woman wearing a black hoodie with the hood up and enormous tortoiseshell sunglasses arrived late, crept noise- lessly into the audience, and sat down in the chair next to Tupper, ignoring his THIS CHAIR LEFT INTENTIONALLY VACANT sign.

Roy continued to read. This was the funny bit.

The rows of rapt listeners giggled and snorted uproariously. They were a good audience. Of course, he knew most of them. If they misbehaved, he could yell at them in the street. But he loved this bunch. He would write *Silver* next. Or *Platinum*. Or maybe *Copper*. And set it here, in Cobble Hill.

He turned the pages. Now for the sad part.

Breaths sucked in with just the right balance of empathy and distress. A few people, Roy included, began to cry.

He stopped reading and looked up. "You're all right," he said. "We're *all* all right. The ending's happy, I promise."

Acknowledgments

This book would never have been written without the constant nagging of my well-meaning family members. "Are you done yet?" "Are you actually writing a book?" "Did you send your book to Bill Clegg?" Thank you to Brooklyn Writers Space for providing me with a no food, no phones, no talking place to escape their nagging, open my laptop, and hope something good would happen. The final result would not have made any sense at all without the intelligence and diligence of Bill Clegg, the real deal. Thank you, Bill.

Peter Borland at Atria gave the book a home as well as his kindness and attention. Thank you, Peter, I owe you lunch. Sean Delone kept me organized and calm when I was freaking out. Thank you also to Simon Toop and the other Cleggers. Thank you, Team Atria, especially Sherry Wasserman, Kyoko Watanabe, Gena Lanzi, and Laywan Kwan for the wonderful book jacket.

I would also like to thank my Brooklyn friends. I'm so lucky to have grown older and raised my children with you.

These pages went into production during a global pandemic and, a little later, a time of tragedy and protest. Our world has changed for good. I'm not sure what happens next, but I am hopeful.

Books are produced in the United States using U.S.-based materials

Books are printed using a revolutionary new process called THINKtech™ that lowers energy usage by 70% and increases overall quality

Books are durable and flexible because of Smyth-sewing

Paper is sourced using environmentally responsible foresting methods and the paper is acid-free

Center Point Large Print
600 Brooks Road / PO Box 1
Thorndike, ME 04986-0001 USA

(207) 568-3717

US & Canada:
1 800 929-9108
www.centerpointlargeprint.com